THE ENTIRE SERIES

UNRAVELING YOU

unraveling you   raveling you   awakening you   inspiring you

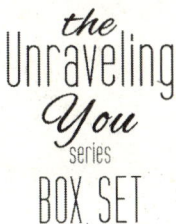

the Unraveling You series
BOX SET

New York Times and *USA Today* Bestselling Author

JESSICA SORENSEN

UNRAVELING YOU ~ THE ENTIRE SERIES
All rights reserved.
Copyright © 2015 by Jessica Sorensen
ISBN: 978-1519159625

This is a work of fiction. Any resemblance of characters to actual persons, living or dead, is purely coincidental. The Author holds exclusive rights to this work. Unauthorized duplication is prohibited.

For information:
jessicasorensen.com

Cover Design and Photography:
Sarah Hansen, Okay Creations
www.okaycreations.com

Interior Design and Formatting:
Christine Borgford, Perfectly Publishable
www.perfectlypublishable.com

UNRAVELING YOU

the Unraveling You series
BOOK ONE

New York Times and *USA Today* Bestselling Author
JESSICA SORENSEN

UNRAVELING YOU
All rights reserved.
Copyright © 2014 by Jessica Sorensen

This is a work of fiction. Any resemblance of characters to actual persons, living or dead, is purely coincidental. The Author holds exclusive rights to this work. Unauthorized duplication is prohibited.

For information:
jessicasorensen.com

Cover Design and Photography:
Sarah Hansen, Okay Creations
www.okaycreations.com

Interior Design and Formatting:
Christine Borgford, Perfectly Publishable
www.perfectlypublishable.com

CHAPTER ONE

16 YEARS OLD . . .

THE COUPLE THAT LIVES NEXT door adopts children like puppies. No joke. The Gregorys are bringing home kid number four today. The adoption process has happened so frequently over the years for them that it's become a routine. They drive off in the early morning, cruising away in their sedan, and then late in the afternoon they return with a small human being sitting in the backseat, looking about as scared as a little puppy getting yelled at.

While I do feel sorry for the little boy or girl, the sympathy quickly wears off. Because within a couple of months, the small human in the backseat will get over their fear and turn into their own person, who more than likely will take it upon themselves to annoy the crap out of me.

I'd be fine with this. After all, they are my next-door neighbors' kids, not my little brothers or sisters. But that's the thing. They *are* kind of like the little brother or sister I never had, since the couple next door are my parents' best friends and close to a second set of parents to me. I even call them Aunt Lila and Uncle Ethan.

"I wonder what this one will look like," I remark as I munch on my toast at the kitchen table. It's late morning, but we're late risers, so we're just starting breakfast, even though it's past ten. "And if it'll be a boy or a girl."

"Lila said he was a boy," my mother answers as she collects her mug and takes a seat across from me. "I think he's about your age, too."

"All their adopted kids are older. Aren't people supposed to adopt younger children?" I ask, reaching for the butter. "Like when they're babies?"

She sips the coffee then places the mug on the table. "Lyric, there are a ton of kids out there that need homes, both young and your age. Even older. You should realize just how lucky you are to have a roof over your head and parents who spoil the crap out of you. Some children don't have it so lucky."

My mother is probably one of the strangest moms ever, but in the best way possible. She uses phrases like, "spoil the crap out of you," and dresses cooler than I do half the time. Plus, she has fantastic taste in music.

"I know how lucky I am," I tell her. "So lucky in fact, that I know you're going to let me paint my room purple and black."

"Let me guess. Purple walls and black skulls."

"Hey, how'd you guess?"

"Because it's exactly how my room looked when I was your age. You're so much like me it's frightening sometimes."

"Well, there goes my theory that I was secretly adopted."

I don't really have that theory. I resemble my parents too much to ever believe I was adopted. I have my mother's striking green eyes, so bright they sometimes startle people at first glance. And I have the same shade of blonde hair my dad does. They're both tall, too, and passed that trait to me. At sixteen, I round in at five foot nine and tower over all of my friends at school. I inherited some of their talents as well, that is, if talents can be inherited.

Like my mother, I have the hand of an artist, although she is way better than I am. She owns her own art gallery and has sold a lot of her paintings. Her work is usually described as raw, emotional, and realistic.

Then there's my dad's talent of music. My father is a musician who used to perform in a band, and then later on as a solo artist. Now, he's mostly retired and owns his own studio. I'm not sure if it was all the time I spent hanging out with him, or the fact that my parents named me Lyric, but music is branded into my bones. I love anything and everything that has to do with it. My favorite instrument is the guitar, granted the violin is a close second. Creating lyrics, though, that's truly my favorite thing to do musically.

"It seems like such a nice day to go out for a drive," my mother comments, bringing me out of my thoughts and back to reality. "Maybe when Lila gets home, the three of us and the new boy can go for a drive. It'll give you some time to get to know him."

I stuff the rest of my toast into my mouth. "What if he's weird, though, like Kale?"

Kale is the latest addition to the Gregory family. He was twelve when they brought him home two years ago, and he still hasn't given up his obsession with comic books. And I mean *obsession*. He frequently dresses up like characters, his favorite being Flash. He also once wore a cape to school, which made him the subject of a lot of bullying.

Then there are the other two kiddos, Fiona and Everson. At twelve, Fiona is the youngest and probably the chattiest. She loves to draw and has a deep fascination with butterflies. Everson is smack dab between Fiona and Kale at thirteen years old. He's quiet, loves sports, especially football, and is probably the most normal of the bunch. They all have their weird little quirks, though, and shady pasts that I never really get to fully hear.

It's not like I have anything against weirdoes and shady pasts—heck, I can be a weirdo and sketchy sometimes—but as the sorta bigger sister, I constantly have to stick up for them, and sometimes it gets tiring.

"Lyric, just because Kale's different doesn't mean he's weird." My mom reaches for the coffee pot. "Need I remind you of your little obsession with that boy band when you were his age."

"You promised you'd never bring that up. You even pinkie swore that you wouldn't."

Her lips curl as she fills her cup to the brim with steaming hot coffee. "Then don't give me reasons to break my promise."

"Fine, I'll stop calling Kale a weirdo on one condition." I swallow a gulp of milk then wipe my lips with the back of my hand. "If you let me go to the concert on Friday with Dad."

Her cheeriness diminishes. "Did he tell you that you could go with him?"

I shrug. "He didn't not tell me I couldn't."

She shakes her head, restraining a grin. "You are way too good of a bargainer for your own good."

I perk up. "So does that mean I can go?"

"Hmm . . . That all depends on if you'll go on a drive with me later and warmly welcome the new Gregory." She raises her glass to her mouth, but only to hide a smirk.

"Touché, Mother. I see where I get my bargaining skills from."

I consider her offer. Going on a drive with my mother may not seem like the most fun thing in the world, but it kind of is. Her and my dad used to drag race, and they still have some of their badass cars we take out when we go for trips. Both of them drive fast, although I think they play it safe when I'm in the car. It's still fun, though.

What makes me hesitate on the offer is the getting to know the new Gregory part. Like puppies, I never know what the new addition's personality is going to be. He could be nice, or he could be a little weirdo who bites. The youngest, Fiona, actually bit me the first day they brought her home.

But I want to go to the concert badly enough that the pros outweigh the cons.

I chug the rest of my milk then agree. "Fine, I'll go with you as long as you let me go with Dad."

"Go where with me?" my dad asks as he strolls into the kitchen carrying his guitar case.

I scoot back from the table and stand up. "To the concert."

My dad drops his guitar case to the floor and lifts his hand for a high five. "See, I told you it'd be better if you asked her."

My mother's head whips in his direction, and she scowls at him. "Did you put her up to that?"

He shrugs as I slam my palm against his. "You have a hard time telling her no."

"So do you." She narrows her eyes. "You spoil her too much."

"And vice versa." He leans down and whispers something in her ear, causing her to giggle and blush.

That is my cue to leave, because in just a few moments, they'll start making out like they always do. *So gross.*

I hurry out of the kitchen and up to my bedroom to change out of my pajamas. I select a black tank top and a pair of cut offs then braid my long, blonde hair before applying a dab of eyeliner around my eyes. I then blast some Rise Against and rock out on my drums for a bit. Uncle Ethan actually taught me how to play, but he says I'm a natural since I caught on really quick.

After the drums comes the guitar. I turn on "Buried Myself Alive" by The Used and strum the strings to the tempo until my fingers are numb. Then I crank up some "Lithium" by Evanescence and go mad crazy with the violin while belting out the lyrics. I stop when I'm hoarse and flop down on my bed to draw covers for the albums I have yet to create.

Once my hands ache, I move on to lyrics. Although it's one of my favorite things to do, I sometimes feel like I lack in the lyrical department. Most of the music I love is angsty, emotional, semi-twisted, and moves the soul. Mine always seem to come out on the exuberant side. I'm hoping with time it will change. I know my dad wrote some of his best lyrics in his late teen years, when he was pining over my mom. He even told me once that the more I experience life, the more emotional my songs will get. Now, if I could just get those experiences like he said, life would be fantastic.

I'm still figuring out how to attain that life, though. For the most part, my life is pretty boring. I have decent, pretty cool parents who support every dream I throw at them, whether it's proclaiming that I'm going to create my own genre in music, or win a Grammy. I get to do a lot of things I want to do, like go to concerts, art shows, meet semi-famous musicians. I've spent a lot of time in my dad's studio, watching artists record. I have a lot of friends, granted none of them I would consider a best friend, but there are still occasions where I feel lonely.

Bored. Ordinary. That's what my life is. And ordinary

doesn't make awesome music.

Plus, even if I miraculously became the most killer songwriter ever, I could never sing in front of anyone. Just playing the guitar for my family makes me want to vomit. Singing is much more raw than playing an instrument. Much more real. Exposes the soul so much more. And as blunt as I am, exposing my soul freaks the living shit out of me, because I fear people won't like what's in me.

By the time I look up from the notepad again, the sun is setting over the city of San Diego, and the sky is shades of florescent pink and orange.

"Lyric, it's time!" my mother calls up the stairs as I'm tucking my notepad under my pillow.

Sighing, I slip on my black boots and trot down the stairs.

"How long of a drive does it have to be?" I ask her as I wander into the living room where she's stacking our entire DVD collection onto the coffee table.

Movie watching is an adoption day tradition. We start off with dinner at the Gregory's, where everyone gets reacquainted with each other. Then we come over here to watch a movie since we have a massive television in our living room.

"I'm not sure yet." She stands up straight and gathers lose strands of her red hair out of her face while she scans the room. She has spots of grey and blue paint in her hair and on her cheek, which means she's been in her studio for most of the day. "I feel like I'm forgetting something."

"Batteries. You've been meaning to change them for like two weeks." I chuck her the remote that I collect from the armrest.

She catches it. "Yeah, that's it. What would I do without you?"

"Probably lose your marbles."

She pats my head as she rushes out of the living room. Minutes later, she returns with the remote and my dad in tow.

"Everyone ready?" she asks as she tosses the remote onto the sofa. "Let's go."

"Do I really have to go this time?" I whisper to my dad as we follow my mom out the door and into the dwindling sunlight. "It's starting to get really old. I mean, I'll get to see the newbie tomorrow. And the day after that. And the day after that."

My dad swings an arm around me as we step off the front porch. "Lyric, I know you don't get it now, but one day you'll see the importance."

I look up at him. "In what?"

"In the family you have," he says as we round the picket fence on the line of our property. We hike up the Gregory's driveway to their two-story home that is very similar to ours. The only noticeable difference on the outside is the shade of the siding—white and grey. "You're really lucky to have *every* single one of us. And you should really get to know the new kid. He's your age, and I'm sure he could use a friend with . . . some of the stuff he's been through. You could be that friend for him. Do something good."

I wonder what he means by *stuff*.

"I know I'm lucky, and I was planning on getting to know him." *Sort of.* "And I do good stuff all the time. I go with Mom and Lila to the shelter every year on Thanksgiving and help out. I give my clothes away sometimes. I even befriended Maggie McMellford last year, despite the fact that no one was nice to her and she didn't know who Nirvana was until I let her listen to them."

"Really? She didn't know who Nirvana was?"

I shrug. "Unfortunately, a lot of kids don't have an old

man musician father who knows all the classics."

"Old man?" His brow arches. "Ha, ha, you're a riot, Lyric Scott."

I innocently grin at him. "I wasn't trying to be a riot. Just telling the truth."

He chuckles and I laugh with him. My laughter silences, though, as the Gregory's enormous sedan rolls up the drive.

I sigh as my gaze instantly drifts to the backseat, searching for the scared little puppy dog. All I find is what appears to be a guy crammed in with the rest of the Gregory clan. I'm not one-hundred percent sure what he looks like, since I don't have a clear view into the backseat, so I wait in anticipation until the sedan parks and the clan piles out.

Normally, the newbie remains in the backseat, too afraid to leave the vehicle. This one just hops right out and rounds the car toward us as if he doesn't have a care in the world.

He doesn't look like the rest of them either. Honestly, he kind of looks like Uncle Ethan in the pictures I've seen of him when he was younger. Black hair, dark eyes, tall. He's dressed head-to-toe in black, wearing a . . . I squint to see if I'm seeing things correctly. Yep, he's wearing a leather collar around his neck.

I'm not sure what to make of this. What it says about him. At my school, the kids who dress like this are the rebellious troublemakers. Is that how he's going to be? Part of me is thrilled at the idea, while the other fears it.

"Everyone, this is Ayden," Aunt Lila introduces him with the proudest smile as she gently places her hand on Ayden's shoulder.

Ayden glances at her hand, and by the hardness in his eyes, I expect him to get angry with her, but he doesn't utter a word.

"And, Ayden, these are our neighbors, Micha and Ella Scott." Lila motions her hand at me. "And this is their daughter, Lyric."

Smiling, I wave. "Hi."

He doesn't say hi back. Doesn't wave either. He just stares at me. And stares. He stares so long that I get a bit uncomfortable, especially because of the sadness radiating from his eyes. It's kind of hard to endure and makes me feel subdued. I consider ducking behind my dad to escape his stare down, but I'm guessing I'd get scolded for being rude so I keep my feet planted and focus on my fingernails, picking at the black nail polish.

I listen to everyone yammer, squirming more and more the longer Ayden's sad eyes remain fastened on me, as if he's daring me to figure out all of his secrets, his weirdo side, his shady past.

Finally, we all file inside the house and I breathe freely again as he stops focusing on me and instead zeros in on his new home.

Lila starts giving him a tour of the house while Ethan leads the other three rugrats into the kitchen with my dad.

I start to go with my dad, but my mom captures me by the back of my shirt and tows me back to her. "Let's go with them." She nods at Lila and Ayden as they ascend the stairway.

I scrunch up my nose as I recollect Ayden's intense, depressing stare. "Do I have to? He looks so sad, and his staring is making me uncomfortable."

"All the more reason to spend time with him." She signals for me to get a move on. I reluctantly obey, but stand as far behind as I can without looking too antisocial.

Luckily, Ayden seems more engrossed with the home and his room than me. He doesn't even glance my way as he takes in each wall, piece of furniture, and framed pictures. But when we all gather around the table for dinner, he ends up sitting across from me, and the stare down begins again.

I attempt to avoid his gaze as he watches me pick at my salad. As I chow down on my burger. As I chat with Fiona about her art obsession. The longer the staring goes on, the squirrelier I become, until I can't take it anymore.

Throwing my napkin onto the table, I slump back in the chair, cross my arms, and stare at him in the same manner.

At first, he appears unfazed, but as the minutes tick by, he starts to look almost amused.

Interesting.

Without removing his eyes from me, he picks up his drink and guzzles a long swallow. I do the same. We simultaneously place our glasses down. He pauses then drums his fingers on the table, either testing me or playing with me . . . I'm still not sure yet.

Intrigued, I thrum my fingers, too.

He fiddles with the small black and red gauge in his left ear. I only have one piercing in each of mine and no earrings in right now, but I still pretend to mess around with an invisible gauge.

He rolls his tongue across his teeth, the smallest trace of a ghost smile emerging. I feel like I've won a game and delve forward, determined to make that sadness crack.

"Oh, Lyric, let me play, too!" Fiona clasps her hands together as she kneels up on her chair. "Pretty please. I've never had a brother to play copycat with before. Kale and Everson always get so angry."

I smirk at Ayden then turn to her. "I think Ayden would love to play with you." I rise from the table, take my dirty dishes to the sink, and sneak outside to get some fresh air.

As I'm sitting on the curb in front of the house with my

legs stretched out, I catch Ayden gawking at me through his upstairs bedroom window. I tip my head to the side, wondering just how long this whole staring thing is going to last. He hasn't even spoken a word yet.

Maybe he doesn't speak.

"Lyric!" my mother suddenly shouts, and I tear my attention away from the window. She's exiting the house with Lila, both of them elated about something. "Ready to go out on a drive with us?"

"Surely durely." I stand up and brush the dirt off the backs of my legs then start to follow them to my house when Lila glances back at me.

"Lyric, would you mind running up and telling Ayden to come with us?" she asks, hopeful. "He seems a little nervous except when he's around you."

My brows furrow. "He hasn't even said a word to me, so how do you arrive at that conclusion?"

"Well, you two were playing that little staring contest game at the table." She adjusts the pale pink strap of her purse higher on her shoulder. "I would really appreciate it, sweetie."

My Aunt Lila is way too nice to argue with, so I reel around to go get Ayden, but then halt before I reach the front steps.

"Aunt Lila, does Ayden . . . talk?" I dare ask, facing her again.

"Of course, sweetie. He's just a little nervous. Things have been hard for him, and I think he's feeling a little overwhelmed."

She turns to my mom and starts telling her about the countless foster families he grew up in and that he has some problems.

"He's been through so much," she says with a disheartened sigh, pressing her hand to her chest. "And still has so much to face in the future."

I stop to listen, but when my mom shoots me a death glare, I hurry into the house and up the stairs to Ayden's bedroom.

His door is wide open and he's sitting on the edge of the bed, staring at a duffel bag on the floor. He looks so morose that I feel kind of sorry for him. *What has this boy been through?*

"You're supposed to come downstairs and go on a drive," I announce as I waltz into the room.

He jumps, startled as his attention darts up to me. He doesn't reply. Simply just stares again.

"I know it sounds really lame." I wander around, observing all the knickknacks Lila put up—sports and band posters, little painted blocks with quotes on them, books on the shelf. It's like she didn't know what he was into, so she just decorated the room with a bit of everything. "It's pretty fun, though. They drive fast and stuff."

He still doesn't utter a word. Just looks at me.

I face the bed and assess him while he studies me back. His head is tilted just enough that his black hair dangles in his grey eyes, so I don't have a clear view of how he's looking at me. He appears uneasy, though, fidgeting with a bracelet on his wrist.

Finally, I can't take the silence anymore. Even though I know I might get in trouble for doing it, if he chooses to tell on me, I march to the bed and stand right in front of him.

When he angles his head back to look at me, his eyes are filled with confusion. I poke him in the side of the ribs, hard enough that he flinches and his body jolts.

"What the hell?" He gapes at me as he cradles his side.

"Ha!" I cry, pointing a finger at him. "You do know how to speak."

His lips part in astonishment. "Of course I know how to speak."

"No, of course you know how to stare. Speaking was getting a little questionable. Either you couldn't speak or you were just shy, but I needed to find out."

He has no clue how to respond to my colorful personality—most people don't in the beginning.

Feeling a little on the adventurous side, I snatch ahold of Ayden's hand and drag him to his feet. "Come on, shy boy." I pull him with me as I march out of the room and downstairs. "The longer we stay up here, the longer this night is going to drag on."

He follows me a lot easier than I expected him to, holding onto my hand, maybe too tightly, as if he's terrified out of his wits.

"I thought you said driving with them was fun?" he questions. "So why would you want the night to end so soon?"

"The driving part is fun," I assure him as I throw open the front door. The cool breeze kisses my skin and it smells like leaves and grass. "But the movie thing at the end is painful to endure. We always have to watch a kid appropriate movie. Either a cartoon or something rated PG." I glance back at him. "Although, maybe because you're older, they'll let us watch something cooler."

"Maybe I like cartoons and PG movies," he counters, holding my gaze as he slides his hand from mine and folds his arms across his chest.

"Do you?"

"Not really. I just wanted to make a point. You shouldn't make assumptions. Maybe I'm a kid at heart who likes kid movies."

"You know what, Ayden? I think you and I might be good friends, if you're lucky." I snatch his hand again and tug him around the fence and up the driveway toward the open garage of my house. "Although, you still have to pass the music quiz."

"Music quiz?" he asks, distracted by my mother's black and red 1969 GTO parked in the garage next to my dad's 1969 Chevelle SS, staring at both of them in awe, like most guys do.

"Yeah. Music. As in instruments and lyrics and stuff. I might not be able to be friends with you if you like some of that cliché pop music they always play on the radio."

He cocks a brow at me. "Do I look like someone who's into that kind of music?"

I release his hand as we near the car then smirk at him. "Well, my initial assumption would be a no, but you told me not to make assumptions."

"But I didn't expect you to listen."

I wink at him. "I'm an excellent listener, along with many other awesome things." I skip around to the driver's side and dive into the backseat, giving the horn a couple of honks on my way.

"Get in!" I call out to Ayden as I push the passenger door open for him.

A second later, he slides onto the leather seat beside me.

"Where are they?" he asks as he settles in the seat, fidgeting with the leather band on his wrist.

"Who knows?" I lean over the console and pound on the horn until the door to the house swings open.

My mom and Lila come wandering out, scolding me for the horn honks. Their scolding is nothing new. I easily shrug it off and sit back in the seat as the drive begins.

My mother does her best not to peel the tires until we're on the freeway, since the last time she did it out of the driveway the neighbors made a complaint. Once we're on the long, curvy stretch of road, though, all bets are off.

"Just take it a bit easy, Ella," Lila begs as she clutches the seat, something she always does when we go driving. "We have a newbie to your . . . um, interesting driving skills."

"Awesome driving skills." My mother smiles at me from the rearview mirror and I grin back, knowing what's coming.

An instant later, she punches the gas and we're off, flying down the road and weaving in and out of cars.

I relax and breathe in the air blowing through the window. Out of the corner of my eye, I catch Ayden picking at his black fingernail polish.

I stick out my hand and wiggle my fingers. "Look. We match."

Again, he nearly smiles, but I've still yet to witness any sort of happiness from him. It's got me curious, way more curious than the other kids Aunt Lila and Uncle Ethan have brought home. They all have their sad moments, but not like this, so sullen all the time. It makes me want to get him to smile really, really badly.

"Hey, Mom," I say, without taking my eyes off Ayden. "Can we turn on some music?"

"Sure. What do you want to listen to?"

"Can I just see your iPod?"

She hands it to me, and I give it to Ayden. "Here you go." I slip off my sandals and kick my feet up on the console. "Impress me."

I wait patiently as his eyes dance between me and the iPod in his hand. He starts sorting through the songs. I swear he just about grins again when he makes his selection and returns the device back to me. I pause as I take it from him, catching a glimpse of a row of thin scars that look like cat scratches on the top of his hand. Noticing the direction of my gaze, he quickly jerks his sleeve over his hand then rotates toward the window again.

I want to ask him about the scars. I want to ask him a lot of things. But I force my curious side to shut up and focus on the music. The song he chose causes me to laugh, because of all things it's by Nirvana. I start singing along under my breath, quiet enough that no one can actually hear me, while Ayden thrums his fingers to the beat, gazing out the window at the houses and stores in the distance.

"Are you sure you're not too hot?" Lila asks Ayden for the millionth time, making her seem way more doting toward him than she was with the other three.

"I'm good," he responds, scratching at the scars on the back of his hand as he turns inward.

"You know what would be cool," I say when the silence gets to me. "If Ayden could come to the concert with Dad and me."

"Oh, he can't." Lila fretfully glances over her shoulder at Ayden, who doesn't say a thing. "Ayden has to take it easy for the first few weeks while he's here, getting adjusted to everything. I don't want to over-excite him."

So strange.

I sit back in the seat as we continue to drive through the city for the next hour before returning home. As we hop out of the car to go inside the house and watch a movie, I snag Ayden's sleeve and draw him back to me. When Lila and my mom step inside, I release his shirt and face him.

"Okay, you passed the music test. Now we can be friends." I would have been friends with him anyway, but it's more entertaining this way.

He stares me down. "What if I don't want to be friends with you?"

I'm unsure if he's being serious or not, but I shrug him off, seeing this as more of a fun challenge than anything else.

"You do. I promise. Not only am I the most awesome person ever, but I can show you the ropes of your new life." I stick out my hand. "So what do you say? Friends?"

He eyeballs my hand then his gaze glides up my body and lands on my face. "All right, we can be friends, Lyric." He places his scarred hand in mine and we shake on it.

His fingers tremor as we pull away, and his smile never fully reaches his eyes.

I know the story. All of the children Lila and Ethan have adopted have been through something terrible. Usually, I leave it alone since it's none of my business, but with Ayden, I'm curious. I have questions. Lots and lots of questions.

I make a vow to myself right then and there that one day, as his friend, I will get to know him and find out his story.

Then, I'll make him smile for real.

CHAPTER 2

Ayden

Just breathe. Just breathe. Just Breathe.
The pressure will crack and shatter
if you just keep breathing.
Life will eventually get easier
if you keep your heart beating.
Just breathe. Just breathe. Just breathe.

I REPEAT THE MANTRA OF words over in my mind the entire drive to my new house, all during the tour, and during the ride with the woman who drives crazier than most teenagers. I chant it under my breath all night long when I don't get an ounce of sleep.

The process is nothing new. This is the sixth time I've lay awake in a new room within the last year. Stability is what's uncertain to me, even before I entered the system. And now, suddenly, they're telling me I have it. That this home is *the* home. That I'm being adopted and will no longer be passed around from family to family.

I don't understand it. Teenagers aren't supposed to be adopted. No one wants them, especially ones that are as ruined as I am, that have been through the things I have. We're stray dogs, scraggily, ratty, bad habits, untrainable.

People want puppies. Cute, fixable puppies. Yet here I am, supposedly wanted by the Gregorys, despite my scars and issues.

The house is strangely quiet at night, and even during the brink of morning. Maybe I'm just too used to a lot of noise, but the soundlessness makes sleep impossible. I end up staring at the ceiling until the sun peeks over the city and heats up the room. Then I climb out of bed and start to get ready for school.

After I pull on a pair of faded black jeans and a matching shirt, I sit on the bed and stare at the few contents inside my bag. A single photo of me with my older brother and younger sister, a rusty pocketknife, and a watch are all that's left of my original life—the one that I was born into. I don't miss that life at all, but I miss my brother and sister, who I haven't seen since social services barged in on that God awful day and yanked us out of that shithole house.

I look down at the scars on the backs of my hands. Marks of my past, branded forever into my body and soul. I can remember clearly how some of them were put onto my body. Others I can't. The freshest ones are the worst. They happened the day I was taken away, a day my mind has somehow blocked.

They'll never go away.
Always own a fragment of my soul.
Own a part of me.
Never let me go.
Yet they won't own the pieces
that live in the darkest parts.
There, but not quite breathing.
Please, please don't let them break me apart.

I put the photo down and pick up the other object hidden beneath the small pile of clothes—a bottle of pills I stole from the last home. I don't even know why I took it.

Not to get high. I'm not into drugs. I just wanted to have them, just in case I can't take this anymore, the pain and darkness and ugliness residing inside me. The loneliness. The unknown.

I wonder if I should take them now. All of them. Then I wouldn't have to face another damn day feeling as though the ground is about to crack apart beneath me. Face the world being friendless again. Alone. Always alone. I hate it, but can't admit it aloud.

"Ayden."

Mrs. Gregory is standing in the doorway with her blonde hair pulled up, wearing a hesitant expression. She has on a red apron over jeans and a long-sleeved shirt. She looks like a typical mom, yet her warming, comforting demeanor is unfamiliar to me.

"I was coming to wake you up for school"—she tentatively steps foot into the room, glancing around at everything still neatly in place like it was yesterday. I haven't dared touch anything except the bed—"but it looks like you're already ready."

I nod as I drop the bottle into the duffel bag and quickly fasten the zipper. Her eyes track my movements, and I half expect her to ask me what I'm doing, but she doesn't.

"Do you want some breakfast?" She points over her shoulder at the doorway. "I made chocolate chip pancakes."

I rake my hand through my shaggy black hair as I spring to my feet and fumble for my tattered backpack on the floor. "Sure, ma'am."

She frowns. "Ayden, you don't need to call me ma'am."

I seal my lips together and remain silent. I've never been much of a talker, nor do I feel comfortable calling her anything but ma'am. Yes, they're officially adopting me now, but we'll see how long that lasts. I give them a week until they want to send me back.

She stiffly smiles then signals for me to follow her as she starts for the door. "Come on. Let's get some breakfast in you while Kale's getting ready. I'll have Ethan drive you all to school. He takes the rest of the kids a little bit later since junior high starts later than the high school."

I nod, slinging the handle of my bag over my shoulder. "Okay."

She seems unnerved by my one-word responses, but I don't know how to give her more.

She pauses when we reach the arch of the kitchen doorway. "Are you sure you're up for school? Because you could always skip a few days and start next week when you're a little bit used to things. And I could take you shopping for some new clothes."

I shake my head. "I'm fine. I'm used to stuff already. And I'm fine with my clothes."

She offers me a sad smile. "If that's what you want."

I freeze, thrown off balance. I'm pretty certain that's the first time someone has said something like that to me. "Yeah, that's . . . what I want."

She whisks into the kitchen, crossing the length of the large room and heading toward the stainless steel stove. The entire house is big and sparkly—fancy. I feel very uncomfortable, because all the other homes I've been in have been small, dull, and broken.

"I'll see if Lyric wants to ride with you," she says as she refastens the tie on her apron. "She's a junior like you. It might be nice to know someone your age."

The suggestion makes me uneasy. Lyric made me feel out of my element yesterday with her blunt, bold attitude. Plus, her green eyes are so unbelievably intense that I had trouble looking away from them. I think I came off even more insane than I normally do. Still, after all the staring, the damn girl seemed determined to be my friend. I haven't had much in the line of friends, and wouldn't even know what to do with one, but I still agreed to be hers, figuring I'd only be here for a week, so keeping my promise wouldn't matter.

"Are you okay with that?" Mrs. Gregory begins stirring batter in a bowl.

I nod as I take a seat at the rectangular table in the nook. "Yeah, that's fine."

I can tell she's about to explode from my limited answers. I wait for her to yell at me—it wouldn't be the first time I've been yelled at by an adult for my silence. Instead, she offers me pancakes, so many that I feel fuller than I ever have, as if she whole-heartedly believes that pancakes are the way to cure my silence.

I wish they were.

Chocolate chips to heal a broken soul.
Cure hunger.
Cure the past.
Cure my amnesia.

Lyric had warned me yesterday, though, that Mrs. Gregory would be like this. That she runs her own catering business on the weekends and loves to do experimental cooking for the family whenever she can.

After I assure Mrs. Gregory that I'm stuffed, she ushers Mr. Gregory, Kale, and I out the door, shoving a granola bar and banana in Kale's hand.

"Oh, and remember you have therapy later today," Mrs. Gregory subtly reminds me on my way out.

I nod, even though I'm not a fan of the idea, and follow Kale and Mr. Gregory out the door. We get into a bulky black sedan that seems more like a chauffeur car than a family vehicle. Then, Mr. Gregory backs down the driveway, pausing at the street where he lays on the horn, staring at the neighbors' house.

"You should get along with Lyric just fine. She's a very outgoing girl." That's all he says. He was the same way yesterday. A man of few words. I think I might kind of like him.

I fasten my seatbelt while we all wait in silence. A couple of minutes later, a very bouncy Lyric comes bounding out of the house with her backpack on. The girl walks like she's on crack, all bouncy and full of sunshine. I find myself both envious and mesmerized by it—by her.

Her long blonde hair is down and blowing in the breeze. She's wearing red cut-offs with a long-sleeved black shirt that has netting for the sleeves. I'm still trying to figure out what kind of person she is. At first glance, I might have gone with Goth—minus the blond hair—but after watching her smile and chat yesterday, she seems too cheery for that type of crowd. Cheerleader doesn't seem right either. Neither does a jock.

"Hello, everyone," Lyric singsongs as she hoists herself into the backseat of the sedan and scoots in next to Kale. She has a violin case in one hand and a Pop Tart in the other.

Orchestra freak? Wouldn't have guessed that.

"Morning, Lyric," Mr. Gregory replies as she slams the car door. He backs out onto the road and drives down the street, past the two-story homes, and toward the stop sign. "What's your dad up to today?"

Lyric briefly flashes Kale a smile, who goes as stiff as a board, then she buckles her seatbelt and peers up front at me.

I realize I'm staring again. I tell myself to look away, but like yesterday, I'm too curious to listen to myself.

"Not much," she tells Mr. Gregory as she munches on her breakfast. "I think he's going to go down to his studio and rock out for a little while. Why? You thinking about having an old man jam session?"

Mr. Gregory shakes his head, but I can tell he's trying really hard not to smile. "I'm not that old, Lyric."

She pats him on the shoulder. "It's okay. I won't tell anyone."

He rolls his eyes. "So, how are the drums coming along?"

She shrugs as she unzips her backpack. "Good. Although I still think I'm way better at the guitar and violin. The drums are fun, though, for letting some steam off."

So she plays the guitar, drums, and violin. Okay, she's not an orchestra freak, just a hardcore music freak. It makes me like her more.

While I don't know how to play any instrument, listening to music is a huge outlet for me and got me through a lot of hard times. Plus, it drowns out screaming really well.

"And how about the lyric writing?" he asks as he veers the sedan onto the main road that centers the small, upper class neighborhood.

She retrieves a pack of gum then sets the bag aside. "Not that great, but I blame it on my parents. They've made my life too easy, and I have absolutely nothing to write about."

"You could always write about the easy stuff," he suggests, looking at me for some reason, as if he knows my not-so-easy secrets.

She pops a piece of gum into her mouth then offers one to Kale, who quickly shakes his head. "I don't want to be that kind of a songwriter."

Mr. Gregory glances at her through the rearview mirror. "You sound just like your dad."

"Thanks." She seems proud of this, something I find

strange. Most kids my age would take it as an insult.

Her eyes abruptly lock on mine. "Do you play anything, shy boy?"

Great. She's already given me a nickname.

I shake my head. "No."

"What do you do, then?"

I shrug. "Nothing."

She leans forward in the seat, chomping on her gum. "Now, that's not true. I mean, clearly you've got a chance for the Most-One-Word-Responses championship title." She blows a bubble, and then smiles at me, making happiness look so effortless.

"Well, obviously there's that," I retort, unable to help myself. "But I'm betting my chances for winning are going to go down the more time I spend with you."

She grins as she reclines back into the seat. "Excellent comeback, shy boy."

I'm on the verge of smiling as I face forward in the seat again, but any trace of happiness dissipates when we pull up to the school. It was clear to me yesterday, when I first saw the neighborhood the Gregorys lived in, that I was now officially part of the upper class society. I didn't even think about what that would mean for the school district.

Instead of a rundown, graffitied building like I'm used to, the school consists of a perfectly structured building, surrounded by green grass and sparkling, crack-free windows. Half the cars in the parking lot look brand new, and the clothes everyone wear look fresh off the racks from some absurdly expensive store.

"Are you going to be okay with Lyric showing you around?" Mr. Gregory asks me as he parks the sedan in front of the drop-off section. "Because I can walk you in if you need me to."

"No way," Lyric interrupts as she shoves the door

open. "As cool as you are, Uncle Ethan, the last thing he needs is you being all awkward, like you usually are around people."

He shakes his head, but he's not irritated, more like mildly entertained. "All right, I'll pick you three up after school, then."

She nods then jumps out at the same time Kale hops out his side. They both slam their doors as I reach for my door handle, but then pause, feeling terrified. I usually like to blend in and typically do. But with my gauges, faded black clothes, and worn boots, I'm going to stick out like a sore thumb.

I open my mouth to ask Mr. Gregory if he can take me home, but my door swings open and Lyric snaps her fingers and points for me to get out.

"You'll be just fine," she assures me as if she's read my mind. She slips her bag on then grabs my hand, giving my arm a tug. "I got your back, dude."

I flinch at her touch and almost jerk back. I hate being touched almost as much as I loathe nighttime. But as I catch sight of the abundance of so-called classy people roaming around, I end up clinging on to her as I climb out of the car, oddly grateful that Lyric doesn't let my hand go as we walk up the wide pathway toward the glass entrance centered below a brick archway.

People are staring at us. At me. At me holding Lyric's hand. At my outfit. My piercings. It brings me back to the day we were pulled out of that house while the entire neighborhood watched the three malnourished orphans as if they were part of a freak show they couldn't tear their eyes from.

"God, it's like no one's ever informed them that staring is rude," Lyric mutters as she slams her palm against the glass door and shoves it open.

Pretty much all eyes land on us as we step inside the narrow hallway lined with lockers. Some people look interested. Others repulsed. Some utterly baffled.

Lyric waves to a lot of people and stops to chat with a couple of girls, never releasing my hand. She introduces me to a girl named Maggie, who looks at me like I'm the rebel she wants to walk on the bad side with. The look is nothing new; a lot of girls do it, except Lyric. She just looked at me like she to be my friend.

"Hey, Ayden." Maggie offers me her hand, fluttering her eyelashes. "So, where are you from?"

"Nowhere important." I don't take her offered hand. Don't want to encourage the fluttering of her eyelashes. Don't want to be looked at like that. Don't want to be looked at at all.

When Maggie's eyebrows bow up, Lyric glances at me with her brow cocked. "You'll have to excuse Ayden," she says to Maggie. "He's a man of few words."

"Oh, the sexy silent type," she says, chomping loudly on a piece of gum. "Nice."

"No, just the silent, doesn't like to chat type," I say, switching my weight uncomfortably, wishing Lyric would end the conversation and just take me to the office so I can check in and get the fuck out of this overcrowded, stuffy hall.

"I don't get it." Maggie blinks at Lyric for help.

"It doesn't matter." Lyric waves good-bye before tugging me down the hallway.

"We so need to work on your people skills," she tells me as she steers me through the mob.

"My people skills are fine."

She snorts a laugh. "Okay."

I sigh, giving up on the argument, and instead focus on what's going on around me. Most of the kids look on the preppy side, except for a group lingering around the benches in the quad. I make eye contact with them, figuring they'll be the best start toward finding my place here. But the tallest guy in the group gives me a hard stare in return, and a curvy girl with purple hair flips me the bird.

The day only gets shittier from there. Everyone at this damn school seems to hate me, and the other half seems overly interested. I don't want that. Don't want their stares. I just want to be left alone, since I'll be out of here when the week passes.

I do my best to keep my distance from most people, and spend lunchtime in the bathroom. When fifth period rolls around, though, things really go to shit. It's PE, which is bad enough, but I also have it with Lyric.

"You have been avoiding me," she says as she waltzes up to the bottom bleacher I'm sitting on, waiting for class to start. She has on a red T-shirt and short, black gym shorts that show off her extremely long legs. "What's up with that?"

"When was I avoiding you?" I ask, fiddling with the drawstring on my own shorts.

"At lunch." She sits down beside me and crosses her legs. "I looked everywhere for you. Where the hell were you?"

I pick at a hole in the bottom of my shorts. "I ate in the bathroom."

Her nose crinkles. "Ew, Ayden. No, no, no. Just no."

I shrug. "It was better than being stared at."

"Who's staring at you?"

I give her a *'really'* look.

She sighs. "All right, I'll give you the staring thing." She rests her elbows on the bench behind us and reclines back, staring at the gym floor. "My school has apparently never seen someone so gothically adorable."

"What does that even mean?"

She smirks at me. "You know, dark, mysterious, sullen, yet cute."

I gape at her. "Do you even have a filter?"

She swiftly shakes her head. "No way. Where's the fun in that?"

I continue to stare at her, impressed and kind of afraid of her. She's so open. So honest. So unlike me, the guy who barely speaks and who carries pills with him, contemplating suicide. Lyric is my polar opposite.

"Hey, Lyric." A guy wearing baggie gym shorts and a school T-shirt comes strolling up to us with a smile on his face. "How's it going?"

"Hey, Lanson." Lyric smiles up at him then leans forward to tie her shoe. "Have you met Ayden?"

Lanson's eyes land on me and the friendliness he conveyed when he was staring at Lyric disappears. "Yeah, new guy, right? I think we have English together."

"Yeah, I think so." Heaviness develops in my chest as more attention is focused on me. *God, I wish this day would just get over with.*

"You two should hang out," Lyric suggests with her head still tipped down as she loops her shoelace.

Lanson sneers. "Oh yeah, I'm sure we can be best friends." When Lyric looks up again, his haughtiness turns into a friendly smile. "In fact, I'm having a party this weekend. You two should come."

Lyric glances over her shoulder at me. "What do you think? Are you up for a party?"

Lanson glares at me. I can't tell if he wants me to agree to go or to say no, but one thing's for sure: my existence is clearly irritating him.

I force a tight smile. "Sure, a party sounds fun."

The death glare vanishes from Lanson's face when

Lyric looks back at him. "Oh, time for class." Lyric springs up and grabs my hand, hauling me to my feet.

That move earns me the darkest scowl from Lanson. I have a feeling things are going to get a hell of a lot worse.

I wish I could follow Lyric, but the teacher splits up the class—boys on one side, girls on the other. Then we're divided into teams of three and handed a basketball. Athletics was never my thing, but I try my best, even when I start to get criticized by Lanson, who of course has to be on the team I'm playing against.

He smirks at me as he throws the ball over my head to another member of the team then "accidentally" elbows me in the gut.

"Where are you from?" he asks as we both jog down the court toward the ball.

"Nowhere important." I dodge to the right when the ball is thrown again and surprisingly catch it.

My shoe squeaks against the floor as he knocks the ball out of my hand before I can even start dribbling. "One thing's for sure; you sure as hell aren't from here." He stares me up and down as if I'm trash. "I heard you were adopted or some shit. Not sure why the hell anyone would want you." He jabs me in the side with his elbow.

It takes all my strength not to clock him in the face.

"And why the hell is Lyric Scott hanging out with you?" Another elbow rammed to the rib cage, this time with so much force it nearly knocks the wind out of me.

For a brief moment, I tumble into a memory from two years ago. The exact same thing occurred then, only it was an adult who took the air from me. As fast as I fall into the memory, it fizzles out like a flame.

"I mean, I get that she thinks she needs to be friends with everyone," Lanson continues, "but seriously, she's sinking to the bottom of the barrel with you."

When he stomps on my foot, I can't take it anymore. I was taught not to fight back when I was younger, but once I entered the system, all bets were off, and I did pretty much whatever the hell I wanted. I was going to try to be better, though, because the Gregorys seemed genuinely nice, but fuck it.

I push him. "Dude, shut the fuck up."

A shit-eating smirk spreads across his face at my reaction. "Or what?" He inches toward me and gives me a shove back. "What are you going to do about it? Because in case you haven't heard, I'm the shit around here."

"Wow, there's an accomplishment," I retort, regaining my balance. "The shit of Glensview High School. I'm sure that's going to get you far in life."

"Way farther than you," he bites back as he glances at my piercings, black nail polish, and gauges. "Seriously, I bet if they searched your room, they'd find dead animals everywhere."

I inhale and exhale, trying to stay calm. "And if they searched yours, I'm sure they'd find steroids."

His smirk shifts to a scowl. Then he's spinning around to catch the ball, but mid-turn, he brings his elbow up and slams it hard into my face. Blood gushes from my nostrils and pain radiates all the way up to my head as I hunch over, groaning.

Fuck that hurt.

Goddamnit, I hate life.

Life always hurts.

I should have just taken the bottle of pills this morning. Spared myself another day's worth of pain.

I'm about to stand upright and go after him—who gives a shit about the consequences—but then I hear a burst of commotion and someone shouting.

When I glance up, Lanson is on his knees, cupping

his own nose, and Lyric's standing in front of him with her hands on her hips.

"Next time, it's going to be my fist, asshole," she says to him then reels around to me. "Are you okay?" She lowers my hands from my nose, wincing at the sight. "We need to get you to the nurse."

"What did you do to him?" My voice sounds all nasally.

"I threw the basketball at his face." She winks at me. "I told you I got your back, dude."

I'm not sure how to respond. No one has ever had my back. Not even my brother and sister, but that wasn't their fault. None of us could take care of ourselves at the time, let alone each other. It feels nice. More than nice. Nice is something new to me. Different. For a moment, I feel different.

And for a fleeting, life-changing moment, I'm kind of glad I didn't take those pills this morning.

CHAPTER 3

"SO WHAT HAPPENED?" IS THE first thing Ayden says when I approach his locker after school.

"Not much. I got detention for a few days, but the principal loves me and always goes easy on me." I slide my backpack on. "What about you?"

He shrugs as he retrieves his bag out of his locker and unzips it. "Nothing, really. I went to the nurse. She put some ice on my nose then sent me on my way."

I squint at his nose. "It looks really gnarly."

He touches the brim of it and winces. "It feels really gnarly." He removes a few textbooks out of his locker, stuffing them in his bag. "How much trouble do you think we're going to be in when we get home?"

"You know, I've been putting a lot of thought into that," I say as he slams his locker. "And I've come up with a plan."

"A plan?" he questions as he secures his backpack onto his back. "What kind of plan?"

"Well, the best bet is to play Uncle Ethan right from the start, because he gets really uncomfortable over almost everything." I link arms with him as we start down the busy hall. I've been touching him a lot today, and while I can tell it bothers him, I'm not going to stop until he asks me to. I like touching him. It feels like he's mine, which makes me feel special. "If we can have him convinced that it was an accident right from the start, then we should be good to go when we get home."

"It kind of was an accident," he points out as we exit the doors and enter the deliciously warm sunlight.

"Yeah, but I kind of have a habit of doing stuff like this," I explain as we cross the freshly mowed grass toward the loading area in front of the school. "You'll get off the hook easily, but I might have to do some time."

His arm flexes beneath my touch. "I'm not going to let you get into trouble over this—over me. I'll make sure of that."

"Aw, so you're the hero type." I playfully bump my shoulder into his. "Never would have guessed that about you."

He comes so close to smiling. Just a little more joking, and I know I can make it happen.

I open my mouth to crack another joke, but snap my jaw shut when I spot the Gregory's gigantic sedan parked amongst the line of cars. "Crap."

"What?" Ayden tracks my gaze to the driver's seat where Aunt Lila is sitting. And in the passenger seat is my mother. "Okay, so now what do we do?"

I overdramatically bobble my head back. "Now, we go face the music."

Aunt Lila is so grateful for my stepping in for Ayden that she actually starts to tear up. She seems heartbroken that someone would want to hurt him. She keeps saying to him, "You've already been through so much. This isn't fair." I can tell Ayden gets really uncomfortable with the waterworks. Thankfully, my mom intervenes and calms Lila down. Then, she turns around in her seat and lays my punishment on me.

The punishment is the stupidest thing ever, though. One week of cleaning my room and one week of hanging out with Ayden after school. Plus, I have to help out at the shelter on Thanksgiving. Like that's a punishment. I have to clean my room anyway and the shelter thing is a tradition.

After we get home, I end up in Ayden's room, sprawled on the bed with the door agape. Lila keeps coming in to check on us, as if she half expects to catch us naked and fondling each other. Fat chance that'll happen. Even though Ayden is ridiculously adorable in a self-tortured artist, gothic, I'm-internally-tortured sort of way, I'm saving myself for someone who will capture my wild soul and tame it. I know I sound like a sap, but I blame it on my parents' undying love story. Even after twenty years of marriage, they're still ridiculously in love, so the bar for my own love story is set pretty high.

"Are you sure you two don't want a snack?" Lila sticks her head into the room for the umpteenth time.

Ayden nods as he situates against the headboard, working on his English assignment. "I'm sure."

She looks at me and I shrug. "I ate a buttload of cookies before I came up here."

"Okay," she says disappointedly then leaves us to get back to our homework.

The soft tune of "Cardiac Arrest" by Bad Suns flows from the stereo as Ayden continues to jot answers down, but. I'm more fixated on him than my assignment.

"So, did the gauges hurt when you got them?" I ask as I doodle thorny vines all over my math paper.

When he glances up from his paper, strands of his black hair hang in his grey eyes. "I don't know. Probably about as bad as your ear piercings."

I touch the rose earrings in my ears then kneel up on the mattress. "What about tattoos?"

"What about them?"

"Do you have any?"

"I'm only sixteen."

"Yeah, so." I arch my back as I stretch. "I bet you do, don't you?" When he wavers, I immediately perk up. "Where are they?"

"There's no they." He sets down the pencil in the spine of the book and flexes his fingers like he has a cramp. "Just one."

"Can I see it?" I eagerly move over to sit down beside him.

His expression plummets. "I don't think . . ." He trails off when my mouth sinks. "Fine, I'll show you, but only if you promise not to ask questions."

I draw an X over my chest with my finger. "I promise."

A nervous exhale escapes his lips as he reaches for the hem of his black T-shirt. Excitement bubbles inside me as he lifts it up and shows me his stomach then his side. Black ink stains his flesh in swirls and patterns that form a jagged circle. The tattoo doesn't look professional by any means. In fact, it looks as though someone branded him with an iron rod then dumped ink into the wound.

"Whoa. Does it mean anything?" I extend my hand forward to touch the tattoo, but he quickly jerks his shirt down.

"I don't know if it does or not, since I can't really remember how it got there," he says coldly. He collects his pencil and returns his book to his lap. "And you promised me you wouldn't ask questions."

He begins working on the assignment again, leaving me with so many questions I feel like I'm going to combust. There's so much I don't know about him, and so much I want to know.

"Can I just learn one tiny thing about you?" I clasp my hands in front of me. "Pretty please. It doesn't have to be about the tattoo." When he sighs, I add, "Okay, I'll tell you something that no one else knows about me first." I deliberate what to divulge. I'm not much of a secret keeper, but there is one thing I never tell anyone. "Okay, so no one knows this, but I totally suffer from stage fright, which is a big, huge problem since I want to be the lead singer in a fucking awesome rock band one day." I pat him on the arm. "See, not so bad. Now it's your turn."

He stares at me with uncertainty.

"Just one thing." I hold a finger up. "That's not so bad, right?"

He considers my proposal, and then in the softest voice admits, "I'm terrified of the dark." His gaze drops to the scars on his hand.

"See, that wasn't so bad." I try to remain cheery even though he looks absolutely horrified that he just admitted that secret to me. "And now I know what to get you for your birthday."

"And what's that?" A frown etches into his face.

I wink at him, hoping to cheer him up. "A nightlight." I settle down in the bed beside him. "Don't worry, I won't tell anyone."

"I wasn't worried about that."

"Then why do you look so upset?"

He shrugs, staring at the foot of the bed. "It's nothing." His gaze collides with mine, and he gapes at me in bafflement. "It's just . . . how can you be so happy all the time?"

His question makes me pause and really think about who I am.

"I'm not that happy, am I?" *Am I?*

"Kind of. I mean, I barely know you, but . . . you just smile a lot." I self-consciously bring my fingers to my lips, but he swiftly catches my hand, stopping me. The contact sends fireworks blazing across my skin and makes me want to smile even more. "I don't mean it as a bad thing. I just wish I could . . . understand it." His shoulders sag as he removes his hand.

Such a sad boy.
With sad eyes.
And a sad heart.
Sad everything.
Too sad.
I need to make him happy.
Somehow.

"I'll make you smile a lot in the future," I promise him after the silence finally gets to me. "You just wait and see. I will drive you so damn crazy, to the brink of insanity, where all you can do is smile. My form of torture will be lots and lots of jokes that will be so hilarious they'll make you pee your pants."

He snorts a laugh but then his eyes widen.

I thought I was being funny, but maybe I scared him. Some people say I come on too strong.

"I was just kidding," I say. "Sort of."

He searches my eyes, his forehead creasing. "I'll be right back," he mumbles as he scrambles to his feet. He bends over to unzip his bag then digs an orange bottle out before running out of the room.

Okay, maybe I need to tone it down a bit. Perhaps he's not quite ready for my sparkling personality and odd sense of humor.

Tone it down, Lyric.
It's not so complicated.

When he reappears in the doorway, his hands are

empty and he seems a bit more relaxed.

"Everything okay?" I cautiously ask as he climbs back onto his bed and opens up his Life Sciences book.

He nods, propping the book on his lap. "Yeah, but could you help me with this assignment?" He avoids eye contact with me, and his fingers tremble as he picks up the pencil. "Science really isn't my thing."

I want to ask him about the bottle. About the fear in his eyes. Crack his head open and see what's inside. Write songs about his inner workings. But I also promised I'd make him smile from now on, and my questions seem to have the opposite effect on him.

So I do what he asks and help him, silently telling myself that one day he'll trust me enough that I'll be able to learn what makes him tick. Then I will write the longest, most meaningful song about everything I've discovered.

Everything about him.

Even his secrets.

CHAPTER 4

Ayden

I'VE HAD THE SAME DREAM for over two years now. Claws. Bleeding flesh. Scars. Scars. Scars. Pain. Metal. Biting. My Flesh. Over and over again. The images are so vague, yet bright as my mind battles not to fully see what happened to me during that week a couple of years ago.

God, I hate this.

The chains were always the worst. They're what I remember the most. Other details are hazy, though, like the people I met while I was trapped. The people who stole everything from me and my brother and sister.

I thought the dreams would go away once I was adopted, or at least hoped they would. But the memories still haunt me most nights, and sometimes during the day when I'm awake. They're extra worse tonight, probably because tomorrow marks a month since I left the shithole of a home I was in before I ended up at the Gregory's. One month since I started my new life. Yet, even a month later, I worry that when I wake up, my nightmares are reality—that this isn't really my life.

Music is the only thing that can calm me down. Well, that and the crazy black light nightlight Lyric bought me for my birthday a couple of weeks ago. She thought she was being funny when she gave it to me, but I was oddly touched that she remembered my stupid confession about being afraid of the dark.

Fortunately, I never told her why I was afraid. Then again, I don't even know the whole reason since I blocked out most of the darker stuff that happened to me. No matter how hard my therapist tries to unravel my mind, they still refuse to surface.

After turning on the black light, everything white in my room glowing neon, I put in my earbuds then toss and turn for half the night until I fall asleep around two in the morning.

Hours later, I'm woken up out of a nightmare by the soft sound of breathing. And not mine. Someone is lying next to me in bed, and for a moment, I have a panic attack, thinking that somehow I've traveled back in time when I was never alone. Then I catch the faintest scent of strawberries and relax. The person lying next to me is the same person who's been climbing into my bed almost every morning since I moved here.

"Are you awake yet?" Lyric asks, ruffling my hair with her fingers. "I'm getting bored watching you sleep."

"Then stop watching me," I murmur with my eyes shut. "It's creepy."

"Hate to burst your bubble, but you're equally as creepy as I am."

"Guess we're perfect for each other, then."

"Of course we are." She flicks me in the forehead, startling me. My eyelids lift open, my gaze meeting her bright green eyes. They're intense to look at, even now after I've known her for a while. I can never seem to stop staring at them. They're beautiful. And it's heartbreaking to feel what my staring at them means. That I like her. A lot. More than I've liked anyone in a long, long time.

"You're doing that creepy staring thing again," she informs me as she sits up in my bed and starts raveling a strand of her hair around her finger. She's dressed in maroon shorts and a dark grey shirt, clearly ready to go somewhere, and knowing our routine, I'm going with her. "You know, it's cool with me. I get it. I'm too dazzling not to stare at." She smiles and my heart misses a beat. Her smile is so perfect and easy. Most days, I envy it. "But you might want to lay off on the staring a little bit in school, at least around Tina Marlelytone."

"I've never stared at Tina Marlelytone." I sit up in bed and stretch my arms over my head.

"I figured, but she thinks you do. So, you might want to"—she points at my eyes—"keep those sad little puppy dog eyes off her."

My hands drop to my lap as I stare blankly at her. "I wish you'd stop saying that about my eyes."

"I'll stop saying that when it stops being the truth." She jumps off the bed and jerks the blanket off me. "Now get up and get dressed. I have big plans for you today."

"You might want to think before you jerk off the blankets like that," I say to her as I drag my butt out of bed. "One day, I might start sleeping naked."

"I think that'd be more embarrassing for you than it would for me," she retorts, backing toward the door. "You blush when someone sees you with your shirt off."

"That happened one time," I call out, but she ignores me, flashing me a sly grin before closing the door.

Shaking my head, I trudge for the dresser to get some clothes. Nothing fazes that girl. It's the most terrifying and fascinating thing to observe. And I've observed her, a lot. Everywhere she goes, she finds a crowd and blends in with them, like a freaking chameleon. Me, I'm like a skittish rodent who never feels at ease, always silent and uncomfortable, making everyone around me silent and uncomfortable. Except, of course, Lyric.

I'm extremely lucky to have met her my first day with the Gregorys. I'm not sure I would have survived without her. No one knows how hard that first day with the Gregorys was, and all the ones before that. I pondered suicide, touched many blades to my wrists, tasted the staleness of pills. Then Lyric sprung into my life with her sunshine attitude and smile, and suddenly my days don't seem so dark. I decided the day she beat the crap out of the guy to defend me that I was going to dump the pills and try to give a go at life, the best that I could.

And I've been working on it ever since.

As I'm searching for a shirt, my fingers skate across one of the three objects hidden in the back of the drawer. The stuff I brought here with me. I still haven't been able to get rid of them. I still think about my brother and sister every day, and wonder where they are.

"Are you still naked!" Lyric laughs as she bangs on the door, interrupting my thoughts.

"Just a second." I slam the drawer shut then tug on a grey T-shirt and a pair of holey black jeans. Then I grab my boots from the closet and throw open the door. "You are the most impatient person ever."

She rolls her eyes at me. "Whatever, shy boy. I'm super patient." She seizes my hand and leads me down the hall toward the stairway. "So, it's going to be a little bit tricky to get out of the house, since the usual tradition for the month marker is to spend the day talking and eating cake and ice cream, but I have an idea to get around it."

Sunlight is flowing in through the massive windows of the kitchen, and I detect the scent of freshly baked cake in the air. The smell is starting to become more and more familiar with each day I spend here, just like everything else. While I embrace it, I also fear that it will all be taken away from me.

"Maybe we should just stay here, especially if Mrs. Gregory has baked." It's not just that though. I always feel guilty whenever I'm about to do something even remotely wrong. The Gregorys were kind enough to put a roof over my head, and I constantly feel in debt to them.

Lyric shoots me an inquiring look over her shoulder. "Why do you keep insisting on calling them Mr. and Mrs. Gregory? It's weird."

"I have my reasons," I mutter as I sit down on a stool to put on my boots.

Lyric watches me lace my boots. I know she wants to ask what my reasons are, but she doesn't. That's the thing with Lyric. As crazy and blunt as she is, she'll never press me too hard for information. I'm grateful that she doesn't, because if she did discover certain details about me, she probably wouldn't want to be my friend anymore. And I need her as a friend, more than anything.

She places her hands on her hips. "So, what you're saying is you'd rather stay here and eat cake and listen to old timers tell mildly embarrassing stories, instead of going on an adventure with me?"

"No, that's not what I'm saying at all. I just . . . feel like it's rude to take off."

"It's not rude. Lila wants you to have fun. I know, because she checks with me all the damn time, always worried about your happiness and wellbeing."

"Well, she *should* worry when I'm around you. Some of the crazy stuff we do . . . I'm surprised we haven't gotten into trouble yet."

"Give us time." She nudges my foot with hers when I frown at her. "I'm kidding. Everything we do is safe."

Safe?
The word still feels so foreign to me.
Nothing like the word *fear.*
Fear is like air.
Breathable.
Because I know it.
I fear the things I don't know.
Like friendship.
And losing it.
Loss.
Like the loss of my memory.
My childhood.

I lace my boot up then stand up, and she has to angle her chin to look up at me.

"Fine, I'll go with you, as long as you promise that I'll come back in one piece for Mrs. Gregory's sake." I don't know why, but the woman seems to like me. Everyone in the house does, even though I rarely talk.

"All right, getting you back in one piece is doable," Lyric muses then spins around and runs through the kitchen, swiping up a dab of frosting from the cake on her way around the island.

We find Mrs. Gregory in the living room, and after a little bit of persuasion—mostly from Lyric—she lets us go.

"Just be careful," Mrs. Gregory says, moving in toward me with her arms out, as if she's going to hug me. Like always, I tense and she promptly backs away. "And be safe, please." She smiles, but it's laced with concern.

I'm still getting used to the whole caring-about-my-well-being thing, so I hesitate as my mind catches up with the scene and the emotions connected to it.

I nod then clear my throat and lower my voice so Lyric won't hear me. "Um, I've been meaning to ask you if you found out how my brother and sister are doing."

Sympathy masks her expression. "I'm sorry, sweetie, but I couldn't find anything out. They said the files were confidential." She comfortingly places a hand on my shoulder. "Maybe when they're eighteen we can start looking again. It'll be more possible to find them then."

Smashing my lips together, I nod then rush after Lyric and out the front door before Mrs. Gregory says anything further.

My chest is still pressurized from last night's dream, and now the whole thing with my brother and sister bears down on me. But after we've been in the fresh air for a few minutes, the pressure starts to alleviate. Always does. Houses do that to me. Rooms. Walls. Confinement.

"All right, here's what I'm thinking," Lyric announces as we hike up the driveway toward the open garage of her house. "Today, we are going to fly."

I gape at her. "In case you haven't noticed, people can't fly."

She grins back at me. "Oh, ye of little faith." She squeezes into the garage between the two ridiculously awesome cars that belong to her parents, ones I long to touch, but have never worked up the courage to.

I notice she has an iPod tucked in her back pocket that I'm sure will serve some sort of purpose later on. When she emerges again, she has her bike.

"We're going to take this bad boy down to Cherry Hill."

"No way. That hill is freaking steep. Plus, aren't we a little too old for bikes?"

"We are never too old for bikes." She juts out her lip. "Pretty please. With a cherry on top."

It's really hard not to say yes to her when she looks like that. Still, I'm torn between coming back to Mrs. Gregory in one piece and making Lyric happy.

"All right, I'll do it, as long as we wear helmets. And take my bike."

"I'll agree to the helmets, but we have to take my bike. Yours doesn't have pegs."

"Why do we need pegs?"

A mischievous grin lights up her face, and I know I'm in for something really iffy when we reach that hill. "You'll see."

Ten minutes later, I'm riding a purple bike, wearing a helmet, and Lyric is standing on the back pegs. She has her hands placed on my shoulders, and I'm both content and uneasy about the touch—always am.

"Okay, stop the bike right here," she says, pointing over my shoulder at the center of the street on top of Cherry Hill.

I aim the bike in the direction and plant my feet onto the asphalt when we arrive at the spot. The inclined road, bordered with lofty, narrow homes, makes me dizzy.

"Are you sure about this?" I warily eye the bottom of the hill, which is an intersection.

Nodding, she pops an earbud into my ear while placing one in her own. "I have to do this, Ayden. It's important to my musical inspiration."

As the lyrics of "Fire Fire" by Flyleaf fill my head, I summon a deep breath, pick up my feet, and position them on the pedals. I don't even have to put pressure on them. The bike takes off on its own and descends quickly down the hill, gaining momentum the further down we go. I start to grow nervous, and my nerves only escalate when Lyric's hands leave my shoulders.

"What the heck are you doing?" I peek back at her while grasping onto the handlebars.

"Flying." She has her arms spanned out to the side, her head angled toward the sky. Her long blonde hair blows out behind her as the wind dances through it. Moments later, she shuts her eyes.

Everything pauses. The freedom she carries is a beautiful, enthralling sight. So enthralling that it feels like I'm falling . . .

"Ayden, look out!" Lyric shouts, her eyes wide open as her hands clamp down on my shoulders.

I look at the road just in time to see a car heading at us. I swerve to the left, but it doesn't help as we barrel toward a thick tree. The front wheel of the bike slams into the truck and I go soaring over the handlebars. Thankfully, I manage to keep my head from hitting the concrete, because even with the helmet on, it would have hurt like a motherfucker. The wind gets knocked out of me, though, and I struggle for oxygen as I lie on my back, staring up at the sky, feeling strangely free at the moment, even with the pain.

"Oh my God. Oh my God. Oh my God." Lyric appears above me, worry written all over her face as she throws her helmet off. "Be okay. Be okay. Be okay." She frantically scans my face and then my body, checking for wounds.

Honestly, I feel fine. My knee and elbow ache a bit, but that's it. I've experienced way more pain than this. I remain still, though, fascinated with how fussy she's being. Normally she's so carefree, but right now she's wound up and panicking. Over me.

I've lived with over six families, and no one has ever cared about me as much as Lyric appears to right now.

Soft lyrics flow through my head.

Let me sing you to sleep.
Kiss your pain away.
Take your next breath for you.
And keep it as my own forever.

Maybe I'm an asshole for doing it, but I pretend to

be hurt, lying still for longer than I should, seeking the fussing just a bit longer. When her eyes meet mine again, I start to feel bad for causing her so much worry. I open my mouth to tell her I'm okay, but the intense look on her face causes me to burst out laughing.

When her eyes narrow, I raise my hands, surrendering. "I'm sorry. I swear. I was just messing around. I'm fine. I promise."

She pinches my arm and I wince, yet continue laughing.

"Seriously, Ayden. That's not funny."

"Oh, come on." I prop up onto my elbows. "Don't pretend like you wouldn't have done the exact same thing."

She crosses her arms, trying to remain pissed, but Lyric never stays upset for more than five seconds, and right on time, she relaxes. "Okay, I'll let you off the hook, but only because I got you to smile." She smiles herself as I reach up and touch my upturned lips.

She's right. I am smiling. And laughing. It's been such a long time that I hadn't even noticed.

"Come on." She stands up, brushes some of the grass off her legs, then offers me her hand. "Let's move on to phase two."

"Phase two?" I question with doubt.

"What, you don't trust me?"

The mangled bike ten feet away should answer that question for me. Regardless of the bent metal and dents in the frame, I still wholly trust her. More than I've trusted anyone.

I nod, lace my fingers through hers, and get to my feet. "But no more hills."

"Deal." She grins.

The day feels so perfect. So real. I just wish I knew if my brother and sister have the same thing.

CHAPTER 5

Ayden

WE SPEND THE REST OF the day doing things a little less dangerous, rolling the mangled bike along with us. We walk down to the local bridge, go get some ice cream, and hang out at the park for a while. By the time we arrive back home, the sun has lowered and the sky is black.

As we're putting the bike away in the garage, Lyric checks her phone. "Oh, looks like we have the place to ourselves. Everyone went out to the movies."

"What are we going to do? Because I know you're already thinking of something."

"You know me way too well."

As she ponders an idea, I dare to touch the shiny black Chevelle in the garage. I remember how one of my foster fathers had one similar to it, only it needed a lot more work. He was one of the mildly tolerable parental figures. He never did let me touch the car, though.

"You know, I could always ask my mom if you can drive it," she unexpectedly says.

I hastily withdraw my hand from the car, as if I've been caught with my hand in the cookie jar. "No, I'm okay."

"Well, you can drive mine when I get it, then. It's

going to be a Dodge Challenger, though. And a fixer upper. At least, that's the plan we've had since I turned fifteen and a half and got my driving permit." When I look at her again, she's got her evil plan face on. "So, do you want to see something really cool?"

"Maybe," I reply cautiously. "It really depends on what it is."

Grinning deviously, she guides me through the house, toward the back section, coming to a halt at a closed door beside the den.

"I've never been in this room before," I remark as her fingers encase the doorknob.

"That's because I'm technically not allowed in here unless my dad's with me."

Before I can protest, she shoves open the door and flips on the light.

All of my objections abruptly dissipate.

"This is your dad's office?" I step over the threshold behind her and glance around the room filled with old guitars, signed albums, drumsticks, photos, and plaques. So much cool stuff my mind goes into overload.

"More like his memorabilia room." She strolls over to a shelf lined with old CDs and starts tracing her fingers along the rows, reading the titles.

I shut the door then stand in the middle of the room, afraid to touch anything. "Maybe we shouldn't be in here."

"We'll be fine as long as we put everything back in its rightful place." She pulls a CD off the shelf, plucks the disc out, then gently places it into a stereo and presses play. Moments later, a grungy song fills the speakers.

"What band is this?" I ask as I roam around the room, examining all the guitars on the walls.

She shrugs as she plops down in the chair behind the desk and collects a guitar propped against the wall. "The front of the CD cover says The Cranberries. I just randomly picked it. Thought a surprise would be fun." She strums a few notes. "I'm wondering if it was one of my mother's CDs, though." Her lips part as if she's going to sing, and her eyes drift shut. But instead of belting out the lyrics, she plays the notes while uttering the words under her breath. When she opens her eyes again, she looks nervous, which is strange. Lyric never, ever looks nervous.

"You okay?"

She nods, setting the guitar aside. "Yeah, just seeing if I could do it around you."

"Do what around me?"

She shrugs as she opens a drawer. "Sing."

I wish I could help her get over her fear, but unlike what she did for me, I can't just buy her a nightlight.

"What were you whispering to Aunt Lila about this morning?" she casually asks as she sifts through a stack of papers on the desk.

"Nothing important." I plop down in a swivel chair in front of the desk and start spinning in circles.

"I heard you say something about your brother and sister." She reads something on one of the papers, but I can tell she's pretending, worried she's crossing a line. "I didn't know you had a brother and sister."

"I did . . . before . . ." I pick up the pace, whirling the chair around and around until I'm so dizzy I feel like I'm going to hurl. "My brother is a year older than me and my sister is a year younger."

"And you haven't seen them since you had to leave your home?"

"No."

"Does it make you sad, that you all had to leave your home and now you don't get to see them?"

I dig my heels into the floor and stop the chair before

I actually do end up vomiting. She's watching me intently, waiting for me to answer, with a drop of apprehension in her eyes.

"I don't miss my old . . . home at all," I utter quietly. "It wasn't even a home . . . at least, from what I can remember . . . but I do miss my brother and sister. That's why I asked Mrs. Gregory if she could find stuff out about them—or at least where they are."

Her head angles to the side and she looks so lost. "You said from what you can remember."

"Huh?" My voice is thick with emotion. Just talking about this is surfacing unwanted memories that are supposed to be forgotten.

"Just barely, you said, 'from what I can remember.'" She shifts in her seat, leaning back. "Can you not remember your old home?"

Seeing no other way out of this than to lie to her—which I won't do—I nod. "Some of my memories are foggy."

"Does Mrs. Gregory know about this?"

"Vaguely. I think social services and the therapist I've been going to told her some details." I clench my fists as my chest starts to constrict.

Links of metal wrapped around my wrist and brain.
Driving me insane.
Begging me to cave.
They whispered they knew the truth.
Marked it forever on my flesh.
Told me to give in.
To surrender.
But I couldn't.

I blink from my thoughts and massage my wrists.

"Maybe I could help you find them," she says, thrumming her fingers on top of the desk.

"Who?"

"Your brother and sister."

"And how would we do that"—my fingers curl around the armrest, desperate to hold onto something, because I feel like I'm about to have a panic attack—"when Mrs. Gregory couldn't even find them?"

She slants forward, crossing her arms on top of the desk. "There's a little thing called the internet, Ayden. We could do some research on our own."

"You would help me do that?"

"I would help you do anything."

Even though the concept doesn't feel possible, I believe her. "Where would we start?"

Her eyes elevate to the ceiling as she contemplates. "You know their last names, right?"

I nod. "My brother's name is Felix, and my sister's name is Sadie. Our last name used to be Stephorson, but I'm not sure now if theirs still is, since mine's changed."

"Okay, we can start there. And it'd probably help if they had something distinct about them."

My fingers travel to the homemade tattoo on my side, put there without my permission. "They have the same tattoo as me."

Her lips part, but no words come out. I've shocked Lyric beyond words, which doesn't seem natural.

"We didn't choose to get them," I mumble, completely clueless why I'm telling her this. "They were put on us, from what I can remember."

She sucks her bottom lip into her mouth, as if she's trying to physically restrain herself from asking.

"What happened to you?" she finally asks.

I grind my teeth so forcefully it actually hurts my jaw. "When I was younger, we were taken by these . . . people who had these really strange beliefs. They put the tattoos on us." My voice quivers almost as intensely as my heart as I speak of the day my mother betrayed her three children. It's the same day that my memories start to break apart into charred fragments that barely make sense.

Lyric swallows hard. "Ayden . . . I . . ."

"Can we please talk about something else now?" I plead in desperation, barely able to breathe. "Please. Something happy." I need my happy Lyric back. Need my happiness before I fall back into the darkness that I carried around for two years after that day.

Silence stretches between us before Lyric says, "Did you hear about Maggie?"

I exhale, my muscles loosening. "No, but I'm guessing she's dating someone new now."

She smiles as she rests back in the chair, making the shift of attitude so breezy. "How'd you guess?"

I give a half shrug. "Because she dates someone new every day."

Lyric giggles, but her laughter silences as she opens the desk drawer. She squints at something inside it, and a pucker forms at her brow. "What on earth?" She pulls out a bottle of scotch along with a pack of cigarettes and an ashtray. "Dude, I know my parents drink"—she shows me the pack of cigarettes—"but I never knew they smoked."

"I'm not surprised. I've smelled it on your dad before." I stretch my legs out and slant my head back at the ceiling decorated with hundreds of guitar picks. "It must have been so cool growing up here," I remark as I spin the chair around, imagining what it was like living here. Probably pretty great since she's so damn happy all the time.

"Yeah, I guess it was pretty fucking awesome." Lyric unexpectedly starts hacking.

My gaze darts to her. I have to bite my lip to restrain

my laughter. "Did you just take a drink of that?"

She wipes her lips, shuddering as she stares at the bottle of scotch in her hand. "Yeah, so what?"

"Have you ever drank before?"

"No." She twists the cap back on. "Have you?"

I shrug. "A couple of times." That's all I say, not wanting to relive the things I've done, like fighting, drinking, and stealing stuff. "You shouldn't start with scotch. That's strong shit right there."

She meticulously eyes me over. "You want a taste?" She extends her arm across the desk, with her fingers enclosed around the bottle.

Even though I probably shouldn't, I snatch the bottle from her and swallow a gulp or two as Lyric watches me with inquisitiveness. When I remove the mouth of the bottle from my lips, she grins.

"You didn't even gag." She grabs a cigarette, along with a lighter that's inserted into the pack.

"I wouldn't do that if I were you. He'll be able to smell it."

"I'm just curious." She reclines back in the chair and pops the end of the cigarette into her mouth.

"Well, you shouldn't be. That stuff is bad for you."

"I'm not curious about smoking," she says, cupping her hand around her face as she flicks the lighter and tries to light the end, "but about you."

"What are you talking about?"

"I can never figure stuff out about you."

"Like what? If I know how to light a lighter?"

She shakes her head, still struggling to light the cigarette. "No. Like what you like to do. If you really are a bad boy at heart. If you've ever smoked before."

I elevate my brows at her. "That's what you want to know about me? Out of all things?" *After the conversation we just had?*

Giving up on the lighter, she rises from the chair and ambles around the desk toward me with the cigarette still resting between her lips. "Well, I have this theory that this good, obedient guy I know isn't the guy who pulled up in that sedan a month ago." She leans over me and taps the hollow of my neck. "I mean, the collar's gone. You took it off at day three, and I could never figure out why—why it was so easy for you to give up your Goth side." She slides her hand to my ear and traces her finger across the lobe, moving her body close enough that I get a straight view down the front of her shirt. I try not to look, but my eyes stray more than a few times, my heart rate quickening. "And the gauges, too. All you have now are these tiny scars." Her hands travel down my arms, causing goose bumps to sprout across my skin as her fingers come to a rest on the tops of my hands. I start to panic, thinking she's going to ask me about the scars there; instead, she grazes the pad of her thumb over my fingernail. "I really do kind of miss the black nail polish."

I shiver from her touch. "I don't." My voice cracks as her fingers graze my knuckles, and I quickly clear my throat.

It's just a simple touch.
A lyrical brush of fingers.
Nothing that can hurt you.
Anymore.

All thoughts vanish, when she straddles my lap. My heart slams forcefully against my chest. I can't figure out what to do with my hands. Definitely not touch her; otherwise, I might lose it. But I look awkward with them out to the side, so I drape them on the armrests and fold my fingers inward.

"How much of that did you drink?" I inspect her face

to see if she could possibly be drunk, but I'm feeling a little woozy myself and my vision is a bit hazy.

"A few swallows." She hands me the lighter, places the cigarette in between her lips again, and waits for me to light it for her.

"This is going to teach you a lesson." I drag my thumb across the top of the lighter and bring the flame closer to the cigarette.

"And what lesson is that?" she asks as the fire crinkles the paper. Moments later, she begins hacking again. She hurriedly removes the cigarette from her mouth as clouds of smoke puff from her lips.

"That smoking is bad for you." I pry the cigarette from her fingers and slant over to put it out in the ashtray, fighting back my laughter.

After she finishes coughing up her lungs, she settles into my lap again. "So have you?"

Again, I question how drunk I am when I start to get a little too happy down south about her sitting on my lap. I've never really been turned on before, not in a welcomed way anyway.

"You're not going to let this go, are you?" I ask, getting squirmy.

She shakes her head, positioning a hand on each side of me. "Nope. Not unless you start freaking out."

I mentally chant the lyrics of the first song I can think of.

You make me dizzy. You make me ache.
You make me burn, burn, burn.
Your touch is toxic. Poison.
Yet I'll never learn, learn, learn.

"Fine," I admit. "Yes, I've smoked before, but not since I moved in with the Gregorys. I went through this phase where I did a lot of things, right after I entered the system."

"I knew it." She sloppily plays with my hair, running her fingers through it. "You were a bad, bad boy, Ayden. Maybe that's what I should start calling you. Bad boy instead of shy boy."

"Is that what you're into now? Bad boys?" My voice comes out deeper than I planned.

"Maybe."

"It's a good thing I'm not one anymore, then, huh?"

Her green eyes sparkle as she taps a finger on her bottom lip. "So, you're saying you don't want me to be into you?" I remain silent, feeling as though I might be walking into a trap. Her lips curve upward as she continues, "Because something might suggest otherwise."

A beat of confusion passes until her insinuating gaze drifts downward. Realization clicks.

"Fuck." I hop out from under her so quickly she ends up falling onto the floor. I face the door, cursing under my breath, completely fucking mortified. How the hell did we go from talking about my past to her teasing me about getting a hard-on? I shouldn't be surprised, though. This is Lyric. Make me crazy, ache, trouble breathing, heart-liberating Lyric.

"Don't worry," she says with an off pitch giggle. "It happens to most guys. At least, that's what they taught us in health class."

I shake my head, telling myself to chill the fuck out. *It's not a big deal. It's just Lyric. It doesn't mean anything. Mean* that. "You seriously have no boundaries."

"Yeah, but that's what you love about me."

I can hear her moving up behind me. I have no idea what's about to happen, or what I want to happen. Thankfully, I don't have to think about it too hard, because a door slams from somewhere in the house.

"Oh shit." Lyric flies into panic mode, running over to the desk where the scotch, cigarettes, and ashtray are. She tosses the bottle and cigarettes into the drawer then stares wide-eyed at the ashtray. "What do I do with this?"

Part of me wants to keep my lips zipped to pay her back for teasing me, but I care about her too much to let her get in trouble. So I rush over and grab the ashtray while Lyric turns off the music and stuffs the CD back into place. I carefully open the window and pour the ashes out onto the back lawn. After closing the window, I return the ashtray to the drawer where I find a can of air freshener. I douse the air with it and tell Lyric to flip on the ceiling fan. We finish cleaning up the best we can, and then Lyric seizes my hand and jerks me out the door.

"Just play it cool," she whispers loudly. I can smell the scotch on her breath.

This is a disaster in the making.

"Just let me do the talking," I tell her as we creep up the hall toward the kitchen. "And don't breathe on anyone."

She gives an exaggerated nod. I sigh.

We are so going down.

The situation only worsens when we enter the kitchen. There is cake, ice cream, and plates all over the countertops. Not only are her parents there, but so is every member of the Gregory family, most of them turning to look at us as we enter. I swear to God it's like they know. Mr. Gregory pauses the longest, his head cocking to the side as he searches both our faces.

Fuck, he knows.

I open my mouth to say something, but Lyric beats me to the punch.

"I think I'm going to throw up." Her fingers slip from my hand as she bolts out of the kitchen toward the bathroom.

Mrs. Scott glances at Mr. Scott, and then she runs after Lyric. Mrs. Gregory looks at me, the disappointment in her eyes making me want to sink into the earth and vanish into the dirt. She sighs then whispers something to Mr. Gregory. His eyes widen slightly as she backs away and ushers the kids out of the kitchen with her.

Then it's just Mr. Gregory, Mr. Scott, and I, in an overly large kitchen that somehow feels overcrowded. The situation is alarmingly uncomfortable. Rarely does Mr. Gregory have to be the disciplinarian, but I have a feeling he's about to.

I want to run out the door. Run away. A year ago, I would have, but I don't think I can do it now—go back in the system. No, I'm going to have to grovel, beg them to let me stay here with them.

"I'm sorry, we just . . ." I trail off, unsure of what to say. The last thing I want to do is get Lyric in trouble, but I'm worried if I take the fall, I'll be kicked out.

Mr. Scott and Mr. Gregory exchange a look then Mr. Scott scoots out the barstool beside the one he's sitting on and pats the seat while Mr. Gregory leans back against the counter and waits for me sit down.

Blowing out a breath, I plant my ass in the seat.

"What exactly were you and my daughter up to tonight?" Mr. Scott asks, watching me like a hawk.

"Um, we went on a bike ride, sir," I answer, but it sounds more like a question than a response.

"What did you do when you got home, though?" This time it's Mr. Gregory that speaks. "Because if I didn't know any better, I'd guess the two of you have been drinking tonight, which would be really, really bad since we set ground rules of no drinking."

"Um . . ." I struggle for a response, glancing back and forth between them.

Rat out Lyric? Get kicked out? What the hell do I do? I don't want to go back into the system. Don't want to go back. Don't want to. Ever.

Mr. Scott leans over and sniffs the air. "Is that my scotch I smell on your breath?"

"I'm sorry, sir." My pulse pounds as I rise from the stool with my head tipped down and my shoulders sagging. "I'll go pack my stuff."

"Pack your stuff?" Mr. Gregory mumbles, confused. The two of them trade a look, and then their expressions soften. "Ayden, we're not going to kick you out, if that's what you're getting at."

My gaze skims back and forth between them. "But I broke the rules."

Mr. Gregory says to Mr. Scott, "See, this is what happens when they give us responsibilities. We fuck things up." Shaking his head, he returns his attention to me, standing up straight. "Son, we're not going to kick you out because you broke a rule, but I do need to punish you." He seems puzzled over what to do next, and seeks help from Mr. Scott. "What do I punish him with?"

He shrugs. "I have no fucking idea. Ella usually comes up with the punishments, and this is the first time Lyric's done something like this. Maybe ground him for a week?"

This is the strangest thing I've ever witnessed. In the past homes I lived in, by this point, I'd be getting yelled at. If I were still at my mother's, fists would have been flying. But that still wouldn't have been the worst part. No, that would come later.

Mr. Gregory considers the idea. "That seems doable." He turns to me. "What do you think?"

I shrug, so damn confused. "Um, it sounds good to

me, sir."

He nods, looking relieved as he stands up straight. "All right, you're not allowed to do anything for a week."

I keep my head down as I breathe in relief. "Okay, sir."

"And stop calling me sir," he sternly adds. "That's part of your punishment, too. From now on, you have to call me Ethan."

I'm relieved he didn't ask me to call him dad. That I couldn't handle, since I've never called anyone dad before. Getting kicked out I can't handle either, not anymore. Hell, I can barely handle the fact that they seem to want me around, despite the fact I've messed up.

"Okay." As I'm starting to relax, Mrs. Scott enters the room, dragging Lyric in with her.

"Your daughter would like to tell both of you something," she says, staring at a very pale looking Lyric.

Lyric sighs then looks at her dad. "I'm sorry that I drank some of your scotch and smoked your secret cigarettes." Her dad's eyes widen, as if he's been busted, while Lyric continues, "And, Mr. Gregory, you should know that it was my idea. I talked Ayden into going into my father's office and into drinking. And he didn't smoke. That was all me." When her gaze flicks over at me, the damn girl smiles and winks.

I got your back, she mouths as she wanders around the counter and takes a seat beside me. She leans in and whispers in my ear, "I'm going to make this up to you by helping you find your brother and sister. I promise."

I want to hug her, but decide it's probably not the best move right now, nor am I sure I can handle a hug. It's a strange feeling, though—wanting to touch someone. It makes me pause. Really think. About who I'm turning into. Could I somehow, after what I've been through, turn out normal? Lose the fear of touching someone? Of the dark? Of the past?

    I stay put until eventually everyone gathers back into the kitchen to eat cake and ice cream, and reminisce about my first month as being part of the family. It's a pretty good ending to the day, and part of me thinks the perfection is going to carry throughout the night. That maybe my nightmares will somehow vanish.

    But the moment I close my eyes to go to sleep, I fall into darkness and my scars start to bleed again.

Bleed. Bleed. Bleed.
Like wilting rose petals.
Against the darkness.
Dripping against the shadows.
Around me. All around me.
The metal bites my skin.
Killing me slowly. Painfully.
Never letting me breathe again.

CHAPTER 6

Ayden

LYRIC BEING LYRIC, SHE KEEPS her promise to me and helps me search for my brother and sister. We spend a lot of time during the summer and well into the beginning of senior year searching. We keep our efforts from the Gregorys and Scotts, though, mainly because it feels like we're doing something wrong.

No article or search gives us any information on their whereabouts, though, even when we try to break into the social service's records—yeah, we're that awesome. Of course, we fail epically with our hacking since neither of us are computer geniuses.

We've been in my room all day. It's late. The stars and moon are shining brightly from outside the window. I'm tired of staring at the computer screen. Lyric looks bored as hell, lying on her stomach on my bed, messing around with her phone.

"I think I need a break," I tell her, swiveling in the chair as I rub my weary eyes.

"Don't get discouraged." Lyric tosses her phone aside and rolls off the bed, tugging the hem of her dress down.

The fabric is black and red with stars on it and it's just the right length that I get an eyeful every time she bends over. I try not to look when she does, but ever since the incident in her father's office a few months ago, I've been struggling with my attraction to her, something I've yet to tell anyone about, even my therapist.

If I were a better guy, I'd tell her to be more careful when she bends over. But I'm not a better guy. I'm a confused guy who got his first welcomed hard-on while she was sitting on his lap. I want her, yet I'm afraid to want her, afraid to feel that way about her, so I try not to look.

"I'm not discouraged." My fingers fall to the keyboard. "I just need a break. I'm bored."

"You're bored. Wow, that's a first." She comes up behind me and places her hands on my shoulders, digging her fingertips into my shirt, massaging my muscles. I tense from her touch, momentarily forgetting how to breathe as her scent immerses me. "You're usually so uptight. You need to relax, dude." She rests her chin on my head as she keeps rubbing, driving my body into a confusion infused frenzy.

"What's up with the constant dude remark?" I ask as I click off the computer screen. "You're always calling me that."

"That's because you're my dude, buddy, bro." She laughs then kisses the top of my head. "Now get up. If you want a break, I'm totally going to give you a break."

"Where are we going to go?" I stand up and stretch my arms above my head, hyper aware that her eyes wander to the bottom of my shirt when it rides up, checking me out.

I feel slightly better about the whole dress thing, but at the same time guilty. And afraid. So fucking afraid all the time, like I have no clue what to do with my emotions for her.

She bites her bottom lip before blinking up at me. "Hmm . . . let me think. Somewhere adventurous, of course." She taps her finger to her bottom lip. "How about the Silver Box? I haven't been there in forever, and I heard there was a few cool bands playing tonight."

"But what if it's noisy and crowded?"

"Don't worry. I'll hold your hand." Her bottom lip pops out as she peers up at me through her eyelashes, using the move she recently learned that gets her way. "Pretty please, come with me."

Sighing, I retrieve my hoodie from the back of the computer chair. "Fine, but I need to talk to Lila about my brother first."

She scoops up her leather jacket from the bedpost. "Why? You're not letting her in on our plan, are you?"

I slip my arms through the sleeves then zip up the jacket. "No. But he turns eighteen in a couple of days, and she said it might be easier to find him then."

"I hope so." She slides her jacket on and opens the bedroom door. "Now, let's get this party on the road."

She links arms with me and we head down to the kitchen. When we stroll in, Kale and Everson are sitting at the kitchen table, eating fruit and arguing about sports.

Everson is more reserved, like me, but freaks out over anything that has to do with football, like now as he talks animatedly about some touchdown by the Minnesota Vikings, one of his favorite teams.

Kale seems mildly interested, but still argues with him. He's always kind of marched to the beat of his own drum, wearing a lot of comic book inspired attire, but thankfully, after he turned fifteen a couple of months ago, he stopped with the capes.

"Hey, have you two seen your mom and dad?" Lyric asks, stealing an apple from the fruit basket on the table.

Everson scowls at her. "Jesus, make yourself at home, Lyric. You can't just come eat our food and interrupt our conversation."

Kale, who's usually a talker, freezes mid-bite of his orange slice, and stares at Lyric with his jaw hanging open as she bites into the apple. I have a theory that the poor kid might have a crush on her, since the mouth agape trait is a common thing when Lyric's in his sight.

"Sorry, Everson," Lyric says, stifling a smile as she wipes a trail of juice from her chin.

"We were talking football," Everson tells her, like it explains his rude behavior.

"Okay. Chillax. I just asked a question, which you never did answer." Lyric skims back and forth between the two of them. "Do either of you know where your mom and dad are?"

Annoyed, Everson points over his shoulder toward the living room. "They're in there, whispering secrets about Ayden. They think they're being sneaky about it, but we heard them when we walked by."

I trade a puzzled look with Lyric, and then we simultaneously duck out of the room and make a beeline for the living room. I'm about to walk right in, but Lyric throws out her arm and pushes me back behind the wall. Then, she places her finger to her lips, shushing me as she huddles against me, leaning to the side to eavesdrop.

I sigh, torn between letting Lyric listen, and not feeling guilty about doing so myself.

"I'm worried the therapy isn't helping," Lila says concernedly. "He's still saying he can't remember anything. And he's been pretty adamant about searching for his brother and sister."

"Baby, I know you want to fix everything, including the world," Ethan tells her, "but you might just have to accept that he may not ever remember. Maybe it's good for him, too. Maybe whatever happened to him is best left in the dark."

"Yeah, but what about finding his brother and sister? What am I supposed to do about that?"

"You try to find them," Ethan replies simply. "If he wants to find them, then he'll find them whether you help him out or not."

"Yeah, you're probably right." She pauses. "I worry about him, though. There's still so much he doesn't know—that no one knows."

A stretch of silence goes by, and then they start chatting about Kale and his problems at school. I don't even realize I've gripped onto Lyric's hand until her thumb grazes the inside of my wrist.

What Lila and Ethan were talking about is nothing I don't already know, but hearing the worry in their voices makes me concerned that I might be more messed up than I thought.

"Hey, are you okay?" Lyric asks, searching my eyes with apprehension.

I nod, forcing down the lump in my throat. "Yeah, I'm fine." I free her hand from my death grip and walk into the living room, cleaning off my damp palms on the front of my jeans.

They're both sitting on the sectional, the television is on, but the volume is down, and a lamp is on. There are stacks of papers and receipts piled on the table, armrests, floor, everywhere really, probably for Ethan's outdoor touring business, or Lila's part-time catering business she runs on the weekends.

"Oh, hey, sweetie." Lila and Ethan appear uneasy at my appearance. She has a bright pink mug in her hand that matches her shirt. When she notes Lyric and I are wearing our jackets, she sets the mug down on the coffee table. "I thought you two were hanging out in your room tonight?"

"We were." I exchange a glance with Lyric. "But we got bored and were wondering if we could go to the Silver Box for a while."

Lila looks at Ethan for his input, but he just shrugs. Her gaze glides to the window across the room. "It's pretty late for a school night."

"We won't stay out for too long," Lyric steps in. "There's supposed to be some really cool bands playing tonight."

Ethan straightens up at this. "Yeah, I actually heard that, too."

Lyric's green eyes start to sparkle, and I know she's already conjuring up a plan. "Hey, here's an idea. How about you and my dad go with us? That could be fun."

Ethan rubs his jawline, musing over the idea. "That actually could be fun." He drops the papers he was holding down onto the couch cushion and turns to Lila. "What do you think?"

Lila sighs as she collects her mug, reclines back in the sofa, and crosses her legs. "Go have fun. Just don't keep them out too late."

When Ethan hurries upstairs to get ready, Lyric faces me. "I probably should go make sure my dad is down. Meet you at my garage in like ten?"

I nod.

She gives me a pressing look before walking out of the room. I know her well enough by now to understand that the only reason she left was to give me an opportunity to speak with Lila. I'm just not sure what I want to say anymore, so I end up sticking to my original plan.

"Um, I kind of wanted to ask you something else." I lower myself onto the edge of the coffee table and pick at a hole in my jeans. "I was wondering if we could start looking for my brother again, since his eighteenth birthday is in a few days."

"I was actually expecting you to ask that sooner, and was planning on visiting social services next week." She smiles as she raises the brim of the mug to her lips, but beneath the mask of happiness is uneasiness.

I'm just not sure what the uneasiness is over. Finding my brother? Or me?

I DIDN'T UNDERSTAND WHY LYRIC was so easygoing about bringing her father and Ethan with us to a club, but I quickly find out once I arrive at her house. After some persuading, she convinces Mr. Scott to drive his Chevelle and to let us drive her mother's GTO so we can race to the club. It's a fairly easy win, though, since Mr. Scott seems to go easy on her.

When we arrive at the building secured in the heart of the town, I learn another reason why Lyric was so enthusiastic over taking the parentals. Mr. Scott is a well enough known musician that he gets easy access through the entrance. We stroll right up to the rope where the bouncer waves us in.

A crowd is already forming around the stage, even though we're here early. The air is hot, suffocating, along with the bodies pressed up against me. The mob is thickening at such a rapid rate that we end up losing track of Mr. Scott and Ethan. I just about get split apart from Lyric, too, but fortunately she presses her back against my chest, grabs hold of my hands, and then wraps them around her waist.

I momentarily seize up by her nearness, but then I realize the alternative—let her go and get eaten up by the throng. I grip onto her and hold on for dear life.

Her hair smells amazing, like strawberries with a hint of perfume. The strands tickle my cheeks, causing my eyelashes to lower.

"Are you okay?" she asks over her shoulder as she stares at the stage where the band members have started to set up.

I force my eyelids open. "Yeah, I'm fine. Why?"

Her shoulders lift as she shrugs. "I just wanted to make sure you were okay after what we heard."

My stomach knots as I remember Lila's suggestion to Ethan about my memories. "I promise I'm fine." But I'm not sure I am.

"Okay." She pulls me tighter against her and remains silent, leaving me to wonder what's going on in her head. I'm about to be daring and ask her, but then she says, "Man, I'm so going to date a drummer one day."

Okay, maybe I don't want to know what's going on in her head.

"You say that now, but next week it'll be the guy from Danny's Stop and Go," I tease. "Then it'll be the quarterback."

She peers over her shoulder at me, the florescent lighting reflecting in her green eyes. "Are you saying I'm flaky?" Her brow arches, challenging me.

"You do change your mind a lot."

"That's because there's too many opportunities roaming around in the world. It's hard to focus on just one." She rotates back around toward the stage and raises her voice as the drummer starts bashing on the symbols. "You know what we should do!" she shouts as the crowd goes wild. "We should join a band! There's these two guys from school, Nolan and Sage, who are looking for band members!"

"I'm not that great at the guitar yet!" I holler as I get

bumped from every angle. *Breathe. Just breathe.* "And what about your issue with stage fright?"

"I'm going to conquer that fear one day!" She lifts her arms in the air and screams as the singer belts sultry lyrics through the microphone. "And you rock at the guitar! It's mad crazy how fast you caught on in just a month's time!"

"Ethan's a good teacher!" I shout, but my voice gets swallowed up by the screams, the singing, the bass, the entire scene of being a rock star.

Lyric gets lost in the rhythm, rocking and bobbing her head. Our bodies are perfectly aligned so every time she sways her hips, her ass rubs against my cock. The sensation is so intense that by the third song, I almost consider bailing.

But the way she moves.
Is breathtaking.
Consuming.
She owns me.
Makes me feel
so alive.
So petrified.
I can't breathe.
Dizzy.
Spinning out of control.
Reckless and wild.
I want.
Want. Want.
Something so
terrifying.

In the middle of my stream of thoughts, Lyric twirls around. Her eyes are large and glazed over, high on the music. I open my mouth to ask her what's up, but she glides her palms up my chest then wraps her arms around my neck. My muscles wind tight as she presses her breasts against me. Then, she stands on her tiptoes and places her lips against my ear.

"*Strip me bare, peel me apart, layer by layer, steal my heart,*" she sings the lyrics of the song playing. Her voice is soft, not to her full potential, yet it's the most incredible sound that's ever graced my ears. I can only imagine what it would sound like if she *really* sang—striking enough to stop my heart probably. "*Let me stand naked in front of you, and pour my secrets out. Unravel me slowly, savoring each part.*" She rolls her body against mine and her fingers trace the nape of my neck. "*Then let me do the same thing to you. Strip you apart.*"

I start to move with her, even though I have no clue what I'm doing. No fucking idea. All I know is I'm left wanting, wanting, wanting.

Wanting her.

Wanting more.

But I'm too afraid to take it.

CHAPTER 7

I'M A SPORADIC PERSON. THAT'S been a given since I first learned how to talk. So when I declare my love for someone, it shouldn't be that big of a surprise. Yet, it always seems to be with everyone. My parents especially. Whenever I proclaim my love for someone new, they seem shocked, like they half expected me to say someone else.

Ayden should know better by now, though, since he understands my little quirks better than anyone.

"I think I'm in love," I announce to him as I stroll into his bedroom.

He's situated on the bed, fiddling with the guitar Ethan bought him for his birthday a few months ago. After a little bit of practice, he's gotten pretty good at it, enough that he joined a band per my suggestion, and now he's living out my lifelong dream. But it's my own damn fault for letting my fear control me.

He glances up from his guitar as I shut the door, his fingers continuing to pluck the strings. "Who is it this time? The drummer from that concert?" He seems more annoyed than usual.

Rolling up the paper I brought over with me, I narrow my eyes at him as I flop down onto the mattress on my stomach. "No, not him. And what do you mean 'this time'?" I prop up on my elbows as the sunlight hits my face through the window. "Are you mocking me, Ayden Gregory, about my frequency in love declarations?"

He rolls his eyes, lays the guitar aside on the mattress, and brushes strands of his black hair out of his eyes as he relaxes back on the bed. "This is the third time in the last four months you've barged into my room and said the exact same thing to me." I pout out my lip, and he sighs, gathering a guitar pick from the pillow. "Fine, who are you in love with?" He fiddles around with the pick, sketching the tip up and down the scars on the back of his hand.

I still don't know where the scars came from. I want to ask him, but any time I even mention Ayden's life before the Gregorys, he gets squeamish, which makes me question how he's going to handle the papers I brought over with me. I have to tell him, though. After spending the last few months searching for his siblings, I finally stumbled across something, not about his siblings, but about his past.

I kneel up on the bed in front of him. "It's William Stephington."

His face squishes in disgust. "Ew, that jock, steroid freak?"

"Hey." I swat his arm. "He's not a steroid freak."

"That's not what I heard." He frowns, staring at me undecidedly. "Lyric, I know you might not want to hear this, but I think you should stay away from that guy. And I really think you should talk to him for more than ten minutes before you decide you're in love with him."

"I've talked to him quite a few times at school. And besides, I agreed to go out with him tonight."

His frown deepens. "Lyric, the guy's got a reputation for being a . . ." He deliberates his word choice while staring at a Pink Floyd poster on the ceiling that I gave him for his birthday. "A manwhore douche."

"Manwhore douche? Wow, those are some colorful words."

"Well, he is."

I scrape at my blue fingernail polish, choosing my next words carefully. "Even if he is, it doesn't matter, because I'm not a douche or a whore. I haven't even kissed a guy yet." I hop off the bed. "But that's going to change tonight."

He pulls a face, clearly irritated, which isn't typical for him. Usually, Ayden is the most agreeable person in the world, always trying to please everyone. "Don't waste your first kiss on that asshole."

"Hey, I've been saving my first kiss for over seventeen years now, so trust me when I say that when it happens, it's not going to be something I do with an asshole."

"He's not the guy who's going to change your soul, Lyric. Or make you write any better. He's not the life experience you're searching for."

I sternly point a finger at him. "Hey, I told you all that stuff in confidence."

His gaze scans the vacant room with his hands spread out. "Am I telling anyone else? No, I'm just reminding you what you told me—that this isn't what you want. You're saving your first kiss for a guy that will make you be able to pour your soul out onto paper, give you something to write about. And I don't believe that that's going to be William Stephington." His face twists with disgust again.

I fold my arms across my chest, and his gaze flicks to the papers in my hand. "Well, even if he isn't, maybe it's time to get this whole kissing thing over with. I mean, I'm seventeen years old, for God's sake. No one is a virgin kisser at that age. Jesus, Maggie kissed her first guy when she was like fourteen. I had my chance, too, but no, I had to hold on to this crazy idea that kisses were supposed to be all romantic and planned."

"It's not that bad of a concept."

"Yes it is. And it's time for me to grow up." I pause. "And why are you even lecturing me? I know you kissed a ton of girls before you came here."

It's just a guess, but when he doesn't deny it, I assume I'm right.

Grief engraves into his face. "Don't do that—change your dreams over some guy or belief based on other people. That's not the Lyric I know and love. Besides, you hardly even know the guy. You're way too trusting sometimes."

I sigh, because he's got me on that one. "Fine, I'll reconsider the kiss, but I'm still trusting him enough to go out on the date, because that's what I do." I back up for the door, knowing that's not true. I've passed up chance after chance of getting kissed, because my expectations are too high. "You know, if it really bothers you, you could always come with us."

"On your date with you?" he says dryly. "Yeah, that sounds like a lot of fun."

"No, to the party we're going to."

I know he won't. He made a commitment to do family movie night tonight, and Ayden hardly goes back on his commitments to the Gregorys, like he thinks he owes them for adopting him or something. Honestly, sometimes I believe that's exactly what he thinks, which is sad.

"I have band practice tonight." He drops the guitar pick onto the pillow and sits up, swinging his feet over the edge of the bed as he stretches his arms over his head. "And then movie night afterward."

I try not to stare when his shirt rides up, but it's always difficult. On top of having a beautiful face, Ayden's body is ridiculously amazing. Not super muscly or anything, just lean and toned.

One of my friends, Maggie, asked me how I can stand being friends with him without wanting to "get some of that." I tell her it's simple, because I don't look at him that way. Just as a friend. She looked at me as if I'd grown a third eye, which I had shrugged off. Yeah, Ayden is hot. That's a huge obvious given. And he's the best friend I could ever ask for. But I haven't felt the butterflies around him or the desire to kiss him. I haven't felt that with anyone yet. Maybe it's because I set the bar too high, but I'm contemplating lowering it tonight.

"So what." I sigh when Ayden finally adjusts his shirt back over his stomach. "Blow off movie night and come after practice is over. Sage and Nolan will probably be there anyway."

He pauses. "Where is it at?"

"Up at Maggie's house." I grip the doorknob, feeling upbeat at the idea that he might go. "Are you seriously considering going?"

He stands up and winds around his bed and over to me. "Yeah, maybe. If Sage and Nolan go there, I might catch a ride with them."

"Good." I have to stand up on my tiptoes to kiss him on the cheek. He flinches, like he always does whenever I touch him, but at least he allows me to. With almost anyone else, he freaks out. The only exception to this being Fiona, and sometimes Lila. "You need to do more fun things in your life, shy boy."

"No, I don't," he says in all seriousness. "I'm just going to keep an eye on you."

I ruffle his hair. "I don't need a babysitter."

"Yeah, you kind of do, and I have an endless list of reasons why. You think too much with your heart, Lyric, and not with your head."

"All right, I'll give you that." Shooting him one last conniving grin, I open the door and strut out of his room, calling over my shoulder, "See you tonight, babysitter."

I halt as I step over the threshold, realizing I still have the papers in my hand. "Oh, wait. There was actually a real reason why I came over here."

"You mean other than make another declaration of love," he jokes as I spin around.

"Yes, my friend." Sucking in a huge breath, I hand the papers over. "I found something out about you on the internet."

"About me?" The papers crinkle as he unrolls them.

"Yeah." I release a deafening breath, worried how this is going to go, but there was no way I could keep something like this from him. "It's about your tattoo."

He glances up from the papers, his grey eyes filled with terror. "I don't understand."

I move around to stand beside to him. "Well, I was typing in random things that I thought might help us figure out stuff about your brother and sister. Then I started typing in homemade tattoos just to see what came up. After scrolling through an assload of images, I found this." I tap my finger against the paper. "I guess it's a pretty common thing to do—put tattoos on yourself. But the one you have belongs to some crazy group of people who believe the tattoo represents some kind of soul cleansing thing. I don't know. It sounds weird to me, but that's what all the articles say. And I guess they've done a lot of bad stuff, too."

He stares at the ink staining the paper in his hand. "Like what?"

"Like . . . kidnappings and things. You said a couple of months ago that you were taken by people with strange beliefs . . ." I trail off, hoping he'll explain more to me. I don't want to push him.

His fingers strangle the paper, the edges ruffling. "I wasn't necessarily taken . . . I was given away."

"By who?"

"My mother." His tone is sharp, his eyes cold, lost. He looks like a scared little boy.

My breath catches in my throat. "She gave you to those people?"

"Left us with them," is all he says. He folds up the papers and chucks them on the desk. "I have a bunch of stuff to do before I head to practice."

I instantly regret showing him the paper, but there's not a whole lot that I can do about it now.

"All right, I'll see you later maybe."

He doesn't respond, so I leave the room, praying that I didn't break him.

CHAPTER 8

I HAVE ABOUT AN HOUR until date time and should be getting ready, but instead I end up getting distracted with my notebook. A lot of the stuff coming out of me today is strange and mainly centered on my worry for Ayden, but since I still don't completely understand him or everything he went through, I feel as though my words are lacking. My lyrics usually do.

Honestly, I'm nowhere near where I want to be in any music area. I've yet to decide which instrument I want to focus on, haven't performed at all, and the idea of performing in front of anyone makes me want to hurl. It gets frustrating. Ayden, who barely talks to anyone, is perfectly fine standing up on stage and playing the guitar, while me, Miss Chatterbox, suffers from stage fright.

Go. Fucking. Figure.

About fifteen minutes before date time, I start the process of getting ready, moving slower than usual as I keep glancing out the window toward Ayden's bedroom. His curtain is shut, so I have no clue what he's doing.

Finally, after going through all of my clothes, I end up stealing a thin-strapped black dress from my mother's closet, and then slip a leather jacket on since it's fall and sometimes the nights can sometimes get a little breezy. I dab on some kohl eyeliner and pink lip gloss, then top off the look with my favorite pair of boots before I go downstairs to wait for my date.

I find my dad lounging on the living room sofa, jotting down lyrics in his own notebook. He glances up when I enter.

"Where are you headed to all dressed up?" he asks, setting the pen and notebook down on the sofa cushion beside him.

"To a party." I drop down in the chair across from him and kick my feet up on an antique trunk that acts as a coffee table.

He puts on his interrogation face. "And where is this party?"

"At Maggie's house." I check my watch. "Mom already went over this with me, Dad."

"And who are you going with?" he continues, ignoring my last statement.

"With a guy from school."

"Which one?"

"Someone you haven't met yet." I lower my feet to the floor. "His name's William Stephington."

"And what does this William do?" he asks, reaching for his soda that's on the trunk.

"He goes to school with me." I fiddle with one of the leather bands on my wrists. "He's on the football team, too."

His grip constricts on the soda can as he frowns. "Football? Really?"

"What? There's nothing wrong with football guys."

"Yeah, but . . . it just doesn't seem like your type."

"I don't even know my type yet." I resist an eye roll. Jesus, he's getting weirder and weirder about guys the more I go out on dates.

He places the can back on the trunk then rests his arms on his knees. "Is Ayden going to this party?"

I shrug, feeling a lump swell in my throat as I remember the coldness in his eyes when I left his room. "I invited him, and he seemed like he might show up, but with Ayden you can never be sure. He might end up feeling too guilty about missing movie night."

Maybe I should go check on him before I leave?

Or at least text him.

I just need to know that he's okay.

My dad ponders over something then sticks his hand into the pocket of his jeans. "I'm going to call Ethan to see if I can find out." He presses a button then puts the phone to his ear while I retrieve my cell from my jacket pocket to text Ayden.

"Yeah, you do that." I jump to my feet when I hear a horn honk outside. "That's my ride. Have fun with your phone call." I scurry for the door with the phone clutched in my hand.

"Lyric Scott, get your butt back here."

Dammit, so close.

I spin around and smile innocently at him. "Yes, Daddy."

"Don't you 'yes Daddy' me." He nods his head toward the window at the driveway where the engine of William's car is rumbling. "I have to meet him before you get in that car with him."

My shoulders slacken. "What, you don't trust my judgment?"

He dithers with indecision. "No, not really. You are my daughter after all."

I blow out a frustrated breath. "Fine. You can walk me to the car and meet him." I aim a finger at him. "But don't be weirdo, strict dad."

He rolls his eyes as he stuffs his phone back inside his pocket. "Lyric, when it comes to you dating guys, I will always be weirdo, strict dad, but only because I love you."

Sighing, I lead him out to William, knowing my dad's already docking points for the Mercedes he's driving. William appears wigged out when I stroll up to the driver's side and rap on the glass.

He rolls the window down. "What's up?" He casts a glimpse over my shoulder at my dad. His appearance is going to be strike two—blonde hair slicked back, a polo shirt, and his somewhat cocky grin isn't going to impress him.

"William, this is my dad." I motion back and forth between them. "Dad, this is William."

My dad eyeballs the sleek lines of the car with his face screwed up tight, like he just tasted something bitter. "How long have you had your license?"

"For about a year." William flicks a *what the hell* look at me.

Things only continue to go downhill as my dad fires question after question at him. By the time we're pulling out of the driveway, fifteen minutes have passed since I first walked out of the house.

"Sorry about that," I say as I buckle my seatbelt. "I'm not sure what got into him today."

William squirms in his seat as he adjusts the mirror. "No worries. I just didn't expect *your* dad to be so uptight."

"What do you mean by *your* dad?"

He shrugs as he shifts gears and speeds up. "I just figured with as laid back as you are that your parents would be pretty chill."

I feel a little bit defensive, which is really out of character for me. Usually I try to stay all peace, love, and sunshine. "He was just making sure his daughter wasn't driving off with a psychopath."

He laughs, kind of snidely. "He seemed a little overly intense, if you ask me."

Okay, maybe Ayden was right. Perhaps I should spend more time with a guy before I proclaim that I'm in love with him.

"Sorry," he quickly says when he catches sight of my disappointment. "I just don't do well with parents." He reaches across the console and wraps his fingers around my bare knee. "Let's drop it, though, and have some fun tonight." He flashes me his infamous dimpled grin.

I smile back, but I'm suddenly not feeling him.

As William starts rambling about sports, I slide my finger across the screen of my phone and send Ayden a text.

> *Me: Hey, so I just wanted to see if u were ok. U looked super upset when I left and I feel like maybe I might have pushed u a little too far . . . If u need to talk or want to meet up later, I'm totally down for it. William might be a bust anyway.*

I slide my phone into my pocket, waiting for a reply. By the time we arrive at the party, I'm still feeling super down and a bit anxious, so when William offers me a drink, I take it, even though I've tried to avoid alcohol since the whole scotch incident.

William flashes me his pearly whites as I guzzle down half the cup in one gulp. "Hell yeah!" he cheers over the pop music I loathe, blasting so loudly I can feel the bass in my chest.

I lick a drop of the spiked punch off the bottom of my lip, slightly more at ease as the alcohol settles into my system. "Want to dance!" I shout, figuring anything will be better than talking about sports some more.

Without waiting for him to respond, I hand him my drink, wiggle out of my jacket and shake my ass toward the dance floor, twirling around and around.

I waggle my fingers at my friend Maggie, who's dancing in the corner with a guy that looks old enough to be in college. She winks at me and wiggles her eyebrows suggestively right as someone places their hands on my waist.

"You dance fucking amazing," William whispers in my ear, his breath hot on my skin and reeking of Bacardi.

I smile at myself then whirl around and really show him what dancing is, rocking and grinding my hips against his. He moves with me, rubbing against me as his hands travel all over my body, gripping at my flesh.

"God, you smell so fucking good." His teeth graze my neck as his hand cups my ass.

The music suddenly screams at my eardrums to the point where I can't stand it anymore.

I'm so not ready for this tonight.

I tense and push back, putting room between our bodies. "Maybe we should slow things down just a bit."

He seems a little pissed, but calms down and says, "How about we go out back where it's a little bit quieter and talk. There are people out there, too, so we won't be alone."

I nod, relieved that he's not being pushy about my stiffness. That's pretty much the only thing he's done right the entire night, so I take it.

He pours us both another drink in the kitchen area before he slips his fingers through mine and steers me through Maggie's house. I've never actually been to her home before, not her father's house anyway. William seems to know his way around as he maneuvers through the throng of people drinking, dancing, laughing, and playing pool. Some I go to high school with, while others look old enough to be in college.

"This house is huge!" I yell over the music as we veer down a narrow hallway lined with shut doors. The lighting is dim, the music softer.

He peers over his shoulder. "Drink up," he says, nodding at the cup in my hand. His expression is darker than it was minutes ago. Oddly enough, he seems extremely relaxed. It makes me hesitate. Red flags go up.

All of a sudden, he's tugging me into a dark room with a bed and a dresser. He doesn't turn the lights on as he closes and locks the door behind us. A little too late, I painfully realize that Ayden might have been right about William. And myself, too. I do think with my heart too much. Do trust people too much.

And now I've walked head-on into trouble.

CHAPTER 9

I HATE PARTIES. GROWING UP in the midst of them gave me an ugly outlook on what can come from too much partying. My mother was a hardcore partier. Her drug of choice was everything and anything she could get her hands on. It aged her quickly and turned her into a nasty person, one who was incapable of loving and did the most awful things to people, including her own children. And that's how she died, a doped-up druggie who hated the world and left scars on her offspring. It was a sad, pathetic waste of a life. At her funeral, I vowed that I would never turn into her.

I almost did, though, as I got lost in the system, getting bitter with each home I was passed through. But then I lucked out and ended up with the Gregorys, who showed me that people could love one another unconditionally and gave me hope that maybe trusting people was a possibility. That perhaps even love was a possibility. That's what my therapist is trying to convince me.

"You're too afraid to feel all the horrible emotions you shut down as a child." He told me that today while I sat in his office, fidgety as usual. You would think after nine months of monthly visits with him I would be more relaxed, yet I never am. "That fear is blocking out all of the good emotions as well as some of your memories."

I hadn't responded.

Part of me agrees with him, but I am doing better with dealing my emotions, not shutting down so much and keeping my feelings to myself. Then I saw that damn paper and was reminded of stuff forgotten. I snapped at Lyric, which is gnawing at me more than anything.

"Ayden, tell Kale to stop teasing me!" Fiona shouts from the kitchen table as Kale throws a pencil at her.

I tear my attention from my thoughts and the cookie I've been nibbling on for the last ten minutes.

Fiona is probably the most spoiled by all of us. I once heard Lila and Ethan talking about how they ended up adopting her. She was born by a mother who was doped-up on heroin. She had a lot of health problems because of this, so no one wanted to adopt her. Like me, she was passed through many homes until she ended up here four years ago. Other than the fact that she's a bit small for her age, she seems normal. Spunky even.

All have their own stories, though.

Everyone does when you really think about it.

It's something I've learned while I've been here. That I'm not as alone as I once thought.

"Kale, leave her alone," I say as I dig a soda out of the fridge.

Kale's shoulders slump as he sets the pencils down on the table. "Whatever." He sulks out of the kitchen.

Fiona flips him the bird then she smiles sweetly at me. "Thank you, Ayden. You're the best brother ever."

I pop the tab on the can, feeling the slightest bit of guilt churn in my gut as I think of my brother and sister, and the paper Lyric showed me with the tattoo on it.

"What are you working on?" I change the subject as I

peek at her drawing. It's of a butterfly—most of them are. "That's actually really good." It's the truth, too. The girl is damn talented at drawing. Equally as good as Lyric and her mother, which says a lot.

"I know. I just wish I could get the butterfly out of my head and draw something else." She sits down and plucks up the pencil. "I can never seem to stop thinking about them. It's like a dream stuck in my head."

My brows furrow. "Is it something from your childhood maybe?"

"Could be." That's all she gives me, and I will never, *ever* press her to tell me more when it's clear she doesn't want to. "Do you think I'll be able to be an artist one day?"

"I think you can be whatever you want," I repeat the words Lila keeps saying to Kale when he asks her a similar question about being a comic book artist. "As long as you work hard."

Fiona works on shading in the wings while humming a song under her breath. "Do you think Mrs. Scott would give me art lessons? She's super good at painting and stuff. And I want to learn to do that. I mean, I like drawing, but I think it's time for an upgrade."

"You could always ask her," I say, trying not to think about Lyric going out with that douche tonight, yet it creeps into my mind and leaves a foul feeling in the pit of my stomach, almost as heavy as when I saw that paper she handed me.

This William asshole has a reputation for treating girls like shit. It's guys like him that will burn Lyric's feisty, trusting, carefree inner fire right out of her. And while that fire has gotten me in trouble quite a few times, I never, *ever* want it to burn out. It's what got me breathing again, brought me back to life, keeps me breathing. As selfish as it makes me sound, I want Lyric all to myself. I just wish

I could give her a little of what she gives me back, instead of freaking out on her all the time.

I sneak up to my bedroom and jot some of my thoughts about Lyric into a notebook. It's something I started doing six months ago when my therapist suggested I find a way to clear out my head. I think that he was aiming more along the lines of a journal, but the pages are filled with song lyrics than my inner thoughts and desires.

Tucking the notebook back into the dresser drawer, I grab my guitar and jog down the stairs. Lila is filling up a pot under the faucet when I enter the kitchen, and fresh vegetables and seasonings cover the counters. She's obviously planning a big meal, so now I feel guilt-ridden about going to the party.

"I'm going to band practice," I tell her as she shuts the water off. "It's still okay if I take the car, right?" I've been a little offish since I overheard the conversation between her and Ethan. I'm not sure why, but it feels like they're keeping something from me about myself or my brother and sister.

"Do you know what time you're going to be back? I want to make sure I have dessert ready and everyone settled down for movie time."

"About that . . ." I shift my guitar case into my other hand. "I was kind of wondering if maybe I could go to a party after band practice."

She carries the pan full of water to the stove. "Is it the one Lyric went to with that William guy?"

"How did you know about that?"

"Micha mentioned something about it just a few minutes ago." She switches the heat up on the stove. "He wanted to know if you were going. I think he's not handling this whole Lyric dating thing very well and wanted you to check up on her."

"So, is it okay if I go?" I ask, opening the fridge to grab another soda. "I mean, I can come home if you want me to. In fact, maybe I should. I promised you guys a movie night."

She sighs as she rounds the counter toward me. "Ayden, you don't need to please us all the time." She circles her arms around me as I'm pushing the fridge door shut. "Go to the party."

I hold my breath and awkwardly pat her back, my grip on the soda can nearly crushing the metal. "Are you sure?"

"Yes." She pulls back, retrieves the car keys from her pocket, and drops them into my palm. "Just do me a favor. When you get there, check on Lyric, and then text me so Micha will stop sending me texts."

"Okay, that I can do." I enfold my fingers around the keys. "But can I ask you one more thing?"

"Of course, sweetie. You can ask me anything. You know that."

I wasn't planning on asking her today, but after the tattoo thing brought up unwanted memories, I need to know for my own sanity. "I was just wondering if you found anything out about my brother yet? I know you said we'd check back when he was eighteen, and now he is, so . . ." I clutch the handle of my guitar case as her skin pales.

"Oh, Ayden." She embraces me so tightly the air gets ripped from my lungs. "I'm sorry . . . I've been meaning to tell you, but I just couldn't figure out how. I guess he ran away from the last foster home he was at, which was over a year ago. No one's seen or heard from him since."

My fingers ball into fists, the sharp edges of the keys slicing into my skin. I want to grasp onto her. Cry. But I can't do that—can't let go in that kind of way—so I pull back.

"Okay, thanks for trying." I start for the door, trying

not to hyperventilate.

"Ayden, are you going to be okay?" she calls after me.

"Not really." The truth slips from my lips, but before she can utter anything else, I'm out the door.

TWO HOURS LATER, I'M FEELING a tad bit better. Playing always does that for me. It helped me to stop thinking of my brother and worrying about Lyric. Lyric also text me, saying she wants to meet up and wasn't feeling William, which made me twistedly happy inside. I had text her back, replying okay, but she still hasn't responded. That's Lyric, though. She's probably gotten sidetracked by someone.

Sage and Nolan are in the car with me as we roll up to the house in Lila's BMW. The fancy car blends in with the rest of others parked around the house. No surprise, since the house is a freaking mansion. I mean, the home I live in is pretty fucking big, but this damn thing looks like it has three stories and a basement. I'm never going to find Lyric here.

I've already sent her multiple texts by the time I enter the home, but she still hasn't responded. As soon as I step foot into the foyer, I discover why. The music is blaring so loud the floors and windows are vibrating.

"Dude, this music sucks balls!" Sage yells over the noise, pulling a repulsed face at a machine pouring fog across the dance area, like we're in a freaking club or something. He rakes his hand through his hair. "I need a fucking drink."

As he vanishes into the crowd and the smog, Nolan stuffs his hands into his pockets. "I'm going to go find Anna. Are you going to be okay?"

"I can take care of myself, man," I say, even though the amount of people crammed into the room is making me feel as if the walls are closing in. This is the last thing I needed tonight after finding out Lila couldn't find anything out about my brother.

I need to find Lyric and get the hell out of here.

"But I know how you get in crowds!" Nolan has to yell in order for me to hear him over the song. "And around people!"

I wave him off. "I'll be fine. Go get some."

He grins then the crowd swallows him up as he dives into the insanity.

I start my search for Lyric, pushing my way through sweaty, intoxicated people, until I manage to find the enormous kitchen that could easily be as big as the entire top floor of my house. I ask if anyone has seen her, but since I usually don't speak until I have to, it's apparent that's made the people I go to school with skittish around me.

Finally, I stumble across Maggie. She's near the dance area with a cup in her hand, her attention fixed on a short, stocky guy that looks like he's in college.

I squeeze past people, moving in her direction across the room. Everyone is dancing, and I get rubbed up on more than once. Add the smoke in the air, and I feel like I'm going to suffocate to death. I still keep going, though, telling myself to suck it up. That this isn't the past. Just a party. Nothing more. But images of my brother and I chained to that damn wall creep up and stab me in the brain. It feels like my skull is bleeding. All I want to do is find a place to curl up and cry.

He disappeared without a trace.
Gone to who knows where.
Lost in a sea of people.
Who will never understand.

Maybe he isn't just lost, though.
Fuck, what if he's dead?

"Hey, have you seen Lyric?" I ask when I manage to get beside Maggie, one of the few people who aren't afraid of me.

Her drunken gaze lights up as she scans me over from head to toe. "Hey, sexy. I feel so special. You never come to parties."

The stocky guy she's with gives me a nasty look, like I'm trying to cramp his style. But one good thing about my intimidation factor is when I retaliate with a dirty look, he backs off.

"I thought I'd come and see what this whole thing was about," I lie. "But I need to find Lyric and check in on her. I promised I would."

"You are so good to her. I wish I had someone like you for myself." She trails her fingers up and down my stomach then flattens her palm against my chest.

As memories prickle at the back of my mind, I almost shove her.

Breathe, just breathe.
Breathe, breathe, breathe.
Into the light, out of the dark.
To the life with Lyric.
Where no one can touch you.
Break you apart.
Where you don't have to see or feel.
What was done to you.
What destroyed you.

I inch out of her reach, and her hand remains suspended in the air as her brows dip.

"Look, I really need to find Lyric," I tell her, stuffing my hands into my pockets to keep from pushing her away.

Her face bunches up as she frowns. "The last time I

saw her, she was heading into one of the bedrooms with William."

My heart hammers inside my chest, my eardrums ringing louder than the song. "Where is this bedroom?" My voice comes out sharper than I mean to, but seriously, what the hell is Lyric thinking going into a bedroom with William Stephington?

Maggie points her finger toward the back of the house. "It's back there, down the hallway." She swigs a mouthful from the cup in her hand. "God, Ayden, you need to chillax. She can go back to a room with a guy without your permission."

I scowl at her then start shoving through the crowd, roughly pushing people out of my way. It takes me a few minutes to get to the hallway Maggie pointed to, but I manage. The first door I open is a closet. The next is a bedroom, but it's empty, so I try the next one. And the next. All are vacant, except for the last one, which has a couple occupying it. They're going at it like rabbits, and I get an eyeful before I get the door shut.

What the hell am I doing? If Lyric is back here doing something with William, then what? I'm going to walk in and tell her to stop? Then she would get pissed off at me, and honestly, I don't think I could handle seeing her doing that with a guy.

Giving up on the bedrooms, I spin back around and make a path for the kitchen again. Halfway down the hall, my phone vibrates from inside my pocket. I pause to fish it out and exhale a breath of relief when I see the text is from Lyric.

Lyric: U didn't by chance come to the party, did u?

Me: Yeah, I'm here right now. Where r u?

Lyric: In the bathroom.

Me: Okay, meet me in the kitchen when u come out.

Lyric: I can't.

Me: Can't what? Meet me in the kitchen?

Lyric: No, come out of the bathroom.

Me: R u sick?

Lyric: No.

Me: Then what's wrong?

When she doesn't respond, I grow anxious.

Me: R u hurt?

Lyric: Kind of.

Me: Lyric, where the fuck r u?

Lyric: I'm in the bathroom on the second floor near the start of the hallway. But, Ayden, u don't need to come up here. I'm fine.

Like hell I don't.

I knock people out of the way as I storm back through the kitchen and toward the massive spiral stairway that coils to the second floor. Different scenarios play in my head as my mind goes wild, trying to figure out what happened. With Lyric, it's hard to say. The girl is a freaking daredevil, but for some reason, I'm betting this has to do with William.

The top of the stairs is much quieter and less populated. Only a group of seven or eight are lurking around, drinking and smoking, including Sage.

"Hey, do you know where the bathroom is?" I ask him

as he takes a deep hit from a joint.

He coughs smoke in my face as he exhales, passing the rolled up paper to the next guy. "Sorry, about that," he says as I fan my hand in front of my face. "Yeah, it's the fifth door down, but I wouldn't bother. Some chick's been locked in there for like an hour."

I'm off before he can even finish his sentence, rushing past doors. When I reach the fifth one, it's locked, so I bang my fist against the heavy wood.

"Lyric, open the door. It's me."

A beat goes by before I hear the lock click. I push the door open and step into the dark, narrow room. Moonlight trickles in from the window above the bathtub, highlighting Lyric's silhouette.

"Why the hell do you have the light off?" I feel around on the wall until my fingers brush against the switch. I flip it on, blinking against the bright light.

"You were right," Lyric says, only her voice sounds so wrong, like it's excruciating to speak, which might be because she has a swollen lip. "I'm way too trusting for my own good."

My lips part in shock at the sight of her. Her cheeks are enflamed and one of the straps of her dress is missing, as if someone ripped it off. The front has fallen down, too, so I can see the top of her bra. Her blond hair is tangled around her pained face and mascara and tears stain her cheeks.

She cups her hand to her cheek. "God, my face fucking hurts."

That yanks me out of my trance.

"What the hell did he do to you?" I pause when her fingers drift to the hem of her dress.

God, no. Please don't let it be that. I don't know if I can handle that. It'll be too much, and I need to be able to handle this for her.

"Did he . . . ?" I can't even say it aloud, as I'm pulled away to a different time, place, life that binds me at the wrists and slices my flesh open.

I don't want to remember it.
Please.
Don't let me remember it.
Right now.
Ever.

She shakes her head, hugging her arms around herself. "No, he didn't get that far."

My breathing comes out ragged as I battle to stay calm. "Where is he?"

She shrugs. "I don't know. Probably icing his balls."

I cock my head to the side. "Huh?"

"Well, I did kick him there enough times that he probably won't be able to have children anymore," she says matter-of-factly, her eyes lacking so much emotion it kills me to look at them.

I miss her fire. Her life.

He better not have stolen that away from her.

Taken *anything* away from her.

I pierce my nails into the flesh of my palms. "How did you get the fat lip and the welt on your cheek?"

She lowers herself onto the shut toilet then drops her head into her hands. "I thought we were going outside and realized too late he was taking me to a bedroom. When we got in there, he locked the door and shoved me down on the bed. I hit my face on the headboard and bit my lip."

I cautiously inch past the sink toward her. "What about your dress? How did it . . . get torn?"

Her breathing quickens and her bottom lip quivers. "I said he didn't rape me, but that doesn't mean he didn't try." She drags her fingers down her face as she stares helplessly at me. "God, I'm so stupid. You were right. I do think too much with my heart."

Something snaps inside me. Breaks. Shatters. I'm not sure if it's because she doubts her heart, or that he tried to rape her. Whatever it is, I can't stop the thoughts from emerging.

House of locks. Walls of metal.
Searing pain. Scorching into me.
Branded forever, like bleeding ink.

I suck in an uneven breath.

William is going to fucking pay for what he did.

"I'll be right back." My voice is low and controlled, despite the fact that I feel more out of control than I ever have. I reel around and yank the door open.

"No, Ayden, don't," Lyric begs, hopping up from the toilet and chasing after me.

But I storm out the door, slamming it behind me with only a single thought in my mind.

Make William pay.
Protect Lyric.

Like no one ever did for me.

I find the douche bag in the kitchen, near the drink section, chatting with some girl from our school, standing a bit awkwardly as he throws back a shot.

Of course he'd be with a fucking girl.

He spots me when I'm about two steps away from him, and by the way the color drains from his face, I can tell he knows why I'm here, and he's afraid. He fucking should be. I had been good at refraining from violence for a while, but I'm making an exception right now for Lyric.

I don't even slow down as I reach him, my feet keeping momentum as I crane my arm back. He starts to stagger back into the counter, but not quick enough, and I bash my knuckles straight into his nose. There's a crack then blood streams from his nostrils, and then he crumples to the floor.

The crowd creates a gap as people skitter away from the scene, some cursing, and a few girls even start crying.

"You're going to fucking pay for that," he growls as he rolls onto his back, cupping his bloody nose.

I crouch down beside him, and his eyes widen and fill with fear. "If you ever so much as look at Lyric again, I will put you in the hospital. You got it?"

He shakes his head, cursing as blood drips down the back of his hands. "I'm going to sue your ass for this."

I lean down in his face. "Do. You. Get. What. I'm. Saying?"

Scowling, he nods. It takes every amount of my strength to stand up without punching him in the face again.

By the time I reach the stairway, my fists are trembling and blood is staining my knuckles and scars. I start to hyperventilate. I try to force the images back, but the flashbacks are too intense this time and emotions overwhelm me.

Claws.
Blood.
The walls are closing in.
They tell me this is how life is supposed to be.
For me to be trapped.
Confined.
A prisoner in a home filled with madness.
That my mother stuck me in.
Gave me up.
Just like that.
As if I was a stray dog she didn't want.

I can almost feel the metal biting at my wrists, and all I can do is grip onto the railing, and pray they'll be over soon.

That I'll forget again.

CHAPTER 10

THIS IS ONE OF THE worst nights of my life. I'm lucky, though. It could have gone a lot worse. William could have gotten what he was trying to steal. He got as far as kissing me and reaching under my dress before I managed to knee the crap out of his balls. Then he collapsed to the floor, and I ran out of the room.

But the damn idiot stole my first kiss!

That I can never get back.

And now Ayden has gone after him to do God knows what. I've never seen him that pissed off before. It has me extremely worried.

I'd been hiding out in the bathroom, embarrassed about how I looked, like everyone would be able to tell what happened by my appearance.

After sending Ayden countless texts, I give up and crack the door open, peering into the hallway. I spot Sage, his bright blue hair making him stand out like a bluebird in a sea of crows. He definitely has his own unique style. Tall and lean, he wears a lot of different shades of clothing, yet all of them are dark with murky tones. He has countless piercings, including three in his brow and one in his tongue.

He's chatting with his buddies, so I open the door all the way and stick my head out.

"Sage," I hiss, waving him over.

When he glances at me, his brows knit as he strides over. He has a joint in his hand and reeks of pot, but Sage is known as the school pothead, so it's no surprise. He can play the drums like a boss, though, so he's cool in my book.

"What's up?" His blue-eyed gaze scans me. "Holy shit. Are you okay, Lyric?"

"I'm fine. But can you go find Ayden? I think he might be in some trouble."

"Yeah, I saw him storming down the hall, looking like he was about to murder someone."

I bite down on my lip, instantly regretting it when pain sears across my face. "I'm kind of worried that he might try exactly that."

He positions the joint between his lips. "I'm on it."

I shut the door as he strides toward the stairs. Then, I sink to the floor and very impatiently wait for Sage to either come back, or hopefully Ayden to return. Seconds tick by. Minutes. Right in the midst of deciding to go out myself, the door finally swings open.

"Oh, thank God." I sigh in relief as Ayden trudges into the bathroom. My gaze immediately drops to his hand cradled at his side, and I jump to my feet. "Why is there blood all over your knuckles?" I grab his hand and jerk it toward me. When his face contorts in pain, I loosen my hold.

"I haven't hit someone since I was fourteen," he mutters, stretching out the fingers of his uninjured hand. "I forgot that I wasn't supposed to use my knuckles."

I gently wipe some of the blood off his skin, surprised he doesn't stop me when my fingertips graze his scars. "But whose blood is this? Because I don't see any fresh cuts."

His gaze bores into me. "Whose do you think it is, Lyric?"

My heart beats wildly inside my chest. "You didn't have to hit him. I kicked him plenty of times."

"Yeah, I did. He *hurt* you." An uneven breath slips from his lips. "I should have done worse to him."

I tell myself to breathe, but my lungs can't seem to figure out how to get the oxygen they need. "But it was kind of my fault. I mean, I had a bad feeling the moment I got into the car with him, but like you said, I don't always think with my head, and I trust people too much."

"Hey." He delicately cups my wounded cheek, his fingers splaying across my flesh. "Bad decision or not, none of this was your fault. He can't put his hands on you just because he's stronger than you. He had no right to touch you." His throat muscles move as he swallows hard then he promptly removes his hand from my face. "No one does unless you want them to."

I'm suddenly hyperaware of how long his eyelashes are and how perfectly kissable his lips look. When did he get so beautiful? I mean, he was always beautiful, but never *this* beautiful.

I rapidly shove the thought from my mind. *Jesus, Lyric, what the hell is wrong with you? Totally inappropriate.*

"Thank you, Ayden." I throw my arms around his neck and latch onto him. "You're the best friend I could ever ask for. No, you're more than that. Way, way more than that."

For the first time ever, he hugs me back. Honestly, it's kind of an awkward hug, because he keeps moving his hands around, unsure where to put them, until finally he decides to circle his arms around my waist.

As his warmth encompasses me, I inhale with a faint smile on my lips. I can almost feel it, the potential for a song surfacing in the back of my mind. Not about this night. Not about William. No, oddly enough it's about this hug.

"We should get you home," he whispers in my hair.

I pull back to look at him. "I don't want anyone seeing me like this." I glance down at the torn strap of my dress and the top of my bra sticking out. "And I lost my jacket, so I can't even cover up."

"We can fix that." He shucks his hoodie off and holds it out for me to put on. After I slide my arms in the sleeves, he snatches up one of the hand towels, gets it wet underneath the faucet, and begins carefully cleaning the smeared makeup from my face as I sit down on the counter, letting my legs dangle over the edge.

I watch him as he works, his intense gaze fixated on what he's doing. I notice the slightest quiver in his fingers and wonder what's causing it. If he's afraid, worried, angry, what? With Ayden, it's always complicated, like trying to figure out a story in a closed book.

"There." He moves back from me and tosses the towel into the sink. "That should be good enough to get you out of here without too many questions."

I twist around and peer at my reflection in the mirror. Besides the welt and cut lip, my face is seamlessly clean, as if tonight never happened. As if it was erased.

At least on the outside.

On the inside, the night scorches vividly inside my mind.

Tears begin to sting at my eyes again as the shock wears off.

Ayden tangles his fingers with mine and helps me down from the counter. "Come on, let's get you out of here." He steers us out the door, saying something to Sage before we start toward the bottom floor.

I stay close to him, clinging to his hand, with my face

pressed against the back of his shirt that smells like his cologne. I focus on his scent as we make our way through the house, counting each step, each racing beat of my heart, each unstable breath.

I only feel safe again when I'm in the passenger seat of Lila's car and Ayden is driving down the road, away from that house, away from the party, away from William and this night.

"I'm going to think with my head more from now on." I rest my swollen cheek against the cool window. "And not trust people so damn much."

"Lyric, that's not what I meant when I said that." He turns down the stereo's volume, so the only noise filling the cab is the humming of the engine and the softness of our breathing. "I love that you don't always think with your head. It makes life interesting and keeps me from going crazy. And if it wouldn't have been for you being so damn trusting toward me, I would have . . . well, life would have been a lot harder."

I rotate my head toward him. "Really? You even feel this way when it gets you into trouble? Like fights. And crashing bikes. Drinking."

His jaw clenches. "It's not the first fight I've been in, or the first time I've drank."

William's blood still stains his knuckles and his scars. I've never flat out asked him where he got the scars from, and quite honestly, I'm afraid to after what happened with the tattoo thing earlier—afraid I'll scare him off again—so I opt for a different route.

"What kind of fights did you get into?" I watch him through the darkness with my knees pulled up, my head resting against the leather of the seat.

When he smashes his lips together, I figure he's going to remain silent and shut down like he normally does, but then his lips part.

"When I was fourteen, this guy from school came after me with a knife because he thought I hooked up with his girlfriend," he starts, staring out at the winding road ahead of us. "I clocked him in the face before he could cut me, but ended up splitting my knuckles open."

I hesitate before I ask, "Is that where the scars on your hand came from?"

His knuckles whiten as he grips the steering wheel. "No, someone else did that to me . . . the same people who put the tattoo on me." His grip tightens even more. "I don't even remember what was done to me, though, so it doesn't matter."

It does matter, though.

Everything about him matters.

His voice is colder than I've ever heard it, so I drop the subject, not wanting to push him any further tonight.

"I can't believe a guy tried to stab you when you were fourteen." I trace circles on the console, wondering what it must have been like for him. "I barely used curse words when I was that old."

He gives me a sidelong glance. "You've had a good life. You shouldn't be sad about it. I know that you wish your life was more complicated so you could write better, but trust me, it's not worth the sacrifice."

"I'm not sad right now because of that." I face forward in my seat and wrap my arms around myself. "I'm sad because you haven't always had a good life; you deserve to have the best."

A beat of silence goes by.

"Life is getting . . . easier for me."

Before I can say anything else, he cranks up the radio again.

We don't speak for the rest of the drive home. I rack

my brain for a way to make him feel better. But by the time we're pulling up to our houses, I still have no clue what to do or say.

All the lights are off at my house so I have some time to think about what I'm going to tell my mom and dad about tonight without them losing their shit.

"You want me to come up and hang out with you until they get home?" Ayden asks, parking in front of his garage and silencing the engine.

I nod then unfasten my seatbelt and drag my butt out of the car.

While we're heading up to my bedroom, I text my parents to find out where they are. Turns out, my mother had to work late and my dad went down to the gallery to spend time with her. The two of them are so adorable that it makes me sick. And envious. I know their story. They grew up together. Were best friends who fell in love. They wrote songs about each other, and painted portraits of their undying love. Usually this makes me smile, but tonight, gag me. Seriously. I feel so bitter.

"I just want to go to bed and forget this night ever happened." I kick the bedroom door open and wrestle the hoodie off. "I should probably take a shower first."

Ayden clicks on the lamp, sits down on my bed, and collects my iPod from my cluttered nightstand. "I'll chill out on your bed and go through your song collection, preparing for your next music quiz." A small trace of a smile graces his lips.

Relief sweeps through me like a gentle breeze. *Maybe I didn't break him after all.*

After I grab some clothes from the dresser, I duck into the bathroom and take a quick shower, scrubbing my skin until it's raw and red, trying to cleanse the icky feeling off. I know tonight could have been a lot worse, but what happened still makes me feel sick to my stomach. Everything aches and my heart feels so dark. I hate the feeling. I want my sunshine back.

Tears spill from my eyes as I sink down into the bathtub and hug my knees to my chest. By the time I return to my bedroom, I'm exhausted, my eyes are puffy, my face hurts, and I'm ready to go to sleep.

Ayden is still in my bed like he said he would be, stretched out on the mattress with his back resting against the headboard. He has my ear buds in, and he's bobbing his head to the music as he thrums his fingers against his knee.

I collapse face first beside him and he quickly tugs on the cord, pulling out one of the earbuds. "Feeling any better?"

I bury my face into the pillow. "Kind of. I just want to go to sleep."

He lies down and rotates on his side, facing me. "Then go to sleep. I'll stay with you until your mom and dad get home."

I close my eyes. "I feel so icky."

There's a pause then he lightly places his hand on my back. My eyelids flutter open at the contact of his warm fingertips. He's so close that his warm breath dusts my cheeks.

"You shouldn't feel icky," he says softly, his hand starting to massage the throbbing muscles of my back. "You did nothing wrong, but trust people too much. That's never a bad thing. Don't ever lose that."

"I'll try, but . . ." I sink deeper into the pillow as tears sting my eyes again. "But he stuck his tongue down my throat, and it was the most disgusting kiss ever. I rinsed and brushed my teeth, but I swear to God, I can still feel it on me."

When he grows silent again, I crack an eyelid open. He's dazing off over my shoulder with undiluted pain in his eyes. The realness of him causes my heart to stutter, and my fingers yearn to jot down unwritten words.

God, what has he been through to create such a look?

When his focus lands back on me, his eyes burn fiercely, as if he's terrified out of his damn mind "Shut your eyes," he whispers, almost horrified.

I do as he says without question, trusting him completely, even though his intensity is enough to make the calmest person in the world feel disconcerted.

He sticks the earbud in my ear and the gloomy, unhurried beat of Radiohead's "How To Disappear Completely" soaks through my wounded soul.

"You picked the perfect song," I mutter as the music engulfs me. "This is exactly what I—"

His lips brush mine, stealing the words right from my mouth. My breath catches in my throat. My first instinct is to pull away, but I don't want to. I want to stay. Let him erase that last few hours from my mind.

I keep my eyes shut, too afraid to open them as his lips timidly start to move against mine. Just a whisper of a graze. A heart-stopping brush. A soul-drowning taste. He does it again and again, taking his time, erasing all the ickiness from tonight.

As I absorb each soft graze, his tongue slowly follows, slipping into my mouth. I gasp, but still don't open my eyes. I barely move. Can hardly think. And when he pulls back, gently biting at my bottom lip, I stop breathing all together.

That burn songs promise.
Blazes in me.
Hot and scorching.
So sweltering and mind-numbing.

I feel it in my veins.
Liquid fire.
Passion.
Driving me insane.
And the bar set so high.
Ayden has soared over.
Past the heavens.
And captured me eternally.

"Go to sleep, Lyric," he whispers, his breathing ragged.

I nod, still terrified to open my eyes. Terrified I'll lose this moment.

A moment I know I'll be able to fill pages and pages with the most powerful lyrics I've ever written. All about him and that kiss.

CHAPTER 11

THERAPY DID NOT GO WELL today, but maybe that's because I was a basket case while I was there.

"Ayden, are you sure there's nothing else you want to talk about?" my therapist had asked, chomping on a mint—the dude always has one in his mouth.

I had raked my fingers through my hair for the millionth time in the last hour. "Yeah, I'm good."

"Are you sure?" he pressed, while jotting notes down. "Are your nightmares troubling you again?"

I gripped at the wooden armrest of the chair I was sitting in. "No, they've been . . . fine." A lie, but I didn't want to talk about them, because then we would have had to talk about other stuff—Lyric stuff.

He had set the pen he was writing with down. "What about flashbacks? Are you having any of those?"

I shook my head. "No, not for a while."

He overlapped his fingers on top of his organized desk, considering something. "You know I can't help you if you don't talk to me."

I wiped my sweaty palms on the front of my jeans. "I'm just stressed out over school," I had lied, to avoid what was really bothering me. Lyric. That kiss. The way our lips touched. The way my heart races in panic every time I even think about it. I could only imagine what would happen if I spoke about it aloud.

He sighed, something he did when he was letting my silence slide, yet wasn't thrilled about it.

An hour later, I'm running around my room like a chicken with its head cut off, searching for my guitar. I can't remember where I left it last night, can't remember much of anything over the last week. My thoughts are scattered, my dreams more vivid, my control gone.

All this from a kiss I can't get out of my head.

But it wasn't just the kiss. It was . . .

Lips. Aching. A touch.
The contact. The connection.
The rush.
It brought my soul back
to life.
And I'm fucking terrified.

I haven't kissed anyone since before I was put into the system. Haven't kissed anyone because I wanted to. I've been kissed a few times—I remember that much about my past—but I can't remember exactly how they happened. Won't remember.

I had cracked open Pandora's Box with the dancing at the club, but it flew right open with the kiss. A kiss I clearly wasn't ready for, even if it was the best kiss I've ever fucking had. Life would have been a lot simpler if all my kisses were like that.

But they weren't.

And life isn't simple.

Now, I'm trapped in a scarred body that cringes whenever it has to endure human contact, except for when it comes to Lyric. I didn't cringe during that kiss. Not once. Which was good. The whole point of it was to try and erase the pain William caused from her eyes. If I could just get over the helpless, out of control fear I feel whenever I'm around her now, things will be golden.

But my soul is out.
Surfaced above the years of pain.
Fuck. I need to stop thinking.
Focus on finding my guitar. Yes, find the guitar. Much more simple.

I look out my window toward Lyric's house. Maybe that's where I left it. But am I that desperate to go over there and find out?

Lyric suddenly appears through her window, jumping around and singing at the top of her lungs. I still have yet to hear her sing, but I can imagine the warm sound of her voice and those incredibly soft lips of hers creating striking songs.

Amazing songs.
That I want to drink out of her.
Taste.
Fuck, I'm losing my Goddamn mind.

My phone rings from my back pocket, and I let out a breath in relief at the distraction. I fish it out, figuring it's Sage calling to see if I'm on my way to band practice.

"I'm on my way now," I answer without checking my screen as I reach for my wallet on the nightstand.

"That's super awesome." It's Lyric's voice that fills the line and my heart flutters. Actually fucking flutters, like I'm some lovesick puppy. "But I just called to ask why on earth you've been staring at my bedroom window. You've been doing it for like five minutes, and it's starting to get a little bit creepy."

I frown when I spot her waving at me through her window.

"What's wrong?" she asks. "You've been acting a

little strange lately. More and more like the shy boy I first met, the one who would barely utter a few stray sentences to me. I'm not losing you, am I? Because we made a deal to be friends, and my deals are unbreakable. If you want out of them, there's this big huge test I have to give you, and I know how much you hate tests."

Lyric has never mentioned a single word about the kiss, which I'm both relieved and upset about. She's been her light, full of sunshine self, acting as if she's completely unaffected.

"I'm fine. Our friendship is fine. Everything is fantastic. I promise." I turn my back to the window, silently begging for my guitar to miraculously appear in my room, but it doesn't. "I just can't find my guitar anywhere."

"That's because it's over here, you goofball. Remember, last night at family dinner when you were playing with my dad and me, which FYI totally made his day. Although he's never actually said it, I think he secretly wishes he had a son sometimes. Or at least a daughter who doesn't suffer from stage fright."

"I'm sure he loves you, Lyric, whether you get over that or not."

"Of course he does. That's not what I meant. I think he's just super stoked that you could become his protégé." She lets out a wicked laugh at the end, the effortless sound splintering the weight on my chest.

"Hey, could you bring my guitar down to the driveway? I'm late for practice, and I know Sage is going to be sending me nasty texts soon."

"Sure thing, shy boy. I'll be right out."

She hangs up before I can say anything else.

I feel like banging my head on the wall, because now I've got to go down and see her again for the fiftieth time since the kiss, and I know I'm going to get all awkward again.

Get it together.

Get it together.

I grab the car keys and jog down the stairs and out to the driveway. Lyric is already waiting for me on the fence with her long legs dangling over the side and my guitar case on her lap. Her blonde hair is braided to the side, and she doesn't have a drop of makeup on, revealing her freckles and perfection.

God, she's beautiful.

"So, I was thinking," she says as I approach her, "that I could go to your practice with you."

I pause at the fence line, stuffing my wallet into my back pocket. "Why?"

She frowns as she hops off the fence. "Well, I didn't expect that sullen reaction." She shoves my guitar at me then adjusts the bottom of her purple shirt lower so her stomach is covered up. She's done that a lot over the last week. She's also worn a lot of jeans, as if trying to cover herself up more, like she blames how she dressed on what happened.

"Sorry." I grasp the handle of my guitar case. "I didn't mean it like that. It's just . . . you've never wanted to go with me before, so I'm just a little confused."

She shrugs as she scuffs her boot across the ground. "I need to get out of the house. I feel like I'm losing my mind. Everywhere I go, one of my parents follows me, like they expect me to break apart at any moment. And I know they're not going to let me go anywhere unless I'm with you."

Despite the sheer awkwardness I'm feeling, I say, "You can always come with me. You know that."

She straightens her shoulders and beams at me. "Thank you. Let me go tell them where I'm going. I'll be right back." She hoists herself over the fence and sprints into her house through the side door near the garage.

With my guitar in my hand, I climb into Lila's Mercedes that she's pretty much given to me at this point. The Gregorys own two other cars, so she always acts like it's never a big deal to let me drive their extra vehicle somewhere. But it is. A. Big. Freaking. Huge. Deal. Because it means they trust me.

"Okay, I'm totally good to go," Lyric says as she slides into the passenger seat. "I just have to be back before eleven, which is so weird. I've never had a curfew before."

"I'm sure they're just worried," I tell her as I back down the driveway, pretending that I'm not hyperaware of her scent filling up the cab. God, she smells so good.

"I know that." She draws the seatbelt over her shoulder. "But I'm feeling a bit smothered ever since my parents decided to press charges against William. I'm hoping things will cool off here in a few weeks when he gets sentenced, or whatever is going to happen to him." The seatbelt clicks into place and she relaxes back in the seat. "Although, if he does get any sort of punishment, I'm sure it'll just be community service, since he doesn't have a prior."

I flip on the blinker to pull out onto the main road of our subdivision. "You say that way too casually."

"I have to be casual about it." She props her feet on the dash and reaches for the iPod docked in the middle console. "Otherwise, it'll pull me down. And I refuse to go down." She pauses as she browses through the songs. "I think my parents might be worried I have a mental illness."

"What?" I gape at her, half expecting her to insert a punch line to her joke. Because she has to be joking.

She shrugs with her head angled forward, her attention fixed on the playlists. "I heard them whispering about it the other day after I momentarily lost my shit and yelled at them."

I tap the brakes at a red light. "What did they say exactly?"

"Well, it wasn't so much *they* as it was my mother." She lifts her shoulders and shrugs. "She just seemed really concerned when I burst into freaking tears for no reason."

"Was this before or after you told them about William?"

"Before. I only actually told them what happened because they seemed super twitchy about my mood swings."

I press on the gas as the light turns green. "What happened when you told them? Did they seem better about it?"

She chews on her bottom lip. "I'm not sure . . . I've heard them whispering a couple of times before about my super cheery attitude. Again, it was more my mother. They never do it in front of me, but I've accidentally heard enough to know she worries about me."

"Why, though? I mean, I've lived with someone who was mentally ill, and that's not . . ." I trail off.

Her concentration floats from the playlists, her eyes falling to the scars on my hand. "Was it the people who did that to you? That weird cult thing I found out about?"

I withdraw my hand and tuck it to my side. "It was."

"I'm sorry, Ayden. About everything. About showing you that tattoo thing. That I haven't found your brother for you yet."

"That's not your responsibility." I return my hand to the wheel. "Besides, it doesn't matter. Lila told me the other day that she looked into my brother, and . . . apparently he dropped out of the system a year ago. I'll more than likely never see him again."

Her eyes widen. "Oh my God, I'm so sorry."

"It's not your fault. It's . . . well, it's my mother's since this whole thing started with her." My hands begin to shake on the wheel as I remember the day she handed us over to those people.

They were actually our next door neighbors, had been for a while. She needed a babysitter so she could go get her next fix. She questioned nothing, not even the chains in the living room. And they were more than willing to take us, needing their next victims.

"What about your mom?" Lyric dares ask. "What happened to her? Maybe finding her could help us find your brother and sister."

"She's dead. And I don't know who my dad is, so that won't help us either. Face it, I'll probably never get to see anyone from my family again."

"Ayden . . ." She clears her throat. "You have a family. All the Gregorys love you. And . . . so do I."

Breathe, breathe, breathe.
With the sound of your heart.
With the whisper of your soul.
Until everything connects.
Composes.
And creates a song.

I can't speak. Can barely breathe. Lyric's eyes refuse to leave mine, even though I'm looking everywhere but at her. I wonder if this is the time she's not going to give up, if she's going to push me until I shatter into a million pieces.

"I think my grandmother had a bipolar disorder," she says, facing forward in the seat and scrolling through the song lists again, going back to the original conversation without missing a beat. "Maybe that's why my mom worries. Perhaps she thinks I'm going to turn out like her."

Air rushes back to my lungs at the abrupt subject change.

As we reach the last house on the street, I turn into the driveway. "Why would she think that? You're like the happiest person I know." I stop at the end of the drive, shove the shifter into park, and slide the keys out of the ignition.

"Maybe I'm a little too happy, though." She places the iPod on the dock without selecting a song. "Besides, some mental illnesses are hereditary."

"I know that."

"I don't believe it's fully true, though," Lyric states, drawing her sunglasses over her eyes. "I think if you don't want to turn out like your parents, then you won't. Look at my mom. She's a pretty stable woman, and I know from bits and pieces of stories I've heard that she had a pretty shitty life growing up."

I swallow the lump in my throat to stop myself from asking.

What happened to her?
Was she broken?
Is she fixed?
Saved from the darkness.
That once grasped her wrists.

"What do you think about when you daze off like that?" she asks curiously. "I've always wondered what goes on inside your head."

If she did know, she'd run.

"Nothing important." Before she can say anything else, I snatch up my guitar from the backseat and bolt out of the car.

I don't look back as I rush up the wide driveway, toward the side door of the detached garage. I free a trapped breath when I hear the car door shut. As much as my emotions are terrifying me, and as much as I know I don't deserve her to, I *need* her to follow me like my heart needs blood pumping through it.

"Hey, man," Sage greets as I stride into the shallow

space of the garage. He's perched on a short stool in front of his drums, twirling the drumsticks in his hands. There's a joint burning from an ashtray on a table near a leather couch, and the air is laced with the pungent stench of weed. He does this a lot in an attempt to hotbox the garage. Says it makes him play better. The problem is, it also makes Nolan and I a little buzzed, and we definitely don't play better when we are.

"Hey." I drop the guitar down on the sofa. "Just so you know, Lyric came with me today."

He purposely drops the drumsticks and stands up. "Dude, so not cool." He heads for the joint burning in the ashtray.

"She's cool," I tell him as he puts the joint out and flips on the ceiling fan. "She won't give a shit if you're hotboxing the garage. *I* might, but she'll be fine with it."

A panicked look crosses his face as he douses the air with Lysol. "That's not what I'm worried about."

I'm so lost. Sage never gives a shit about anything, even his mom finding out he's high. "Then what are you worried about?"

He sets the can down on the table. "Don't you think Lyric's just kind of, I don't know, s—" He gets cut off as the door swings open and Lyric strolls into the room.

I start forming every *S* word I can think of.

Sunny?

Strange?

Sweet?

Sassy?

Sexy?

It better not fucking be the last one.

Lyric's nose instantly scrunches as she gets a whiff of the air. "Dude, it reeks of pot in here." She closes the door behind her and spins around to face us, her eyes skimming the room. "Is that what you guys secretly do here?" she asks suspiciously, her gaze dancing back and forth between Sage and me. "Is this whole band thing a ruse to be closet potheads?"

"Nah, Ayden doesn't do that shit," Sage tells her, leaning over to gather his drumsticks from off the floor.

"You do, though. I know that," Lyric remarks as she circles the room, studying all the framed albums on the wall. "Was your dad a musician or something?"

Sage glances at me for some reason then strolls up to her with his hands tucked into his back pockets. "Nah. He just wishes he was. And actually, the albums are my mother's. She just bought all of them a year ago after my dad cheated on her. They're all of his favorite albums signed by his favorite bands, and he will never get to see a single one of these, other than the one time my mother brought him over here to rub it in his face."

"That's so sick and twisted," Lyric mumbles as she leans forward to inspect one album in particular. "Aw, Micha Scott. He's pretty good for being old school." She casts a sly glance over her shoulder at me.

"Yeah, he's okay." Sage playfully bumps his shoulder into hers, filling me with the strangest sensation of jealousy, enough that I want to bump into him a hell of a lot harder, maybe even knock him down. "Hey, any relation?" he jokes.

"He's actually my dad."

Sage starts to laugh, but then his eyes widen when he notes the serious expression on Lyric's face. "You have got to be shitting me."

She shrugs as she scratches at her arm then rubs her eyes, probably because of the abundance of smoke swirling around the air. "Nope. I'm totally being one hundred percent shitting free serious right now."

I can't help but chuckle.

His eyes enlarge even more. "Let me get this straight. Your father is Micha Scott, rock star slash music producer who owns Infinity Studio, and he's been your father this entire time."

Lyric shrugs again, shuffling her feet back and forth across the carpet. "Yep, pretty much."

Sage shoots a baffled look at me. "Did you know about this?"

Nodding, I sink down on the couch and unlock my guitar case. "I don't know why you're freaking out so much, though."

"Um, because you have a connection," he says, confounded.

"No, Lyric has a connection." I sweep my hair out of my face as I position my guitar on my lap. "Not me."

He shakes his head, still flabbergasted. "You could have said something at least."

"It wasn't my something to tell." I pluck my fingers across the strings, tuning the guitar while tuning Sage out.

He twists around, facing Lyric again. "So can you do anything?"

"Oh, I can do a lot of things," Lyric replies in her flirty tone that causes my jaw to tick. She plops down on the sofa beside me, slips her hands under her legs, and leans toward me, her hair brushing my cheek. Her eyes are slightly bloodshot and her pupils are unfocused.

I reach back to open the window while Sage drags a stool over to us.

"I mean, can you play anything?" Sage wonders, plopping down on the stool.

"I can play a lot of things," Lyric replies, resting her head on my shoulder.

Sage flashes me a puzzled glance and I shrug.

I have no clue what she's doing, other than maybe she's high. What I do know is that the feel of her is driving me absolutely crazy in the best way possible. Her touching me is nothing new. She's usually got her fingers laced through mine, but this feels different somehow, as if she's trying to read me through the connection of our bodies. Maybe it's all the freaking pot in the air, or maybe it's because of the kiss. I'd be fine with it—I'm usually good at keeping myself in control—but my breathing has gone erratic and my heart's lost its Goddamn mind.

"Like what?" Sage asks Lyric, reaching for the lighter on the floor near his feet.

"The violin, guitar, drums. I used to play the piano, but I haven't practiced in a while."

"What about singing?"

She hesitates. "Singing is subjective, so I can't answer that."

Sage assesses her closely. "So, you're saying you think you can sing, but you're unsure of your voice." He flicks his lighter on and off as he deliberates something. Then he hops to his feet and ambles over to the microphone. Picking it up off the floor, he twists up the volume of the speaker. "Let's see what you got, Scott." He tosses the microphone at Lyric.

As she catches it, her face drains of color. "Um, I'm not going to sing for you." She chucks the microphone at him. Instead of catching it, Sage skitters out of the way and it ends up crashing against the symbols.

All three of us stare at it as it threatens to topple over.

He rips his focus off the vibrating metal. "Why not?"

Lyric glances at me for help, but I have no idea what to say to her. I've never heard her sing. Hell, she barely lets me hear her play the guitar and she rocks at that. But I know she does it all, sings, plays, writes lyrics.

"I'd really like to hear the answer myself," I tell her, shifting the guitar off my lap. "Because I've been really curious for a while."

She glares at me, and I shrink back. "I already told you I have stage fright."

Right. She has told me that. Maybe I'm higher than I thought.

Sage flicks his hand at her, waving her off. "That is totally curable."

Lyric crosses her legs, and her gaze glides across Sage's facial piercings. "And what's your cure? Should I dye my hair and pierce my skin to make me believe I'm a true rock star?"

Sage points at his chest. "I'm not a rock star. I can't sing at all, but I can play the drums like a badass."

Lyric folds her arms across her chest with a sway of attitude in her body. "So can I."

I catch Sage peeking at her cleavage popping out of her shirt. That's when I realize the *S* word he was about to drop when Lyric walked in was probably sexy. It pisses me off, and my reaction is surprising as shit.

But Lyric isn't sexy. She's fun, ridiculously happy, effortlessly beautiful, life-saving, and mind-blowingly amazing. Sexy doesn't even begin to sum her up.

"Yeah, but our band doesn't need a drummer." He scoops up the microphone from the floor and presents it to her like it's a bouquet. "We need a singer."

Lyric folds her fingers around the mic as she takes it from him. "I can't. I'll seriously throw up if I even try."

He holds up a finger as a slow grin curves at his lips. "I have an idea for that."

When he disappears through a door at the back of the room, I say to Lyric, "You don't have to do it. Sage just gets crazy about this stuff. He lives and breathes music and thinks everyone should do the same."

"I live and breathe music, too," Lyric reminds me, anxiously chewing on her bottom lip. "I just can't do it in public . . . You really think he's got some magical cure for stage fright?"

I line my fingers against the guitar strings and strum a chord. "Probably not. But if he does come out with a brownie, please don't eat it."

"I won't, but I think I might be a little bit high already."

"Yeah, me, too."

A nervous giggle escapes her lips then she relaxes back on the sofa and kicks up her feet on the stool. "So, can I ask you something?"

My fingers tense and I miss the next chord. "I guess so."

"It's about the other night . . . about the . . . kiss." She pauses, and an enormous lump wedges in my throat. "I think it might be the weed talking, because I promised myself I wasn't going to bring it up, but now I suddenly feel like I need to."

I squeeze my eyes shut. I still have my head down so she can't see my face. Thank God, or otherwise, who the hell knows what she would see.

"I just wanted to make you feel better about that asshole stealing your first kiss," I say, messing around with the knob on the bottom of the guitar. "It was the only thing I could think of to do."

Liar.
In the darkness.
You are.
The biggest.
Liar I've ever seen.
Pretend it doesn't exist.
Like everything else inside you.

She cracks her knuckles. "So it was just a friend kiss, then? Because Maggie has a theory that our friendship might have blossomed into love." She laughs like she thinks the idea is funny.

Me, I find it terrifying.

Love.

The word souls burn for.

People die for.

Live for.

Breathe for.

But for me, it's simply poetry, lyrics, an emotion I'll never understand.

Can't.

I swallow hard and force my voice to be equally as light. "Yeah, of course. And I really think you should stop listening to Maggie. It's what started the whole thing with William to begin with."

"Hey." She cups my chin and forces me to look up at her. "I'm totally cool with you kissing me to cheer me up, just as long as we stay friends. I never want anything to get weird between us."

"Of course." I bob my head up and down. "I want the same thing."

"Good." She smiles as she reclines back in the seat.

The scatteredness in my head begins to clear. This was my problem—it had to be. I was so worried I'd lose her as a friend that it fucked with my head. Thank God, I'm cured.

"You and I"—she points back and forth between us—"we're going to be one of those people who are still friends when we're super old, like our parents." A laugh bubbles from my lips and her smile expands. "You know, I always feel so special whenever I get you to smile. Like I discovered some sort of rare gem."

I want to kiss her right there, eternally seal my lips to hers.

Okay, maybe I'm not cured.

Maybe I can't be cured.

Of anything.

"You're special, Lyric. You should know that by now."

"So are you." She pats my leg then rises to her feet when Sage strolls back into the room.

"So, what's your huge plan to cure me?" she asks him.

He holds up a brownie in his hand. "This will cure all your stage fright." He draws and X over his heart and winks at her. "I promise."

Shaking my head, I set my guitar down and rise to my feet. "No way." I push Sage's hand back. "How about I blow off practice and we do something fun," I suggest to Lyric. "Nolan isn't even here anyway."

"He's always late," Sage intervenes, munching on the brownie. "He'll show up in like ten minutes or so."

"I was kind of hoping coming here would cure me of my stage fright." Lyric stares at me with hope in her eyes. "I don't know why, but I thought it would help somehow, like maybe being around you and seeing how much fun you guys have when you play would force me to conquer my fear."

I rub my jawline, trying to conjure up an idea. I remember when I was afraid of the dark, how I used to cover my ears and shut my eyes to block out my surroundings. It didn't cure me, but it got me through the night. Now I use music and that silly nightlight Lyric gave me forever ago.

"I have an idea," I say, my voice unsteady from a memory long forgotten of me as a small boy begging to be let free. "But it might be a little weird."

She smiles excitedly. "Lay it on me. Whatever it is, I trust you, Ayden."

Her words crash into my heart, more than in a just-friends way. I wonder just how much of a lie I told her when I said that it was just a friend kiss. It doesn't matter, though. Lyric is the sunshine in my world. She keeps me going when things get really dark. I'm not even ready for a relationship. I can barely handle myself right now, even something as simple as kissing her sent me into panic attack after panic attack.

I suddenly realize something makes my scars throb, that I'm not ready to handle the emotions clipping their way to the surface. That even though I have a new life, the cuffs and chains are still there, trying to pull me down into the darkness of memories, begging to haunt me. Of myself. My brother. My sister.

What was done to me? Stuff I can't even remember, but can somehow still feel the fear connected to the experiences.

And I'm not sure if I'll ever fully be able to escape them.

CHAPTER 12

*In the silence of my soul, there is a breathless ache
desperately seeking air.
Like I'm dead, yet alive.
Breathing yet suffocating.
Then I felt your lips.
The softest touch
kissed my mouth,
and my soul sang to life.
For the very first time
you showed me a taste of life.*

THAT'S WHAT I WROTE AFTER Ayden kissed me. That's what constantly floods my thoughts day and night, over and over again. I want another taste of it—of what his kiss brought me. But he's been acting so strange since it happened. Twitchy. Smiling less. And I have no idea how to act around him other than be super happy twenty-four seven, even after what I discovered about him tonight while searching around on the internet—an article about his past.

"Are you sure about this?" I ask Ayden as I stand in the middle of the room with my eyes closed. I have earplugs in my ears, a microphone in my hand, and my heart's thudding like a jackhammer.

"Not really!" he shouts out. "But it doesn't hurt to try it out!"

"True." I dither, trying to decide if I want to do this.

Suddenly his fingers circle my wrists, and I feel his face dip toward my ear. "Relax. It's just me and Sage in the room. Two people. That's all." His breath is hot on my cheek, making the air sweltering.

I nod as my fingers grasp the microphone. "Okay."

"Okay, you're ready to do this?"

I nod then fist bump the air. I hear him chuckle, but the sound gets lost as he moves away from me.

A heartbeat or two later, the music is cranked up. Lyrics by Flyleaf surround me and it's perfect. I know for a fact that Ayden picked out this song, because he knows how much I love the band. The thought relaxes me for about two seconds until it's time for me to sing then my voice locks up in my throat.

Shit. I'm so going to throw up.

My eyelids start to lift up as panic sets in, but warm fingers touch my wrists again.

"Relax!" Ayden shouts over the music. "I've got your back, dude."

I snort a laugh then relax.

Calm. That's all I feel.

I don't know why, but I open my eyes.

My gaze meets Ayden's grey eyes.

I think about the lyrics I wrote the other day.

My inspiration.

The stuff I dreamed about for years.

Friends or not, I'm using our kiss to my benefit.

I put the microphone up to my mouth.

Then I start to sing.

I sing like my life depends on it. Sing like I've always dreamed of doing. Sing as though my heart is going to burst if I don't scream out every emotion through the lyrics.

I'll admit, for the first thirty seconds or so, my voice is wobbly and off pitch. I start to grow concerned that maybe my life dream of singing is going to be a behind-closed-doors sort of thing. I pop the earplugs out, so I can hear myself. It helps. My voice gains stability. I unstiffen. Loosen up.

I begin dancing around the room, and Ayden laughs at me, his smile so bright his eyes crinkle around the corners. There's something in his expression, something I've never seen before, and it causes the room to spin. So I spin with it, jumping up and down, belting out the lyrics until I finally let go and get really crazy.

I shove Ayden back on the sofa and straddle his lap, singing and putting on a show for him. His eyes widen at my overly friendly touch, and his arms tense out to the side. I'm excited, rubbing my hands up and down his chest, thinking about that kiss, how amazing it was, how it exceeded the bar I set and then some. If only I could have him, but after what I found out . . . I'm not sure I ever can.

I know I'm pushing him right now, and usually I'd stop, but I can't stop. I love this moment. Touching him. Singing. Being in the moment. So I keep going, shoving aside any self-protest until the song ends.

And the moment ends.

And I feel so sad for him again.

I'm sweating, exhausted, and fucking content as I climb off Ayden's lap.

"So, how'd I do?" I pant, moving the microphone away from my mouth.

Sage is staring at me with his arms crossed over his

chest. I don't know him well enough to read him, but if I had to guess, he kind of looks impressed.

Sage trades a questioning look with Ayden. "You think we could rock the girl singer image?"

I sternly point at Sage. "Don't insult my girliness. I rocked the crap out of that song."

He fiddles with one of his eyebrow rings. "That you did." His eyes scroll over me then he sticks out his hand. "What do you say, Lyric? You want to be the singer of Hearts and Scars."

I'm starting to reach out to take his hand, but withdraw. "I will, but on one condition."

His expression twists with confusion. "And what's that?"

"We totally change the name to something way less cliché."

"Change the name? Are you kidding me? We spent two months coming up with that name."

"And it sucks balls, so maybe you should let me come up with one. I can even ask my dad for input," I add enticingly.

His eyes light up as he considers my offer. "All right, you have a deal, Lyric."

We shake on it, and he holds onto my hand way longer than necessary. Who knows why, nor do I care.

I turn to Ayden, grinning like an idiot. He doesn't seem as happy about the agreement as I am, though.

"What's wrong, shy boy?" I wipe the sweat from my brow.

He collects his guitar from the couch. "Nothing."

My hand falls to my side. "I totally should have asked you if you were okay with this, right?"

"Why wouldn't I be okay with this?" He slides the guitar strap over his head with his head down, his black hair shielding his eyes from my view.

"Because this is your guy thing." I gesture around the garage. "And I just crashed it with my girliness." Or is it about my inappropriate touching?

He shakes his head. "I can assure you that's the last thing I was thinking. I love your girliness."

"Then what are you thinking?" I smooth my thumb between his brows, trying to erase his worry.

His fingers strangle the guitar. "Lyric, I think we should—"

Sage clears his throat from behind us. "Nolan just pulled up." He points over his shoulder, appearing uncomfortable as fuck, like he just caught Ayden and I having sex. "You two better be ready to play."

"Okay." I direct my attention back to Ayden. "What were you going to say?"

"Nothing." Ayden strains a smile. "I'm fine. I promise. Now quit worrying and go rock your ass off." He plugs the cord into the amp and focuses on tuning his guitar.

I hate this. This last week has sucked big time, and now he suddenly seems even quieter. I want my Ayden back.

"Are you sure you're sure?"

All he does is nod.

It hurts that he might be upset with me. Makes me want to curl up in a ball and cry.

But Nolan strolls in before I can utter a word.

"Who's fucking ready to get this . . . ?" He trails off mid-sentence as he kicks the door shut. "Why are you here?"

From what I understand, Nolan rocks the bass. He looks more like a lead singer in a boy band than anything. Spikey blond hair, blue eyes, these crazy full lips that don't seem like they should belong to a guy, yet they do. He wears a lot of skinny jeans, too, and fitted shirts, more hipster than rock star.

"Wow, hello to you, too," I joke as I rotate the volume knob on the amp.

He rolls his eyes as he shucks off his jacket then drapes it on a hook near the door. "As much as I adore you, Lyric, I don't find your sarcasm funny."

I pull a face. I've known Nolan since ninth grade, and while we're not technically friends, I know him well enough that I can mess around with him. "Yes, you do. Don't lie."

He snorts a laugh as he weaves around the sofa to collect his guitar from the corner of the room. "Fine, you're amusing." He picks up the guitar and slides the handle over his head. "But seriously, why are you here?"

"Because she's our new singer," Sage intervenes as he materializes from the back room with another brownie in his hand.

"Really?" Nolan asks, glancing from Sage to Ayden, then his gaze lands on me. "You decided to follow in your father's footsteps, then, huh? I'm crossing my fingers you can sing as good as him."

"Of course I can," I say confidently, but my stage fright momentarily creeps in and puts the tiniest hint of doubt in me.

"You knew who her father was, too?" Sage asks incredulously as he heads for the amp.

Nolan shrugs. "I thought everyone did."

"I guess I'm the only idiot out of the loop, then," Sage mutters as he nibbles on the brownie.

"Are you cool with me being part of the band?" I ask Nolan, because I know enough about bands to understand my initiation will only work if they're all on the same page.

He briefly contemplates my question, but the hesitancy

is more for show than anything. Because moments later, he grins and pats me on the arm. "Of course. Welcome to the band. Now, let's get this show on the road and see what you got." He plugs his amp in and twists up the volume.

I try to catch Ayden's eye as I move the microphone up to my mouth to sing, but he keeps his chin down, his eyes focused on the guitar strings.

I spend the next hour singing my heart out with the guys, doing my best not to focus on Ayden and instead on the music. By the time we're finished with practice, my lungs ache in the best way possible.

The drive home is soundlessly painful, though. Ayden will barely utter a word to me. I grow more anxious that the kiss might have changed our friendship in a negative way, but at the same time, I'm excited that I was able to sing and finally found a band to be part of.

By the time we pull up in the driveway, I'm ready to bounce into the house and announce the news to my dad.

"That was so much fun," I tell Ayden as he shuts the headlights off. "Thank you for letting me tag along. You should come up to my room and watch a movie with me. We can celebrate." I cross my fingers, praying he will.

He shakes his head, rotating around and reaching into the backseat for his guitar. "I can't. I have homework." He hurries out of the car and up the driveway toward the house.

"Was it because I sucked?" I call out in desperation as I stumble out of the car and out beneath the stars. "Was Sage just being nice and I'm really not that good?"

He pauses then gradually turns around. When the porch light hits his face, I can see the shock in his eyes.

"Lyric, you have a fucking beautiful voice. It's crazy how amazing it is . . . unreal. But I . . ." He appears completely terrified as he turns away and rushes into the house, shutting the door behind him and leaving his words echoing in my head.

A beautiful voice.
That someone can finally hear.
Let my words spill out into the world.
Let my soul drench the air.
Let it change lives.
Let it bring my best friend back.

But he doesn't come back, and I stand alone in the dark, desperate to chase after him, yet terrified what will happen if I do.

I turn for the door and trudge into my house, less eager to tell my dad the news now. I honestly think about going straight up to my room, but my parents are at the kitchen table eating cake when I walk in.

"Hey, sweetie," my mom says, but instantly frowns when she sees the look on my face. It's the same expression she wore when I had my meltdown the other day. They had both looked at me like I was going to liquefy into a crazy puddle on the hardwood floor. One day I will make her confess why she looks at me that way sometimes. "What happened?"

Sinking into the chair, I reach across the table to steal a glob of pink frosting from her slice of cake. "Nothing. Ayden and I are just having a little spat." If I can even call it that. I honestly have no clue what the hell is going on in that boy's head anymore.

"I'm sorry." My mother discreetly glances at my father as he shovels a chunk of cake into his mouth. "But don't worry, you two will get over it. Best friends always do."

"Ayden and I aren't you and Dad, Mom." I lick the frosting from my finger. "We just . . ." I trail off. We just what? Spend every waking hour together? Kiss in the darkness of the room? Sing solo performances while grinding on each other. "So, I have some news." I change the subject. "I'm officially a singer in a band."

My dad's back straightens, and he beams with pride. "Oh, really? When did this happen?"

I shrug as I roam over to the cupboard. "Tonight. One of Ayden's band members convinced me to sing, although Ayden was the one who actually helped me." I grab a glass from the cupboard then open the fridge. "But it doesn't matter. The important thing is I'm officially cured of my stage fright and can live out my lifelong dream." When I remove the jug of milk out of the fridge, I notice how edgy my father is. "What's wrong, weirdo Dad?"

"It's nothing." He takes a swig of his milk. "It's just that . . . I just want to make sure you're careful. If you really get into this band thing . . . well, the environment is intense."

My mom nods in agreement. "It's not that we don't trust you, but we just want to make sure you don't get into too much trouble."

"I get into trouble all the time," I remind them as I fill the glass with milk. "But if you're talking about drugs, sex, rock 'n' roll, and all that shit, you should know I'm good with staying away from that stuff."

"Okay, but there will be rules," she says as she cuts into the slice of cake in front of her.

"What exactly do you guys think I'm doing?" I ask as I take a seat again. "I just joined the band; I'm not starring on stage yet."

"But if it's your lifelong dream, you will eventually," my father chimes in. "And I just want to make sure you do things the right way."

"Like using my father's awesome connections to get my foot in the door?" I grin sweetly at him.

He tries not to smile, but it slips through. "Maybe. I'll have to hear you play first."

I press my hand to my chest, mocking being offended. "Father, I'm shocked. You seriously don't believe that with my awesome genetics, I don't have the voice of an angel." He wavers, and I throw a napkin at his face. "So insulting." I rise from my chair. "I'm going to bed. I'll let you two finish off your cake."

When I get to my room, though, I don't go to sleep. I write.

Kiss me goodnight. Throw me away.
Hug me tight. Then let me fray.
Pieces of you. Unraveling me.
Weakening, so desperate to be free.
Ready to break. Ready to tear.
I can see you breaking, and it's so hard to bear.

I finish the last sentence then peek out my window at Ayden's home. The lights in his room are off, but I'm only half convinced he's asleep, since his room isn't glowing with the black light I gave him.

I move over to my desk and open up the webpage I was looking at earlier today before I went to band practice. I'd been so shocked when I found it that I actually had to get up and scream the lyrics of the most intense, angry song I could find, just to feel like I could breathe again.

After months of investigating, I finally managed to find an article that I think was linked to Ayden's past. It happened in San Diego, and there's a mention of a woman that has the same last name as Ayden's old one who died.

After a complaint was made about noise disruption, police were led to a home where three abused children were found, appearing to be beaten and starved. No arrests have been made, but the case is heavily under investigation. While reports haven't been confirmed, the case has been linked to three other abuse cases in the area over the last three years. All the victims suffered from the same injuries and subjection.

It makes me wonder exactly what happened to Ayden. Makes me afraid for him. Makes me wonder if the people who tortured him were ever captured.

Is that why he's always afraid?

Or is it something else?

Something worse.

CHAPTER 13

Ayden

EVEN THOUGH IT'S KILLING ME, I've been keeping my distance from Lyric. It's almost impossible, though, when she lives right next door and our families spend a hell of a lot of time together. Plus, there's the whole band thing. Whenever we practice, she's there, and Sage is there staring at her. The dude clearly has a thing for her. Thankfully, she doesn't seem too interested.

I'm not going to lie, I'm fucking miserable. I miss her way more than I thought was ever possible. But I can't help my distant behavior.

That night Lyric sang, jumping on my lap and touching me, caused me to shrink within myself, because I liked it. Wanted more. And it fucking terrified me as I remembered what more felt like.

I remember the touches that singed my skin.
The way they touched me.
How I begged them to stop.
But my voice was hollow.
Resonating.
A sound no one seemed to hear.
The world was merely a shadow
as they tied me up.

Cuffed me.
Used me.
Drained my soul.
Spilled my blood into the earth.
Then left me for dead.
To rot away with the others.
Rot away with their sins.

"Ayden, did you hear me?"

I focus back on reality as I listen to my band members, trying to figure out a plan that will get our foot in the door of the music industry.

"We should definitely have a talk with Lyric's dad," Sage puts in his two cents as he puts away his guitar.

"Wow," Lyric states, appearing offended. "Sometimes I feel like I'm being used for my dad's connections."

Sage swiftly shakes his head. "No. Not at all." He props his guitar against the wall then faces her. "You have a killer voice, Lyric. Seriously. We're going to be badass." He scratches at the corner of his bloodshot eye. "I'm just saying that we shouldn't waste a good connection like that."

Lyric unplugs the microphone and winds up the cord. "Well, I'll bring it up to him, but he won't do anything until he hears us. We have to be good."

"We are good," Sage presses, checking out her ass as she bends over to stick the microphone onto the bottom shelf of a cupboard. When he notices that I catch him, he offers me a tense smile and shrugs, like *what are you going to do?*

"Yeah, we'll see." Lyric stands upright, tugs the elastic out of her hair, and then combs her fingers through her locks as she ponders over something.

Even though I've tried not to, I end up zoning in on her every move, the relaxed expression on her face, the way her chest arches the slightest bit, the way her glossy lips part . . .

"What do you think, Ayden?" Lyric asks me as she gathers her hair back into a messy bun on her head and secures it with the elastic.

I realize I'm staring at her, holding my breath, and clutching the life out of my guitar.

"About what?" I ask her dazedly.

She holds my gaze, silently begging for something I don't fully understand, nor do I think I can give to her. "About asking my dad for help?"

I shrug as I slide the guitar strap over my head. "If you want to, then do it. I'm sure he'll be okay with it." I don't look at her as I speak. Instead, I concentrate on putting my guitar away, checking my phone, the clock, anything to keep me busy, hyperaware that she's watching me, like she has every day at practice and at school. Our time has only been filled with formal conversation and polite smiles, and I think it's starting to get to her. It's definitely starting to get to me.

"I have to go," I lie when her stare becomes unbearable. "I have some stuff I'm supposed to do at home."

I continue to feel her eyes on me as I hurry across the room, grab my jacket, and dart out the door. Only when I step out into the cool night air can I breathe again.

Lyric and I haven't been driving to band practice or school together, so I make the short drive home by myself, with only my thoughts for company. I'm lonely. Sad. Lost.

On the one hand, I want to remain in my little bubble, because it's easier to breathe and exist. Then again, my bubble isn't really giving me the shelter it used to. It was easier being lonely when that was all I knew. Now that I've gotten a taste of the other side, where I can coexist with people, putting myself in solitude isn't as simple.

By the time I arrive home, I'm miserable and sullen. Lila notices my depression the moment I trudge into the house—she has for the last couple of weeks now. Like always, she convinces me to help her out with something to keep me from locking myself into my room.

"Help me bake Everson's birthday cake," she tells me when I wander into the kitchen, looking for something to eat.

"I'm not that good at baking," I point out as I hunt the cupboards for something to fill my appetite. "Remember when I tried to make those cookies?"

She kindly smiles as she pulls out a carton of eggs from the fridge. "I'll put you on egg duty. It's hard to mess that up."

Closing the cupboard, I take a seat on the barstool and do what she asks, breaking and separating eggshells. Something in the process and the way the yolk falls out of the egg strikes up a distant memory.

Thick, like yolk.
I watch the blood drip.
Over and over.
A repeated pattern.
Driving me mad.
The way it splatters.
Across the floor.
The sound is like nails.
Pounding into my skull.
Drip. Drip. Drip.
Even when I shut my eyes
the dripping still exists.
Over and over.
Never a miss.
I'd lift my hands.
Cover my ears.

Suffocating the dripping out.
But my wrists are tied.
Weighed to the ground.
So I'm stuck
with the torture
weighing me down.

"Ayden, did you hear me?" Lila asks.

I flinch out of my daze, returning back to reality. What I'm supposed to be doing. The food on the counter. The eggs in front of me.

"Um, no, I didn't. Sorry." I pick up an egg and crack the shell against the edge of the bowl while she turns down the heat on the stove.

I'm not sure why I suddenly remembered the sound of the blood dripping, or who the blood even belonged to. I wish I could figure out why I'm having a sudden onset of memories so I could come up with a way to forget again.

"I asked you if you wanted to go help Lyric and her dad work on the car he bought her." She moves a pan of boiling water to an unheated burner. "I'm sure cooking is getting boring."

I split the egg apart and let the yolk drip into the bowl. "Nah, I'm cool here."

Trepidation creases her face. "Are you sure? Because you seem like you're not having that much fun."

"I'm fine." I set the eggshells down on the counter and wipe my fingers on a paper towel.

She dithers, pulling a drawer open to retrieve a spoon. "You and Lyric seem . . . I don't know. Did you have a fight or something?"

"No." It's technically not a lie. We're not exactly fighting. I'm just avoiding her. And she's tried to get me to talk to her. A lot.

"Then why aren't you two hanging out anymore?"

"I don't know."

She's growing frustrated, her cheeks reddening. "Well, I don't care what's going on." She suddenly goes from kind, caring mom to annoyed, get-your-shit together mom, a side I've never seen before. She shoves a plate full of cookies into my hand and shoos me toward the door. "You will go over, and give Lyric and her father some of these cookies."

She has got to be shitting me.

"But—"

"No buts," she cuts me off, snapping her fingers as she points toward the doorway. "Either you go over there, or I make you go talk to the therapist. Maybe he can get to the bottom of why you two suddenly aren't speaking to each other."

Unsure how to respond, I do as she says and start for the backdoor.

"Oh, someone got in trouble, didn't they?" Fiona teases as we cross paths in the foyer. She's got her dark brown hair up in butterfly clips, and her lips stained a fiery red that match her dress.

"Does Lila know you're wearing that much makeup?" I ask as I maneuver the door open, letting the cool November breeze gust in.

She blows me a kiss. "Of course." She's probably lying, though, and will also lie her way out of it when Lila gets mad at her. "Oh, and make sure to make up with Lyric while you're over at her house. I'm seriously getting tired of your sulking." She flashes me a crafty grin then skips out of the foyer and into the kitchen.

Painfully aware of how much I've changed over the last few weeks, I step outside and shut the door behind me.

The sun is set, the sky black. Almost every house on the street is lit up with Christmas lights and flashing signs that promise Christmas cheer. I'm not a big fan of the holidays, but I've gotten better over the last year that I've spent with the Gregorys. I've gotten better at a lot of things while living with them. I just wish things could have remained that way. That the memories had stayed locked away, instead of clawing their way back into my mind.

The garage door of Lyric's house is open when I round the fence. Light and music filters into the night, engulfing me the moment I step foot on the property. The sight of Lyric slams against my chest as the kiss we shared a month ago overwhelms me.

I almost spin around and run, but Lyric spots me and waves.

"Hey," she says in astonishment when I approach the open garage. Her hair is braided, and she's wearing a leather jacket, holey pants, and black lace-up boots. Her cheeks are flushed, and her lips are tinted blue from the chilly breeze.

"Hey," is all I can think of to say back, because I can still feel it. That stupid flutter in my heart, the one that showed up after we kissed. And the emotions associated to the last time someone kissed me.

She sets down a wrench she's holding and meets me around the back of the car. Her gaze drops to the plate in my hand. "Did you bring me cookies?"

I stare at her for way longer than necessary, only ripping my gaze away when she looks up at me. "Oh, yeah, Lila sent them over."

"Can I have one?" she asks, acting coyer than normal. "A cookie, I mean."

"Yeah, of course." My fingers fumble as I lift the plastic off the plate.

She selects one of the snowmen caked in frosting and sprinkles. "These look so good." She dunks her fingertip in the frosting and licks it off, causing a rush of adrenaline to pulsate through my body.

God, I want her.

I need to get out of here.

"Is your dad around?" I frantically scan the garage. "I was supposed to give the plate to him."

She bites off the head of the snowman. "Nope, he ran out to get a part for my car," she replies with her mouth full. "Hey, do you want to see my car? I know you've been . . . busy, and haven't had a chance to see it yet."

"I really need to get back to the house." I set the plate of cookies on the trunk of the car, ready to bail.

"Ayden, please don't leave," she begs, nearly splitting my heart in two.

I freeze. It's the last thing my sister said to me that day we were split apart.

When I glance over my shoulder and see the tears in her eyes, I whirl around. "Lyric, I don't . . ." I trail off, my mind racing with what to say to her. When I come up with nothing, I cautiously inch toward her. "I'm sorry. Please don't cry. I'm so fucking sorry."

She sucks back the tears as she stares at the star dusted sky. "I just don't understand," she says, dabbing her fingertips under her eyes, wiping away some smeared eyeliner before she looks at me again. "You just stopped talking to me for almost a month, with no explanation. And I don't know how to fix it—fix us."

"It's not your fault," I promise her. "I'm just . . . confused."

I let her twine our fingers together, even though her touch makes me ache all the way down to my bones.

"About what?" she asks. When I open my mouth to give her a vague answer, she cuts me off, like she knew what I was going to say before I spoke it. "You know you can tell me anything, right? I got your back, dude, remember?"

Unable to help it, I crack a smile. "Yeah, I remember. Anyone who messes with me gets a basketball to the face."

She laughs then tugs me into the garage toward a rustic 1970 something Dodge Challenger with a dented fender, bumper, hood, dented everything really. "Come on. Come see my new ride. I've been dying to show it off to you."

I allow her to lead me to the car and push me down into the passenger seat. Then she skips around the back, swiping another cookie before dropping down into the driver's seat.

"So, what do you think?" She pats the top of the torn steering wheel. "Pretty beat up, right? But it makes it so much more super awesome. My dad promised that we'd have it finished before graduation."

"Seven months, huh?" I cock a brow at the tattered backseat and caved in bodywork.

"Hey, he's really good with cars." She playfully pinches my arm then frowns when I flinch. Still, she manages to put on the nicest fake smile I've ever seen. "So is your dad."

"Who . . . ? Oh, you mean Ethan. Yeah, I've seen some photos of the cars he used to fix up. They're pretty cool."

She rests back in her seat with her head turned toward me. "You should have him fix one up for you, then we can be twins." She wiggles her fingers in my direction. "Remember the black nail polish we were both wearing the first day you came here."

I smile at the memory. "You seemed so proud of the fact that we matched."

"I was proud," she admits, tucking a strand of hair behind her ear. She flutters her eyelashes as she peers up at me, but I can't tell if it's intentional or not. "You were so intimidating that day. I needed something to say to you."

"Intimidating?" I snort a laugh, the sound echoing around us. "You seemed so at ease. I was the one who felt intimidated."

"But you kept staring at me."

"Not at you. At your eyes. They were—are"—I shrug—"beautiful."

"You've said that to me a lot lately," she whispers softly. "At least, before you stopped talking to me."

"I'm sorry, Lyric. It's just . . ." I start to get choked up. "There are still so many things you don't know about me—that I don't even know about me. If you did, you probably wouldn't want to be my friend anymore."

"Try me." When I gape at her, she sits up and props her elbows on the console. "How will you ever know the answer to that if you don't tell me stuff?"

I scratch at my arm, feeling fidgety and erratic. "I can't tell you everything. I can't even tell myself everything. But . . . the whole touching thing freaks me out."

"I know it does," she says simply. "I could tell that from the first day we met."

"I don't even know why it does. I mean, sometimes I see things, and . . ." I jerk my fingers through my hair. "I just feel all wrong inside."

"Ayden, I get that you've been through stuff, but I want you to always trust me. This whole fighting thing . . . well, it's been killing me. The last month without you has been killing me."

"I wasn't fighting with you." My voice weakens as she leans in, as if she's about to hug me. All my instincts scream at me to back away, but I can't move. All the emotions I've been running away from emerge and magnify, more potent and toxic than ever. "I was just confused . . . about stuff." As she moves in to wrap her arms around me, something crumbles inside me—my self-control.

Before I can even comprehend what I'm doing, I angle my head to the side and press my lips to hers. She tenses, but only for a fleeting second, then she melts into my touch. I realize right then and there that I can keep running from her, but I can't run away from my emotions. They'll always exist under the surface, maybe even longer than I'll admit.

"Oh my God," she groans against my lips as I slide my tongue into her mouth.

She taste like frosting and feels so warm. My fingers begin to shake as I place my hands on her waist, needing her closer, yet fearing her closeness. I grab at her shirt, both pushing and pulling her against me while I kiss her with passion, heat, trying to suffocate the memories that scar my mind.

But they mix together.
Light and dark.
Fear and lust.
Liquid and fire.
I can't get enough.
Yet I have too much.
I'm overflowing.
About to combust.

I start to protest, push back, because my mind is going into overdrive, but suddenly Lyric scrambles over the console and straddles my lap. Her warmth drowns me, seeps through my skin, and singes my veins. And when she presses her chest against mine, all the cold inside me flares. I tangle my fingers through her hair, tugging at the roots, and slide my hand up the front of her shirt.

"Ayden." She bites at my lip, causing my entire body to quiver.

I'm so confused.

My mind wants one thing.
My body the other.
Fear.
Want.
Fear.
Want.
Past.
Future.

She rolls her hips against mine, and I gasp in desperation. In desire. In a million things I don't understand. My body feels like it's about to explode as my fingers inch up the bottom of her bra, and then graze her nipple. I have no clue what I'm doing. Absolutely no idea. *Want.* I know that I want something, so I continue to caress her, gasping and groaning as her nipple hardens under my touch. She bites at my bottom lip again, stabs her nails into my arms, holding onto me, or holding me up—I'm not sure.

I've never purposefully touched a woman like this. Feared it for three years. Yet I want to touch Lyric more than I've wanted to touch anyone, so I cup her breast, feel her delicate flesh, and lick her soft lips. She tastes so good, her skin is so warm, and the whimpers coming from her make my heart slam against my chest, almost painfully.

I'm not sure how long it goes on, us in the car, exploring each other, but it feels like forever.

I could have gone on forever.

Eventually, Lyric pulls away, but keeps her forehead pressed against mine as she traces a finger up and down the back of my neck.

"I've missed you," she utters with her eyes shut. "I'm sorry I upset you."

"I've missed you, too," I openly admit as I struggle to get oxygen into my lungs. "But it wasn't your fault I got upset. I was—am just confused."

Her eyelids lift open and she leans back. "About what?"

"About . . . stuff. There's things about me, Lyric, that even I don't understand sometimes."

"You know you can tell me, right? Tell me anything."

"I wish I could . . . but I can't even remember everything myself."

Strangely, she looks terrified, her eyes widening. "I've been trying to figure out how to bring this up to you, but right before you stopped talking to me, I found an article on the internet that I think is about you."

I swallow hard, scared to death, yet needing to know. "What did it say?"

She secures her arms around me, as if she's afraid I'm going to run. "It just talked about three kids being pulled out of a house. That they . . . had some injuries."

"Lots of injuries," I whisper, scared to death that this conversation is going to trigger what happened before I was pulled out of that house. "More than I think the reporters realized."

Her chest rises and falls as she fights to breathe evenly, her sympathetic gaze drowning me in emotions I can barely comprehend. "Ayden, I . . ." She trails off as her gaze wanders to something over my shoulder.

"What are you looking at?" I track her gaze out the rear window and see a cop car pulling up to my home.

All the fear I had been battling suddenly explodes and smothers me.

CHAPTER 14

FOR ONCE, I CAN'T THINK of a single word to say. Can't smile. Can't breathe.

Everything had been so perfect for about five minutes. That kiss and those touches were the kind that artists crave, like a drug addiction. The moment was perfect, and a song was already forming in my head.

Then the cop car had pulled up to the house and everything went to shit.

I followed Ayden over to his house when he jumped out of the car. Then I sat in the living room with Lila, Ethan, and Ayden while the police started talking. My mom and dad quickly took Kale, Everson, and Fiona out of the house when they realized what the conversation was about.

They found Ayden's brother. Not just found, but discovered his body in a ditch not too far away from their childhood home. And from what it sounds like, he might have been murdered. There is an ongoing investigation, and while they didn't flat out say it, I got the impression that his brother's death might have had something to do with whatever happened to them a few years ago, that there were some marks on his body that led them to believe this, along with some other evidence they wouldn't divulge.

"If you can think of anything at all," the taller of the two officers says, directing his question to Ayden as he hands a card to Lila. "I know in the initial investigation you told the detective that you couldn't remember anything, but if you do, please call us."

"Of course," Lila replies, tucking the card in her pocket, struggling to keep it together.

"And you might want to be a bit more cautious over the next few weeks while we gather more evidence," he tells Lila as she walks them to the door. "It's just a precautionary measure, but it's better to be safe."

I try to catch Ayden's eye as Lila finishes chatting with the officers, but he won't look at me. Won't look at anything, except the scars on his hands.

Lila is sobbing by the time she returns to the living room. Ethan looks like he's about to throw up. And I feel as sick as Ethan looks.

"I'm going to go do my homework." Ayden abruptly stands up from the sofa and walks out of the room at a normal pace with a relaxed expression.

So normal.

Like nothing's wrong.

Lila's shoulders shake as she reaches for a tissue on the table, her eyes filled with tears, and her makeup running everywhere. "Oh my God, this is so horrible. I need to go check on him." She starts to get up, but Ethan drapes an arm around her and pulls her back down. "Let Lyric do it, okay? You need to calm down before you talk to him." He looks at me for help.

I nod, getting to my feet. "Of course." I leave the living room and start up the stairs, but pause when I hear the two of them whispering.

"We knew this was a possibility when we took him in," Ethan says in a gentle tone. "We knew that those people were never caught, and that something might happen one day."

"But I never expected it to happen like this." Lila sniffles. "And did you see the look on his face. It was the same look he had when we picked him up that first day. God, what if he goes back to barely speaking." Tears flood her voice. "I just want him to be happy."

So do I. More than I want my own happiness.

I rush up the stairs and pause in front of Ayden's shut bedroom door, hesitating before I knock.

"Come in." His voice sounds so hollow that I almost start crying as hard as Lila. Instead, I collect myself and push the door open.

"Hey," I say as I tentatively enter.

He's lying on his stomach on the bed with a math textbook opened in front of him, doing his homework just like he said, as music thrums from the speakers of the stereo. He's grasping something in one of his hands.

He finishes writing out the problem before he glances up at me. "Did you need something?" he asks, the life in his grey eyes dead.

I press my lips together. "I just wanted to see if you were okay."

He shrugs, returning to his paper. "I'm fine. It's not like I didn't expect that to happen."

"You expected your brother to die?" I question as I close the door. "Why?"

He shrugs again, continuing to move the pencil across the paper. "I don't know. I just thought it could be a possibility after I found out he disappeared. I honestly am surprised any of us are alive, so . . ."

I should just walk out. Give him time. The space he seems to want. But I can't leave him. So I sit down on the bed, highly aware when his grip on the pencil constricts.

"Ayden, talk to me." I suck in a breath before I dare place a hand on his back.

He goes as rigid as a board. "I don't know what to say." His voice cracks, and then he starts to cry, tears spilling out as he hunches over, hiding his face from me. "I don't think I can do this again—say goodbye." His hands free the object he was clutching, and a few tears slip from my eyes. It's a photo of him when he was younger, along with a young teenage boy and a girl. Probably his brother and sister.

All those years I spent wanting to experience life to the fullest, feel love and heartbreak, and now I feel so grateful that I haven't. Haven't been through what he has.

"Yes, you can." I rub his back as each of his sobs ruptures my heart. "I'm here for you. Whatever you need. I got your back."

But this time, it might not be so simple.

This time, I might not be able to help him.

CHAPTER 15

SOMEHOW IN THE MIDST OF the chaos, I manage to fall asleep. When I wake up, my limbs are tangled with Lyric's, so much so that I can't tell where my arms start and her legs end.

Her head is nuzzled in the crook of my neck, her arm resting on my stomach, and her fingers are splayed across my rib cage where the tattoo is hidden beneath my shirt. The branded flesh scorches like it did the day it was put on me. The pain is one thing I've always been able to remember.

Charred skin.
The scent of dying flesh.
Listen closely.
You'll hear the scream.
Of someone breaking.
Burned alive from the inside.

I lie awake until the sunlight hits the window, watching Lyric sleep, trying to figure out how I managed to drift off with her in my bed.

I'd been such a mess last night, cold, distant, then I freaking lost it and cried in front of her. She'd held me, and instead of panicking, I'd felt better.

Felt safe.

Eventually, I leave the bed.

After slipping into the bathroom to change, I go downstairs, hoping no one else is awake. The moment I catch the scent of bacon, though, I know Lila is up and cooking.

I hesitate before I enter the kitchen, debating whether to run or stay. The obvious choice is to bolt. I used to do it all the time, and it was easy. Run away, live on the streets for a few days, then by the time I was found, the foster family didn't want me anymore. I have a feeling that things aren't going to be that uncomplicated with the Gregorys.

So, summoning a deep breath, I walk in.

Just as I guessed, Lila is standing near the stove, watching bacon sizzle from the pan. She's still in her pajamas, her hair unkempt, and her eyes have bags under them. She probably slept like crap last night, all because of me.

"Oh, hey," she says, startled when she sees me. "I didn't know anyone was up. I was actually about to wake you."

"I just woke up." I rub at my wrists then trace the long, thin scars on the back of my hand. "I'm not sure how much trouble I'm going to be in, but you should probably know Lyric's asleep in my bed."

She reaches to turn the burner off. "Yeah, I know that. So do the Scotts. We thought it'd be okay for the night, considering." She moves the pan off to the side, then wipes her hands on a paper towel. "How about we have some breakfast and talk? There's a few things we need to discuss."

I stare at her with wariness as she crosses the kitchen to the table where there's a plate with eggs and a fork on it. She takes a seat then pats the chair next to her, and I reluctantly sit my ass down.

"How are you feeling?" she asks, inching the plate of

eggs toward me.

I pick up the fork, but I don't feel very hungry. "Okay."

She tiredly sighs. "Ayden, I know you're not okay. You just lost your brother—you can't be okay."

"I lost him once before." I stab the fork into the eggs.

"Yeah, but this is different."

I stuff a bite of eggs into my mouth and slowly chew, killing time so I don't have to say anything. If I speak, I'm afraid I'll break again, like I did in front of Lyric last night.

"Ethan and I were talking last night, and we think you should start seeing the therapist a little more." She covers her hand over mine. "I know you've been doing well, but we just want to make sure you're okay." She pauses, and I know there's more. "There's something else. Something the cops mentioned when I walked them to the door."

I stop chewing. "What did they say?"

She squeezes my hand. "They think it could be beneficial if we tried some stuff to strike up your memories. They think it could help with the case if you could remember some of the details."

I clutch the fork so firmly the handle bends. "But how can they even know for sure that my brother's death had anything to do with the people who took us? It's been like, three years."

"They said there was some evidence that linked the two incidences together." She offers a sympathetic look. "I'm sure they'll be able to give us more information later on."

I inhale a large breath then exhale. "I don't want to talk about this anymore, if that's okay."

She moves her hand away from mine, nodding. "That's fine. We don't have to right now." She scoots the chair back from the table to stand up. "But, Ayden, I just want you to prepare yourself for, because it might be brought up the further they get into the case. Ethan and I will do everything we can to keep it as easy as possible on you, but some things might be out of our hands."

She returns to the bacon, leaving me with my eggs and my thoughts. There is a reason why I refuse to remember the week we spent in that home chained up. And while I can't actually recollect it, I know it has to be bad; otherwise, I wouldn't have suppressed the memories in the first place. But what if it could help with my brother's case?

After I finish my eggs, I head back upstairs. The house is still quiet when I slip back into my room, the only noise coming from the kitchen. I figure everyone is still asleep, so I'm surprised when I see Lyric sitting up on my bed, wide awake, the blankets tangled around her legs.

She's still wearing the shirt and jeans she had on yesterday, her blond hair surrounding her face, and she looks drained of all her sparkling energy.

"Hey." She sits up straighter as I shut the door. "Where did you go?"

"To eat some breakfast." I pause at the foot of the bed, staring at her. Through all the madness of last night, I haven't had time to think about what we did in the car. How we kissed. How I touched her. How I felt when she touched me back. I'm still so confused about it. So lost. About everything.

"Is everything okay?" She kicks the blankets off and scoots down the bed until she's kneeling on the mattress in front of me. "I don't want to push you," she starts, "but I need you to know that I'm here for you if you decide you need to talk."

"I don't feel like talking," I tell her then completely contradict myself seconds later as words pour out of my mouth. "They want me to try to remember stuff about three years ago."

"Who does?"

"The police. Lila . . . She didn't flat out say it, but I can tell she thinks I should. That it could help the case."

Her forehead creases as she combs her fingers through her hair. "How does that even work? If you can't remember, then you can't remember, right?"

I shrug as I sink down onto the bed beside her. "There are ways. My therapist's mentioned a few before, but I always turned him down."

"What are you going to do?" She sketches a soothing path up and down my spine with her fingertip.

My instinctive shudder from her touch reminds me of what I face if I decide to do this. I want to, if nothing else, for my brother; but I'm also terrified out of my Goddamn mind.

"I don't know what I'm going to do."

"Well, I'm here for you, whatever you decide." She hugs her arms around me and pulls me closer to her.

I close my eyes, and for the briefest instant, try to allow my mind to remember. But as soon as my body begins to quiver, I give up. Instead, I lean into Lyric's touch, knowing that it's only a temporary fix, and that eventually I'm going to have to make a choice.

Face my future.

Or completely shut down.

RAVELING YOU

the
Unraveling
You
series
BOOK TWO

New York Times and USA Today Bestselling Author
JESSICA SORENSEN

RAVELING YOU
All rights reserved.
Copyright © 2015 by Jessica Sorensen

This is a work of fiction. Any resemblance of characters to actual persons, living or dead, is purely coincidental. The Author holds exclusive rights to this work. Unauthorized duplication is prohibited.

For information:
jessicasorensen.com

Cover Design and Photography:
Sarah Hansen, Okay Creations
www.okaycreations.com

Interior Design and Formatting:
Christine Borgford, Perfectly Publishable
www.perfectlypublishable.com

CHAPTER 1

"I THINK WE SHOULD GET one of the dead ones." A smile curls at my lips as I pluck a brown pine needle off a tree veering toward eternal death. "Just think about it. We'd be the only ones in the entire neighborhood with a brown Christmas tree. We'd really stand out amongst the masses."

Ayden's lips quirk as he flicks a tree branch. "As much as I'd love to let you have your way, I doubt Lila or your mom would be too thrilled if we came home with a fire hazard for a Christmas decoration."

"It wouldn't be the first time. One time, Uncle Ethan and my dad brought home this baby pine tree that had hardly any needles after Aunt Lila told them to bring home the cutest Christmas tree they could find." I tug my beanie lower onto my head and zip my jacket all the way up to my chin. "They thought they were so funny, but she was so mad she threw the tree in the fireplace."

Even though we live in San Diego, where it never snows, the December air has a nip to it. We're at a tree lot, trying to figure out which tree is considered "flourishing." The area smells like forest and pine nuts, and the red and green twinkly lights on the sign and fence glimmer across our faces, evidence that the holidays are spritzed everywhere; trees, yards, streets, stores.

I generally enjoy the spirit of Christmas, but after attending the funeral for Ayden's brother, Felix, yesterday, this year seems less cheery. Ayden hardly showed any emotion at the graveyard. I held his hand through the eulogy, and he gripped on for dear life, as if the connection was the only thing keeping him on his feet. I tried my best to keep it together for him, to stay upbeat.

Still am.

"She set the angel tree topper on fire, too," I continue when Ayden doesn't crack a smile. "You should have seen how the dress went up in flames. Looked like a little devil toward the end of it."

"You're so full of it," he says with a ghost of a smile. "But thank you."

"For what?"

"For trying."

His words don't make me feel any better, since he still appears depressed.

I tip my head up to the night sky and spot a shooting star glimmering across the sky. Under my breath, I utter a wish that Ayden will be able to overcome all of his obstacles. Not just with the passing of his brother, but with his sister not being at the funeral. No one will give him any information about where she is, either. He's frustrated, although he rarely complains about his hardships—never has.

On top of all of that, he's dealing with a tremendous amount of pressure from the police to seek therapy to try to restore his memories. He's conflicted with what he feels is right and wrong; not helping means turning his back on his brother's memory and helping means facing the demons of his past.

Although he has never flat out told me the specific details of what he can recollect about his time before foster care, I've come up with my own speculations, and all are horrible. The homemade tattoo they branded on his flesh tells me how mistreated he was while he was held captive.

"What do you think about this one?" Ayden draws my attention back to him.

He's standing by a tall, puffy tree propped against the fence.

I move beside him and angle my chin up to stare at the tip of the towering tree. "It might be a little excessive and will probably barely fit in your living room. Remember how super frustrated Aunt Lila was with Uncle Ethan last year when he brought home that one that was too big for the living room? The top nearly touched the damn ceiling, and there was hardly any room for the angel."

"Yeah, I forgot about that." His frown deepens. "I guess you're right. It'll probably be better to get a smaller one this year." His head falls forward and strands of black hair drift into his dark eyes.

He's so beautiful and sad, like the haunting portrait my mother painted of her mother's grave surrounded by black mist and bleeding rose petals. I wanted to cry every time I looked at it. She ended up selling it for a ton of money. Guess people have a thing for depressing and slightly morbid stuff.

I need to cheer him up somehow.
Come on, Lyric. You can do better.

I place my hands on my hips. "All right, dude, what's with the poutiness?"

He gives me a sidelong glance. "Dude? Are we really going back to that?" A playful tone edges into his voice. *Finally.*

"Um, hello. You will always be my dude, even when we're super old." I flash him my pearly whites. "You'll be all badass—old with a cane and a hunch, but rockin' your boots and black, studded clothes. And, sometimes, you'll even smile and make all the ladies in the old folks' home giggle like they did when they were sixteen. You'll totally be grandpa dude worthy."

Laughter escapes his lips. "So, you're putting me in an old folks' home, huh? Nice to know where I'm headed."

"Yeah, well, I had to. Your cane was cramping my hot Grandma swagger."

His lips twitch as a full smile threatens to break through. "Oh, my God. I would love to know how you come up with this shit."

"No, you wouldn't." I put the tip of my two fingers to my temple. "Trust me, you're way better off not knowing what goes on in here." When he laughs again, I dare ask, "So, are you going to tell me why you got all sad puppy eyes when I said this tree might not be the way to go?"

"It's not a big deal." He skims over the trees then nods his head to a shorter one near the entrance of the tree shop. "We should probably go for one like that."

I catch his sleeve before he can wander off. "No way. We're totally getting one of the tall ones."

"Nah. You were right. They're too tall."

"Nope, they're just right. Besides, Uncle Ethan will make it work, and he'll love every second doing so. And then we can get me this bad boy," I point at an equally tall and fluffy tree leaning beside the one Ayden picked out, "so we can be twins." I waggle my eyebrows at him. "And we both know how much you love being just like me."

"Yep, it's my secret wish," he finally, finally jokes back. "In fact, every night when I go to sleep, I look out my window, find a shooting star, and beg it to please let me wake up and be exactly like Lyric."

"Ha, ha." I aim a finger at him and force a falsetto laugh. "I knew it."

"You are such a weirdo." He's totally smiling a big, ol' grin from ear to ear.

"Yeah, but a weirdo that you're so in love with." As soon as I say it, I instantly want to retract it.

Ayden massages the back of his neck tensely, looking everywhere except at me.

Can you say awkward?

It used to not be this complicated between us, but that was before the kissing and touching we did in my car. Since then, stuff between us has gotten slightly uncomfortable if certain subjects come up, like love.

I don't feel bad about it at all, though. Ayden doesn't even tell the Gregorys he loves them. I honestly don't think he can say that word and mean it, not yet anyway. There are several things he can't do, like allow anyone to touch him more intimately than holding a hand or a hug. While we have kissed twice, our lip-locking has come to a grinding halt ever since his brother's death. He's not cold toward me—he cuddles and holds my hand more than he used to. I think his brother's mysterious death has messed with his mind, though, because that dark place he forgot about for over three years is trying to reenter his life.

"Okay, this weirdo right here is getting hungry." I rub my tummy. "So, how about we load up these lovely trees and stop to get a burger on the way home before I starve to death?"

"Fine, but only if you let me pay this time." He relaxes, and so do I. "You always pay."

I link arms with him. "Okay, I'll let you pretend to be the man for tonight." When his lips tug upward, I press on, "Man, I'm so funny. What would you do without me?"

He stares at me, dead serious. "I honestly have no idea." With a sigh, he wiggles his arm from mine and gently drapes it over my shoulder. A simple gesture but out of the ordinary for him. "Come on. Let's go pay for the trees and get you your burger so we can get back. Otherwise, we'll be late for band practice."

We pay for the trees and load them in the back of my Uncle Ethan's truck, who really isn't my uncle, not by blood anyway. Uncle Ethan and Aunt Lila are just close to my parents, best friends to be exact. I've known them since I was born and sometimes call them aunt and uncle.

Once we hop into the cab and pull out onto the road, Ayden turns on the radio, flipping on some Brand New. I've learned over the last year of our friendship that his music choices portray how he feels. Tonight, he's stuck in his own head. I'd ask him what he's thinking about, but I know him well enough to understand he more than likely won't tell me.

The Christmas tree shop is about a ten-minute drive from our neighborhood, so after we pick up some takeout, we still arrive home with a decent amount of time to spare before we have to leave for band practice.

The moon is a glowing orb and the stars sprinkle like pixie dust across the sky. A scenic night to be decorating the house, which is exactly what Uncle Ethan is doing when we pull up.

"What's with the inflatable Santa?" Ayden nods at Ethan who's inflating a massive Santa near the border of where our properties meet. "Last year, he put it that close to your house, too."

"It's because my dad's afraid of them." I unbuckle my seatbelt. "I guess he got stuck under one during a teenage prank gone wrong. Every year, Uncle Ethan puts it up to torture him. They're so crazy and weird, maybe weirder than me."

"Yeah, but it's nice, I guess. To have Christmas traditions like that, something you guys have done for years."

He silences the engine and unfastens his seatbelt.

Suddenly, his deal with the big tree makes sense. He wants to keep tradition by getting a large one like the Gregorys did last year during his first Christmas with the family. He was so quiet back then, and I was awkward, trying to push him out of his comfort zone. I wanted so much for him to be my friend. This year, I want him to be more than that. But with what he's going through, I can't expect anything more than friendship.

"You know, my mom is having one of her holiday art shows like she did last year on New Year's Eve," I tell Ayden as I open the door to get out. "We could go again, but this time we can try sneaking off with a few glasses of eggnog. Get buzzed. Add to the tradition."

"I thought you were going to go to that party with Sage?" Ayden's brow arches as he glances at me. "That one Maggie invited you guys to."

Sage is the drummer of our band. With his blue-dyed hair, multiple piercings, and tattoos, he fits the part of what most people think a drummer should look like. After two months of jamming with him, I'm still deciding if he's a walking cliché or just an expressive person.

"Well, she invited you, too, silly. But I think the art show would end up being more fun. Besides, parties still make me uneasy. And I could very well run into William there."

William is the guy who assaulted me and attempted to rape me at a party a few months ago. Thankfully, I was able to get away before he got too far, but the thought of being near him makes me uneasy.

"You shouldn't worry about running into him," Ayden says. "*He's* the one who should be worried, not you."

"I know, but unfortunately, that's not the way it works. I saw him at school after he did his community service.

The douche had the nerve to grin at me."

"I want to punch him in the face," Ayden growls through gritted teeth, gripping onto the steering wheel, his knuckles turning white.

"You already did that." I gently touch his arm, hoping to calm him down. "We just need to move on now. Stewing in what he did only gives him more power."

"You got that from my therapist."

"Yeah. He said that to me when I went to visit him."

I went to one therapy session after what happened with William, mainly because my parents needed to know my head was okay. Talking about what happened was therapeutic, but not enough for me go to weekly visits like Ayden does.

"So, what do you say?" I ask, clasping my hands in front of me. "Does an art show sound New Year's Eve worthy? Pretty please, say yes."

"Sure. An art show sounds good." He offers me a small, grateful smile. "But only because you said pretty please."

"Awesome." I shove the door open all the way, and a chilly breeze gusts inside the cab. "I'm going to go tell my dad to come get the tree. Then I'm going to take a shower. I smell like pine needles and greasy burgers, not a great combo." I pause before I jump out. "Are you driving tonight or am I?"

"I can . . ." He appears distracted, his attention on the garage ahead of us.

"Hey, are you okay?" I search for what he might be looking at, maybe hidden in the shadows, but I don't see anything.

"Yeah, I'm fine." His gaze finds mine and he blinks dazedly. "I was just thinking about some stuff I have to do tonight."

"Anything you want to talk about?" I swing my legs over the edge of the seat to hop out of the truck.

He shakes his head then forces a stiff smile. "I'll go take care of the trees and then head over to your house in about a half an hour."

I suppress a sigh, jump out of the truck, and close the door. Giving a quick wave to Ayden, I round the fence between our driveways and enter the warmth of my home.

My dad is in the kitchen when I walk in. He has a notebook in his hand, intently reading one of the pages as he nibbles on a cookie. His blond hair is sticking up, and he looks stressed out.

"Yo, Daddy-O." I slam the door with an excessive amount of force to scare him.

He jumps and drops the cookie on the floor. "Jesus Christ, Lyric." He shakes off his jumpiness and scoops up the cookie from the hardwood floor. "You scared the shit out of me."

"That's what I was going for." I unzip my jacket and grab a cookie off the plate in the middle of the table. "Nice hair by the way. Did you just get out of bed? Or were you going for that bedhead/fauxhawk look all the cool kids are wearing nowadays?"

He places his palm on the top of his head, flattening his hair down. "Is it really that bad?" When I nod, he puffs out a frazzled exhale. "I was just going through some things for work, and I guess I took my stress out on my hair." He pulls out a chair and sits down at the table.

I rest my arms on the back of a chair and lean over the table to get a glimpse of what's on the pages. "Anything I can help with?"

He fans through the pages then rakes his fingers through his hair, making the ends stand right back up and solving the culprit of the bedhead/fauxhawk look. "Nah, it's just club stuff I'm trying to figure out."

"Like what?"

His brows elevate. "You really want to hear about my business problems?"

I stuff the rest of the cookie into my mouth. "That all depends on if it has to do with the music business side of it."

"It does." He seems hesitant to embellish.

I drop down in the chair across from him. "Then lay it on me. I'm all ears."

"Okay, but you have to promise me one thing," he says with reluctance. "That you won't mention your band at all during the conversation."

"My lips are sealed." I drag my fingers across my lips, pretending to zip them up.

His mouth is set in a firm frown, as if the last thing he wants to do is discuss whatever he's stressing about. "It's about one of the bands I had lined up for the opening." He waits for me to go back on my word and react, and I almost do, but forcefully smash my lips together, instead. "The lineup's pretty cool, but one of the opening bands backed out at the last second, so my big plan to carry it out all day isn't going to be possible. I mean, I still have a lot of good ones lined up." He reads over a scribbled list of band names. "I just wanted seven total." He flips the page, muttering nonsense, while I struggle not to put my two cents in. "It really isn't a big deal, except that it is since the flyer and advertisement said there'd be seven bands."

I raise my hand in the air like I'm in grade school.

"And it's too late notice to find someone else. The opening is less than three weeks," he carries on, ignoring my raised hand. "I'm already in the lineup, and I'll be way too busy making sure things run smoothly to try to take on two sets."

I bounce up and down in my chair, waving my hand in front of his face. "Hello? Can't you see my hand?"

"I can." He closes the notebook. "And I know what you're going to say. The answer is no, though."

My shoulders slump as I plant my ass back in the chair. "No to what?" I fake pout. "You haven't even heard what I'm going to say."

"But I already know what you're going to say."

"How so?"

"Because we share the same musical DNA, and twenty-five years ago, if I'd been sitting in your spot, I'd have asked the same question you want to ask right now."

I jut out my lip. "You're cruel."

"No, I'm being a good father." He shoves his notebook aside and rests his elbows on the table. "There's no way I'm going to let my seventeen-year-old daughter and her band play at a club with a bunch of hardcore rock bands."

"FYI, I'm almost eighteen." I cross my arms and slump back in the chair. "You haven't even heard us play yet. Maybe we're as good as those hardcore rock bands."

"It's not that I doubt your ability, Lyric. I've heard you play and sing behind closed doors. You're fucking talented." I start to beam. "But . . ." he adds, and I frown—there's always a but—"it takes a lot of prep time to play onstage. And I'm not just talking about practice time, but mental prepping."

Aw, my parents and their concern for my mental stability. The worry seems to be expanding, too, ever since Ayden went into his depressive state, as if they believe we're so in sync I'll shut down with him.

I narrow my eyes, getting defensive. "Hey, we're ready. More than ready. We fucking rock."

"Yeah, but I'm not sure I'm ready for you to grow up that fast yet." He scoots the chair away from the table to stand up. "The environment at these things . . . it's intense."

"You played when you were my age," I argue. "Maybe not at clubs, but I've heard the stories about the parties you and Mom went to back in the day."

He gapes at me. "When did you hear stories?"

I rise from my chair. "Every time you, Mom, Uncle Ethan, and Aunt Lila get drunk, you sit in the living room and reminisce about the good old days. And you're really loud drunks." I snatch up another cookie and stride for the doorway.

"Lyric, please don't be upset," he pleads. "This has nothing to do with your ability."

"Of course it doesn't." I pop a chunk of the cookie into my mouth and raise my chin in confidence. "You've never really heard me sing. And I mean *really* sing. Because, if you did, you'd be overlooking your overprotective father thing you've got going on right now and let me own your opening."

He opens his mouth to say something, but no words come out. I've struck him speechless, which was exactly what I was hoping for, even though I'm totally being overconfident. Our band doesn't even have a name, at least one we all agree on, and we haven't played anywhere other than inside the four walls of Sage's garage. But confidence can carry you a long way. Believe in yourself, and other people will, too. At least, I'm hoping that's where this conversation goes.

"And P.S.," I add, "a fantabulous Christmas tree is waiting in the back of Uncle Ethan's truck for you."

I walk out of the kitchen, leaving my father to stew in his thoughts, and go upstairs to take a shower. Afterward, I blow-dry my long, blonde hair straight, apply some kohl eyeliner, and then tug on a pair of black torn jeans and a red shirt. It's nearing eight o'clock by the time I finish getting ready.

I glance out the window at Ayden's bedroom. The lights are on, with the curtains shut. He's kept them consistently closed for the last week, and I often wonder if he's hiding something behind them. I could be overanalyzing his distant behavior, but I don't know . . . There have been moments since his brother died when he'll suddenly announce he has to go home, even if we're in the middle of a movie or at band practice. He always goes into his bedroom and locks the door; at least, that's what I heard Aunt Lila whispering to my mother the other day.

"I'm getting worried," she said while they were unloading Christmas presents from the car, "about what he's doing in there. Like, maybe drugs."

They didn't know I was listening from the garage, but I stepped out and gave them my input. "He's not on drugs. You guys are overreacting. He probably just needs his space." I didn't bother mentioning that Ayden and I technically get high on secondhand smoke every other night at band practice since Sage insists he plays better when the garage is being hotboxed.

As I'm gazing out the window, I suddenly notice something odd on the sidewalk below. A middle-aged bald guy with a beer gut and a gnarly looking scar on his jawline is walking his dog. He pauses in front of the Gregory's home and stares at the house. He could easily be gawking at the freshly hung twinkling lights and decorations, but his attention lingers on Ayden's bedroom window for far too long in my opinion. Then the man scurries away, tugging his dog along with him.

I make a mental note to mention the guy to my mother when I see her later tonight. I'm sure he is just some random dude being a gawker. But, with how worried everyone's been lately and with the police telling Lila to keep a closer eye on Ayden, it feels imperative to at least bring it up.

After the guy vanishes, I turn from the window and collect my phone from my dresser to text Ayden.

Me: U about ready to get this funfest on the road?

Ayden: Yeah, I'll be over in like ten. I'm in the middle of something.

Even though we're already running late, I don't push him to hurry his butt up. I slip on my leather jacket, tuck my phone into the pocket, and pop in my earbuds. I crank up a little "For You, And Your Denial" by Yellowcard and flop down on my bed with my notebook I jot lyrics in.

Despite how collected I am around Ayden, my composure crumbles and splatters across the pages the moment I pick up a pen. Penning lyrics has become my outlet and my sanctuary, a time when I feel okay not being so cheery and smiley.

Can you hear me crying?
Silent agony that will completely vanish.
A scorch in my heart,
Singeing into embers.
My veins char to ash.
Hardly a flicker of fire left
To ignite life into me again.
Eventually the cold settles
Through my skin into my bones.
The embers drown with mourning,
Stealing the last breath of air.
And that silent cry dies,
Takes its final breath of air,
Caves to the chill.
Nothing is left, left, left.

Fading, withering, dying.

I pull the pen away. Okay, maybe my parents do need to worry about my mind.

I scratch my head as I reread my gloomy and slightly morbid lyrics. I don't know why, but I kind of like them.

Feeling satisfied, I tuck my notebook away then turn to the window again to check on Ayden. His bedroom light is off, so he has to be heading over. Down in driveway, Uncle Ethan and my dad are sawing off the bottom of a tree. Kale and Fiona, Uncle Ethan and Aunt Lila's other adopted children, are with them, gathering the stray tree branches and carrying them inside the Gregory's home to make wreaths like they do every year.

Ayden is nowhere in sight.

Me: Dude, where are you at?

He doesn't respond.

About a minute later, I spot him hurrying up the sidewalk from the direction of the main road with the hood pulled over his head. Instead of cutting across the front lawn, he hunkers down behind the neighbor's fence then climbs over it into his side of the yard. With his back pressed against his house, he inches toward the front door like a ninja, clearly trying to go unnoticed. But why? And where was he for the last ten minutes or so?

To make the situation sketchier, the instant he slips into the house, he texts me back.

Ayden: Just got out of the shower. Be over in a couple.

"That little liar," I utter under my breath.

I wait near the window until he exits through the backdoor. He waves to my dad and his, then jogs around the fence to my yard. Like always, he knocks on the door before walking in.

My dad turns to him from the driveway and hollers, "Ayden, you can just go in!"

I pull my earbuds out and wait for him to walk into my bedroom. When he strolls in with damp hair, as if he actually took a shower, my jaw ticks with irritation.

"All right, buddy." I stare him down hard. "What are you keeping from me?"

He averts his gaze to the floor, ruffling his hair into place. "What are you talking about? I've been at my house." He scratches at the corner of his eye, and I notice a phone number on the back of his hand.

What the hell has he been up to tonight? And, better yet, who has he been with?

And why is he lying to me?

SHE HAS A VERY UN-LYRIC like expression on her face when I walk into her bedroom. She's upset, maybe with me. After a week of being extra nice and agreeable, her determined attitude instantly throws me off. Then she bluntly calls me out on keeping something from her, and I know it's only a matter of time before I spill my secret, because upsetting her will quickly wear me down.

"What do you mean?" I mess with my damp hair. Since I texted Lyric that I'd just gotten out of the shower, I actually had to get it wet in the bathroom sink before I headed over. I ended up getting the collar of my shirt wet in the process, making the back of my neck cold.

"Don't 'what do you mean' me, looking all innocent." She strides across the room then pokes me in the chest. "You know, usually I'm cool with you not telling me stuff, but when I see you creeping up to your house all ninja style then lying to me about where you were, telling me you were taking a shower," she rolls her eyes, "that's when I start pressing for info. So, tell me, where'd you sneak off to tonight?"

"I . . ." I trail off as she elevates her brows at me.

For the last two weeks, I've spent night after night

wondering if my brother's death was a murder caused by the people who held my siblings and me captive three years ago. His body had been found near the house we'd been held hostage. If it was the same people, I worry they'll eventually try to kill my younger sister and me. My sister who I wish I could see again, if for nothing other than to know she's safe.

Fear, toxic fear,
driving me insane.
Flooding me with rage.
Fear, toxic fear,
I wish you'd just disappear.
Leave me alone.
Get the hell out of here.
But I know you'll never go away,
let me breathe again,
until I know my sister's safe.
Until I know the demon has paid.

On day five of barely sleeping at all, I decided I'd had it with the constant worry and started searching around on the Internet. I'd stumbled across a hacker and met the guy tonight in the park near my neighborhood because he refused to have business meetings over the phone or computer. Not the smartest thing to do on my part, but I'm getting desperate.

Of course when I met him, my worries of whether he was a serial killer or not dissolved. Rebel Tonic—an online name—is a gangly guy younger than me. If he tried anything, I could have taken him if I had to.

He insisted he can find my sister's whereabouts by hacking into social service's records. His fee is more than I have stashed away, so I'm trying to figure out where to come up with the money, and if I can even trust him not to screw me over.

"I can't tell you." I offer Lyric an apologetic look, wordlessly begging her to please be understanding like she normally is.

Her mouth plummets to a hurt frown. "Why not? You know I'll keep whatever you tell me a secret."

"I know you will . . . that's not the problem." I tangle our fingers together and guide her to the bed, drawing her with me as I sit down. "Trust me, it's not because I don't want to tell you. I just don't want to get you into trouble if I get caught. It's better if you don't know what I'm up to just in case our parents find out . . . It's better if you're in the dark, at least for now."

"You're worrying me. Is it . . . ?" She bites on her bottom lip. "You're not doing anything illegal or dangerous are you? Like . . . drugs?"

"What! Drugs . . . do you really think that about me?"

She looks shamefaced. "No, but . . . I heard Aunt Lila whispering it to my mom the other day. I think she's worried about you because you seem so . . . depressed." Caution creeps into Lyric's voice, probably worried she's crossing a line with the remark about my emotions.

"I know she is." And I feel bad. The last thing I ever want is for anyone to worry about me. I wish I could be happier so my family could relax, but I feel so depressed all the time. "I'm not doing drugs, though."

"I figured you weren't, but I had to ask." She intently studies me with her green eyes then her bottom lip juts out into a full-on pout. "You really won't tell me what's going on?"

It's difficult to tell her no when she looks as adorable as she does right now. I just want to kiss her lip, suck it in my mouth . . .

"Lyric . . . I . . ." Her pout deepens, and I sigh. "You know, when I first met you, I thought you used to do the whole pouting thing unintentionally." I tuck a strand of her long, blond hair behind her ear, highly aware of how badly my fingers tremble and the way her breath hitches in her throat. "But now I'm starting to wonder if you know exactly what you're doing."

"So does it work?" she asks, hopeful. "Does it mean you'll tell me where you were?"

"Not yet . . . but soon . . . maybe. If I feel like it's safe to."

"How soon is soon, though? Because you've got me really, really worried about you, to the point where it's hard to think about anything else."

"I don't want that. You don't need to put so much . . . effort into being my friend all the time, especially with how much of a burden I've been lately."

"Like I could simply just quit." She shakes her head and her smile brightens. "You're my favorite person. And it's hard to just stop thinking about my favorite person. But think of it this way, the sooner you tell me what's up, the less time I'll have to spend stressing."

"I wish I could tell you now." I withdraw my hand from her hair as the compassion in her eyes becomes unbearable to look at. The way she looks at me sometimes, like I'm everything to her . . . No one has ever looked at me that way, and it feels unnatural. "I just don't know if it's okay yet." Safe yet.

"So vague." Her gaze drops to my hand as I flex my fingers. "Can I just ask one more thing, though?"

I nod. "Of course."

"You're . . . You're not seeing anyone, are you? Like dating someone or something?" She angles her head forward, her face blocked by her hair.

"Huh?" I'm so confused. I haven't shown signs of wanting to heat up our friendship boundaries again, but that doesn't mean I've shown signs of wanting to be with anyone else. "No. Again, what's with the weird assumption?"

"Because of this." She flicks the back of my hand.

My expression sinks. I didn't have my phone or any paper when I met Rebel Tonic, and he wanted to leave me with his private phone number. I found a pen in my pocket and jotted his phone number on my hand with every intention of transferring the digits to paper when I got home, but then I got sidetracked with rushing over here and forgot to wash the number off.

"God, I just made things super awkward, didn't I?" Lyric mutters with a disheartened sigh. "After being like the coolest person ever, I've resorted to an awkward, unsure girl." She stretches her fingers out and focus on her hands. "Can we pretend I didn't just act like a jealous weirdo? It could be your early birthday present to me."

My heart thuds deafeningly from inside my chest as I hook a finger under her chin and tip her face up. "You're not acting like a jealous weirdo. You're acting like a normal person. I'm the one who's been the weirdo, shutting you out like I have. It's not fair." My heart rate quickens even more as she wets her lips with her tongue and briefly glances at my mouth.

God, if I could just kiss her without freaking out . . .

I'd kiss her all the time.

"So, just to be clear," my voice wobbles embarrassingly, "I'd never go on a date with someone else. I don't want to date at all. I mean, I do want to date, but I just can't yet. I don't think so, anyway." I clear my throat. Nothing I'm saying is coming out right. "Okay, let me try that again. I don't want to go out on a date with anyone other than you. I just don't think I can handle dating right now." I roll my eyes at myself. Man, I am the least smooth person ever. "See, now I'm the one who just made things awkward."

"You didn't make things awkward." She searches my eyes, her own sparkling, a sign that my cheery Lyric is about to emerge. "So, my dad had a band cancel for his opening."

Her abrupt subject change throws me off, but I latch on to her offering. It's one of the reasons I love her so much . . .

Love her?

I shake my head at my thoughts, and Lyric's face twists with perplexity.

No, I like her.

A lot.

I don't even know what love is.

I can't.

Can I?

"Did you offer up our help?" I absentmindedly twist a strand of her hair around my finger, shutting down my thoughts before I freak out.

"Well, duh." She rolls her eyes then grins. "Of course I did."

With each soft tug of her hair, her eyelids flutter and her lips part.

And with each eyelid flutter and lip part, my pulse throbs.

I don't stop.

I don't want to stop until it becomes too much for me.

"And what'd he say?" My voice is surprisingly husky.

She moans, and that's when I finally lose it, when I know I've pushed my emotions too far. Images start to creep into my mind; a brush of hair and caresses of fingertips I don't want touching me.

I untangle my fingers from her hair as a breath falters from my lips.

Lyric frowns disappointedly but doesn't say anything.

"The same old, same old." She makes a flapping motion with her hand as she pulls a face, pretending to mimic her dad. "He yammered about my mental stability, said I needed more stage preparation, and that *he* needed more preparation for his daughter to freakin' rock the socks off a bunch of people."

My lips twitch in amusement. "And what did you tell him?"

"I told him we rocked, and if he heard us, he'd beg us to be in his lineup. I gave him something to really think about." She winks at me. "Now, we should probably go practice for when he asks to see us play." She laces her fingers through mine, rises from the bed, and then pulls me up with her.

"You really think he's going to?" I question as we head for the door.

"Oh, yeah. I could see it in his eyes." She points at her own. "He was totally wondering just how talented his daughter really is. In fact, I bet by tomorrow he'll be asking to hear us play."

"You really think we're ready, though?" I ask as we descend the stairway toward the main floor of the two-story home. "I mean, we don't even have a band name yet."

"I have a few ideas for that." She peers over her shoulder at me, her eyes sparkling mischievously. "Have a little faith in me and my awesomeness, would you?"

"I have a ton of faith in you and your awesomeness. It's the rest of the band I'm worried about."

She squeezes my hand reassuringly. "We're all doing well. Granted, Nolan's a little less motivated than you, Sage, and me. Do you ever get the feeling that his interest in the music industry is solely based on getting laid?"

"I've thought that a lot," I reply as we enter the dimly lit kitchen that smells like vanilla with a hint of cleaner.

A plate of cookies Lila sent over this morning is on the countertop along with a stack of neon pink flyers for the opening of Infinite Bliss, Lyric's dad's new club.

"He's so old school," Lyric remarks as she picks up a flyer.

"He didn't do any other promoting?" I steal a cookie off the plate.

"No, he did after I made a suggestion that flyers don't work that well anymore." She drops the flyer back onto the stack. "See, he totally owes me." She grabs two cookies off the plate then steers us out the back door and to the driveway. "I just wish he'd realize that." She puts the cookies in her mouth so she can open the garage door without letting go of my hand.

The night sky is lit up by the moon and the countless stars and matches the illuminated neighborhood covered with Christmas lights and decorations. I've lived here for over a year and still can't get over how different it is from all the other homes I stayed at. So bright, cheery, welcoming. All the other homes were full of despair and were energy draining.

"Who is that?" Lyric suddenly asks.

I track her gaze to a man with a dog on a leash wearing a tracksuit. He's slowly walking down the sidewalk with his attention on my house, specifically focusing on the second story, right on my bedroom window.

"I don't know. He's probably just some neighbor wondering why we have a half-deflated Santa near the front door of the house."

My thoughts laugh at me, whisper another story, remind me that it was my neighbors who took me into their home and broke my brother as well as my sister and me.

Sharp objects, have you forgotten?
All those days forced into restraints.

All the blood spilled across the carpet.
The stench of rust hanging in the air.
Trust. Trust. Trust.
How can you still be so naïve?

Lyric looks at me with concern. "Yeah, I guess so . . . but he's not even looking at the front door. And I think I saw him earlier, too, and he looked like he was staring at your window."

I squint through the darkness to get a better look at him: middle-aged, going bald, a beer gut, and what looks like a scar on his jawline. For a brief moment, I pause, trying to connect the guy to my past. But my effort is worthless. The people who kidnapped me are buried in the darkest parts of my mind along with the memories of what they did to me.

"He looks like almost every other guy who lives on the street." My inner voice laughs at me again. "I'm sure it's nothing." Even I don't sound that convinced by my words, though.

"Maybe." Lyric sounds doubtful. "Ay, I don't want you to be upset with me for bringing it up, but . . . I was thinking about how those detectives said that maybe Aunt Lila and Uncle Ethan should keep an extra eye on you until they can figure out who was behind . . ." She anxiously waits for me to say something. When I don't, she tacks on, "Maybe we should mention something to them, just in case."

My eyes wander back to the man and I realize the he's looking right at us. I instantly stumble back into the shadows and pull Lyric with me. Then I position myself in front of Lyric to protect her from being seen.

"Do you think he can see us?" Lyric whispers, fisting the bottom of my shirt as she peers over my shoulder.

"Not now." My body convulses with spasms as her

knuckles graze my lower back, but she doesn't appear to notice, too preoccupied by the man. "But I'm sure he did before we ducked back here."

I observe the man from around the corner of the garage. He continues to stare in our direction, before finally fixing his attention back on my house. Then with a jerk on the dog leash, he scurries down the sidewalk toward the end of the block and out of sight.

"That was weird." Lyric steps around me, the absence of her warmth leaving me oddly cold inside. "We should definitely mention it to Aunt Lila."

"Yeah, I guess we should. If you think so, anyway." When I face her, she scowls at me. "What?"

"Not you guess," she scolds. "You *will* tell her, or *I* will. I don't care if it's nothing. After . . . what happened, I'm not going to risk it, risk something happening to you."

"There's no use arguing with you, is there?"

"Nope. Not about this."

"All right. When we get home from band practice, I'll make sure to bring it up to Lila. Only for you, though. I'm not worried."

Liar, liar,
all the time.
Worry dances in your mind,
round and round,
a broken record.
A song stuck on repeat,
singing through veins
as you lie restlessly in bed.
Liar, liar,
all the time.
Always worrying they'll return,
and death will burn your skin again.

A few minutes later, when we're satisfied the man isn't

going to return, we pile into Lyric's dad's 1969 Chevelle since the Challenger her dad bought her a little over a month ago is nowhere near ready to drive yet. Then we buckle up, turn on the radio, and Lyric slams the gas pedal down. The tires squeal as she backs down the driveway and onto the road.

"If you're not careful, one of these days, someone is going to call the cops on you about your driving," I tease as I relax back in the seat. Just being with her gives me a little bit of inner peace sometimes.

"If it happens, it happens." She cranks the wheel and fishtails the car onto the main road with an up-shift. "I mean, what are my parents going to do, get mad at me? My mother's gotten more tickets than I can count."

"True." I pick up the iPod from the dock and start browsing through the songs. "But they could—"

My phone vibrates from inside my pocket. I fish it out and swipe my finger over the screen to read the text message.

> *Lila: We need to talk about something important when you get home.*

> *Me: Okay. What's it about?*

I grow anxious that perhaps she found out I met with a hacker tonight. I haven't been punished very much by the Gregorys—I've tried to stay out of trouble as much as possible ever since they adopted me. I'm guessing with something as severe as illegal hacking, their relaxed approach at parenting would disappear.

> *Lila: I really just want to talk to you about it when you get home, not on the phone.*

> *Me: Okay. I'll be home in a few hours. Can you at*

least tell me if I need to be worried?

Lila: No, no need to be worried.

I start to put my phone away when another text comes through.

Lila: I don't want you to worry all night, and knowing you, you will. It's about the police. They want to talk to you again about your brother. Please don't panic. I'm sure it's nothing.

I probably should respond to her message, at least to tell her I'm okay, but I can't think of what to say.

"Everything okay?" Lyric asks.

I concentrate on the song list again. "Yeah, of course."

She watches me instead of the road. "Who was that text from?"

"Lila. She just wanted to let me know she needs to talk to me about some stuff when I get home."

"Are you sure that's all she wanted?"

I nod, unable to look her in the eyes, knowing she'll see right through my lie.

Liar, liar, alone in the dark,
Hide the truth from your heart.
Lock your soul in a box.
Melt the key.
Set the box on fire.
And burn it into oblivion.
Let the ashes scatter the ground.
And never utter a sound.
Liar, liar, alone in the dark.

Lyric's chest rises and falls, as if she's struggling to breathe. "If you don't want to tell me, then that's fine. But just say so. Don't lie to me, please."

God, I'm the biggest asshole ever. I really am.

"The police want to talk to me." The words are difficult to say.

Her gaze glides to mine and her grip tightens on the wheel. "When do they want to talk to you? Tonight?"

I shake my head. "I don't think so, but Lila didn't say."

"Are you . . . Are you going to be okay? I mean, with talking to them."

"I don't know," I admit honestly. "I guess it depends on what they want to talk about. She said something about my brother, but I'm not sure if it's details about his death or my"—I swallow hard—"memories."

I think I already know for sure, though. Lila warned me the morning after we learned the news of my brother's death that the police may want my help in solving his murder by remembering what happened those weeks we spent with our captors. They believe if I can remember then maybe I can help identify them.

If that's what they want me to do . . . Well, I'm not sure I can handle it. I locked up the memories for a reason.

Dying flesh.
Ruptured heart.
Scars searing.
Flaming soul.
The touch of death
burns through my skin
and strikes at my bones.
Resuscitated and revived,
but not without sacrifice.
Close up my mind.
Forget what I saw.
What I heard.
What was done to me.
Remember and give up my soul.

Remember and submit to the pain.
Remember and wither away
into nothing.

CHAPTER 3

IT'S BEEN TWO DAYS SINCE I saw the strange man hanging out in front of Ayden's house, and I've been working on a drawing of the guy just in case it's needed. I don't know why, but I have the strangest feeling that the man was more than a just a neighbor passing by.

I've been having trouble sleeping the last couple of nights because of the man. Every time I close my eyes, I see him in the tracksuit with his dog. The twisted part is that his outfit sometimes transforms into a cloak and the dog shifts into a scythe, and I'm suddenly staring at the Grim Reaper.

No more horror movies for me for a while.

I debate whether or not to tell Ayden about my dream. In the past, he'd have found it amusing, but with everything going on, I doubt he would anymore. He still hasn't spoken to the police, nor does he know when he's going to, only that it'll be someday this week.

My family and all the Gregorys get together every year to decorate the tree. After we're done, we'll all go over to my house and do the same thing. It's a strange little tradition that started during my first Christmas ever. Back then, though, Uncle Ethan and Aunt Lila hadn't adopted any children yet.

The massive tree Ayden and I picked out sits in the center of the Gregory's living room, trimmed and decorated with shiny silver and red balls that glimmer against the glow of the flames burning in the fireplace. Our parents are drinking eggnog in the kitchen and have already exceeded the tipsy point. Kale is eating popcorn and watching a Christmas movie while Fiona and Everson fight over who gets to put the star on the tree. Ayden and I sit in front of the computer doing a little research on his brother, ignoring the commotion going on.

He'd been so reluctant to even speak his brother's name that I was honestly surprised when he brought out the computer and said he wanted to look up stuff on him. But I wasn't about to ask him, too concerned I'd hit a nerve.

"I still don't get why we're looking this stuff up." I skim the paragraph on the computer screen. "Everything we've found out about your brother's case online is the same stuff the police have told you, right?"

"Yeah, but it seems like there's something else," Ayden mumbles, clicking the mouse on the Page Back arrow. "Like why he would even go so close to the house in the first place. It doesn't make any sense. Either he had to be kidnapped or his body was placed there for a reason." His voice cracks and he quickly clears it.

"Maybe he was just there revisiting his past . . . Did he have amnesia like you?" I rest my chin on his shoulder then immediately regret it when his muscles constrict.

"Not that I know of." Ayden taps a few keys. "But I didn't really see him after we were taken out of the house. We went straight to the hospital and were placed in the system not too long after."

"I'm sorry," I say, unsure why I feel the urge to apologize over something that has nothing to do with me.

"Sorry for what . . . it wasn't you're fault." He twists around, causing my chin to fall off his shoulder. "You shouldn't be apologizing for anything." He sketches a finger across my cheekbone.

An evanescent contact of skin to skin, but my body still flushes with heat. I lick my lips—I don't even know why. It's not like I'm about to kiss him in the living room in front of everyone.

His breath hitches in his throat. "Maybe we should—"

"Hey, it's my turn to put the star on the tree!" Fiona shouts, causing Ayden and I to blink. She plants her hands on her hips and glares at Everson. "You did it last year."

"Liar. You did it last year." Everson is holding the silvery star and reaches his arm up high. Fiona, being on the short side, jumps to get it, but misses it by at least a foot.

"Everson! Give me that star." Fiona moves to tackle Everson, and he dodges out of the way, laughing.

"Everson, you did put the star up last year," Ayden intervenes without looking away from me. "Give the star to Fiona."

Everson curses under his breath, shoves the star at Fiona, and stomps toward the doorway. "Whatever. She's too short anyway. She'll never get it up there."

"I will, too!" Fiona shouts after him, glancing from the star to the tip of the tree.

Ayden sighs, sets the computer down on the coffee table, and gets up from the sofa. "I'll go get you a stool," he tells Fiona. "Hang on."

After he leaves the room, Fiona reels around and faces me with a haughty bob of her head. "So, what are you guys doing on the computer anyway? Just seeing what was up with Ayden's brother."

"Sort of."

"Well, you're not going to find anything on the

computer," she says, chipping at a chunk of glitter on the base of the star. "Ayden's just going to have to remember."

Fiona's always been on the strange side, so I don't put too much thought into what she said. Instead, I reach across the sofa to steal a handful of popcorn from the bag on Kale's lap because I'm starving. With how tipsy the adults are, I'm guessing this night is going to end with takeout.

Kale's eyes instantly pop wide as I bump his leg on my way back to the side of the sofa.

"Whoops. Sorry." Curious to why he looks so terrified, I add, "You okay?"

He mutters a "yes" then tosses the bag onto the table and bolts out of the room like it's on fire.

"What was that about?" I stuff a few pieces of popcorn into my mouth.

Fiona shrugs. "He's just weird. Like Ayden. We all are really." She ravels a strand of her long hair around her finger as she gazes at the lights flashing on the tree. "I've always kind of wondered if Lila and Ethan did it on purpose."

"Did what on purpose?" Ayden inquires as he enters the room carrying a stool, along with two cans of soda.

"If Lila and Ethan purposefully adopted weirdoes." When Ayden places the stool in front of the tree, Fiona climbs on and stretches her arm toward the top. With a slight sway of her balance, she gets the star on then jumps backwards off the stool. "There. Look at how pretty it is." She admires the tree with a tip of her head.

Ayden returns to his place beside me, but doesn't pick his computer up. He hands one of the cans of soda to me then pops the tab on the other. "I think I'm getting tired of researching."

I tap my finger on top of the can before opening it

up. "We can take a break, if that's what you need." I take a swig of soda, the fizz tickling my nose. "Anything you want to do in particular?"

"Want to go get your guitar?" he asks. "Then we can go upstairs and play for a little while."

I grin a goofy grin. "You know the way to my heart, Shy Boy." He really, really does.

I just wish I knew the way to his.

THE NEXT MORNING AS I lie in bed, staring up at the ceiling as the sun begins to rise and warm up my room, I try to think of a good present to get Ayden, one that will cheer him up. Last Christmas I got him a signed album, but this year I want to get him something special. Something that will make him smile like he made me do yesterday when we'd spent over four hours last night jamming out to our favorite songs. It was a nice. I wish we could do that more often.

Knock. Knock. Knock.

"Lyric, I need to talk to you," my mother says through the door with another soft rap. "Are you decent?"

"Yeah, you can come in." I sit up in bed and stretch out my arms as she opens the door and enters.

She's sporting a holey pair of jeans and a faded black shirt splattered with neon pink, yellow, and green paint. Her auburn hair is pulled up, and her phone is clutched in her hand.

"Man, since when did you become an early bird? You know that's a sign of getting old," I joke, glancing at the clock on my nightstand.

She smiles tiredly. "I have to get some pieces done for the art show in a few weeks. And I've been up all night, so technically, that doesn't make me an early bird."

I plant my feet onto the floor. "Nope, it just makes you a crack-head."

She sighs her *oh Lyric* sigh.

"What?" I ask innocently. "Too early for jokes?"

"Or too late." She sighs again. "Lila and Ethan had to take Ayden to the police station this morning, so you're going to have to drive yourself to school today. And you need to take Kale with you."

"Oh." I fight back a frown. Ayden and I always ride to school together, and we stop by this little coffeehouse that has the best cappuccinos ever. Usually, he drives us in one of the Gregory's cars, although my parents occasionally allow me to borrow one of theirs when they're feeling particularly awesome. It's our morning ritual and I love it, just like I love seeing him. "Do you know when he'll be back? I mean, will he be at school at all today?"

"I'm not sure. They weren't sure how long they'd be there."

"Do you know why they're there? What they wanted to talk to Ayden about?"

"I didn't ask." She sits down on the bed beside me. "I figure it's really none of my business unless Lila wants to talk to me about it." Her stern expression presses that it should be none of my business, either, unless Ayden wants to talk about it with me.

Sometimes I feel like she knows more about Ayden than I do. I've overheard Lila whispering stuff about his past to my mom. I'm not sure what since they either shoo me away or leave the room themselves when they noticed I'm listening, and prying it out of my mother was impossible.

"I'm his best friend." I pick at a loose string on the hem of my pajama shorts. "He should want to talk to me about it, but he never seems to want to."

She pats my leg. "Unfortunately that's not how it always works. Sometimes even best friends need to keep stuff from each other. At least until they're ready to talk about it."

"Did you keep stuff from Dad? I mean, back when you were best friends."

Traces of remorse haunt her eyes. "There was a lot of stuff I didn't tell him. I kept more from him than I wish I would have."

I hug my knee to my chest. "Then why did you do it?"

She shrugs, uncomfortable. "I was afraid of what I would feel if I said stuff aloud. Afraid that your dad wouldn't love me anymore if I told him everything about me."

I rest my chin on my knee. "Just what kind of secrets did you have, Mom? You sound super sketchy right now."

She shrugs again and her eyes well up. "It doesn't really matter anymore. What's in the past is in the past." Sucking back the tears, she stands up. "You can drive my car to school if you want to, but you'll have to gas it up." She starts to leave, dabbing her eyes with her fingertips.

"Mom, wait." I spring from the bed and hurry over to her. "I'm not sure if I need to tell you this, but it kind of feels like I should, since I'm worried Ayden himself might not tell Lila or Ethan."

I quickly tell her about the guy standing outside the house, giving her the details of what he looked like, and giving her the sketch I drew of guy the night I first saw him. I omit that Ayden snuck out for a while, not wanting to get him in trouble. He still hasn't confessed what he was doing and I've given up on trying to get the information out of him. For now anyway.

"I'm glad you told me," my mother says when I'm

finished. "I'll make sure to mention it to Lila. She'll want to know about it."

"You don't think he's bad, do you?" I gather my hair into my hand and fasten it into a ponytail with an elastic from my dresser. "Like maybe one of those people the police are looking for?"

"I doubt it." But concern masks her face. "But it's better to be safe than sorry." She glances down at the phone in her hand. "You should get ready for school; otherwise, you're going to be late." She walks out of my room and closes the door behind her, leaving me to stew in my own worry.

I decide to text Ayden to make sure he's okay; something short and simple, knowing that he's probably stressed out from being at the police station.

Me: Hey! If u need anything, give me a holler.

Then I put my phone down and get ready for school, waiting for him to respond and trying not to stress out when he doesn't.

CHAPTER 4

THREE HOURS AND ONE SILENT ride to school with Kale later, Ayden still hasn't given me a holler, which should be a good thing, right? Means the visit with the police went okay?

Doubt resides in the back of my mind, though. Knowing Ayden, his silence could mean he's shutting down. Like my mother told me this morning, even best friends keep secrets from each other.

While I attempt to remain understanding, it still makes me sad. I barely know what's going on with him at the moment. If he's hurting while dealing with his brother's death, and what on earth he was doing when he snuck out of his house the other night.

"Earth to Lyric. Have you heard anything I've said at all?" Sage waves his hand in front of my face, interrupting my thoughts.

Startled, I jerk back in surprise and chuck the pencil in my hand. Our desks are facing each other, so the pencil ends up zipping by his head, missing his eye by an inch. Thankfully, we're in fourth period English, and the teacher, Ms. Reltingly, loves doing group projects, so most of my classmates are distracted and don't notice my crazy ninja reflex reaction.

Sage, of course, does since he's the one who caused it. He cautiously raises his hands in front of him and leans back in his seat. "Jesus, Lyric. You don't need to get all crazy and try to stab my eye out." He leans over his desk, scoops up my pencil, and flips it through his fingers like a baton before handing it to me.

"Sorry." I check the time on the wall clock. *Holy shit! Lunch is in ten minutes.* "How long have I been zoned out?"

Sage shrugs as he flips a page in his textbook. "For about twenty minutes."

I casually glimpse around at the rest of the class; everyone is partnered up and working on the assignment. "Dude, I suck. I'm like the worst partner ever."

Sage fiddles with a silver barbell in his brow. "It's just class, no biggie." He releases his piercing and starts doodling skulls on the top of his notebook. "Do you want to talk about what's bothering you, though?"

I peek at the page he's on and turn to the same one. "Who said anything was bothering me?"

His brow cocks. "Lyric, you've been staring at the wall for the last twenty minutes and haven't said a word. Something definitely has to be wrong for you to remain that quiet."

I press my hand to my heart, pretending to be offended. "Are you saying there's no way I can just be quiet without something being wrong?" When he presses me with a look, I sigh. "Okay, you're right. But I promise it's nothing. I'm just waiting for Ayden to text me. That's all."

"Yeah, where the hell is he today? We were supposed to meet up before school to chat about something, but he totally blew me off and ignored my text, too."

"He had an appointment or something, and I think he

must have forgotten his phone," I lie because I have no clue what to tell him. No one outside of the Gregorys and my own family knows what's going on with Ayden and the police. They don't even know about his brother's death.

"Yeah, if he's not texting you, then he's definitely forgotten his phone. What's going on with you two, anyway? You seem a little," he rubs his jawline, "offbeat lately."

"Whoa, nosy much?" I squirm, something I'm not a fan of doing. Usually, I'm comfortable in every situation.

"I'm just curious what's going on with you two . . . for the band's sake." He shrugs and waits for me to answer his question. "You know, the last thing we need is some sort of lover's quarrel that causes us to split up."

I shoot him a dirty look. "Ayden and I aren't lovers."

"You sure about that? Because I can never tell with you two."

"Hmmm, let me think," I sarcastically say, thrumming my fingertip on my lip. "Well, there was that one time when we kissed under the bleachers and I nearly swooned on the floor. It was so magical." I roll my eyes. "What are we, gossiping girls?"

"Hate to break it to you, but you are a girl." He scans me over, his gaze remaining a little too long on my chest.

I cross my arms and decide to put him on the spot. "Okay, so why were you two meeting up before school? Because I'd really like to know for the band's sake. I mean, for all I know, you two could be having a bromance quarrel."

He stares at me blankly, clearly unimpressed. "You're too clever for your own good, Lyric Scott." He tucks his pencil into the spiral of his notebook then leans back in his chair with a lazy grin on his face. "And I'm not telling you my secrets unless you tell me yours."

I scrunch my nose at him. "Well, this game isn't fun if

you're not going to play."

"Sorry." He seems very unapologetic. "Besides, I don't want to talk about this with anyone until I chat with Ayden first."

"You're being very cryptic." I examine him intently. "You're not thinking about springing the band, are you? I know we haven't gotten any gigs yet and everything, but working my magic takes time."

"I know it does." He reaches into his pocket for his phone. "And it's not that. Trust me, I'm way too comfortable with you guys to ever start over with a new band." He reads something on the screen of his phone then smiles. "Well, looks like our boy got his phone back."

"Ayden just texted you?" I lean over my desk to look at the screen of his phone, but Sage quickly presses it to his chest.

"Dude, that's private shit right there, Lyric." He stuffs his phone into the pocket of his blue hoodie. "I know you and Ayden don't have boundaries and everything, but seriously, you can't just read people's phones whenever you want."

"Sorry." I'm not, though. I'm actually really curious to read what's on his phone, more than I was before.

"It's cool." He shuts his book, giving up on us finishing the assignment. "We should probably finish the project up after band practice or something since we wasted so much class time."

"Sounds like a plan." I close my textbook and shove it into my bag.

For the next seven minutes, I mentally chant the lyrics of an angsty song I wrote during first period, trying to cool off and not get jealous over the fact that Ayden texted Sage before me.

Am I another obsession?

An aching in your brain?
Am I a complicated attraction?
Driving you insane?
Tell me why I can't get you out of my head!
What it is you've done to me?
Why do you drive me so fucking crazy!
Please, please, tell me
Something.
Anything.
That will help me think
Clearly agaaaaiiiin!!!!

By the time the bell rings, I've chillaxed a smidgeon. I enter the busy hallway and spot Ayden leaning against the lockers across from the classroom. He's texting on his phone with his head angled down so he doesn't see me right away.

Sliding the handle of my bag over my shoulder, I push people out of my way as I march up to him. "Hey, what's up, buddy?"

His head jerks up at the sound of my voice, and he almost drops his phone. "You scared the shit out of me." He presses his hand to his heart and his breathing turns ragged.

My lips tug upward. "Clearly."

"Hey, we'll talk at practice later!" Sage shouts to Ayden as he walks backwards down the hallway. "I seriously have something important to talk to you about, so no blowing me off again!"

Ayden holds a thumbs up in his direction as he finishes sending his text.

I scroll over his black jeans, red logo T-shirt, his soft lips, dark eyes, and inky black hair to make sure every inch of him is okay. The last thing I ever want to do is be angry with him if he's hurt or something. When every visible part of his body checks out okay, I place my hands on my hips. "So, what's up with texting Sage before me?"

He scratches at the scars on the back of his hand, a nervous habit of his. "I texted him because I wanted to talk to you in person. Not through a text. I wanted us to go have lunch so we can talk in private. I want to . . . well, try to tell you what happened today."

"Oh." I feel so silly and kind of douchey for being irritated. "Sorry. I feel like an ass now. And kind of childish. I was thinking you liked Sage more than me."

"That will never, ever be true." He reaches for my hand. "And I'm pretty sure you could never be an ass, even if you tried."

I hold up a finger. "That isn't true. I'm pretty sure your brother thinks I'm an ass."

His brows knit. "My brother . . . ? Oh." He shakes his head. Again, I feel like an asshole. He probably thought of his real brother, the one he just lost. "You mean Kale or Everson?"

"Kale." We start down the crowded hallway with our fingers linked together, like we have every day since Ayden entered my life. "I had to give him a ride to school this morning. I think the kid is totally terrified of me. He wouldn't say a word, and every time I said anything to him, he scowled at me."

Ayden snorts a laugh as he weaves us around a group of cheerleaders blocking the middle of the hallway.

"What's so funny, Shy Boy?" I tuck my elbows in as we squeeze by a group of jocks.

I find myself searching around for William in the midst of them, since he generally hangs with the athletes. Thankfully, he's nowhere to be seen.

Hopefully, it stays that way.

"It's nothing." Ayden's lips expand into an amused

smile. It's been a while since I've seen that smile, so even though I have no idea what's causing it, I smile, too.

"Tell me what's so funny." I prod his side with my elbow. "Or else I'll tickle you until you pee your pants."

His muscles spasm, and I worry that I've crossed a line again.

"I'd like to see you try." He flashes me a genuine smile, and I relax.

"I accept that challenge." I poke him in the ribs.

"Lyric," he chuckles, wrapping his arm around his midsection for protection. "I can't tell you. Kale would get pissed off at me."

"I wouldn't tell him that you told me. Jeez, who do you think I am? Maggie?"

As if she senses us talking about her, Maggie suddenly appears in front of us with her hands on her hips and determination in her eyes.

"The date for my New Year's Eve party has been changed," she says to me as Ayden and I slam to a halt in front of her. Then she grins in Ayden's direction and not so discreetly pushes her chest out. I love the girl to death, but she really needs to stop drawing guys in with her breasts. "It's going to be December thirtieth."

"How can you have a New Year's Eve party that's not on December thirty-first?" Ayden's smile fades. He's unfriendly and cold to a lot of people, except me. For some reason, I've always been good at bringing out his inner sunshine. "It makes no sense."

"It makes perfect sense." She tucks her elbows inward to push her cleavage even higher. "A party's a party, right?"

Ayden shrugs. "I guess. But technically your party is a New Year's Eve Eve party."

"Clever." Maggie smiles then her gaze flicks to me, as if seeking some sort of confirmation that I'm okay with her trying to show Ayden her goodies. I'm not okay with it. At all. But I'm not about to get angry with her since I haven't been that honest with what's been going on with Ayden and me.

She searches my eyes then her posture relaxes and her cleavage sinks back into her shirt. "But, as clever as that is, I'm still calling it my New Year's Eve party." She points a finger between the two of us. "A party that you two better show up to."

She reels around and shimmies her butt down the hallway, drawing in a lot of the male population around her. She instantly zeroes in on her next target, the varsity quarterback. Rolling her shoulders back, she approaches him with what she calls her "vixen swagger walk."

"Man, she knows how to work those bad boys, doesn't she?" I mutter, peeking down at my own breasts.

I'm barely a B cup, not that I care. Big breasts aren't going to get me what I want in life, but I have wondered what it would be like to overly fill out my shirts.

"Work what?" Ayden glances confusedly at me.

I point back and forth between my breasts. "These bad boys."

Even after being around my constant unfiltered mouth, Ayden still blinks in shock.

"Trust me, you could work yours, too, and get way more attention than she does." His attention drops to my chest fleetingly then he looks away as his skin turns bright red.

My own skin warms as I recollect when he reached up my shirt and brushed his fingers across my nipple. The torrid sensations I felt that night were like nothing I've ever experienced before.

I wish you would do that again.
Touch me like that

In my car,
In my room,
In my bed.
Touch me, touch me everywhere.

Instead of touching, Ayden and I silently head down the hallway with the buzzing of voices flowing around us. His palm dampens in mine or maybe mine does in his . . . It's hard to tell. We're tense, sexually frustrated as Maggie would put it.

"I'll tell you what I know about Kale," he unexpectedly sputters, breaking the tension between us. "But only on one condition." He releases my hand to push the door open and moves aside to let me through.

"Okay, what's the condition?" I step outside into the cool winter air, and goose bumps sprout across my skin.

Ayden lets go of the door then promptly returns his hand to mine, as if the ten second break from our flesh touching nearly drove him to a panic attack. My body, although cold, warms inside.

"That you never, ever repeat to Kale what I'm about to tell you," Ayden says as we start down the sidewalk and through the people eating lunch around the front area of the school.

"Okay . . ." I stare up at him, squinting against the sunlight peeking through the cracks in the tree branches above our heads. "You've got me worried."

"It's not anything to worry about." He grows quiet, spacing off as we hike across the freshly cut grass toward the parking lot. "But it's private enough that I need you to pinkie swear on it."

My lips part in mock shock, and I cover my mouth with my hand. "Ayden Gregory, don't you trust me?"

He stares up at the sky, stifling a smile. Eventually, his amusement gets the better of him, and he ends up grinning from ear to ear. He stops in the middle of the grass and raises his free hand with his pinkie hitched.

"Wow, where's the trust, Shy Boy?" I give an exaggerated stomp of my foot then link my pinkie with his. "I promise that whatever you tell me will stay between us. But, just so you know, that's always the case."

"I know; I just need to make sure, for Kale's sake." He tightens his hold on my pinkie when I try to pull away. "Just like I need you to promise you'll go easy on him."

"Okay, I promise, even though I have no clue what you're talking about."

Satisfied, he frees my finger, and we start walking again.

"I think Kale might have a crush on you." He glances at me from the corner of his eye. "I've actually thought it for a while."

"No way." I wave him off. "Kale's the kind of guy who will get a crush on someone equally as adorably nerdy as him. Someone who's in love with comic books and wears capes on non-Halloween days."

"Clearly, you don't understand how a guy's mind works."

"Hey, I do, too," I say, this time genuinely offended. "I'm totally running on the same brain waves." Ayden's brows elevate questioningly, and I playfully swat his arm. "You seriously just lost cool points for that move."

He shrugs, unbothered. "Sorry, but I'm glad you don't run on the same brain waves as me. It would be weird."

"Yeah, you're right." I pause, contemplating what he said. "He really has a crush on me?"

"It's just a guess, but as a guy who's had crushes on girls before, I'm guessing that his awkward silence thing he does whenever he's around you means that he likes you."

I've known Kale since Lila and Ethan adopted him a few years ago. He's like a little brother to me, which makes the situation kind of weird.

"You get awkwardly quiet around every girl we cross paths with," I point out to Ayden after we climb into Lila's BMW. "Which, by your theory, would mean you have a crush on all of them, including Maggie."

"Yeah, but I'm a freak of nature." He turns the key in the ignition, and the engine grumbles to life.

"So am I. I make love declarations about every guy I cross paths with."

He shoves the shifter into reverse. "You haven't done that in a while."

I draw the seatbelt over my shoulder and strap myself in. "Ever since William." *And since you kissed me.*

He rotates in his seat to glance behind him, but when our gazes collide, he pauses.

"Have you seen him again?" he asks with hesitancy.

I shake my head. "Not since that last time. What about you?"

"I saw him in gym. He didn't say anything to me, but he did try to hit me in the face with a ball during dodge ball."

"What a dick," I grumble. "I'm so sorry for bringing you into this drama."

"It's just a ball, nothing like a fist. And you didn't bring me into the drama. I chose to walk in it because I care about you." A faint smile rises at his lips, one that warms me from my head to my toes. "Did you know his nose is crooked now?"

I perk up. "Really?"

He nods, his eyes burning fiercely. "I wish I would have broken more, though."

"The nose is good." I sketch my fingertip down the

brim of Ayden's nose. "You did well, Shy Boy."

We exchange a meaningful moment, and then he backs the car out of the parking spot and steers toward the road.

"So, are you going to tell me what happened this morning?" I ask as he drives down the road lined with fast food places and restaurants.

"Yeah . . . Let's go pick up some lunch and park up near the bridge." He flips on his blinker to make a turn. "I want to be able to talk to you privately about some stuff before we head to town, anyway."

"Head to town now?" I ask, and he nods. "What about class?"

We only have a thirty-minute lunch break, and we wasted ten minutes getting to the car. Driving to the city limits of San Diego takes about twenty minutes, give or take a half of an hour for traffic.

"We're skipping the rest of school."

My nerves bubble inside me. *What the heck is going on?* "Why?"

"Because . . ." He nibbles on his bottom lip, mulling over something. "We're . . . We're taking a self-defense class, instead."

"Why?"

"Because my parents and yours want us to be safe, to make sure we can protect ourselves if we need to."

I'm not sure what to make of that.

Protect us from what exactly?

CHAPTER 5

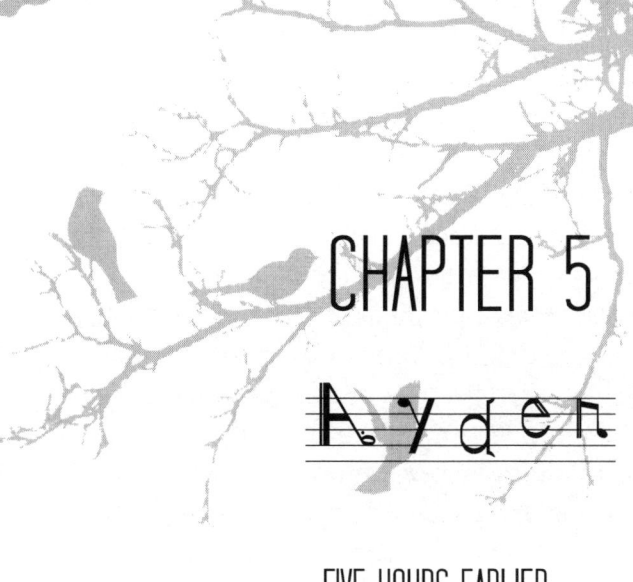

FIVE HOURS EARLIER...

THE VISIT WITH THE POLICE turns out to be exactly what I was dreading. To move the case forward, they want me to try a few sessions with an amnesia therapy specialist.

"If it turns out to be too much for him or shows no signs of working within the first few sessions, then we'd like to try a few more aggressive methods," a detective who goes by the name Rannali explains. "I know this might seem a little extreme, but—"

"A little extreme," Lila cuts him off, her tone razor sharp. "You're showing no sympathy for Ayden, who's been through enough already and just lost his brother."

"Sympathy isn't my priority," he replies straightforwardly—he has been that way the entire visit, "solving this case is a priority. We truly believe that if Ayden can remember those days he spent in the house, he could help us identify some of the suspects."

"But I thought you weren't positive it was the same people," Lila points out. "That maybe he was just in the same area by coincidence. You said a lot of homeless people migrated to that area because the vacant homes were good shelter."

"Right now, tracking down those people is the best lead we've got," he responds vaguely, appearing mildly annoyed by Lila's excessive questioning. "And right now, your son is the last known person alive who's seen what these people look like. It's becoming a priority that he moves forward in his therapy. I know some therapists who come highly recommended for these types of things."

Lila's expression simmered with rage. "You don't need to be so coldhearted about it. You're speaking about him like he's not even a person. Just a tool to help solve your case."

"Help solve his brother's murder," he pressed as he coolly reclined back in his seat. "Do you know anything at all about this group of people?" He reaches for a folder on a filing cabinet then straightens in the chair. Opening the folder on the desk, he removes a paper and places it in front of the Gregorys. "They call themselves soulless mileas or warriors. Worshippers of evil, the list of the horrendous crimes these people have committed goes on and on."

Soulless mileas.
Soulless mileas.
Soulless mileas.

The name screams repeatedly in my head, but the noise is minimal compared to my accelerating heart rate. In the folder is a letter written in sloppy handwriting that looks an awful lot like my sister's. When I lean forward to get a better look, the detective hastily shuts the folder. He's not quite quick enough to stop me from seeing the signature on the bottom, though.

Sadie Stephorson.

My sister.

Detective Rannali avoids eye contact with me, focusing on Lila and Ethan as if I don't even exist.

"Wait? I don't understand," Lila says perplexedly to Detective Rannali. "Why are you mentioning these people?"

"We believe that someone in this group is responsible for the kidnapping of your son three years ago." He pauses with a brief glance in my direction. "And that they might have played a part in Felix Stephorson's murder along with several others over the last decade. It would make sense with his body being found close to the home Ayden and his brother and sister were removed from."

I want to shout at him to tell me why on earth he has a letter from my sister in the folder.

"Why would he have been there, though?" I ask. "Did they kidnap him again?"

"There were no signs of kidnapping," the detective answers. "But we haven't ruled out that theory either. We also have a theory that maybe your brother was looking for the people himself."

My back straightens in the chair as an icy chill slithers up my spine. "Why would he do that? It would make no sense."

Ignoring me, he drones on until I can't take it anymore. I need to know what that letter was.

After a while, I lose my cool and snap, "What was that?"

All three of them jolt at the sound of my voice.

"What was what?" The detective feigns being clueless.

I aim a finger at the folder. "That letter in there . . . It looked like it was from my sister."

"What's in that file is confidential," is all he says.

I turn to Lila and Ethan for help, but they only look at

me with pity. Then Lila gently pats my knee and directs her attention back to the paper, leaving me to stir in frustration.

Why would they have a note from her? Is it old? New? Did she have something to do with this? Are they using her to help solve the case, too? Or is there more to it?

Ethan clasps Lila's hand when her eyes start to water. "Honey, relax. Everything's going to be okay." He looks at me. "We'll get through this together."

I know right then that the police are going to make me try to remember, that I don't really have a choice in this, even though they say I do. Besides, if I don't go through with it, I'm willingly making a choice not to help solve my brother's murder.

My throat thickens and my lungs constrict.

Force the memories up.
Then what?
What will happen?
To you?
To the person they all knew?
To the person you are right now?
He'll be gone,
as the chains wrap around.
Bind you in.
Make your head spin.
You'll lose your mind.
Lose control of your life
Again.

I only speak again when we're back at home.

I unstrap my seatbelt and say, "I saw that letter, and I want to know what it says. Is my sister helping the police, too?"

Lila and Ethan trade a concerned look, and then Lila rotates in her seat.

"Ayden, there's some stuff we don't feel like you're

ready to learn just yet," she explains to me.

I don't want to get angry, but I feel the emotion scorching under my skin.

Before I can react, though, Mrs. Scott comes barreling around the fence and over to the car. After a lot of hushed talking between her, Lila, and Ethan, they take me into the kitchen and inform me that Lyric told them about the guy staring at our house. Then they inform me that, for safety purposes, I'm going to take Lyric with me to a self-defense class this afternoon.

Even though I'm upset, I don't argue. The class will be a good thing. Lyric knowing how to protect herself will be a good thing, especially with guys like William walking around.

Honestly, I can't wait to pick Lyric up from school. I feel so frustrated and know she will settle me down. Even in the midst of my darkness, through a storm of pain, Lyric brings me calm.

CHAPTER 6

THE PRESENT...

LYRIC SPREADS HER SUNSHINE ACROSS my gloom the moment we reunite. Even when I tell her about the police visit, omitting the letter about my sister for the moment, I feel more at ease. The comfort remains during the entire drive to the self-defense class, but then the reminder of why we're there to begin with creeps up on me.

"Wait, I'm not dressed for something like this," Lyric says after I park the car near the back of a small brick building located about fifteen miles south of our quaint neighborhood secluded in the burbs.

I shut off the engine and slide the keys out of the ignition. "You look perfect to me."

"I'm sure I do, but as for being able to move around, which I'm sure is required in this class, these," she flips her fingers against her jeans, "aren't going to cut it."

"Yeah, your mom figured you'd probably need a change of clothes." I reach over the console to the backseat and grab a bag. "She sent you this."

Lyric takes the bag from me and unzips it. "Where

did she even get these?" She holds up a pair of black yoga pants and a purple tank top made of some kind of stretchy fabric.

I tap the tag still stuck to the fabric. "She must have just bought them."

"Wow, they must have been preparing for this." She tears the tag off, drops it into the bag, and tosses the empty bag onto the backseat. When she turns around, she starts undoing the zipper of her jeans.

"What are you doing?" My panicked gaze darts between her jeans and her face.

"Getting changed." She unfastens the zipper, lifts her hips, and then tugs down on her pants.

"Right here in the car?" With a lot of effort, I manage to keep my eyes on her face, even though my instincts beg to look downward.

She shrugs, shimmying her hips out of her jeans. "It's just underwear, no biggie. I'm even wearing my boy-cut panties that cover up more than my swimsuit."

Her pants are so far down I can see those black boy-cut panties along with her upper thighs. Her skin looks so soft, so touchable. My hands quiver just thinking about brushing my fingers over her legs.

She suddenly halts her torturously slow strip tease. "Wait, am I crossing one of those boundaries again? I never know sometimes."

To Lyric, changing in front of her best friend is probably on the same level as wearing a swimsuit, completely innocent. But her swimsuit doesn't have lace at the bottom or a tiny pink bow on the front.

God, I just want to touch her.

My breathing accelerates with my thoughts as I desperately try not to panic.

Lyric must sense my anxiety because she begins

pulling her jeans back up.

"Do you want to go find a bathroom at a gas station so I can change?" she asks, inching the fabric back over her thighs.

There are probably locker rooms in the building where the class is. I should tell her that or just take her to a gas station. But even in the midst of my semi-panicking, I'm so turned on I can't bring myself to utter those words.

"No, you're fine." I rip my eyes off her body and dig my phone from my pocket to busy myself with something other than gawking at her. "Unless you really want me to."

"I'm good changing wherever," she replies hesitantly. "And you don't have to look at your phone if you don't want to. I'm comfortable with you, Ayden."

I believe her. She's made it pretty clear that she wants to be with me as more than a friend. Right now, I wish I wasn't completely fucked-up so I could have her that way.

Have her on the backseat.
Touching her everywhere.
Her warm body underneath me.
Flesh to flesh of blazing heat.
Drowning me in warmth.
Taste it.
Drown in it.
Beg for more.
Kiss her like my life depends on it.
Like the blood running through my veins.
Kiss her until the darkness fades.
Kiss her, kiss the hurt away.

"Ayden?"

My attention drifts back to Lyric. *Fuck.* She doesn't have a shirt on. Her bra has the same lacy trim as her panties do, with a pink bow right between her breasts.

"Are you okay?" she asks, fiddling with the bow in the

center "You've been zoning out."

"Huh?" I blink away from her chest. "Yeah, I'm fine."

"Are you sure?" She bites the tag off the shirt. "You seem really out of it. And I'm worried the visit with the police is," she lifts her arms to pull her shirt over her head, "messing with your head."

The visit with the police . . .

Where stuff happened . . .

Where I was reminded of my past . . .

My head becomes foggy . . .

She hasn't pulled the shirt over her bra, still struggling to get the super tight fabric over her chest.

"The police visit did mess with my head a little, but that's not what's making me so out of it right now. It's just . . . I mean, it's you . . . and . . . you changing in my car in front of me." My cheeks warm.

Her lips form an *O* as her gaze drops to the shirt stuck on top of her breasts.

"It's really distracting," I add, feeling like an idiot when my skin burns hotter, "to see you like . . . that."

Instead of tugging the shirt down to cover up, she leaves the fabric up and bites on her bottom lip. "Good distracting?"

Her bluntness shouldn't surprise me—this is Lyric—yet I am. I'm stupidly surprised to the point that I just gape at her. She stares back, thoroughly amused.

What I wouldn't give to be like Lyric.

So at ease with life.

So comfortable in my own skin.

I sneak another peek at her chest then face the steering wheel and open my texts, even though I have no messages. "Of course it's a good distraction. You're gorgeous." My voice is low and husky in a way it's never been before.

Lyric is breathing so ravenously I expect her to say

something dramatic and sexual. She never utters a word, though. When I finally look up at her again, her shirt is on, and she's putting her hair up.

"You ready to get this show on the road?" she asks coolly.

I nod and open the door, the cool air sweeping in and swirling around the cab, adding fog to the already fogged up windows.

"Wait. What about you?" She points at my black jeans, T-shirt, and combat boots. "Aren't you going to change, too?"

"Into what? Tight yoga pants?" I crack a smile for the first time today, but it still takes a lot of effort.

"Hey, you might look good in them with that cute, little butt of yours." She extends her hand toward me to pinch my ass, but I jump out of the car. She hops out, too, laughing her ass off as she shuts the door. "You should have seen the look on your face. It was adorable."

"And what would you have done if I hadn't moved?"

She skips around the front of the car and snatches hold of my hand. "Um, totally copped a feel, and I'd have been damn proud of it."

I roll my tongue along my teeth as a massive grin threatens to reveal itself. There are times when I wish I could spend every waking hour with Lyric. I'd smile a hell of a lot more and be way less depressed.

"You're blushing," she teases, moving in front of me and walking backwards without releasing my hand. "It's cute."

"No, I'm not." A lie. My cheeks are blazing hotter than the sun.

"Okay, if you say so." She turns back around and walks beside me, gazing up at the blue sky, musing over something.

"What are you thinking about?" I ask as we approach the back entrance of the building.

Her fingers wrap around the door handle. "Nothing." Her head tilts to the side and I can see the wheels turning in her head. "It's just that . . ." Without warning, she reaches around and pinches my ass.

"Shit." I skitter back, my fingers falling from hers.

"Ha! Don't pretend you didn't like that." She yanks the door open and scurries inside, laughing.

I did like it. And I didn't like. I'm conflicted. Confused. Dizzy. Sick.

There's been so much touching today.

So much happening . . .

So much going on . . .

So much stress . . .

I think it might have been too much . . .

Too overwhelming of a day . . .

Something's wrong. I gasp for air as I shove the door shut, remaining outside, hoping Lyric won't see me like this.

My chest compresses, suffocating me. My vision gets spotty, and my surroundings are growing blurry. My bones ache, feeling as though they're going to collapse.

A young mother with children,
dancing on her grave.
Every day a battle,
never to be saved.
She can barely keep her head,
let alone her children fed
as she battles the monster
living inside her,
pushing her deeper into insanity.
She hangs on the edge
about to tumble into an abyss,

never to see daylight again.
Her skin cracks apart.
Her heart bleeds and rots.
She doesn't want this.
She wants to be saved.
Taken away.
That's what they *promise her.*
Saviors of the dark,
with empty promises of tomorrow.
Give into us, and you'll feel no sorrow.
Pathetically, the mother surrenders,
gives up her children to feed the monster within her.
They *take the children,*
drag them into their tomb,
cuff them up so tightly,
so achingly
they can't even move.
The pain sears their souls.
But that's just the start
of an unthinkable torture
that will shatter the children apart.
First, they take a hammer
and bash in their bones.
Then comes the needles
that dig into their skin.

"Ayden, can you hear me? Oh, my God. Please look at me. Ayden . . ." Lyric trails off as my vision comes back into focus.

It takes me a moment or two to process where I am; sitting on the asphalt, hugging my knees to my chest, and gasping for air. Lyric is crouched in front of me. Her skin is pale and her eyes are wide in horror. My head is throbbing as adrenaline pounds through my body. The worst part of the situation is the tears falling out of my eyes.

Crying for myself.

For my brother.

For my sister.

Crying because I almost saw the capturers' faces. And I don't want to see their faces, don't want to remember.

"I'm sorry." I quickly wipe my eyes with the back of my hand. *I can't believe I just cried in front of Lyric again.*

"Sorry for what?" She cups my cheek in her hand and tenderly smoothes her thumb across my skin.

"For freaking out in front of you." I put my hands on the ground to stand, but my legs wobble, weak like me.

Lyric places a hand on my arm and gently guides me back down to the ground. "You shouldn't stand up yet," she insists. "You were breathing pretty hard before you fell."

"Fell?"

She slides her hand up my arm to my shoulder then along my neck all the way up to my head. "Can't you remember what happened?" She softly combs her fingers through my hair as she studies me.

"No. I can only remember getting ready to walk inside. That's it." I rack my brain for what happened.

Lyric opened the door to walk inside. Then she pinched my ass for fun. The contact broke something inside my head, something I thought I'd locked away to be forgotten. Add that to the stress of the police visit, and I lost it, completely crumbled. It's been a while since a blackout has happened, the last time being at the party where William assaulted Lyric.

"You're shaking," she whispers, scanning over every inch of my body. "Oh, Ayden. I'm sorry. I shouldn't have touched you like that. I set something off, didn't I?"

I shake my head, not wanting her to feel responsible for my mental instability. "It wasn't you. I honestly don't know what happened to me. I just sort of zoned out and sank to the ground."

"I think I should take you home." She stands to her feet then offers me her hands.

"No, you need to take the class." When I set my hands in hers, she helps me up.

The world spins around me as I get my feet under me. The blood rushes from my head, and I stagger around as I try to get my balance.

"I'll take another class later or find another way to learn some defensive skills." She slips a hand around my back and steers me toward the car.

"I didn't hurt my legs," I say, forcing a confident tone as my stomach churns. "I can walk."

Her grip only tightens. "I don't care. I don't want to risk you collapsing again."

Tired, I relax against her. Her warmth and scent brings comfort. Safe and cared about—that's what I feel whenever I'm with her. I'm lucky I have her—have this. I just wish I knew my sister had someone who made her feel safe and cared for, that she is okay. That the letter to the police was just her helping with the case, nothing more.

When we reach the passenger side of the car, Lyric moves her arm away to open the door then motions for me to get in. "I'm driving. You look too sick right now to be behind the wheel."

"What about your car?"

"When my dad gets home, I'll have him drive me to the school so I can pick it up. You shouldn't be driving right now."

I hand over the keys then duck inside. Lyric shuts the door and climbs into the driver's seat. I stare at the back of my hand as she revs up the engine. A lot of people think the scars on my skin are cat scratches, but they're from fingernails.

Put there by blood red fingernails.

A quiet humming builds in my skull, and my skin feels charred. I rest my head against the cool glass of the window as Lyric pulls out onto the freeway. I concentrate on breathing. Breathing, I can handle. Breathing is easy. Deep breaths, in and out.

We make the thirty-minute drive listening to Rise Against. My nerves settle the closer we get to home. But Lyric seems to grow more restless. By the time she parks the car in front of the garage, she's practically bouncing in her seat.

"Do you want me to come in with you so I can help you tell Aunt Lila and Uncle Ethan what happened, since you can't remember?" she asks as she silences the engine.

I shake my head. "I'll be fine. This has happened a couple of times, so they sort of know the drill by now." Only partially a lie. They know about my panic attacks, but the one I just had was more than that. It caused me to remember why tiny scars dot my legs and why two of my toes are crooked. Pins and hammers were used to inflict injuries on me.

I'm remembering.
Please don't let me remember.
I can't.
It hurts too much,
Will break me more.
And I need to be whole for the moment
So I can take care of some stuff—
Find my sister and make sure she's okay.

Nodding, Lyric extends her hand to the door handle. The pain emitting from her eyes tears my heart apart.

I catch her arm to stop her from getting out. "Lyric, I'm so sorry."

She sucks in a sharp breath before peering over her shoulder at me. "For what?"

I clutch onto her in desperation. "For being a shitty best friend, for making you sad all the time."

She rotates in the seat, facing me. "You don't make me sad all the time." She leans over the console. "You make me happy, Shy Boy. More than anyone ever has."

"Then why are you crying?"

"Because you're hurting, and I hate seeing you hurting."

My head slumps forward as guilt crushes my chest. "I just wish I could be a better friend to you," I whisper, squeezing my eyes shut.

Her forehead touches mine, her warm breath dusting my cheeks. "You're the bestest of bestest of best friends."

I smile, but the movement aches. Being happy right now feels wrong and energy draining. "There you go, making up words again."

She chuckles. "Didn't I tell you once that I'm that awesome?"

"You did." I don't open my eyes. Just feel her breath, her heat, allow her strawberry scent to encompass me. I want to kiss her so bad. I want to press my lips to hers in a soft brush, a quick taste, before I get out of the car and deal with everything waiting for me.

Everything about her sends my body into a mad frenzy. I'm walking a dangerous line right now, pushing myself far enough that I'm starting to remember some of the details of what happened three years ago. But fuck it. The police are already going to force me to split open my mind and let my memories out.

Just one moment with her. That's all I want.

Without opening my eyes, I dip my mouth forward and brush my lips across hers. She sucks in a sharp breath then lets out a soft whimper that causes both our bodies to quiver. Her lips willingly part, and my tongue slips deep inside, swallowing the taste of her. She groans in response, her fingers finding my waist and gripping tightly.

I gasp from the contact and instantly feel the memories scorch, bright and vivid, like hot iron on my flesh.

"I should go inside," I whisper breathlessly after I break the kiss.

"Okay," she utters raspingly.

A moment ticks by where neither of us budge, then we simultaneously move apart. Lyric climbs out of the car and heads to her house while I hurry into mine, wishing I was going with her. Wishing I was just a normal guy who could hang out with his girlfriend without flipping out.

But I'm not. I'm scarred, broken, cracked apart, bleeding out, and I don't know how to make it stop, how to fix myself.

I need to try, though. I have to try to get my life together and fix myself. Starting with my sister. If I can find her and know she's out of harm's way, then maybe I can have some peace of mind. Maybe I'll have hope that getting better is possible. Maybe seeing the images of my past can be just that—my past.

Maybe I can be fixed.

CHAPTER 7

I HAVE NEVER BEEN SO scared in all my life as when Ayden fell to the ground. Then he looked up at me with tears in his eyes, and I just about died. My beautiful, sweet friend was crying and in pain. Seeing him like that was heartbreaking.

After we part ways at our houses, I start to wonder what caused the meltdown. Could it have been stress from the police visit, the stress of them insisting he has to try to remember his past? I don't know for sure, since he still hasn't told me much about his past. With Ayden, everything is in the present, which is fine—I'm all about seizing the moment—but it makes me wonder exactly what kind of terrible things happened in his past.

Needing to take my mind off stuff, I track down my father in his office to bug him some more about his club opening.

"Knock, knock, knock," I say, rapping my knuckles on the doorframe as I enter his office. The usually tidy room is a mess. Papers are scattered on his desk, records are strewn carelessly on the floor, and empty energy drinks overflow the trashcan. "Whoa, did a tornado blow through here or something? Or is this just what happens when you hit stress mode?"

"What?" He closes his laptop then blinks around at the room as if he's just noticing the mess. "Oh, that. Yeah, I haven't had time to clean up in a few days."

I raise my brows at the mess that is clearly from more than a few days. "Want me to clean up?"

He shakes his head as he stands up, rubbing his eyes and yawning. "Nah, I need to get up anyway. I've been sitting at the desk all day." He stretches out his legs and arms. "What are you up to? I thought you were supposed to be at a self-defense class or something."

"That didn't work out." I plop down in a chair in front of his desk.

He starts stacking some papers. "Why? What happened?"

I shrug, spinning around in the chair. "I'm not sure."

He pauses. "You're not sure, or you don't want to tell me?"

"Both," I say, and he looks at me funny.

"Lyric, you need to go to those classes. With everything going on with Ayden and what happened with William," his jaw tightens, "you need to know how to protect yourself."

"Technically, I did protect myself from William. I'm the one who got myself out of that room after kicking the crap out of his balls."

"I'd still feel better if you took the classes. Ayden needs to take them, too."

"I was planning on it—we both were—but . . . I think Ayden had a panic attack or something, and we had to come home."

"Really?" He doesn't seem all that shocked.

"Did you know he has them?"

"No, but I'm not surprised with the stressful life he's

had." He picks up the stack of papers and sets them in the desk drawer. "Your mother used to have them when she was younger."

I stop spinning in the chair. "Really? Why have I never heard about this?"

He glides the drawer shut then moves to the trash bin to clean up the cans. "Because she hasn't had them in a long time. And she doesn't really like to talk about it too much."

"Is that why you guys worry about my mental stability?"

He drops the can he's holding. "Why do you think we worry about that?"

I push up from the chair and scoop up the can he dropped. "Because I heard you guys talking about it once. That I was *too* happy." I chuck the can in the trash bin. "You guys seemed pretty convinced that was a bad thing."

He collects another can from the floor and crunches the metal. "You misunderstood us." He tosses the can into the trash. "Your mom . . . she just worries."

I start gathering the records on the floor. "Over what?"

He sighs, scratching the side of his head. "You know about your grandmother, right? Your mom's mom?"

"I know she committed suicide, if that's what you're getting at. But only because Grandpa let it slip out in one of his stories, not because you two told me."

"Well, she was bipolar."

"And . . . ?"

He sighs again then takes the records from me and stacks them on the shelf. "Don't take this the wrong way, but sometimes, your grandmother would get in these moods. These really, upbeat, happy moods that almost seemed unnatural."

I study his uneasy demeanor and a theory develops.

"Wait a minute. Do you guys think I'm bipolar?"

"No," he says quickly, tense and guilty. "That's not what I'm saying at all."

"Then why do you look so guilty?"

His stiff posture loosens. "Lyric Scott, we don't think you're bipolar. Yes, we had to worry since it can be hereditary, but that's it."

"Well, to stop your worry, I'll just be blunt with you. I'm overly happy because I've had a super good life and I'm happy. That's it." I head for the door to leave. "And just so you know, I do get sad sometimes. I just choose not to be mopey for very long because life's too short to waste my energy on being sad."

I exit the room, even though I haven't discussed our band playing for his opening yet. But I'd wanted to cheer up, not sink farther into a bummer mood.

I go up to my room and rock out on the violin for a while, seeking comfort from music. The soft tunes and channeled energy soothe my restless soul. By the time I put the bow down, I feel content enough to jot some lyrics down.

I grab a pen and notebook then flop down on my bed.

Look at the stars, staring upon the souls.
Watching them wander. Little pieces of their own.
Lost in a sea of others. Drowning in pain.
But there are too many to hear all the silent cries.
So we keep drifting, drifting, drifting
As the stars keep shining, shining, shining.
Watching, watching, watching us all fade away.

I withdraw the pen from the paper. "Okay, I'm not sure if I love what I'm writing or am terrified of it."

I decide to give my hand a break from my head. I hide the pen and notebook under my pillow then sit up. Outside my window, the sunset paints the greying sky with hues of pink and golden orange. I still have a few hours until band practice. I could work on my homework, but I want to check up on Ayden first to make sure he's okay.

Grabbing my phone from my nightstand, I pad over to the window and send him a text.

Me: How r u feeling?

While I'm waiting for a response, the Gregory's sedan backs out of the garage and down the driveway. I can't tell who's in there, but I wonder if Ayden is.

Ayden: Yeah, I'm fine. Just resting now.

Me: At your house?

Ayden: Yeah.

Me: By yourself?

Ayden: I'm with Kale. Lila and Ethan just took Fiona and Everson to soccer practice.

Me: Want some company? I'm super bored.

Ayden: Lila actually told me I couldn't have anyone over.

Me: But I'm not just anyone. I'm your best friend.

Ayden: Sorry.

Sorry? What is that? A brush off or something?

Before I can think about it too deeply, Ayden walks out of his house and hurries down the driveway toward the sidewalk. His hood is down, and he keeps peering around as if he's nervous. When his eyes land on my window, I duck for cover and peer over the windowsill.

He lied to me again, snuck out of the house again.

"That little liar," I mutter as he veers right toward the

end of the block, the same direction he wandered up from the other night when he snuck out.

Even though it might be wrong, I make the choice to tail him, worried he might be in trouble. Worried he'll blackout again like he did earlier. More than that, I'm just generally worried about him.

I snatch my leather jacket from my bedpost then run downstairs and out the door. I slip on my jacket as I jog across my lawn and turn right when I reach the sidewalk. I can't see him anywhere, so I pick up the pace, sprinting to the end of the street. Glancing left then right, I finally spot him crossing the street in a hurry.

Hunching down, I race after him, zigzagging behind trees and parked cars, trying to stay out of sight as much as I can. I check left and right before I dash across the street and hunker down behind a chain link fence near the park as Ayden slips through the gate.

I count to five under my breath then stand up and peek over the fence, crossing my fingers, hoping he hasn't spotted me.

He's striding across the grass toward the playground. No one is around, except a guy perched in the middle of the merry-go-round. As Ayden approaches him, the guy hops to the ground. They meet under an oak tree and start talking about something, their lips moving as they huddle together. Then Ayden sticks his hand into his pocket and retrieves a silver object out that looks like a knife.

Something snaps inside me. Worry, fear, anger—perhaps a mixture of all three. Without any forethought, I leave my hiding spot, march through the gates and toward Ayden and his friend.

The guy spots me first. He says something, and Ayden reels around. Shock crosses his face, and he quickly shoves the object back into his pocket.

"Oh, don't stop whatever you're doing on my account," I say to Ayden as I reach the two of them. Up close, I get a better look at the guy. Lanky and on the younger side, with squared framed glasses and a pen tucked in the front pocket of his plaid shirt, he looks kind of nerdy. "What's going on?" My gaze travels back and forth between the two of them

"That's none of your damn business, little girl," the scrawny guy states, crossing his arms and narrowing his eyes at me.

"Little girl?" I mimic his move, folding my arms. Then I arch a brow and stare him down until he squirms. "Look, I think we both know I could kick your ass, so there's no use trying to be all badass." I turn to Ayden who's all squirrely himself. "What's going on?" The only thing keeping me calm is that maybe he has a good reason for lying to me. "Why are you sneaking off," I nod my head at the other guy, "to meet him?"

Ayden gulps. "Lyric, you need to go home. You shouldn't be here."

"Ouch. That stings." I press my hand to my chest, noting that it actually does ache.

"I'm sorry, but you do." His eyes narrow. "Wait. How did you even find me?"

"I followed you here when I saw you leaving the house after you texted me, telling me you had to stay in," I say coldly, shocking both him and myself. I hardly ever get angry, but right now, frustration simmers under my skin. "I'm sorry for getting snippy, but I'm worried about you, and until I'm not worried about you, I'm not leaving."

"Look, I know this seems a little sketchy, but I'm keeping you out of the loop for a reason." With a glance at the guy, his fingers circle my arm, and he steers me toward the gate. "You need to leave before you get into trouble."

I dig my heels into the ground. "Are you in some kind of trouble? Is that what this is about? Because I can help you if you are. But you have to tell me what's going on or else I can't do anything for you."

"I'm not in trouble." He withdraws his hand from my arm then rakes his fingers through his hair. "I just don't want you involved in this. If you knew what I was doing, you wouldn't want to, either."

"Well, tell me and I'll let you know if you're right."

He blows out a breath, his hand falling to his side. "I'll tell you, but you have to promise that, as soon as I do, you'll leave."

I shake my head. "I'm not going to promise that."

We silently stare at each other while the wind howls and kicks dead leaves across the dry grass and around our feet.

"It's about my sister," he finally surrenders.

My heart misses a beat. I wasn't expecting that.

"What about your sister? Is she in trouble?"

"That's what I'm trying to find out." He peeks over at the guy, who is texting on his phone, and then leans in and lowers his voice. "Today at the police station, I saw a letter in one of the files that was from my sister. When I asked the detective about it, he told me it wasn't any of my business."

"Did you tell Lila and Ethan?"

"Yeah, and they pretty much gave me the same attitude."

"You think they know what it is?" I ask, astounded. "That they're keeping stuff from you?"

"I'm not sure. I mean, I'd like to think they don't keep secrets from me, but there's been a couple of times I've overheard them whispering about me, and I have to wonder if maybe they know more about my past, this case, and my sister."

"But how would they know?" The wind picks up and blows strands of my hair around my face. "And why would they keep it from you? It makes no sense."

I suddenly remember something I overheard the night the police broke the news to Ayden about his brother. A short conversation between Lila and Ethan when they thought I was out of hearing range.

"Ayden, I think maybe I should tell you something I heard Aunt Lila and Uncle Ethan talking about, but after you take care of whatever you're doing with that guy, because he's staring at us right now and looks really, really creepy."

Ayden tracks my gaze to the guy then inches toward me protectively when the guy shoots me a nasty look.

"Who is that guy, anyway?" I ask, plucking pieces of hair out of my mouth.

"On the Internet, he calls himself Rebel Tonic," Ayden says. "I don't know what his real name is."

"Rebel Tonic?" I question with a *really* look.

"He's supposed to be really good with computers," he tells me as if it explains everything. "Good at hacking, too."

I try piecing everything together. "Is that why you're meeting him here, to have him hack for you? And is that what you were doing the other night, meeting him then, too?"

He warily nods. "I want him to hack into social service's records and track down my sister. I met him the other night and have been trying to figure out if I wanted to risk it and how the hell I was going to come up with the money." He pauses, frustrated. "After seeing that letter, I have to do this, Lyric. I need to know she's okay." He looks at me, pleading for me to understand where he's coming from.

I'm glad I can't understand, at least in the same context as him. I've had a really good life and will never fully comprehend what it's like to go through what Ayden has. I remember how I used to envy him, because he's experienced life. Now I'm grateful for what I have.

"How much does it cost?"

He stuffs his hands into his pockets and kicks the tip of his boot against the grass. "The fee is a thousand dollars."

"A *thousand* dollars!" My eyes widen. "Where the heck did you get that kind of money?"

"I don't have it all. I've saved up six hundred from the times I helped Lila with her catering events. The other four hundred I was going to pay off with . . ." He pats his pocket.

I eye him suspiciously. "What's in there?"

"A knife that belonged to my brother. It's rusty, but the brand is pretty high quality. I'm honestly not even sure where he got it from."

Tears instantly prick in my eyes. Here Ayden is, doing something highly illegal, risking getting into trouble, giving up something that belonged to his deceased brother, and he does it so simply, so matter-of-factly.

"You need four hundred dollars, then?" I mentally count what I have stashed in my sock drawer. After my last record shopping spree, I'm guessing about four twenty-five, give or take ten bucks.

"I'm not taking your money, Lyric." He pushes me in the direction of the gate and points for me to go. "Just like I'm not letting you get involved in this."

"Tough shit for you, but I'm already involved." I stand my ground. "You're my best friend. I care about you. And I'd be a freaking jerk if I just bailed out now."

"You'll still be my friend if you bail. You'll always be

my friend."

"No duh. That's the most obvious statement ever. But I'm still going to go get you four hundred bucks so you can pay that asshole over there and keep your brother's knife."

"Lyric, I—"

I conceal his mouth with my hand. "Ayden, it's just money. It means absolutely nothing compared to our friendship." I remove my hand from his lips. "Now, go tell Mr. Rebel Tonic," I roll my eyes, "that I'm running back to the house to get some cash and not to go anywhere."

I raise my pinkie to make him swear he'll wait for me. Once he does, I start to jog toward the exit of the park but stop near the gates.

"Ayden," I call out, and he turns toward me. "*We'll find her, okay? You don't need to do this alone.*"

He mashes his lips together, nods once, and then heads back for Rebel Tonic.

I run like hell for my house before Ayden can back out on our pinkie promise.

By the time I return to the park with a ball of money in my pocket, I'm sweaty and breathless. Relief washes through me when I spot Ayden and Rebel Tonic hanging out on the merry-go-round. He hasn't left, which means Ayden didn't break his promise.

I approach them, reaching into my pocket for the money.

Ayden quickly jumps to his feet and blocks me from Rebel Tonic's view as I hand Ayden the cash.

"I'm going to pay you back every penny," he promises as he stares at the bills in his hand.

I wave him off. "Let's just get this guy paid and go home." He turns toward Rebel Tonic, but I capture his sleeve. "Are you sure you can trust him?"

He lifts his shoulders and shrugs. "I don't know, but

it's the only idea I have."

I free his sleeve and Ayden gives Rebel Tonic my wad of cash along with a crumpled stack of his own. Rebel Tonic counts it out, and then a greedy grin forms on his acne-covered face.

"Fan-freaking-tastic," he says, balling up the bills and stuffing them into his jacket. "Give me like a week, and I should have the information for you."

"How are you going to contact me?" Ayden asks as Rebel Tonic backs toward the gate.

"By email," he tells him, pushing his glasses up the brim of his nose. "And don't try texting me on that phone number I gave you the other day. My mom took my phone away."

"*His mom?* How old is he?" I frown, doubtful that this ordeal is going to end well with Rebel Tonic. The only thing that stops me from chasing his skinny butt down and snatching the money back is the glimmer of hope in Ayden's eyes.

"I'm not sure," Ayden mutters with his eyes still fixed on Rebel Tonic. "Maybe like fifteen?"

"As old as Kale?" Yeah, I highly doubt this is going to end well.

Ayden finally looks at me when Rebel Tonic disappears out the park gates. The sky has shifted to stardust, darkness blankets the land, and the streetlights have clicked on, highlighting the way home.

"So, what were you going to tell me about Lila and Ethan?" he asks.

I scuff my boot across the grass. "The night we heard the news about your brother, I overheard them talking about how they knew your brother getting . . . killed was a possibility, that the people were out there, and they could come for you guys or something like that."

He rubs his hand across his forehead. "I knew that, too. That it was a possibility."

"Oh," I say at the same time he adds, "But . . ."

"But what?" I press with interest.

"But I don't know. I'm starting to wonder if they know more about my sister, brother, and me than even I know."

Silence encases us.

"What are you going to do?" I finally ask, zipping my jacket up all the way to my chin.

"I don't know." He draws the zipper up his own jacket then glances up at the moon. "We should get going before Lila and Ethan get home and notice I'm gone."

"Were you supposed to leave the house?" I ask as we hike across the grass.

"Not after what happened today. At the class, I mean. Plus, they're worried about that guy we saw watching my house."

"Yeah, I'm sorry I told my mom about that. I just felt that, with everything going on, they should know."

"It's okay. I'm glad you did. I should have told them myself."

I twist a strand of my hair around my finger. "Ayden, do you think what happened today . . . Was that a panic attack?"

He's quiet before he answers. "I was remembering stuff."

My head whips in his direction. "*What?*"

He exhales. "It happens sometimes . . . when I'm stressed out . . . or when things happen that remind me of my past."

We arrive at the iron gate and veer down the sidewalk, past the homes sparkling with Christmas lights, wreaths, inflatable globes, and even some with artificial snow.

"Was it the stress of today?" I scoot over as one of our

neighbors strolls by, giving us a friendly wave.

"Yeah, kind of," Ayden replies, waving back.

"Kind of? Was it the letter from your sister?"

"Yes and no." When I stare at him, silently pressing for more, his shoulders slump. "I don't want to lie to you anymore."

"Then don't," I say frankly. "When I told you that you could tell me anything, I meant it."

He contemplates what I've said. "It was because of all the touching we've been doing." His voice is barely audible and crammed with apprehension.

"Oh." My shoulders sink along with my mouth. "I get it."

He abruptly slams to a halt, grabbing my arm and stopping me with him. "No, you don't get it." Panic floods his eyes. "I want to touch you. I think about it all the time . . . Have ever since that day in your dad's office when I . . ."

I can't see his cheeks, but I can picture how red they are, like every time he talks about something sexual.

"When you got turned on," I calmly finish for him.

On the inside, I'm a wreck.

All the way back then,
His heart danced for me,
Spun a longing for my soul
And sought the taste and feel of me.
All this time, all this time, all this time,
He wanted me.

He bobs his head up and down. "You're the first girl who ever made me feel that way."

"The first that's ever turned you on?" I ask, astonished.

I've often wondered how sexually experienced he is, if he's still a virgin. The first time I met him, he was wearing all black along with a leather collar, gauges in his ears, and he was sporting black nail polish. I assumed back then that, because of his rough appearance, he was experienced. Then I actually got to know him and discovered how much he hated being touched, and I questioned my initial assumption. I still don't know for sure, since he never offers to talk about his past.

"You're the first girl I've ever wanted to turn me on." He chokes up, his hand on my arm trembles, and his fingers dig into the fabric of my jacket. "It's not the first time I've ever been turned on . . . just the first time where I wasn't . . . being forced . . ." His voice cracks.

His comment rolls over me like a vicious wave. What he's trying to say without actually saying it. That he thinks he's been sexually abused.

The reality of how harsh his life has been knocks the wind out of me. Why hadn't I thought of this before? With the way he hates being touched.

"Ayden, I . . ." I'm speechless, unsure what to say to him and freaking terrified I'll say the wrong thing.

"I don't know if anything actually happened to me in that house. All I know is that, at fourteen-years-old, I went into that house feeling okay with being touched. But, when I came out of the house . . ." He skims a finger along my jawline. "Sometimes, something as simple as a handshake can make me feel like I'm going to throw up. But I'm working it, working on getting better," he whispers, sounding as if he's trying to convince himself more than me.

My lips part as I prepare to ask him how he's working on it, but then his lips come down on my mouth. I stumble back from the unexpected contact and grab onto him to stop from falling. My fingers grasp his shirt, and I end up pulling him back with me. Losing our balance, we slam against the fence, but our lips remain fused together, even when Ayden moans.

"I'm trying," he whispers through kisses. His tongue tangles with mine as his hands find my waist and he pulls me toward him in desperation. "I want to be able to kiss you like you deserve to be kissed."

I have no clue what he's talking about, because I am being kissed like I deserve.

This kiss, it makes my body pulsate.
Makes flames blaze under my skin.
Steals my breath from my lungs.
But it's not really stealing
When I'm giving the air to him.
Willingly giving him anything he wants.
Just say the word, Ayden, and it's yours.
My heart.
My soul.
Whatever you want.

"Ayden," I gasp into his mouth as his body starts to quiver, "it's okay. I'm fine with how things are. And I love our kisses."

He abruptly pulls away, his solid chest heaving as he struggles for oxygen. "No, it's not . . . okay . . . nothing is." He avoids looking at me, staring at the corner of the street. The Christmas lights reflect in his eyes, making it appear as if he's tearing up. "You deserve so much better than some guy who can't even touch you."

"You *can* touch me." I grab his hand, lace our fingers together, and pull him. I refuse to let him go. Ever. "See."

His gaze drops to our linked hands. "It's not the same as if you were with someone else who didn't have so many problems."

"Of course it's not." I swing our hands. "It's so much better."

His Adam's apple bobs up and down as he swallows

hard. "You say that now, but you'll change your mind eventually."

"No, I won't. You leaving my life would crush my heart, and I refuse to let my heart get crushed."

"It may take forever for me to get over this. And it could get worse when I start seeing the therapist for my amnesia."

"I don't care." I stand firm, knowing that, through all my indecisiveness and sporadic choices, I do want Ayden. I decided that the moment he kissed me for the first time to try to erase the painful memory of my first kiss that William stole from me. "I want this . . . want you."

His hand shakes in my hand, but he nods his head once. I'm not positive what the nod means. If he wants this—wants me, too. If he's giving us a shot. I'm hoping so, hoping what he says is true. Because what I've said is the truth.

He'll crush my heart if he leaves my life.

Will I live? Sure. I'm not going to become overdramatic and think I'll drop dead if Ayden decides he can't be with me. Will my life be destroyed? For a while maybe, but eventually, I'll get over it the best I can. But there will always be a scar on my heart connected to every memory of Ayden. And I'd rather not have a scar.

I'd rather just have him forever.

CHAPTER 8

OVER THE NEXT COUPLE OF days, things are a little awkward between Lyric and I after I confessed that I might have been sexually abused. But I think we're just confused where our relationship stands. Are we friends? Boyfriend and girlfriend? I have no idea. I'd like to believe, after the conversation we had the other night, that we're the latter. But we haven't really said anything to confirm it. We behave the same as we always do. Still holding hands. Joking. She makes me smile. I'll take whatever she'll give me. I'm not even sure I could take more if she offered it. I wish I could offer her more, though. I meant what I said that night I kissed her near the park. She deserves better than what I can give her.

I don't have too much time to overanalyze what's going on between us because my amnesia therapy sessions begin this week. I'd be lying if I didn't say that I'm absolutely frightened out of my goddamn mind.

It's late in the evening and I'm lying in a lounge chair inside my therapist's office. My arms are tensely overlapped on my stomach and my heart is pounding like a freaking drum, thrashing against my chest.

"Now, Ayden," my therapist, Dr. Gardingdale leans

forward in the chair and hovers over me. A string quartet flows around me and the ceiling light flickers about every two minutes or so. "I need to make sure you want to do this. Because the last thing I want is for anyone to push you into this. It could make your Severe Post Traumatic Amnesia worse."

Inhale. Exhale. I nod, even though I don't. Want is too strong of a word. Am I going to do this? Yes. But only for my brother.

"Alright then. I'm going to record our session for the police to review." He relaxes in the chair and reaches behind him to press the on button of a recorder. He taps the top of a timer. "And I don't want to keep you under for too long."

He had explained when I first came in that this was a lot like hypnotherapy. I'd never tried it before but had watched someone get hypnotized at a fair.

I suck in a deep breath and nod, my nerves jarring. "Okay."

"Now close your eyes."

"Okay."

"And relax."

"Ok . . . ay."

"Do you hear that, Ayden," my sister says. "Cop sirens. We're saved."

Saved? Is it possible?

"It'll never be possible," a woman whispers. ""You'll never be saved. Because if you escape, we'll come back for you . . ."

I rub my eyes as I open them. Blinking against the inadequate lighting, I sit up. "Did it work?" I ask the doctor. "Did I say anything?"

His sympathy tells me all I need to know. "Unfortunately no, but did you remember anything different?"

"Just my sister saying we were saved." I drag my fingers along the scars on the back of my hand. "And a woman telling me we weren't ever going to be saved."

"Well, that's a tiny bit of progress then." He stops the timer. "I don't want you to immediately get discouraged that you only were able to remember a little. These things can take time."

He continues explaining the details of hypnotherapy while I zone out and focus on the short memory I did see. See might be a stretch. Heard is more like it. No one ever has faces in the faint memories that return to me. They're just blurs, shells of people and places that I pretend don't exist.

After the session, I return home in a sullen mood and feel exhausted. I go straight up to my room to relax and play the guitar until Lyric comes bounding into my room, sporting one of her heart-warming smiles.

"I have an idea," she singsongs as she bounces onto my bed.

"And what's that?" I pluck a few guitar strings.

"Even though it's Christmas Eve and we're supposed to exchange presents," she kneels in front of me, "I think we should wait."

"Wait? But you love, *love* opening presents."

"True, but I was thinking it might be fun to do it later when life is a bit more cheery." She situates beside me and tugs the hem of her dress down as she stretches out her legs. Her hair is up, her deliciously looking lips sheen with gloss, and her green eyes radiate enthusiasm. "And it could be like a weird little tradition we do. Instead of being cliché and exchanging them on Christmas Eve, like a ton of people are doing all around the world."

I ponder her offer. "All right, you have yourself a deal."

"Good." She grins. "Because I can't think of a damn thing to get you."

I shake my head, faintly smiling. "I knew there was an ulterior motive." I strum the strings of a song I've been working on.

"What's that tune you're playing?" Lyric wonders, sliding her legs up and facing me.

"Just a song that's been stuck in my head."

"I like it . . . it's pretty."

"Pretty isn't very rock n' roll."

"Neither are you." She slumps her head against the headboard. "You're sweet and sensitive and piercing free." She touches the tip of her finger to the corner of my eye, causing me to miss the next chord. "You have such long eyelashes . . . They're gorgeous."

"So let me get this straight." I set the guitar down on the foot of the bed and turn to her. "You tell me I'm not very rock n' roll and that I have gorgeous eyelashes. I'm not really sure how to take that."

"You should be happy," she insists, her gaze momentarily flicking onto my mouth. "Being rock n' roll in a band is cliché and your gorgeous eyelashes make your eyes stunning."

My cheeks flame. I'm blushing.

"You're cute." She swipes her finger down the brim of my nose. "I remember the first day of school how I held your hand. I felt so special that you were all mine."

My heart flutters like an upbeat song when she declares that she pretty much claimed me a year and a half ago. "You are special," I say, wishing I was brave enough to kiss her right now. But after therapy, the doctor had said to take it easy with anything severely emotional. Just being with Lyric sparks emotions to life. Good ones like happiness and longing.

I pick my guitar up while Lyric fluffs a pillow and lies down in my bed. She watches me play for a while, running her fingers through her hair.

"So, how did your therapy go today?" she finally dares to ask as I play a song.

I shrug. "Not too bad, but that's probably because nothing really happened."

"You didn't remember anything at all?"

Another pluck, another strum. "Maybe a little."

"Okay."

I know she wants to ask what I saw, but she seals her lips together, suppressing her questions.

"It was when the police found us." I cease playing. "It was the last time I saw my sister . . . and she seemed so happy that we were saved." His jawline tautens. "One of the women that was holding us there . . . she said we'd never be saved . . . she warned me she'd find us again." My fingernails enfold into my palms, biting my flesh. "What if that's what happened to my brother? What if they went back for him? What if it's only a matter of time before they come back for me?"

"Ayden, you're safe." When I try to look away from her, she captures my face between her hands. "You have a family who loves you—people who love you. Nothing is going to happen to you."

Life would be less complex if I could wholeheartedly believe her. But after my brother's death, I can't fully accept that nothing will happen to me.

I rest my forehead against hers and take a few shallow breaths as she slips her leg through mine and aligns our bodies.

"What do you want to do for the rest of the night?" she asks, playing with my hair.

"Can we just stay like this? Can we just pretend that

everything is okay for a while?"

"Of course."

She wiggles around until we're both lying down face to face. She keeps her leg between my legs, her hand on my cheek, and her forehead against mine. We fit together so perfectly it's mind-boggling.

How is this possible?
To completely fit with someone.
Our bodies creating lyrics
Perfectly composing
As our hearts dance together.
Nothing makes sense.
Yet everything makes sense.
Perfect is so confusing.
A dizzy spell inside my head.
Thirsting for answers.
With nothing to drink.
Where do I go?
To find out who I am?

CHAPTER 9

I TRY NOT TO WORRY over the failed attempt of restoring my memories and instead concentrate on the band. It's not like that session was the only chance for me to remember. Plus, part of me is relieved the session didn't work. Relieved I didn't have to relive the hellish nightmare. But another part of me feels guilty, like I'm not doing all that I can to help track down my brother's killer.

A couple of days later, I'm sitting in Sage's garage with Lyric, listening to music, attempting to focus on chords, notes, and the strum of my fingers. It's still Christmas break. December thirtieth to be exact. Everywhere I look still screams, *the holidays aren't over yet! Cheer up! We're starting a new year!* On top of everything going on with therapy, I haven't heard anything back from Rebel Tonic yet and cheering up seems impossible when the possibility that he ripped me off gets higher.

Things remain pretty quiet for the first ten minutes or so while we wait for Sage and Nolan to show up so we can get band practice started. They were supposed to be here fifteen minutes ago, but Sage texted me and said they were picking up pizza on their way back from a concert they went to over the weekend. He also still needs to chat with me about something. He's been texting me for about a week now, but has never gotten around to actually telling me what he needs to discuss. I'd probably worry about it a little bit more, but I've had other things on my mind.

"Self-defense class should be called kick-your-ass class. I'm so sore," Lyric says, massaging her shoulder. "I feel like such a wimp."

"That's because you are a wimp," I joke as I strum a few chords on my guitar.

She shifts on the sofa and lightly punches my arm. "Whatever. I could so kick your ass if I wanted to."

"I was holding back on you in class."

In class, I'd been Lyric's partner, which required a lot of touching and human contact. I didn't flip out too badly, so I felt pretty proud of myself. I kept reminding myself that it was important for Lyric to be able to learn to protect herself, and in order to learn, I had to be a good partner. After everything she's done for me, I owe her so much.

"I could so tell, too." She fiddles with the microphone cord. "You're such a softie when it comes to me."

God, if she knew how right she is.
How much I melt just from just a simple look from her.
A glance in my direction
Sends my pulse racing.
Her green eyes melt away
The chill always in my soul.
I'm liquefying into something else,
Someone I don't understand,
Someone different.
Someone not so handcuffed to my past?
I wish.
God, I wish, that were true.
That the stress of my life was coming to an end instead of just beginning.

She prods the tip of her boot against mine. "You are doing okay with that, right? I mean, with all the touching we did in class?"

I twist the tuning pegs on the top of the guitar handle. "I'm fine. I promise. You don't need to constantly worry about me."

"That will never happen, so get over it."

Quiet stretches between us as I work on tuning my guitar and Lyric gets up to mess with one of the amps. She's wearing a short black dress with red flowers on the bottom. Every time she bends over, she flashes me. I don't look away. I have tried too many times and realize how pointless it is to fight my attraction to her anymore.

"Oh, I thought of a name for our band." She stands up straight, tucks a strand of her hair behind her ear, and then her brows dip. "Wait. Were you just checking out my ass?"

I shrug, staring at my guitar. "Maybe."

She laughs as she plops down beside me. "I so just busted you."

"Well, I wouldn't call it busting me since you willingly stripped down in front of me in the car. I've seen pretty much everything already."

She teasingly bumps her shoulder into mine. "Are you trying to flirt with me right now, Shy Boy?"

"Maybe a little."

She sweeps my hair out of my face. "You're so adorable."

I restrain a smile. "You do realize guys don't like being called adorable, right?"

"Yeah, right. You totally love that I do. Love that I give you little nicknames that no one else gets. Admit it."

"No way am I giving you that much power over me."

She grins wickedly. "Oh, yes you will." She tickles my side and my pulse soars erratically. "Because you love giving me what I want."

"True," I easily admit.

Her lips part to speak, but the buzz of her phone interrupts her. She scoops it up from Sage's stool, reads the message, and frowns.

"Who is it?" I set my guitar down on the floor.

"My dad." She texts something back then sets the phone down on the cushion next to her. "He was wondering where I was, like he doesn't know. I'm at the same place I am every Friday night."

"Are you two still fighting over the club thing?"

"That and the fact that he and my mom think I'm bipolar."

"I'm sure they don't really think you are. They just worry about you."

"Yeah, but instead of whispering about it behind my back, they should have told me." She reclines back on the sofa. "All my life, I've been taught to just say things how they are, not to hold things in or keep secrets. I was taught to be honest even when it's hard. They should be the same way with me."

"I know. I'm not saying what they did wasn't wrong." I relax beside her. "But don't be mad at them forever, especially when they care so much about you."

"I won't, at least over the bipolar thing. The band thing, on the other hand . . ." She faces me, bringing her leg up onto the cushion and tucking it under her ass. "I just really wish he'd give us a chance, you know? I'm starting to wonder if he has confidence in my talent at all. Maybe this whole concern for my mental stability is an excuse."

"I'm sure that's not what it is. He knows how talented you are," I assure her. "He's probably just worried about you entering that life. He does know firsthand how intense it is to be a rock star."

"I'm not trying to be a rock star to get famous." She flops her head back and stares at the ceiling. "I just want to perform onstage and share my art with people who want to listen."

"You're too beautiful for your own good."

"So are you."

We stare at each other until the heat of the moment becomes too much.

Looking away, I collect my guitar from the floor. "Lyric, we *will* get to perform. Even if it's not at your father's club opening; we'll get our chance one day."

"I know we will. I just wish it were sooner. You know how impatient I can be."

"Yes, I do," I agree, positioning the guitar on my lap.

She narrows her eyes at me, but then laughs. "I'm just anxious. That's all. No biggie."

"Anxious about what?"

Her attention drifts to the wall covered in albums. "I don't know. Stuff."

"Lyric Scott." I splay my fingers across her cheek and force her to look at me. "What's going on?"

"Did you just last name me?" She elevates her brows accusingly.

"Call it payback for all those times you've called me Shy Boy and dude. Now, fess up. What's going on? I can tell something's bothering you."

"I'm just worried that I might not have it in me, and then all of this," she gestures around the garage covered with albums, instruments, amps, and ashtrays, "will just have been a waste of my time."

"You do have it in you. Your voice, it's . . ." I don't even know how to describe the sound of Lyric singing. The sultry tone of her voice is almost unreal. "It's unearthly. Unreal. Beautiful."

A grin curves at her lips. "Unearthly? Wow, that's poetic. If I didn't know any better, I'd guess you were trying to flirt with me again."

I give a half shrug. "I'm just being truthful."

Her green eyes bore into me, and desire pulsates through my veins, desire I'm terrified to act on.

Just grab her and kiss her.
Crush your lips to hers.
Drink her soul
And give her yours.

"I know you are," she says. "And it's not a lack of confidence in my ability that I'm worried about. It's my confidence in my ability to perform in front of people other than you, Sage, and Nolan."

"You'll be fine, and I'll be there to help you."

"I know you will." Her grin broadens as she shifts her body toward mine, nearly bursting with excitement. "You should just start singing duets with me. Then I wouldn't have to worry about being up on stage, singing solo."

"You should probably hear me sing before you start making plans," I tell her, but she just stares at me expectantly. "I'm not going to sing for you." I lean over the armrest to prop my guitar against the wall. "I'm not a singer."

"Have you ever tried?" She inches closer, and strands of her hair tickle my cheek.

The feel of her warm breath and nearness sends a shiver through my body. Images of laying her down on the sofa and kissing her passionately flood my mind and make it almost impossible to breathe steadily, let alone reply to her question.

Swallowing hard, I shake my head.

"But you write lyrics."

My lips part in surprise. "How do you know?"

She chews on her lip, looking guilty. "Don't be mad

at me, but there was this one time when you left your notebook open on your bed. I honestly thought it was just schoolwork and was going to shove it out of the way. Then I saw what was written on the opened page."

"Did you read the entire book?"

She places her hands on the armrest behind me, pinning me between her arms as if she's afraid I'm going to run. "I would never do that. I just read the one page then set it aside. It was good, though, what I read. Sad, but really, really moving. You have a hidden talent, Shy Boy. One I'll admit I'm a little jealous of." She wets her lips with her tongue.

I'm uncertain exactly what she's attempting to do—if she's unintentionally trying to turn me on or not. Regardless, my cock is getting hard inside my jeans. My body only gets more muddled when she moves near enough that her chest brushes mine.

"Which one was it?" I struggle to concentrate on the conversation as her body heat clouds my thoughts.

"Huh . . ." She's as equally distracted as I am.

"Which song was it that you read?"

"I think it was called 'You Devour Me.'" She stretches her arms farther toward the armrest, arching her back and aligning her chest, hips, and legs with mine.

I can't fucking breathe.

Focus.

Focus on something else.

Focus on the song.

"You Devour Me" is a song I wrote about her not too long after we shared our first kiss, when I was confused about what was going on inside me and thought I was going to lose my mind. So damn confused all the time, all I could do was write to free myself from the confusion. I ended up writing a lot. And wrote about Lyric frequently.

You seep into my skin, devour me whole.
Beg me to cave in, give in to what I fear.
You make my body burn. Make my heart bleed.
Make me feel alive. Make it so fucking hard to breathe.
Nothing feels right whenever you're near.
Everything feels wrong whenever you disappear.
Fuck, I can't figure out what you're doing to me.
What you make me feel. Was never supposed to be.

"We should sing it," she breathes against my mouth. "I could play guitar for one set, and you could sing." She sucks her lip between her teeth as her gaze zeroes in on my lips.

"I'm pretty sure I'm tone deaf." I fight an internal tug-of-war with my mind and body.

Take and devour her.
Deal with the consequences later.
Or push her away.
And drift farther away from having her.

"Then I could sing it," she says in a raspy voice I've never heard come out of her mouth before. It's like we're talking dirty without actually talking about anything dirty. "Unless that's weird."

"Weird?" *I have no idea what we're talking about anymore.*

"Yeah. I mean, it seemed like you wrote the song about someone. Maybe it's personal."

"I'm not sure I'm ready to sing it aloud. Maybe one day I'd be okay with you singing it, though." Maybe one day I'll be okay enough to admit the lyrics are about my true feelings for her. Maybe one day I'll actually be able to fully admit them to myself.

She hooks her arms around me. "I'm so glad you said that. It's such a good song." She squeezes me, crushing the air from my lungs.

My arms enclose around her waist and I nuzzle my face into the curve of her neck. She sighs contentedly as my fingers travel down her spine and sketch a delicate path along the bottom of her back. I bite my lip to restrain a moan when she shudders. "The Window" by Mars Volta fills up the silence between us as she nips at my earlobe with her teeth, and my body quivers uncontrollably.

"I know we never actually fully reached a conclusion to what was okay between us," she whispers with another graze of her teeth, "and what was not, but—"

I cut her off, turn my head, and press my lips to hers so roughly our teeth clank together. Probably the least sexiest kiss ever. Add that to the fact that I can't figure out what to do with my hands—never seem to be able to—and she should leave me high and dry. Instead she presses closer, rolling her hips against mine as she nips at my lip and tugs at my hair.

"You feel so good," she moans breathlessly as she rocks her hips again. "Is this okay? You're not feeling anxious, are you?"

Not this time. This time, I am way less stressed out. I feel way more in control over my head, at least for the moment, anyway.

Another mind-blowing movement of her hips and I damn near explode. Something possesses me—an urge I don't understand—and I'm suddenly flipping us over.

A quiet whimper escapes Lyric's lips as her back hits the sofa cushions.

"Are you okay?" I wiggle my body over hers, still feeling out of my element.

Push or pull?
Want or desire?
Stay or flee?

Her blonde hair looks like a halo around her head, her

green eyes are glazed over, and her lips are swollen from the intense kiss. She's the most beautiful sight I've ever laid eyes on. Will ever lay eyes on.

"More than okay." She cups the back of my head and guides my mouth to hers for another passionate kiss.

Our tongues twine together as I grind my body against hers. A shudder then another grind. I feel like I'm dying inside, yet at the same time, fully alive. My body and mind are a walking contradiction, never wanting the same thing.

For the moment, my body ends up winning as I glide an unsteady hand up Lyric's dress. Her legs part, and I settle between her with my hand on her ass. She shivers, and her head falls back as she gasps.

Terrified, I start to pull away, but she reaches between us and places her fingers over mine, holding my hand there. I kiss her fiercely until my lips feel swollen then move my mouth down her neckline. Little whimpers and moans keep escaping from her lips the lower I delve. By the time I reach the top of her dress, I'm pulsating with need.

She rolls her hips against mine again as she grabs my hair. Glancing up, I slide one of the straps of the dress down while watching her expression. When her chin dips down, her hungry gaze collides with mine. She wants this, wants me. I don't even know how to process that fact, so I try not to, try not to think about anything as I slip the strap down and expose her breast.

"Oh, my God," I whisper. I'm as hard as a rock. Through the yearning, the fear is there, residing under my skin.

I won't give in. I won't give in.

Lyric grasps my hand that's still on her ass, but I manage to pull away. I take her other hand, and with our fingers linked, I move her arms above her head, then I lower my mouth to her breast, and suck her nipple into my mouth.

Her back bows, our bodies meld together. I'm about to lose it, yet somehow, I continue going, sucking and tracing circles with my tongue. Lyric gasps and moans and writhes underneath me until she finally cries out, stabbing her nails into my hands as she comes apart.

The pierce of her nails almost causes me to tumble into a memory.

See the darkness eating around you.
It will one day consume you.
Because we're not going to let you out of here
Until you're so ruined you'll never be good again.
No, no, no.
I don't want to see it.

I force the images out of my mind, returning to reality just in time to see Lyric blinking up at me.

"Are you okay?" she asks as she traces her finger across my collarbone.

I nod, still in shock over what just happened between us. "Are you?"

"I'm more than okay." Her hand glides down my spine to the bottom of my back, just above the waistband of my jeans, and her fingers play with the fabric of my boxers.

Every single one of my muscles wind into knots, and the moment begins to crumble.

I don't—can't—be touched.

She must see the terror on my face because she quickly removes her hand. "I'm sorry. When I go too far, just say so, okay—"

The sound of the door swinging open cuts her off. I swiftly jerk the strap of her dress over her shoulder, and then we both bolt upright, tugging our clothes into place. We don't move fast enough, and Nolan and Sage get a clear idea of what's been going on.

"Oh," Nolan says, glancing between Lyric and me.

Then he busts up laughing, hunching over and cradling his stomach. "Dude, next time, lock the door."

Sage doesn't appear as amused. In fact, he seems really irate. I think about all the times I've caught him flirting with Lyric and checking her out and worry this might end up being one of those issues that breaks up the band.

"Do you want us to leave so you two can finish up?" Sage says flatly as he kicks the door shut.

Lyric combs her hair into place, calm as can be. "We're good, but thanks."

Sage's eyes land on me, burning holes into my head. "What about you? You good? Or do you still need to go into the bathroom and finish off?"

"Knock it off." I hate drama, and Sage is trying to stir it up.

A pucker forms at Sage's brow, but the confusion quickly disappears as he turns around. "I'm going to go outside and smoke." He storms out of the garage, slamming the door behind him.

An awkward silence forms between the three of us.

"I should go talk to him." I get up and head for the door while Nolan sits down on one of the stools and starts tuning his guitar.

"Are you sure you want to?" Lyric calls out after me. "It might be better to just let him have his hissy fit and get over it."

If Sage likes Lyric, then I'm not sure he's going to get over her. Lyric isn't the kind of girl you just get over.

"I'm just going to make sure he's okay." I slip out the door before she can say anything else.

When I find Sage, he's sitting on the hood of his truck, puffing on a joint.

"Are you sure you should be doing that?" I hoist myself on the hood and prop my feet on the bumper. "What if someone sees you?"

He takes a drag, traps the smoke in his chest, and then exhales. "I really don't give a shit who sees me." He holds the joint between his fingers, staring at his neighbor's house in the distance. "So, you guys are like a thing now?"

"I don't know." I tensely massage the back of my neck, unsure of what else to say to him.

He glances at me and arches a brow. "You don't know?"

I shrug. "We haven't really talked about it. Why are you so pissed about the idea, though?"

"Because I like her," he says simply as the stench of weed circles around us. "That's what I was actually trying to talk to you about. To see if you'd be cool with me dating her."

"Oh." I have no clue what to say to him.

We're quiet for a while as he tokes up. He offers me a drag, but like always, I never take it.

"Well," he finally says when we hear Nolan and Lyric blast the amp, "we should probably get inside."

We hop off the hood, and I follow him toward the garage.

"Are we cool?" I ask as he grips the doorknob.

"Sure." He shrugs as he takes another hit from the joint. "It's probably my own damn fault for waiting too long, especially when I could be where you two were headed."

How could he possibly know where Lyric and I are headed when I don't even know myself?

He opens the door. "Besides, I probably shouldn't get all tied up. Leaves room for groupies, right? That is, if we ever get a gig."

I laugh, even though I think he's only half joking.

When we enter the garage, Nolan and Lyric are

rocking out on the guitars. Lyric is using mine, sitting on the edge of the sofa, while Nolan is the middle of the room, head banging.

As her fingers pluck the strings, Lyric's gaze finds mine. *Everything okay?* she mouths, playing chord after chord.

I shrug and mouth, *I think so.*

I cross the room and sit down beside her. They finish the song, and when the room goes quiet, Sage clears his throat.

"I'm sorry for being a dick," he apologizes to Lyric as he picks up his drumsticks.

"It's okay," she says with a small smile. "Just as long as you don't do it again. And you let us use my name for the band."

Sage plops onto the stool behind the drums and twirls his drumsticks. "What's the name?"

"Alyric Bliss?"

"How'd you come up with that?" Nolan asks, unscrewing the cap from a bottle of water.

Lyric shrugs. "I just played with some words."

"It has your name in it," Sage points out with a bang of the symbol.

"So?" Lyric shrugs again. "My name is awesome."

Sage considers the name, bobbing his head up and down. "I kind of like the sound of it." He looks to Nolan who shrugs.

"I'm good with it." He takes a swig of water then sets the bottle down on the floor.

Sage glances at me. "What do you think?"

"I'm good with it." I grab my guitar from Lyric.

"I'm also going to work on creating a band logo," Lyric adds, cracking her knuckles. "Put my art talent to use."

"You're an artist?" Sage questions. "Since when?"

"Since forever," Lyric replies. "My mom's one, too."

"A woman of many talents," Sage muses thoughtfully as he taps a drumstick against the symbol.

"FYI, I put the *A* at the front of Alyric Bliss to stand for your name," Lyric whispers to me when Sage isn't paying attention. "Don't say anything, though. Sage won't use it if he knows. He'll make us change it to an *S*."

I can't help laughing.

Sage raises the drumsticks in the air and hollers, "Alyric Bliss." He moves to slam the drumsticks down, but freezes when the door swings open.

"Dad?" Lyric rises to her feet as Mr. Scott walks in. "What are you doing here?"

Sage's eyes widen and his lips part, completely star struck by the sight of the retired rocker. Nolan seems a little more at ease, but he still gapes.

Mr. Scott briefly glances at me, and I feel like he somehow knows what I was doing with his daughter, even though there's no way he possibly could. Our parents are clueless about our stolen kisses and heavy making out. If they did know, I'm sure they'd start making us keep our bedroom doors open when we're together and stop allowing Lyric to occasionally fall asleep in my bed.

Mr. Scott tears his attention off me and focuses on Lyric. "You said I needed to see you play. That, if I did, I would be begging for you to be in my lineup." He drops down in a fold-up chair near the door, reclines back, and folds his arms. "So, let's see your awesomeness."

Lyric looks at me helplessly. She's terrified of messing up, of her stage fright, of not impressing her father.

With my guitar still in hand, I step behind her and lean over her shoulder. "You've got this," I whisper, grazing my finger along the inside of her wrist. "It's just like the first time you sang in front of Sage. Pretend it's only you in the room."

She turns her head toward me, our lips almost touching. "Can I pretend you're in the room with me?"

I nod as my heart swells in my chest. Her words pierce my soul. How much she trusts me. How much I want her to trust me. How much I'm pretty sure we're not just friends anymore.

We're so much more.

CHAPTER 10

I FEEL LIKE I'M GOING to throw up as I raise the microphone to my mouth and prepare to sing in front of my dad. I'd rather run out the door and hide. What keeps my feet planted on the floor is what Ayden whispered in my ear.

Just him and me in the room.
No one else is here.
No one at all.
No one.
No one.
No one.

The music starts playing, a cover song we jam out to a lot. And with a deep breath, I open my mouth and sing.

Like the first time I sang in front of Ayden and Sage, my voice is slightly wobbly. I stabilize my tone quickly, though, and before I know it, I'm rocking out, putting on a show. I hit pitches I've never reached before and carry notes longer and more in control. Smooth is the first word that comes to mind when I'm finished. I performed smoothly.

"Well, what do you think?" I ask my dad after we finish the song.

I'm panting and sweaty like I always am after I sing. My heart dances lively in my chest as I wait in anticipation for his response. Usually, I can pick up what he's feeling, but right now, he appears neutral. I start to grow worried that maybe he didn't like it, that perhaps he's trying to figure out a way to let us down gently.

Stop being so self-doubtful!

I square my shoulders while I wait. When a grin spreads across his face, I release a trapped breath.

"You guys have a name yet?" he asks, leaning forward in the chair.

"Alyric Bliss," Sage responds, dropping his drumsticks to the floor.

"Well, Alyric Bliss," he stands to his feet, "you just got your first gig."

I run over and hug him, even though it's probably super unprofessional.

"Thank you, Daddy," I say, hugging him tightly.

"Don't thank me." He hugs me back. "As much as I love you, I wouldn't have let you be in the lineup unless I thought you were good enough."

"Well, thanks for thinking we're good enough."

"More than good enough. You're really talented." He embraces me tighter and lowers his voice. "And I'm sorry for what happened the other day. You were right. Your mother and I should have told you."

"You're totally off the hook." I pull back to look at him. "Just as long as you never do it again."

He draws an *X* across his chest. "I promise."

I smile and step back. "Do you want to stick around and play with us for a while?"

"I was supposed to go home and help your mother with something." He rubs his jawline, tempted by my offer. "But I guess I could spare a few minutes."

A few minutes stretch into a few hours. By the time he leaves the garage, it's nearing eleven o'clock. He tells me to be home by one then adds that we might want to consider at least singing one of our own songs next week.

My stomach churns at the idea. Yeah, we've played a few of my songs, but the idea of spilling my soul out to a room full of people adds to my stage fright.

Fortunately, I don't stress about it for too long, because Sage suggests that we go to Maggie's party. Suddenly, we're piling into Aunt Lila's car and heading toward the ritzy side of town near the docks.

"Who's DD?" Sage asks as we pull up to Maggie's dad's three-story mansion.

The party has moved outdoors; people are crammed on the front lawn and around the garage, and some have gathered near the numerous cars parked in the driveway. Music blasts from inside and flows through the air. Twinkle lights cover all the trees and dimly light up the yard.

"I'll be," Ayden and I say simultaneously.

"You two are no fun," Sage comments as he hops out of the car.

Nolan follows and the intoxicated people swallow up the two of them.

"So, tonight's been interesting." I remark when it's just Ayden and me in the car.

"Definitely." He stares at the party, and the lights from the trees reflect in his eyes.

"I mean, my dad randomly shows up and gives us our first gig. Sage gets mad for some silly reason when he catches us making out . . ." I trail off as Ayden raises his brows.

"You really don't know what that was about?" he questions skeptically.

"Should I?"

"Lyric," he starts.

I heave a sigh. "Fine, I know what it's about, but I don't want it to be about that. I don't want to have drama in the band." I pick at my sapphire nail polish. "Besides, I don't think of him as anything more than a friend, never have, especially when I like someone else." I smile at him, but my mood plummets when he frowns. "What's wrong?"

"Are you sure that you . . . ?" He huffs out an aggravated breath. "Are you sure you want this—want me? We'd have to move really slow." He looks away, embarrassed. "I'm not even ready for you to touch me yet, at least not intimately."

"Of course I want you," I climb over the console and straddle his lap, "slow or fast or simple or complicated. I'll take whatever, just as long as you'll give it to me." I smile thoughtfully. "Hey, I'm totally putting that in a song when I get home."

He chuckles. "It would sound pretty good, wouldn't it?"

"It would," I agree. "You know, one day, we should write a song together and then sing it as a duet."

He chuckles again. "You are so ambitious sometimes."

"That is the best compliment you've ever given me." I lick my lips and move in to kiss him, hoping he doesn't lean away.

"What are we going to tell our parents about us?" he asks as my mouth inches toward his.

"I think we should hold off on telling them for a while; otherwise, they might put restrictions on our time together, and I don't want that."

"Agreed."

Our lips connect, breaths mingling.

I'm about to dive into the kiss when someone taps on the window. When I turn my head, I see William grinning at us from the other side.

"So, this is why you wouldn't hook up with me?" he asks with a shit-eating grin on his face. "Wow, I knew you were all about being nice to everyone, but seriously, you've lowered your standards to him?"

"You're just pissed off because he kicked your ass," I say haughtily. "Nice nose by the way."

"You little cunt." He reaches for the handle.

Ayden shoves me back into the passenger seat and gets out of the car as William opens the door. Ayden has him by a few inches, but William is definitely bulkier. Ayden once called William a steroid freak, and with his moodiness, I'm starting to wonder myself. Or perhaps he's just an asshole.

"You're going to walk away, back to the party, before I bash my knuckles into your face again." Ayden's voice is low and firm, and his hands are balled at his sides as he struggles to remain cool.

William's fingers dart to his crooked nose, probably remembering what happened the last time Ayden punched him. "Whatever. You two can go fuck yourselves," he spats, then storms back to the party.

Ayden slides back into the driver's seat and shuts the door, locking us in.

"Well, at least I got my first encounter with him over with." I blow out a shaky breath. I don't like the vile feeling stirring inside me.

"Tonight's been full of drama, hasn't it?" He tucks a strand of my hair behind my ear, and his fingers linger on my cheeks. "I won't let him hurt you."

"I can take care of myself, Ayden, but thank you. For protecting me."

A smile touches his lips then he leans over the console to kiss me. But before our lips can reunite, his phone vibrates.

Sighing, he moves back to retrieve his phone and check the message. A frown etches on his face as he glances at the screen. "We have to go home."

"Why . . . We still have an hour and a half left before curfew."

"Because . . . the police are after a man that fits the description of the guy we saw that night standing in front of the house."

"Why are they after him? Was he hanging around outside your house again?"

His eyes are wide, sheer terror radiating from his pupils. "No he broke into my house."

CHAPTER 11

WE TEXT SAGE AND NOLAN, telling them they have to find their own ride home, then we leave the party. By the time Ayden and I arrive at the house, my parents and the entire Gregory family have gathered in the living room of my home because Fiona, Kale, and Everson are too scared to go home. So scared, in fact, that they all brought their sleeping bags and pillows over to spend the night.

After we walk in, they sit us down and tell us what happened.

When the Gregorys came home from dinner, Uncle Ethan caught the guy snooping around in Ayden's room. Before they could do anything, the guy dove out the window. Uncle Ethan chased him for a mile but lost him in the park where a neighborhood Christmas party was taking place. The police are currently searching for the man and dusting for fingerprints even though Uncle Ethan is pretty sure the guy was wearing gloves. The worst part, though, was the tattoo Ethan saw on the back of the man's neck—black ink and circles around solid lined symbols. While he didn't get a really good look at it, he's pretty sure it's the same tattoo that Ayden has branded on his side.

"We're going to find a way to get that tattoo off you." Uncle Ethan says to Ayden as he paces the living room, more riled up then I've ever seen him. "We'll get you laser surgery or you can go get it covered up, but it's coming off."

"Fine by me," Ayden mutters, shutting his eyes and sucking in a breath.

"The police also want you, Lyric, and Ethan to go in and look at pictures," Aunt Lila says. "See if maybe someone can identify him."

"Okay," all three of us mutter simultaneously.

The room grows quiet as reality seeps in. The guy had the same tattoo, which means he has to be part of the group that held Ayden hostage three years ago.

"We should turn a movie on," Aunt Lila suggests to my mother, breaking the silence. "It might take everyone's minds off this and help them fall asleep."

My mother agrees and the two of them start rifling through the DVD collection while my dad and Uncle Ethan wander into the kitchen to make a snack for everyone.

Ayden remains pretty quiet as Lila asks everyone what they want to watch. His silence is concerning me. He says stress sets off his panic attacks.

I scoot close to him on the sofa. "Want to go up to my room and talk?" I whisper in his ear.

Ayden nods once then gets to his feet, pulling me up with him.

"Where are you going?" Everson asks. At fourteen-years-old, the kid is sassy for his age, but I prefer his sassiness over Kale's gaping, especially after what Ayden told me.

Lila glances up from a stack of DVDs on the coffee table. "Ayden, you can't go anywhere, not for a while, anyway."

"Lyric and I are just going up to her room, if that's okay?" he asks politely. "We need to work on some songs."

"Songs?" Lila asks, her face contorted with puzzlement.

"Did your father hire you, then?" my mother asks as she searches the couch cushions for the remote.

"Yep, he sure did." Even though the night ended stressfully, I still glow with excitement and nerves, knowing that, in less than a week, I'll be doing my first performance.

"Good. I'm proud of you." She discovers the remote near the fireplace. "Just make sure you're careful, okay? The environment at those kinds of things is very adult."

"Mom, I turn eighteen in two months. I'm pretty much an adult already."

"You'll always be my little girl, Lyric Scott."

"Aw, are you getting soft on me, Mom?" I dramatically touch my hand to my heart. "Usually, you're the tough one and Dad gets all emotional."

"I am the tough one." She sternly points the remote at me. "But I love you just as much as him, which is why I'm going to come to the performance and keep an eye on you."

I dramatically stomp my foot. "Crap, there goes my plan of doing drugs and hooking up with guys all night."

"Lyric Scott." Her eyes enlarge as she shoots a warning look, pressing that we have an audience. "There are children in the room."

"Not really." Fiona's been doodling in her sketchpad the entire time we've been home but stops drawing to chime in. "I'm the youngest and I'm almost fourteen, which hardly makes me a kid anymore."

"You are a child." Lila sternly points a finger at her. "No matter how hard you try, Fiona Gregory, no matter how much makeup you put on, you are still my little girl."

"You know," I intervene, offering my two cents. "I've often wondered why my mom and you and even Uncle Ethan and Dad use our last names when you're angry. I mean, it's not like we don't know who you're talking to if you just say our first names."

"Lyric Scott," Aunt Lila scolds me, but then smiles. "Fine, you have a good point, but like how you and Ayden hold hands all the time, using your last names when we're angry is something we're going to do." She glances at my and Ayden's clasped fingers.

Kale tracks her gaze and frowns, like he's just realizing Ayden and I do such a thing. On top of feeling awkward, I feel bad for him. I've had a ton of crushes over the last few years, and it never feels all that great when you realize nothing will ever happen with the person you're momentarily obsessed with.

Ayden's grip on my hand strengthens. "We should go get that thing done," he says to me.

"Thing?" Her attention descends to our hands. "I thought you guys were going to work on a song."

"We are," I say, hurrying toward the doorway before they can stop us.

"Keep the door open!" she calls out after us.

"Do you think she knows?" I hiss as I steer Ayden toward the kitchen to grab a snack before we head upstairs.

"About what?" Realization clicks and his jaw drops to the floor. "You mean about us . . . kissing?"

I nod as we enter the kitchen. The air smells of cinnamon and hot chocolate and makes my mouth water. "Yeah, it seemed like she might have known about us."

"Known what about you?" my dad asks, his voice scaring the bejesus out of me.

I slam to a stop near the island, quickly realizing he and Ethan might have overheard us.

"Um, that Ayden and I haven't gotten any of our homework done over holiday break," I lie poorly.

My dad pops a chunk of chocolate into his mouth then trades a look with Ethan. "You two seem awful nervous right now."

I rack my brain for what to say and catch a whiff of cigarette smoke. *Jackpot!* My out.

"About as nervous as you two," I retort, scooping up a couple of pieces of fudge from off a platter on the countertop.

"What do you mean?" The microwave beeps. "We're not nervous."

"Maybe you should be." I hand Ayden a piece of the fudge and stuff one into my mouth. "I can smell you from all the way over here." The chocolate melts in my mouth. So delicious. Aunt Lila makes the best fudge.

He removes a bowl from the microwave, then tenses. "I have no idea what you're talking about." He exchanges another look with Uncle Ethan.

"I can smell it on you, too," I tell Uncle Ethan and his expression plunges, his back stiffly straightening like a bolt of lightning just zapped him. "I'm not going to nark or anything. Just thought I'd let you know." I shovel a handful of candy from a glass dish then tug Ayden out of the room with me before anything else can be said.

"You've always known how to talk your way out of things," Ayden says as we ascend the stairway. "But I've never seen you make them squirm like that."

"If I didn't try something, then they would have pried the truth out of us with their parental mind control skills," I joke, pushing open my bedroom door.

I flip on the lights, wrestle out of my jacket, and scarf down the remaining candy. Then I kick my boots off and flop down on the bed.

"You want to talk about why you're so quiet?" I ask with my mouth full of candy gooeyness.

He shuts the door and slumps against it. "I'm just trying to process everything." He lets out a shaky breath. "Why the hell was the guy in the house? A guy who clearly has to be part of that group." He touches his side where his tattoo is hidden beneath his shirt.

I stretch out on my stomach, pondering the possibilities. "Maybe he wasn't part of the group," I say, trying to remain optimistic. "Maybe he just had a tattoo that looked the same. Maybe he was just breaking in to steal stuff and Uncle Ethan scared him off before he could take anything."

Ayden frowns. "There seems to a lot of maybes."

"I know." I sigh and bend my knees so my feet are in the air. "But I still don't get it. Say he's one of those people."

"Soulless mileas," he mumbles as he sinks to the floor, brings his knees up, and slumps his head against the door. "That's what they're called."

Hearing the name of them makes the situation even more unsettling. "Okay, let's say he is part of this group and he was the guy outside staring at your window. He's obviously been watching you and the house, but then why break in when no one's home? To just go in your room? There had to be a point."

"Maybe he thought I was in there and was coming after me?"

"Maybe, but Aunt Lila and Uncle Ethan usually turn off all the lights when no one's home." I trace my finger across my lips. "What if he was looking for something else besides you?"

"Like what? I don't have anything. Nothing important anyway."

"What if he left something then?"

He lifts his head and cocks a brow. "Have you been reading mystery books again?"

"Yeah, so what?" I push up from the bed and kneel down in front of him. "It wouldn't hurt to look around your room, would it?"

He traces the scars on the back of his hand. "It might."

"I'll go look then." I start to get up.

He snatches hold of my arm and pulls me back down, swiftly shaking his head. "I'm not going to risk your safety over mine."

"They don't want me," I remind him. "I'll be okay."

"They want everyone." He continues to trace the pale scars, while dazing off over my shoulder. "They came from fingernails."

"What did?"

"The scars on the back of my hand. That and metal cuffs." When our gazes weld together, his grey eyes fiercely scorch. "Still want to go over there?"

My lips quiver as I nod, telling myself that it's just next-door and our parents will be only a yard length away. Everything will be fine. But Ayden seems like he believes the exact opposite, as if at any moment someone is going to charge through the door and steal us both.

"In the morning, we'll check things out," he says with uncertainty. "I'm not taking you over there when it's dark. And only hours after the guy was in the house. Besides, maybe the police will catch him by tomorrow."

"So, what do we do for the rest of the night then? Because we have to do something. Otherwise, we'll just sit around and drive ourselves crazy with worry." I sound innocent, but my body and mind are hyper aware that we're in my room with my bed only a few feet away.

He straightens his legs and rises to his feet. "We really could work on a song."

I perk up. "You want to write one with me?"

"We could try." He cracks the door, leaving it open like Aunt Lila said. "I'm not sure how good it'll be, though."

"I think we might rock it." I cross the room to my bookshelf. The bottom row is lined with a collection of CDs my dad gave me. "What's your choice of poison?" I ask as I skim the titles.

He crouches down beside me. "Something relaxing. I don't think I can handle any more stress tonight."

"Hmmm . . ." I thrum my finger against my lips then select a CD. Going over to my nightstand, I open the case, remove the disc, and feed the player my disc.

"What is this?" Ayden walks up behind me, causing my skin to tingle.

The sensation is insignificant to what I felt earlier today on Sage's couch. My very first orgasm, and it was better than any scenario I'd ever conjured up in my very creative mind.

I skip through the songs and land on one of my favorites. "'Civilian' by Wye Oak."

"Do I get a mark against me because I don't know them?" He tangles his fingers through my hair and sweeps the strands aside. Then he does something unexpected but amazing. He rests his chin on my shoulder. A gesture so small and plain an outsider wouldn't think twice about it.

Me, I think a lot about it.

So much my mind sparks like a hot-wired car.

"This is nice." I rest against his chest and his arms enclose around my waist. His nerves are still evident with the fumbling movement of his hands and his heart pounding against his chest and my back.

He places delicate kisses on my shoulder, savoring the taste of my flesh. My head uncontrollably falls back, my neck arched and exposed, seeking more of his gentle touches.

"Lyric," he whispers, his mouth moving against the arch of my neck. "I need you to promise me one thing."

I bob my head up and down, my eyes rolling into the back of my head as my eyelashes flutter. I would promise him anything right now.

"Promise me that if this gets to be too much—if at any point you feel like I'm bringing you down—you'll walk away."

"That will never happen."

"Just promise me, okay. I need to know that I'll never ruin the amazing person that you are."

Shaking my head, I spin around and loop my arms around the back of his neck. "You'll never ruin me. You add to my amazingness, not hinder it." His lips part in protest, but I talk over him, "But if you really need me to promise then I will. Just know that I'll never feel that way."

He seems somewhat satisfied by my answer.

"Now, no more stress." I grab his hand, push him back, then raise our arms and spin around like a ballerina. "Let's write beautiful lyrics together."

He laughs and twirls me around again. My dress spins around my waist, dancing with me, and my hair flows behind me like a flag in the wind.

After a few more twists, we hop on my bed and get situated with some pillows, a notebook, and a pen.

"I'll write the lyrics with you, but it's up to you to sing them." He fluffs a pillow then lies down beside me.

I prop up on my elbow. "For right now, I will. But one day in the future, I will get to hear you sing, Shy Boy."

"And what if I suck?"

"Then you suck, but at least I'll have gotten the chance to hear you."

"All right, just know that you've been warned."

I salute him. "You've done your duty, my dear friend. Now, what should we write about?"

He shrugs, rotating on his side and propping up on his elbow. "I don't know. What do you want to write about?"

We ponder our options while the song plays through and changes to the next.

"I never knew it could be like this," Ayden finally says, his lips quirking.

I'm not sure if he's talking to me or mumbling a lyric, but I write it down anyway.

His eyes drift to the ceiling as he ponders the next line. "Kissing the air from her lungs."

"*Her,* huh?" I pen what he said down. "Guess I'm a lesbian in this one."

He chuckles and I grin.

"And the heavens rain stars down on us." I scribble across the paper.

"Pieces of shimmering gold around us."

"Pouring warmth all over us."

"Kiss me until I can no longer breathe."

"Raveling me up with you until I can hardly think."

That's how far we make it before we start making out on my bed. We stick to kissing and getting tangled in the sheets, but we break our lip lock the moment Ayden starts having trouble breathing.

I can tell he's upset that he has to force us to stop. I talk around the subject and eventually manage to sidetrack his thoughts.

A little past two o'clock, Aunt Lila pokes her head into the room and tells us we should go to sleep. She doesn't make Ayden leave, but she does open the door all the way.

We start to drift off a while later, lying face to face

while Ayden strokes my cheek and stares deeply into my eyes.

That's the last thing I remember before the screaming starts.

CHAPTER 12

SCREAMING.

Screaming.

Screaming.

At first, I think I'm dreaming.

But when my eyes shoot open, I realize I'm not.

I search frantically for where the noise is coming from. But the lights are off and nightfall is heavy and thick against my vision. The yelling is coming from somewhere close. Somewhere in my room. But I have no idea where.

I sit up in my bed and fumble around in the dark until I feel my lamp. I tug on the cord, clicking it on. Light flows around my room and I realize Ayden isn't in my bed. The screaming has stopped, though.

I hold my breath, waiting anxiously for someone to run into my room, because someone had to have heard it. But my house is fairly big and the walls are fairly sound-proof and sometimes sounds get muffled.

When no one shows up, I stumble out of bed and peek under my bed, then head for my closet, the only other place he could be in my room. When I open the door, Ayden is huddled in the corner with his arms wrapped around his knees. He's rocking back and forth, staring at the wall. His eyes are huge, glossy, dazed, and out of touch with reality.

I cautiously approach him, worried I might spook him if I move too quickly. The closer I get, the more I realize he's not awake; he's sleep walking. Everson used to do it when he first arrived at the Gregory's. He actually walked over to our house one night and tried to get inside. My mother thought it was an intruder and almost called the police. Thankfully, Aunt Lila found him before that happened. She gently guided him home, telling my mother that, if it ever happened again, to not wake him up; he'd get hysterical if she did.

Deciding I need to find Aunt Lila, I turn around.

"Where are you going?" Ayden mumbles. "You can't leave here."

I freeze and peer over my shoulder. He still seems in the same condition, spaced off in dreamland.

"I'm just going to get your mom," I say quietly, turning to leave again.

"Your mom's dead," he utters. "She's dead, and she left you here to rot with us."

An eerie chill slithers up my spine, like a bolt of electricity zapped me in the back.

"Ayden, my mom's fine. She's just asleep like everyone else."

"There's no sleeping in this house." His eyes are fastened on the spot of carpet in front of his feet. "We don't sleep, not until the ritual."

A massive lump wedges in my throat. Absolutely terrified and with no clue what to do, I leave him there and race down the hallway to my parents' room, hoping he doesn't go anywhere. I give my mother a shake to wake her up then tell her what's happening. She immediately stumbles out of bed and runs into the guest room to wake up Aunt Lila.

"Where is he?" Aunt Lila asks, hopping out of bed and throwing on her robe.

I point down the hallway. "In the closet in my room."

She races into my room with my mother and me following. She sticks her head inside the closet, and her shoulders relax.

I relax, too, but only a little because I can still remember what Ayden said to me. His words are an echo in my head. His mother was dead while he was with those people. He wasn't allowed to sleep until the ritual.

What the hell?

"Come on, sweetie," Aunt Lila speaks tenderly as she holds onto Ayden's arm and guides him out of the closet. Ayden is still asleep and can hardly stay on his feet as they make a winding path to my bed.

Once he's lying down on the mattress, Lila turns to me. "Lyric, would you mind if I slept on the floor?" she asks in a hushed tone. "I want to keep an eye on him, but I'm worried that, if I try to get him into the guest room, I might wake him up."

"Lyric can sleep on the sofa." My mom pets my head like she used to do when I was child.

"Yeah, of course." I grab a folded up quilt from the trunk at the foot of the bed.

"Thank you." Aunt Lila draws the comforter over Ayden.

"I'll go get a sleeping bag for you," my mother tells Aunt Lila then hurries out of the room.

I start to follow her but Aunt Lila calls me back.

"What exactly happened?" She momentarily stares out the window then tugs the cord and closes the blinds.

I shrug, hugging the quilt to my chest. "I was woken up by a scream and found him in the closet."

"Did he . . . say anything to you?" Her question is casual as well as her demeanor, but it almost looks forced.

"He was muttering some stuff." I omit the details, figuring I'll tell Ayden in the morning and let him decide if he wants to tell her.

"Are you sure you couldn't understand what he was saying?" She studies me from across the room.

I shake my head. Something feels off. It's like she already knows the answer to her question and only wants me to confirm it. "I'm going to get set up on the sofa."

I leave the room, feeling strange and really uncomfortable in my own home. The feelings amplify when I realize I'll be sharing the living room with Kale, Everson, and Fiona.

The three of them are sprawled out on the floor, fast asleep in their sleeping bags. It's like a maze to get through them to the sofa.

"Is he going to be okay?" Fiona suddenly asks while I'm making a bed on the couch near the fireplace.

I jump from the sound of her voice. "I thought you were asleep."

"I was, but then Ayden woke me up." She rolls over in her sleeping bag and stares at me. A fire is crackling, my parents' heat source during the mild winters in California. Fiona's eyes glow orange, the flames reflecting in her pupils. Dark strands of hair poke out of her braided hair at every angle.

"You heard his screaming?" I ask.

She shakes her head. "No, I felt it."

My brows knit. "I'm not sure what you're talking about."

"Most people don't." She turns over like nothing about the conversation is strange.

Although, it is.

The entire night has been strange.

I just cross my fingers, hoping that, by morning, things will have returned to normal.

CHAPTER 13

Ayden

"I DON'T KNOW WHAT TO say," I mumble to Lyric the next day after the break-in.

It's late in the evening and the pale pink glow of the sunset streams though my window. We're in my bedroom, searching for something the guy might have left, but so far, we have come up empty-handed. For the last five minutes, Lyric has been explaining to me what happened last night, how I talked to her in my sleep. The things I said to her . . . I feel so embarrassed. She has to be afraid of me now, right?

While I don't give a reason aloud as to what caused my sleepwalking and talking, I have a theory that perhaps it has something to do with the amnesia session. My therapist told me that it could cause an increase in night terrors and problems with sleeping

"You don't need to say anything," Lyric says as she hauls my dresser away from the wall and peers behind it. "I just wanted to let you know what happened so you can decide if you want to tell your mom and dad."

"You said Lila was acting strange?" I flatten myself on the floor on my stomach to check under my bed. Having no idea what I'm searching for, the task seems pretty much pointless, though.

"She was acting like she knew you told me stuff about your past." Lyric purses her lips as she glances around my room. "If I was a creepy guy trying to leave something in a room, where would I put it?"

I push to my feet. "I don't know. I'm still not convinced that's why he was in here, anyway."

"Maybe." She flops down on my unmade bed, seemingly unsure about something. "Has Fiona ever said anything weird to you before?"

"Like what?" I rummage around in my nightstand drawer, but the only thing in there is my notebook full of lyrics.

"I don't know." She shrugs. "She just said something strange to me last night, something about feeling you scream instead of hearing it."

"That's strange, but she kind of marches to the beat of her own drum." I shut the drawer. "Ever since I moved in, I've noticed she draws butterflies obsessively. She says she can't get them out of her head."

"What's her story?" Lyric asks, looking under my bedspread. "I know she came here when she was seven, but that's about it."

"Her mother was a drug addict like mine. She got taken away and ended up here. That's about all I know."

"Strange." Lyric contemplates something as her gaze deliberately sweeps my room. "Wait a minute . . . Are you sure he didn't *take* anything? Like maybe something Aunt Lila and Uncle Ethan didn't know you had?"

"I have a couple of things . . ." I open the top drawer and my heart skips a beat. "My knife is gone."

"The one you were trying to give Rebel Tonic?"

"Yeah, but why would he take that," I glide the drawer shut and rub my jawline, "out of all the things in this house that have value?"

"Maybe it wasn't for value purposes." Her skin suddenly pales as her eyes widen.

"What's wrong?" I ask, sitting down on the bed beside her.

"Don't be mad, okay, but last night, after the incident, I couldn't sleep, so I did some searching on the Internet about the soulless mileas." She collects my laptop from the nightstand, sets it on her lap, and boots up the screen. "I think I remember something about rituals and needing an object that belongs to the person the ritual is for."

"Why?"

"Hold on." Her fingers hammer against the keys as she types something in the browser then pulls up a page. "Read here." She taps her finger against the screen

Leaning over her shoulder, I skim the paragraph then frown. "Where did you find this website?"

"After like ten searches, it popped up." She shudders. "It says they need something off you too . . . like a belonging you carry or fingernails—weird stuff like that. It's so crazy. That people do this . . . it gives me chills."

I rub my eyes and reread the paragraph again. "It's pretty vague about what the rituals are for."

"You talked about a ritual last night," she says cautiously. "Do you remember anything about it?"

A hot branding iron,
melting the flesh.
Forever marking you with our sins.

Little images sear inside my brain, ironically while I'm not in therapy. My fingers graze the homemade tattoo hidden beneath my shirt and distorted memories jolt through my mind. This mark was their mark. The mark of their group . . . What I would give to get rid of the ink on my skin, forget it was ever put on me, forget what it symbolizes—pure evil. "It might have something to do with this, but that's about all I can remember." I lower my head into my hands as my temples throb. Between this, the guy breaking in, and still no response from Rebel Tonic, I have a headache. "We need to tell Lila and Ethan about this."

Lyric slams the laptop shut. "Okay, but you also need a break." She stands up and slips a hand around my wrist, giving my arm a gentle tug. "How about we go get ready for the art show? We probably can head out there soon, too, if you're ready?"

"I'm not sure I'm allowed to go to that anymore. Lila said something about me staying home as much as possible."

"She's going to the art show, so I'm sure it'll be okay."

"How do you know that?"

"Because I was eavesdropping on her and my mom this morning and heard them talking about it?" She frees my wrist when I finally get up from the bed. "I guess Aunt Lila is catering the event."

"Hear anything interesting?" I grab my blue hoodie from the closet.

"Not really." She frowns, disappointed. "They mostly just talked about the type of cake to serve and what wine my mom wants."

"I really should press her more about that letter." I slide my arms through the sleeves of my jacket.

"But you won't." She opens my bedroom door. "Because you're too nice."

"I just don't want to come off sounding ungrateful." I follow her out of the room and down the hallway. "Especially with everything that's been going on. They have to be stressed out and I'm the one causing that stress."

"I'm sure they don't look at it like that." She slips her

fingers through mine as we head downstairs to the kitchen. "I mean, my parents have put up with a lot of shit from me over the years, and I know for a fact they still love and want me. It comes with being a parent. Unconditional love no matter how much of a pain in the ass your kids are. And besides, this thing going on isn't your fault. It's completely out of your control."

"I still brought it into their lives."

"Yeah, but like I heard Aunt Lila say that night, they knew it was a possibility that this could happen and they still chose to adopt you." She gives my hand a comforting squeeze. "That's how special you are."

Even though I don't entirely agree with her, I brush my lips against hers. "Thank you."

"Thank you," she says, then she grabs the back of my head and fiercely kisses me back.

Her tongue slips out and parts my lips, causing a shudder to ripple through my body. A good shudder. One that makes me excruciatingly ache inside, long for more.

Suddenly, the door bangs shut. Lyric and I jump apart, breathless and gasping for air. Lila strolls into the kitchen with grocery bags in her hands.

"Oh good, I was just about to go look for you two," she says, dropping the bags on the countertop. "I need your help."

"With what?" Lyric asks, still holding my hand as she roams over to the counter.

Lila undoes the buttons on her coat and shucks it off. "With my event tonight. I had a few waitresses cancel and I need fill ins."

"You want us to mingle with my mother's pretentious clients." Lyric scrunches up her nose.

"They're not pretentious." Lila digs around in the bag and starts pulling out cans of condensed milk and stacking them on the counter. "They're artists, like you."

Lyric sits down on a barstool. "And I'm very pretentious."

Lila shakes her head, but smiles. "Oh Lyric, you remind me so much of your father sometimes. Always so full of sarcasm."

"Why thank you," Lyric replies, beaming with pride. "Because of your compliment, I'll give you a free night of my ever-so-awesome waitressing skills."

A laugh slips from my lips as I sit down beside her. "Guess that means you get mine, too," I tell Lila. "But mine aren't so awesome."

"That's okay." She throws the empty bag into the drawer. "At this point I'll take whatever I can get."

We start opening the cans of milk while Lila whisks eggs in a bowl, giving us directions on how to make cheese fondue. After a few minutes, Lyric whispers for me to tell Lila about the knife.

I loathe giving her more bad news, knowing she's only going to get more stressed than she already is. I still recap the details, and Lila rushes out of the kitchen to call the detective and tell him.

"She seems upset." I open the fridge to grab a stick of butter.

"Of course she's upset." Lyric takes the butter from me and drops the stick into a small plastic bowl. "You're her son and some creepy dude snuck into your room and stole a knife from you because he believes in some icky ritual."

"We don't know that for sure," I tell her as she places the bowl into the microwave and presses the timer.

"I'm betting that's what the detective will say to her. They're investigating this group, right? They have to know about their rituals."

I hate that she's probably right about the group and the rituals. That she knows so much about this. That stuff like this exists in our lives.

When Lila returns to the kitchen a minute later, her eyes are bloodshot and her cheeks are streaked with the remnants of tears.

"Ayden, you need to make sure that you have someone with you at all times for the next few days." She goes right back to mixing.

Lyric and I trade a look from across the kitchen island.

"How come?" Lyric aligns the lid of the can with the opener and opens the top. "Because the man still hasn't been caught?"

"Yes. It's just a safety measure until they can track down the guy and find out if he's part of this group—get a positive ID on him. They dusted for fingerprints but nothing came up." Lila taps an egg against the side of the bowl and separates the shell. "The detective brought up the therapy sessions and wants to have another visit to discuss how they're going. He said we could do it when you guys go down to look through some photos."

"I don't know why he wants to visit about that. Nothing's changed. I still can't remember," I mumble as the microwave dings.

"Honey, that's not your fault." Lila retrieves the bowl of melted butter from the microwave. "You're doing everything you can by trying."

I nod, unable to speak. I feel like such a failure over the fact that I've gotten nowhere with my memories because my fear of remembering is hindering the progress.

"Ethan's going to have to go to the concert with you guys," Lila adds as she pours the butter in with the eggs. "I mean, we were going to go already, but he's going to have to be backstage with you, to keep an eye on things."

"Are you sure this is just for safety measures?" Lyric questions as she pries the top of another can open, trading a suspicious glance with me.

"Of course. What else would it be for?" she asks, wiping her hands on a towel.

Excellent question. If they're not even positive who this man is or why he broke into the house? I think of my brother and how his body was found by that house.

Maybe that's what this is about.

Maybe Lila knows the real reason the man was in the house.

Maybe he was coming after me.

CHAPTER 14

THE NEXT WEEK PASSES RATHER quickly, but that might just be because I'm stressed out. We all are. Even at my mother's slamming art show, we were all a wreck. Fiona kept saying she had a feeling someone was watching us, or more specifically Ayden. After what she said that night, the girl has utterly creeped out.

Most days, everyone just kind of hangs out at the house, waiting for news that never gets delivered. Ayden and I are only allowed to be by ourselves when we're at band practice, a place that's quickly becoming our sanctuary through all of this, even though we work our butts off to learn one of the songs I wrote. Actually, the one Ayden and I wrote together.

After a lot of contemplating and Ayden refusing to let us sing one of his songs, I decide we should do the one we wrote. We had to complete it first, though, which took us an entire night, a six-pack of Dr. Pepper, and an endless amount of gummy worms.

But we did it.

Saturday night the tension in our lives briefly lifts like thinning fog. Because Saturday night is club opening night and our band's first gig. I'm ecstatic the entire day until we're actually at the club. Then reality kicks me in the face.

"Oh, my God, I think I'm going to puke," I whisper as I peek out onto the stage. "There are so many people out there."

"You'll be fine." Ayden rubs my back. "And just remember, only you and I are in the room."

Easier said than done when there are two hundred plus people buzzing with energy all crammed into one room. We're the first band up, too, something I sarcastically thanked my dad for.

"I'm suddenly wondering why I begged to do this so much." My eyes remain fixed on the floor. In the midst of the madness, near the bar, I spot my mom and Aunt Lila throwing back shots. Awesome. Guess Ayden and I are going to be DD since they were our ride here.

Uncle Ethan and my dad are around, shuffling people here and there, dictating what to do. The last time I saw my dad, he looked like a wreck, his bedhead/fauxhawk look in full form. I'd feel bad for him, but he's always said opening a club has been a dream of his for the last ten years, so I figure all the stress has to be worth it.

Most dreams are, right?

"Because it's your dream," Ayden reminds me as his hands travel up to my shoulders. His fingers work their magic, unwinding the knots in my muscles. "You can do this, Lyric. I know you can. You're the bravest person I know."

"Then you clearly don't know yourself."

"I'm not brave at all," he utters quietly. "I couldn't even make it through the start of my amnesia therapy without freaking out."

I embrace his touch as his arms circle my waist. "You'll get there. It'll just take some time."

"Tell that to Detective Rannali. He's getting super pushy about doing more sessions, like the entire case is riding on it. I don't get it, though. Even my therapist says the therapy isn't a guarantee, that there's a chance it won't work."

"Fuck Detective Rannali. It's easy for him to be pushy and expectant when he's not the one lying in that chair, facing what you are."

"But I don't even know what I'm facing." He rests his forehead against the back of my head, and his erratic breathing tickles the back of my neck. "I'm scared of what I'll see."

It's the first time he's flat-out admitted he is afraid. I wish I could take away his fear, wish I could free him from his pain.

"I'm here for you if you ever need to talk." It's all I can offer him, but I hope it's enough.

"I know." He grazes his lips across the back of my head. "Can we talk about something else now? Before I get all riled up."

I nod. "Um, did you see all the freaking musicians when we walked in? I seriously about died."

"Yeah, your dad's got mad connections."

"Sage is totally working it, too. He went right for the first girl he saw. I think she plays drums for one of the bands. I'll give it to him. She's pretty hot."

Ayden chuckles under his breath. "I love how you can openly say stuff like that, but just so you know, you look hot," he whispers in my ear, his breath hot on my skin.

I shiver from the caress of his breath and glance down at my boots, netted tights, and plaid dress that hugs my body. My hair is down, black liner frames my eyes, and my lips shine with gloss.

"So do you." I whirl around to face him. His black hair

hangs in his eyes, he's wearing the leather collar because I suggested it would be fun to wear for one night, and he has on a red shirt and black jeans held up by a studded belt. "My gothically adorable friend."

"You know, I think we should create a Lyric Scott dictionary and sell it online."

"We'll definitely have to look into that," I agree, fiddling with the collar on his neck. "I have so many more words sloshing around in my head."

I angle my head up towards his face. When our gazes fasten, our mouths magnetize toward each other. My breathing quickens and so does his. His dark eyes smolder with passion, and my skin hums with nearly unbearable heat. God, I want to kiss him all the time. It's crazy how much I want to kiss him.

This is how it's been between us for the last week. The moment we look at each other, we start making out and are unable to keep our hands off each other. I seriously feel like I have no control over myself anymore, and I'm kind of glad. I love, love, love losing myself in him.

I always have to be careful, though. Ayden has no problem with touching me, but I can't even slip my fingers up his shirt without sending him into a panic attack.

"You guys about ready to go on?" Uncle Ethan's voice instantly puts a lid on the moment.

We push apart, our breathing ragged. We turn to the side, and Ayden immediately withdraws his hands from my waist the moment he catches sight of Uncle Ethan's questioning expression.

"Um . . ." Ayden struggles with what to say.

"You're on in five." Uncle Ethan's attention flicks between the two of us before he hurries off toward the hallway where the rest of the bands are hanging out.

"Do you think he saw us?" Ayden asks worriedly as

he faces me again.

I shrug. "I'm not sure. It kind of looked like it."

"What are we going to do if he did?"

"I don't know. He might not say anything to anyone. This is Uncle Ethan we're talking about. He rarely says anything."

"Yeah, but us about to kiss . . ." Ayden makes a wary face. "I kind of doubt he'll keep quiet about that."

I open my mouth to tell him not to stress about it when Sage and Nolan come strolling up.

"This is so fucking awesome." Nolan bounces up and down on the balls of his feet, pumped up.

Sage leans around me to get a glimpse of the crowd. "Dude, the place is packed."

Place.

Crowds.

People watching me.

Watching me sing.

What if I suck?

I'm suddenly reminded that I have bigger problems than whether or not Ethan is going to out my and Ayden's relationship.

My stomach churns. "I think I'm going to throw up." I slap my hand across my mouth and push past Ayden, running into the restroom. I lock myself in the stall, drop to my knees, and puke up every ounce of the chicken I ate for dinner.

My belly is empty by the time I sit down on the floor. "I can't do this," I mutter. "I really can't."

A moment or two ticks by, then I hear the click of heels on the other side of the stall.

"Lyric, are you in here?" my mother hisses.

"Yeah," I say with a groan. "I think I'm too sick to go on stage, though."

She gives the stall door a shake. "Open up. Now."

I kneel up and unlatch the door then sit back down. She walks in with a glass half full of wine, and I notice her eyes are a little glazed. She takes one look at me then shuts the stall.

"You have to do this." She tears some tissue from off the roll and hands it to me.

"I know. I know. Or Dad will hate me." I dab the sides of my mouth and under my eyes then toss the tissue into the toilet.

"No, because you'll regret it if you don't." She pats the top of my head. "Trust me, your dad will forgive you if you bail. Will he be upset? Probably for a while, but he loves you too much to stay mad at you. But trust me when I say that regret is much harder to get over."

"You're speaking from personal experience, aren't you?" I stare up at her, the woman who shares the same eyes as me and is probably one of the coolest people I know. I look up to her for living her dream of becoming an artist.

She nods. "I am. There's a lot of stuff I have and haven't done in the past that I wish I could do differently."

I heave a weighted sigh. "Fine, I'll do it, but only because your pep talk is scaring me." I get to my feet, and then we exit the stall. I stop by the sink to wash my hands while my mom sets her wineglass down on the counter to fix her lipstick. While she's not paying attention, I pick it up and take a few swallows.

"Lyric Scott," she scolds, but I can tell she's working hard to be angry. "Don't ever do that again."

"Okay." I hand the glass back to her as the alcohol swims through my veins. I feel slightly mellower, but not a whole lot. I still manage to exit the bathroom and walk backstage where Sage, Nolan, and Ayden are waiting.

"You going to be okay?" Ayden asks, brushing my matted hair from my forehead.

I nod, but don't say anything as vomit burns at the back of my throat again. "No regrets. No regrets. No regrets," I chant under my breath.

"What are you saying?" Sage asks, semi-distracted by the stage.

"Nothing." I turn my back to him and keep chanting until we're called out.

"This is it," I whisper to myself. Then I raise my chin, square my shoulders, and march out onto the stage.

The lights are blinding, and the crowd is eagerly cheering, even though they have no clue who we are. I remember all the times I've cheered bands on and wonder if this is how any of those singers felt, as if they'd swallowed a thousand butterflies on crack.

Ayden and Nolan plug their guitars in and do a quick tuning and sound check. Sage does a few warm up beats while I stand in front of the microphone and adjust the height of the stand an unnecessary amount of times.

Then the strum of a guitar ripples through the amp and floats over the crowd. The entire room silences and people stare at me, waiting to be dazzled by my talent.

I'm supposed to say something. My dad told me what it was, but I can't remember.

"Um . . . we're Alyric Bliss," I murmur into the microphone, and my dad's words gradually come back to me. "And thanks for coming out. This one's called 'Raveling You.' "

Something as easy as a few sentence makes my knees threaten to buckle. I grasp the stand with my sweaty palms as Sage taps his drums. Then the three of them are playing, creating a flawless tune that swirls together and kisses the air. I just hope I don't fuck it up when I open my mouth.

The intro is pretty long, so I have to wait a seemingly endless amount of time before I sing, but the moment finally arrives.

I take a deep breath and part my lips.

"I never knew it could be like this, never thought such desire was possible, kissing the air from his lungs." My lips quirk at my slight word variation. "And the heavens rain stars down on us, pieces of shimmering gold around us, pouring warmth all over us. Kiss me until I can no longer breathe. Raveling me up with you until I can hardly think. God, please fucking kiss me before I crumble to pieces."

I move back as Ayden's guitar takes over. I suck in a few breaths, feeling less nervous. My voice is balanced, surprisingly smooth. Although, the next part will test it. The words move fast, and I have to push my voice to a near scream. In practice, I rocked it, but I'm worried now. My throat feels like sand paper after puking.

I step up to the mic again, grip the stand, and run my fingers through my hair as some guy whistles at me from the crowd. "You make me weak. You make me strong. You make me ache. You make me feel so wrong. You make me burn for just a taste. You make me, make me, so fucking insane!" My voice carries flawlessly over the room.

And I can't help myself.

I smile, realizing this dream of mine just might be possible.

I create magic for the next forty-five minutes, and by the time we're finished, I feel like I'm glowing.

"Thank you!" I shout into the microphone then bounce off stage with the biggest smile plastered on my face.

My skin is damp, I reek of sweat, and I'm the happiest I've been in a long time. I hug Sage and Nolan after we make it backstage, and then I throw my arms around Ayden and hug the crap out of him.

"That was so much fun," I say, then throw my head back when he lifts me up off the ground and spins me around and around.

"You were amazing," he whispers in my ear, sneaking a bite of my earlobe.

"So were you." I kiss his cheek, and then he plants my feet back down on the floor.

"Who wants to celebrate?" Sage's pumps a fist into the air, grasping a bottle of champagne.

"Where'd you get that?" I ask. "Did you steal it from one of the other bands or sneak it out from the bar?"

"Does it really matter?" He moves to pop the cork, but to no avail, showing his lack of experience with champagne bottles.

"Dammit, let me go find an opener." He strolls off, putting swagger in his step as he passes by a few older women batting their eyelashes and grinning at him.

"Oh, the life of a rock star." Grinning, I shake my head. "He's going to be a handful. Isn't he?"

"Probably," Ayden agrees with amusement. "Every band has one, though."

"So what do we do now?" My mind promptly conjures up very creative and vivid images.

"We could exchange our belated Christmas presents," he suggests. "It might be fun."

"I thought we were going to do that later? When we are happy."

"You look pretty happy right now."

"But what about you?"

"I'm happy just seeing you happy." When I hesitate, his brow cocks. "Do you really want to wait even longer? Or are you just procrastinating because you don't have mine?"

"I actually do." Which is the truth. But the present

isn't bought so I'm uncertain how much Ayden will like it. Still, it did come from the heart. "Alright, let's do this. Hand it over."

"I don't have it with me." He nods his head at the bar. "But we can go get our moms and head home and I'll give it to you. Lila's looking pretty tipsy anyway."

I stick out my elbow and he links arms with me. "Sounds like a deal."

AN HOUR LATER, AYDEN AND I are in my bedroom on my bed with the door open. Music is floating from my stereo and a soft trail of light flows from my lamp. My mom and Aunt Lila are downstairs with Kale, Everson, and Fiona, drunkenly chatting so loud we can hear them all the way upstairs.

"They're trashed," Ayden remarks as he tosses my present in the air like a baseball. It's small, about the size of mine, with shiny silver and purple wrapping paper.

"Not as bad as they were that one New Year's." My present for Ayden is secured in the palm of my hand. I'm nervous to give it to him. I don't know why. Maybe because the gift kind of means something? "Remember how giggly they were. The sounded like two silly teenage girls."

"You're a teenage girl," Ayden reminds me with a clever grin.

I smack my forehead with the heel of my hand. "Duh. Thanks for reminding me. I almost forgot."

He shakes his head, half grinning. Then he shoves his hand in my direction, presenting his gift. "You open yours first."

I snatch the present from him, tear open the paper, and lift the lid from the box. Inside are two leather bands with the words *Endlessly Yours* engraved on them.

"You mentioned once that your parents used to have leather bands that said forever on them and how they used to be best friends like us," he explains as I stare inside the box. "I remember how happy you looked when you told me about it and how you said that one day you were going to be with a guy that would get you something like that. I didn't want to make them exactly the same, though, so I went with endlessly yours."

I'm quiet for a lengthy amount of time, mainly because I'm way too emotionally overwhelmed to speak.

"You don't have to wear it if you don't want to," he says self-consciously. "Or you can keep them both and give the other to someone else one day."

I finally find my voice. "You said 'how they used to be best friends like us.'"

"Huh?"

"Just barely. You said that we used to be best friends like how my parents used to be friends."

Pink colors his cheeks. "Well, I didn't really mean it like that. We're still best friends now, like your parents are, too. I just meant that we were like them in the sense that we used to be friends but now we're . . ." He scratches at the back of his neck, glancing at the door like he wants to bolt.

I place my hand on his arm. "We're more than friends, Ayden." When I withdraw my hand, he turns his head and looks at me. I take the bracelets out of the box, slide one on my wrist, then slip the other on his. "And I think this is going to prove it even more." I hand my present to him.

He gingerly rips off the paper then opens the tiny box. "We think so alike it's frightening." He removes the two faded leather bracelets. Each one is engraved with *Forever*.

"Definitely, but I like that we do."

He puts the band on his wrist, then his fingers circle my arm and he slips the other bracelet on my wrist. His fingertips are right above my pulse and I wonder if he can feel how rapid my heart is racing. "Endlessly yours forever," he says, staring at the bracelets together.

"The ones I gave you actually belonged to my parents," I say when he doesn't release my wrist. "My mom gave them to me the other day when I asked her for present ideas. It kind of makes me wonder if she knows about us, since the bracelets are so symbolic to her and my dad's relationship."

"After tonight, I'm pretty sure Ethan might be wondering if something's up, too."

"I hope they don't know yet." My gaze flicks to the door then a smile curves at my lips as I lean in. "I like being able to be in my room alone with you." I stop when our lips are an inch away. "Thank you for my present."

"You're welcome . . . And thanks—" He eliminates the space between our mouths, cutting himself off.

I grab at his shirt and pull him down as I lie back on my bed. Our tongues entwine as our bodies align. When our chests collide, my heart slams inside my chest and knocks against his unsteady heartbeat. His hands skate across my body, along my curves, the arch of my breast, and my hips, his fingers tremulous as he rocks against me.

I moan and my fingers form a mind of their own, wandering, wandering, wandering to the bottom of his shirt. I want to touch him. Savor the feel of his skin, bask in every part of him like he's doing with me. My fingers delve under the hem, caress his skin, fleetingly relishing his smooth, solid muscles. But then those muscles tauten along with the rest of his body.

I quickly pull my hands out. "Sorry," I breathe against his lips.

"It's okay." His voice is raspy, his chest forcefully rising and falling. "Can you just touch me on the outside of my shirt?"

"Of course."

"I'm sorry," he sputters, battling for oxygen.

I cup his face between my hands. "Don't be sorry . . . You're perfect . . . Everything's perfect." *And I think I might be in love with you.*

The thought strikes me like bolt of lightning. Out of nowhere. So startling that I don't dare utter it aloud. Too afraid. Of how he'll react. Of how I'll react.

Instead, I just keep kissing him and falling.

Deeper, deeper, deeper
Into another world.
Where I don't even know who I am anymore.
But it's not a bad thing.
Just terrifying and confusing.
My head is so foggy yet clear.
My heart so alive, so vibrantly beating.
My body so needy, desperately seeking.
Him.
It's all about him.
Endlessly his.
Forever.

CHAPTER 15

THE NEXT COUPLE OF WEEKS fly by rather fast. Life begins to return to normal as no more incidents happen with the strange man who broke into the house. The police are still looking for him, but the more days that go by, the less likely it seems that they'll find him.

I hardly spend any time alone anymore. Someone is always with me, except for the rare occasion when I'm driving somewhere by myself, like to therapy. The Gregorys had an alarm installed in their home, which shows how worried they are, not just about the break-in, but because I've been sleep walking more frequently. I think they worry I'll wander off in the middle of the night.

On a positive note, the band is doing pretty fantastic. After our exceptional performance at the opening, Mr. Scott is allowing us to play every other Friday night and wants us to put together some songs to hopefully record in the future months.

And Ethan hasn't mentioned anything about catching Lyric and I mid kiss. I think he does know about the relationship, though, because every time he sees Lyric and I together, a suspicious look crosses his face.

I have therapy once a week after school, both my

regular sessions and my amnesia one. After all the sessions, my mind is as empty as it was to begin with. Dr. Gardingdale thinks it's because my fear is blocking my memories. I agree with him, but until I can figure out a way to eliminate that fear, there's not much I can do.

After school, I make the ten-minute drive to the office. We start out with my normal session. Dr. Gardingdale asks me the same questions about how I've been doing, and I give him the same answers. I try to stay away from the Lyric subject, not ready to discuss her with him. Yet I somehow accidentally imply that I'm seeing someone.

"I didn't know you were dating anyone." Across the desk, Dr. Gardingdale gapes at me, stunned.

I shake my head, ready to deny it, but then hesitate. Maybe it's time to tell someone about Lyric and me, get the secret off my chest. Make it more real. Besides, it's not like the doctor can tell anyone.

"Well . . . I might be, but I just haven't said anything about it."

"Why not?" His overly bushy brows furrow as he jots something in the legal pad he uses to take notes.

"I don't know . . . I guess I'm confused and worried." I fiddle with the leather bands on my wrist. Endlessly yours forever. My heart still races just thinking about that night, my emotions a jumble. That night had meant something. To me. To Lyric. To both of us. I'm really falling for her. But I still feel so guilty, still feel unworthy of her.

"Worried and confused about what?" The doctor interrupts my thoughts.

"About how my parents will react." I realize I referred to Mr. and Mrs. Gregory as my parents.

That's a new one . . . I don't even know what to make of it. What it means about me. That I'm progressing? I shouldn't be so surprised since I'm progressing with Lyric as well.

I trace the cracks in the wooden armrest of the chair I'm sitting in. "And I'm confused because . . . I don't know, even though I love Lyric's company, I'm still afraid."

"Of what?"

I narrow my eyes at him. "I think we've talked enough that you know what I'm afraid of."

He drums his pencil on his desk. "I know we've talked about a lot of fears, so I'm not positive which one you're referring to right now."

Even though I know he's trying to heal me, I hate when he makes me say things I don't want to say aloud.

"My fear that I've been sexually abused at some point in my life . . . At some point when I was in that house. And I'm afraid that I'll never fully be able to get over it—that I'll never be the person Lyric deserves." My fingers curl around the armrests. "I don't know why you make me say it when you already know what I'm going to say."

He scribbles in the notepad the sets the pen down. "Because I believe it's important for you to verbalize them instead of keeping things locked in like you've done in the past."

I roll my tongue in my mouth, aggravated at myself for being so messed up. "So you think it's been a good thing for me to go to this amnesia therapy? I mean, it's gotten me to speak about stuff aloud, even though it hasn't really done anything to strike up the right memories."

"You seem really agitated today."

"I'm agitated every day that I have to come to these amnesia sessions."

He loosens his tie that has smiley faces on it, conveying happiness that never happens while I'm in these four walls. Our sessions have been about splitting me open and bleeding me dry. Coming here is emotionally exhausting, but as long as Lila and Ethan want me to continue seeing the doctor, I will. They gave me a roof over my head. Got dragged into a police investigation. Got dragged into a mess with a group of people who worship evil.

"You shouldn't push yourself too hard." He gathers a large blue mug from his desk and takes sip of coffee. "If it's becoming too much for you to handle then it's too much for you to handle."

"The police aren't really giving me a choice." I anxiously jiggle my leg up and down. "Well, they are, but if I don't do it, I'm pretty much refusing to help track down my brother's killers . . . and the people who tried to ruin my life. They've been really pushy, too, calling Lila all the time and asking for reports."

"I'll suggest he not call so much the next time I speak to Detective Rannali. He needs to understand that these things can't be rushed and that it takes time." His phone vibrates on the desk, and he silences it without checking the screen. "How are things going with the Gregorys? You haven't really said much about them lately."

"They're going good. I feel bad that they have to go through all this stuff, but they seem okay with it for some reason." It feels late, well past the normal hour I usually spend here. Out the window, twilight has risen and kissed the sky with silver stars. Usually our session ends before the sun fully sets. "Did we run late today? Shouldn't we be starting the amnesia therapy already?"

"Yes, but Lila just requested that I spend an extra hour with you today before we delve into that." His phone hums again. This time he picks it up and presses a few buttons. "She felt that with everything going on, you might need some extra time to discuss how you're feeling."

"How I'm feeling about what?" Removing my keys out of my pocket, I trace the jagged edge of across the palm of my hand, trying to channel my restless energy stemming from knowing that shortly we'll be trying to crack open my head.

He sets down the phone and overlaps his hands on his desk. "The fear that your capturers might still be out there."

"That's not a new revelation. I've always known they were out there."

"I know, but in a way, the loss of your brother has brought the memory of that back into your life. And the incident with the break-in—it has to be hard to deal with."

"The police don't know for sure if our kidnappers were the ones who killed my brother or broke into my house." A lump swells in my throat at the mention of my brother's death.

"I also heard you played your first concert." He avoids my statement. "That had to be stressful."

"Not really. Playing relaxes me more than anything. Lyric was pretty nervous, though."

"Lyric, the girl you're dating?" he asks, even though he knows her. Not only because I talk about her sometimes, but because she had a session with him after William assaulted her.

I nod. "That would be the Lyric I'm talking about."

He opens a file and glances at a paper inside. "Does she know what's going on with you at all?"

I nod again. Lyric knows more than most people. Maybe even more than my therapist.

"Do you talk to her about your past a lot?" he asks, shutting the folder.

"Sometimes."

"About what exactly?"

"Everything I can."

He meticulously examines my expression over,

hunting for cracks in my façade. Like always, I grow uneasy. What does he see? A broken shell of a guy that may never be fixed?

My phone abruptly vibrates from inside my pants pocket, giving me an excuse to look away from his scrutinizing gaze.

Lila: Hey, when is your therapy going to be done? I want to know when I should start dinner.

Me: We should be starting the amnesia therapy soon. It usually only takes about fifteen minutes.

Lila: K. See u soon. And drive careful, sweetie.

"We should wrap this up." I stand up and stretch my arms above my head, ready to get the next part over. "It's getting late and Lila needs me home anyway."

"Alright, lie down on the sofa then." He motions at the leather couch nestled in the corner of the room near his filing cabinet and the window.

The ceiling has an unpainted spot where the plaster shows through. I don't know why, but whenever I lie down, I always find myself picturing it caving in and the sheetrock raining down on me.

The doctor turns on some mellow music, a symphony of violins. Then he turns on the camera, sits down in a chair in front of me, and clicks on a timer.

"Close your eyes, Ayden," he begins with a droning tone. "You're in a safe place, where no one can hurt you. Now, let your mind relax."

Like always, I fleetingly feel like I'm falling.

Down.

Down.

Down.

Then I crash into a wall.

You can't think about it.
You aren't allowed.
There was a reason for your amnesia.
You think we'd let you off that easy.
You think we'd really let you go.
Don't think too much.
Or you're going to lose control.
We're going to come after you.

Dark eyes . . . thin bodies. . . . yellow teeth . . . blue and red lights flash as sirens get closer to the home. Someone is banging on the door, shouting, "Open up!"

My sister lifts her head and there's life in her eyes for the first time. My brother is curled up in the corner, though, thin, frail, so close to death.

Our capturers flee, but not without an impending warning.

"No one escapes," a woman whispers as she stabs her fingernails into my hands. "We'll come back for you." Her face . . . blurred . . . but the pain . . . is excruciating.

My eyelids spring open to the patch on the ceiling. The room is quiet, but my heart thunders like a storm inside my chest.

Dr. Gardingdale waits patiently at my side with pen and paper in his hand and hope in his eyes that I'll tell him I remembered the identities of the people.

"I saw a few images, but everyone's faces are blurred over, and honestly, none of what I'm seeing makes sense," I tell him as I sit up and plant my feet on the floor. As usual, the room twirls around me in hazy colors and shapes. "They threatened us, though, when we left the house. Said they'd come back for us." Invisible fingers wrap around my neck and my oxygen supply dwindles. "You should probably tell the police that. Or I will."

He nods his head at the camera. "They'll see this when

I give them the video tomorrow."

I massage my aching chest. "Did I say anything aloud to you by chance?"

He sighs heavily. "Unfortunately no, which I find strange, especially considering you've been sleep walking and talking so much at home. It's like your mind opens up after the sessions."

"Is that common?"

"It's hard to say." He removes his glasses and cleans them off with the bottom of his shirt. "This therapy—hypnotherapy as a lot call it—isn't something performed that frequently. And your case is extremely complex." He slides his glasses back on. "But, Ayden, if this doesn't start working . . . I . . . there might be some other treatments you might consider trying . . . they're a bit more experimental and have risks, though."

My brows furrow. "What kinds of experimental treatments?"

He pushes his feet against the floor, wheeling his chair back toward a printer. Then he collects a thin stack of papers and hands them to me.

"Shock treatment." Words jump out at me from the pages. Ice cold water. Injections. Electricity.

"They're risky procedures," he explains, looking as though he doesn't really want to be discussing this with me. "I honestly don't believe it's a great idea, but I want to give you the choice. I think that's important. Just like I know it's important to you to find out who killed your brother." When I don't respond, he sighs. "You can throw them away if you want to. I just want you to be informed. Since you're still a minor, though, I can't do anything without your parents' consent, so you'll have to talk to your parents."

"I'll be eighteen in a couple of weeks," I tell him, even

though I want to throw the papers away.

Some of the treatments are appalling. But as I think of my brother lying dead in his own blood outside that home that stripped us bare, I fold the papers up and stand up to leave.

"I better go. It's getting late."

"Ayden," he calls out. I pause, twisting around. "Remember, if you ever need to talk, I'm here. Even when it's not a session, you can always call me."

I bob my head up and down then exit the office, pretending his words don't affect me as much as they do. But the fact that I have people in my life who care about me still gets to me and makes me feel warm and cold inside. Warm, because it's amazing to have people in your life rooting for you. And cold, because it's terrifying having people in your life, putting themselves in harm's way to help you.

My thoughts drift to my brother who probably had no one in his life. Who died all by himself.

"Why were you there?" I whisper to myself as I enter the crisp night. The moon is crescent in the dusky sky and a haze conceals most of the stars. "Was it because they had you against your will?"

A depressing thought occurs to me. I might never get the answers to those questions. I might never know what happened to my brother.

But I can still find out about my sister. If I can find her.

On my way to the car, I check my email on my phone, hoping there's a message from Rebel Tonic. Almost three weeks later and still no word from him, I've pretty much lost hope that he'll ever get back to me. More than likely he played me, and like a sucker, I fell for it.

No new messages so I stuff the phone away and speed up across the vacant parking lot. The sole lamppost that usually lights up the area has burnt out so I can scarcely make out the outline of my black BMW. As I find my way through the dark and approach the vehicle, I pat my pocket for my keys but can't find them. Wondering if I left them in the building, I flip around to head back inside. Mid turn I notice something in the trees lining the property. Movement? A figure moving? I can't quite tell.

I dodge to the right and skitter for the door. It has to be a dog or something. No need to get paranoid. With everything that's happened over the last couple of months, my mind's just playing tricks on me.

Then I hear a bloodcurdling scream reverberate from nearby.

Fuck, dogs don't scream.

Freezing, I scan the trees, the closed stores across the street, and the office building, but I can't see anyone or anything around. I jog for the door, my boots thumping against the pavement. As I reach the curb, I hear another scream. This time the noise fractures my heart into a thousand pieces.

This time I recognize the scream.

"Sadie?" I frenziedly whirl around again. Branches snap and leaves rustle. I fumble for my phone as I inch toward the tree line, prepared to dial nine-one-one if needed. "Sadie, are you in there?" I call out as the tips of my boots reach the border of where the parking lot shifts to a shallow forest. I squint through the darkness, but it's pitch black. Too fucking dark.

Darkness settles
a heavy quilt
suffocating.
I can't breathe.
Whisper the words,
They say,

Whisper them and we'll free you.
Whisper.
Whisper.
Whisper
that you worship us.
Belong to us.
That you'll do anything for us.
We're coming back for you.

I swipe my finger to unlock my phone and illuminate the screen. Then I aim the light toward the forest. A screech echoes from amongst the thick leaves then a figure zips from the trees at me. I stumble back, clumsily drop the phone, and darkness smothers me.

Find the fucking phone.

Footsteps rush around in soft pitter-patters.

I collapse to my knees.

Find the fucking phone.

"Ayden, Ayden, Ayden," a low chant echoes around me. "You think we'd let you get away that easy?"

Ayden, Ayden, Ayden,
do you hear us calling your name?
Feel the cuffs around your wrists.
We own you now, Ayden,
there's no getting out, even when you leave these walls.
Ayden, Ayden, Ayden,
Do you see what we can do?
Do you see the blood that stains the ground?
If you leave, we'll come after you.

"Ayden, Ayden, Ayden." Whispers mix with the wind. "We have her. Your sister. And we're coming for you."

"It's just your imagination." I cover my ears with my hands. "You're just remembering again. Nothing is happening . . . Nothing . . . There's nothing out there."

I feel a tug on my hair, strands getting ripped out, then

nothing. With a deep breath, I lift open my eyelids. Nothing but darkness and trees and I lower my hands from my ears.

"Ayden." A voice slams up from behind me.

I stagger to my feet and spin around, only to find Dr. Gardingdale standing there with shock frozen on his face. "Where did you . . ." I reel back around. The area is silent. The trees still. As if nothing happened. "I don't . . ." My mind races a million miles a minute.

What the hell just happened?

Did I just imagine it?

Or was it real?

They said they're coming back for you, like they did when you were pulled out of that house. Is this it? Are they returning to me? But then, why taunt me instead of taking me? Why scare me, rip out a chunk of my hair, and break into my house to take my knife? Is this part of the ritual? And what is the ritual for?

"What's wrong?" he asks as he surveys the parking lot then the forest. "Did you see something out there?"

I face him and shift my weight so the trees are in my peripheral vision. Then I give the doctor a recap of what I think I just saw, trying to explain to him the best I can.

"It could have been a homeless person or some kids messing around." He scratches his balding head as he stares at the trees and shrubbery. "Both have caused commotions around here before."

"But they said my name." I lower myself onto the curb and drop my head in my hands. "Or at least I think they did . . . Maybe that was just part of a memory surfacing. Maybe the amnesia therapy was delayed or something." I grip the back of my neck. "I don't know though. I thought they pulled my hair. And it actually hurts right now."

"Pulled your hair?" A pucker forms at his brow. "I think we should at least report the incident to the police, just to be on the cautious side." He sits down on the curb next to me. "I wish you'd have told me how bad the memories were—that you were having a hard time grasping reality while they are happening."

"It's never been that bad before." I raise my head and stare out at the cars on the road ahead of us.

"It might be wise if I prescribe you something," he suggests. "Just until you get a better grappling with remembering."

"I'm not taking drugs," I reply in a clipped tone. But after seeing my mother turn into a monster when she was doped up, I made a vow never to use drugs of any kind.

"It's just a mild sedative that you can take if you have another episode." He pushes to his feet and cautiously moves toward the trees. "You don't have to take it all the time, only when needed." He bends over and scoops something up before returning to me. "Let's go inside so we can report this." He hands me the object he picked up—my phone. "Then we'll call Lila."

I follow him back inside his office, take a seat in the chair, and listen to him recount what happened to the police. Everything that "allegedly" or "possibly" happened. I agree with him to an extent. I'm not positive of what was real after I heard the scream.

The sound could have easily triggered a nerve and sent me to the most vivid places in my mind. Places I never knew existed. But then again, it could be the same person who broke into my house.

One thing I am sure of. I know what I heard. That scream rang familiar to my sister Sadie's. I know her scream well. Heard it day in and day out while we were locked up.

As I wait for Dr. Gardingdale to finish the police call, I check my email again. The screen is cracked from dropping it onto the asphalt, and I have to press each button at least five times just to get into my inbox. I open the app and hold my breath as I scroll through the messages. My heart stops when I reach the fifth line down in my inbox. A message from Rebel Tonic. I open it, praying that he's been able to find her.

Sorry it took me so long to get this to you. For some reason there was no record of a Sadie Stephorson social service's records. I did manage to track an address through her school records, but it took a long time since there are so many districts. The last place she was listed living at was 40499 Faring Lake Ave. Street in San Diego. Hope that helps and good luck.

P.S. Remember to delete this message from your email when you're finished.

I do a map search on the Internet for the address. It's fairly close to where I am now, on the route home if I take the long way.

I do exactly as he instructed. After I type the address in the note section of the phone, I delete the email. Then I wait very impatiently for the doctor to finish up his call.

After he chats with the police, he calls my parents to update them on what happened. When he hangs up, I receive a text message.

> *Lila: Ayden, Dr. Gardingdale is going to walk you to your car. Lock the doors and drive straight home. And if you see anything that's suspicious, call me.*

I'm getting ready to put the phone away when another text comes through.

> *Lila: Better yet, just stay there. I'll have Ethan come get u.*

> *Me: I'll be fine. It's a ten minute drive.*

Lila: Just check the backseat, okay? Sometimes people can hide back there.

Me: You've been watching too many horror movies.

Lila: Maybe so, but u still need to.

Me: Okay.

I close up my phone then the doctor walks me to my car, telling me that the police will probably be in touch with me sometime tomorrow after they've done some investigating around the area. He waits near the curb as I check the backseat, climb in, and turn on the engine. Then he starts for the door as I drive out of the parking lot and onto the nearly vacant street.

My fingers thrum restlessly as I steer past stores, houses, and gas stations. The closer I get to the address the more jittery I become.

Ten minutes later, I near the location of the address. I'm not positive what I'm even going to do when I arrive. Knock on the door? I wasn't even supposed to take the detour let alone leave the vehicle. And it feels wrong to put myself into danger by getting out of the car at night in some strange area. I should just drive by then maybe return during daylight. Perhaps bring Lyric with me.

Just a quick peek then it's home for me.

Faring Lake Ave. Street is in a subdivision near a shopping mart and a park. When I turn down the road, the first thing I notice is that a lot of the single story homes are abandoned. A lot of the structures appear old and outdated, paint peeling off the siding, mailboxes knocked down. I don't think too much of it until I pull up to the house with the numbers 40499 next to the door. Like the other homes, this one appears vacant. Shingles are missing from the roof, the porch is collapsing, and the windows are all covered with plywood.

I start to choke up, the wind getting knocked out of me as I turn around and the headlights beam across the home. Painted across the wood, in various colors are circular marks.

Marks that resemble my tattoo.

CHAPTER 16

"YOU SEEM REALLY HAPPY," MY dad remarks as he stuffs half a roll into his mouth. "Like extra happy."

"You really do," my mother agrees as she adds a glob of butter to her potatoes. "I wonder why." Her tone insinuates something. What, I'm not sure.

Either she's speculating that I might be bipolar, or she's trying to get me to fess up as to why I've been almost stupidly happy over the last couple of weeks.

I shovel a spoonful of corn into my mouth. "I'm a normal happy, you guys, so don't start."

"We weren't starting." My mother works with a knife to slice her steak. "And I'm sorry for ever bringing that up. I'm really sorry about that, Lyric. I should have never said anything."

"Okay, good." I smile at her, and she returns it.

At the moment, all feels right in the world.

Despite all the drama, life has been good, something I ponder as I eat my mashed potatoes.

Things really have been great.

And calm.

As if the world is attempting to prove my thoughts wrong, all hell suddenly breaks loose as the back door flies open and bashes against the doorstopper.

Aunt Lila comes barreling into the kitchen, her eyes

massive and jam-packed with terror. "I need you to watch the kids," she sputters to my mother as she winds a scarf around her neck. "Something happened with Ayden at therapy, and he was supposed to come straight home, but it's been over an hour since he left. Ethan's already out looking for him, but I'm going to go check a few places, too."

Fear pulsates through my body. I quickly check my phone to see if there are any messages from Ayden, but I have no new texts.

My mother shoves back from the table, the chair legs making a godawful scratching noise against the hardwood floor. "Let me just grab my coat and I'll be over."

I stand up so abruptly I damn near tip the chair over. "I'm going with you," I say to Lila.

"Okay, that's fine." Aunt Lila is distracted as she glides her finger across the screen of her phone, checking for messages. "I don't know why he's not answering my calls or texts . . . he never does stuff like this."

"I'll drive around with Lyric, and we can check some places, too," my dad adds as he hurries for the stairs. "Just let me grab my phone and wallet."

I send Ayden a text.

Me: Where the hell r u? Everyone's freaking out.

Then I head to grab my jacket from the coat rack when the back door opens up behind me.

"I found her house," Ayden says to me as he enters the foyer and closes the door.

"You're okay!" I throw my arms around him, unaware until now how worried I was. "Everyone's freaking out." I pull back. "Wait, found who?"

"The last address my sister lived at." His hair is disheveled, there are dark circles are under his eyes, and his shoulders are hunched, as if the weight of the world is crushing him.

"Rebel Tonic got back to you?"

He nods. "With an address."

"And?"

His throat muscles work as he swallows hard and fights back tears. "It was a vacant house with this," he lifts up the bottom of his shirt and taps his finger on the rough tattoo on his side, "painted all over the boarded up windows."

I gulp. "Why . . . I don't understand."

"Neither do I." He grips ahold of my hand. "But we're going to go find out." He marches across the room toward the kitchen.

"Where are we going?" I ask as I shuffle to keep up with him.

"To my house. I need to talk to Lila to find out what that letter was about."

"Lila's here, in the kitchen. She was about to go look for you," I tell him, which only makes him quicken his pace.

When we enter the kitchen and Aunt Lila sees Ayden, a choking sob wrenches from her throat.

"Oh, my God, we were so worried about you." She crosses the kitchen and wraps her arms around Ayden.

He stands with his listless arms to his sides, still holding my hand. "I need you to tell me what that letter was about." He doesn't have to explain what letter he's speaking of. The reluctant expression on Aunt Lila's face reveals she already knows.

"Ayden, Ethan and I already explained that there's some things you aren't ready for yet," she reminds him sympathetically.

"I tracked her last address down," he states bluntly, firmly holding her gaze. "It was about ten miles away from here. The house is boarded up and has these marks spray painted on it, ones that match my tattoo."

"Ayden . . ." Her face contorts with emotional agony. He tugs me closer to his side. "Just tell me."

Aunt Lila seals her quivering lips together as tears fill the corners of her eyes. Ayden's fingers clench around my hand as he watches her unravel in front of us.

"Your sister was kidnapped again not too long after you guys were . . . found in that house." She lowers herself into a chair. "She's been with those people for the last two and a half years. The police honestly thought she was dead until they received a note from her over a year ago on the day we brought you home."

"What did the letter say?" he chokes out hoarsely, and I feel him sway, as if his legs are about to buckle.

"I don't know," she replies as tears stream down her cheeks. "The police won't release that information."

"Is that what happened to my brother, too?" he whispers in horror. "Was he kidnapped? Did they kill him?"

"All I know about your brother is what you do. He vanished out of the system a couple of years ago. Social services assumed he'd ran away. The next time he was found . . ." She reaches out to touch his shoulder, but he moves away. More tears bubble in her eyes. "I'm so sorry."

"Why didn't anyone tell me this?" Ayden starts to sit down even though there's no chair around. I quickly usher him to a nearby barstool before he ends up falling on the floor.

"Because we wanted you to have a normal life." She fights back a sob, her chest heaving as she verges toward hysteria. "Oh, sweetie, I'm so sorry you have to go through this."

She runs over, wraps her arms around him, and squeezes him tightly. Ayden stares like he sees a ghost in the space in front of him, those dark eyes of his completely haunted with his past.

"You're going to be okay," she promises him, smoothing her hand over his head. "We'll get through this. The police are looking for her."

Still clutching onto my hand, my arm ends up getting crushed between their bodies. I wiggle it, but Ayden refuses to let go. Finally, I relax and let him hold on.

"I want to try to remember," he croaks. "Do whatever it takes to find those people . . . Doctor Gardingdale . . . he said there were other methods . . ."

"Yeah, the detective mentioned those to me, too," Lila's tone is uneven, "and they're too risky."

"Leaving my sister with those people, hoping she'll make it out alive is too risky . . ." His fingers enfold around the back of his neck and grip tight. "I swear I heard her scream in the parking lot tonight . . . She was there . . ."

"Oh, honey." She pulls him nearer, like she has no clue what else to do but hang onto him.

I want to stop the pain in his life and make him feel safe, but I don't have that power.

Right now, everything relies on what the people after Ayden want. Until we find out exactly what that is, no one's going to feel safe again.

AWAKENING YOU

the
Unraveling
You
series
BOOK THREE

New York Times and *USA Today* Bestselling Author
JESSICA SORENSEN

AWAKENING YOU
All rights reserved.
Copyright © 2015 by Jessica Sorensen

This is a work of fiction. Any resemblance of characters to actual persons, living or dead, is purely coincidental. The Author holds exclusive rights to this work. Unauthorized duplication is prohibited.

For information:
jessicasorensen.com

Cover Design and Photography:
Sarah Hansen, Okay Creations
www.okaycreations.com

Interior Design and Formatting:
Christine Borgford, Perfectly Publishable
www.perfectlypublishable.com

CHAPTER 1

"I WANT YOU TO CLOSE your eyes and relax," my therapist instructs in an even, soothing voice I've heard at least a dozen times.

I'm lying in a lounge chair in front of him with my arms overlapped on my stomach, and my heart is slamming against my chest as I prepare to be put under for my amnesia therapy. The soft flow of the ocean drifts from the stereo, and birds chirp just outside the window beside me.

"Relax," he repeats. "Clear your mind."

Clear my mind.

Clear my . . .

Body . . .

And . . .

Mind.

I fall deep into my thoughts, a blanket of darkness wrapping around me.

Around.

Around.

Around.

"Ayden!" my sister cries from the recliner. "Stop spinning me so fast."

I continue to lap circles, pushing the chair she's in.

"You asked me to spin you, so I'm spinning you."

"Not this fast, though!" she cries through her laughter, gripping onto the torn armrests. "I'm going to throw up!"

"Oh, fine." I stop moving and hop back, watching the chair continue to twirl until it gradually slows to a stop.

"That was fun." She bounces from the chair, her arms spanning to the side as she staggers toward me. "Whoa, I'm so dizzy." She braces her hand against the sheetrock wall beside her. "Everything looks all blurry."

I laugh, sitting down on the edge of the scuffed up coffee table. "Give it a minute, and it'll stop."

She nods, sinking back into the chair. "So, I heard a rumor about you."

"Oh, yeah?" I ask, vaguely interested as I pick up the remote and turn on the television. The service has been turned off, though, probably because my mom forgot to pay the bill again, so I turn it off.

"Yeah, I heard you kissed Laura Flemming on the lips." She giggles.

I set the remote down. "So what? It's not that big of a deal."

"That's not what I heard." Her eyes sparkle mischievously. Sadie has always been the kind of sister who likes to tease me about everything. "I heard that she wants to be your girlfriend."

I roll my eyes. "Well, she can tell me that herself, then."

"That's such a boy answer."

"If you haven't noticed, he is a boy." My older brother enters the living room from the hallway. He's wearing plaid pajama bottoms, and his hair is messy, as if he just woke up, even though it's six o'clock at night. "Where's Mom?"

I shrug. "Out."

He shakes his head, aggravated and exhausted from the late hours he's been putting in at his job and school. *"Probably doing drugs."*

"She doesn't do drugs," Sadie spits. *"Stop saying that she does."*

"You're just in denial," my brother replies, winding around the chair and heading for the kitchen attached to the living room.

"I am not."

"Am, too."

"Would you two knock it off," I intervene, being the peacemaker as always. *"Just let her be, okay? It's not that big of a deal."*

"Yeah, it is." He motions around us at the shithole we've called home for about a year now. *"Look around you. If you can't see how bad things are, then you're dumb as fuck."*

"I'm not dumb." Tears overflow from Sadie's eyes. *"Why do you always have to be such a jerk?"*

He sighs. *"Look, I'm sorry, okay? I just want you to see how things really are so maybe you can have a chance at a better future."*

"I know things are bad," she mutters, *"but it doesn't mean I have to be all mopey about it all the time."*

I hate when they fight. Life is bad enough already.

"How about we go outside," I suggest to Sadie, *"and see what kind of trouble we can get into?"*

Sadie beams as she springs from the chair. *"Can we go see Miss Tammy's puppies?"*

"Sure. Why not?"

She bounces off toward the door while I shoot my brother a look as I head for the front door.

"Don't ruin her happiness yet," I mutter under my

breath as I pass by him. "Let her be a kid for a little while longer."

"She's thirteen-years-old." He grabs a bowl from the cupboard then lowers his voice when he realizes Sadie is still lingering near the front door. "She needs to start growing up and realizing just how shitty our lives are. And how shitty our mother—"

"My babies!" The door swings open violently, and my mother bursts into the narrow living room with her arms wide open. Her attention falls on Sadie, and she lazily grins. "Come give Mama a hug."

"Speak of the devil," my brother mumbles under his breath.

Sadie gives her a nervous, one-armed hug. "I missed you."

She trips in her heels as she staggers into the small living room. "Where have the three of you been?"

"Right here." My tone is clipped. "Waiting for you to show up and pay the damn bills."

She frowns as she slumps against the wall with her head tipped back, her droopy eyes on the stained ceiling above. "I've been busy . . ." Her eyelids lower as if she's about to pass out. "How long was I gone?"

I bite down on my tongue until the rusty taste of blood fills my mouth, hating myself for detesting her so much. "Four days."

"Four days," she murmurs sleepily. Her head starts to angle to the side, and I think she's about to pass out, but she suddenly gets a second wind. Her eyes pop open as she jumps away from the wall. "I need you guys to come with me."

"I have to go to work," my brother snaps while pouring cereal into a bowl.

"Work, shmirk." She waves him off, staggering over

her own feet as she jerks open the front door. "Come on. This is important."

I exchange a quizzical look with my brother, and he shakes his head and slams the box of cereal down onto the counter.

"Fine, what do you want?" he asks, striding to the front door.

"It's outside," she whispers, her gaze darting from left to right.

My brother rolls his eyes, but steps outside, anyway. "I'm getting so tired of this shit."

My mom stumbles down the rickety porch to the gravel driveway, and we all follow her. The sky is clear, the sun gleaming brightly, but there's a chill to the air.

"What do you think she's on this time?" he asks me as we hike down the windy road, past trailer homes, and toward the field surrounding the area we live in.

I shrug. "I really don't care anymore."

Which is the truth. I may hold it together on the outside, but I was done with my mother and her drug and alcohol addiction a long time ago. I have four more years of this shit, and then I'm getting out. The moment I graduate, I'm packing my shit and leaving. And I'm going to take Sadie, too.

My mother leads us on a wild goose chase up through the field and around the fence line before heading back toward the house.

"I have a bad feeling about this, Ayden," Sadie whispers to me. "In fact, I had one of my feelings this morning that something bad was going to happen today."

"It's going to be okay." I squeeze her hand, trying to comfort her, but I'm pretty fucking worried myself.

By the time we've reached the road again, I figure my mother probably forgotten the purpose of why she brought us out here—if there was even a purpose to begin with—and is going to take us back to the house.

But she makes a right at the smaller home just next door, and the three of us begrudgingly trail after her, exhausted and cranky and ready to go home. Even Sadie has grown quiet.

"Just wait right here," my mom instructs as we reach the bottom of the rotted, wooden steps that lead to a crooked front door. She climbs up the stairs and fixes her dress into place before knocking.

The door swings open, but I can't see who's inside the house. For the most part, the three of us have tried to stay away from our neighbors, considering most of them deal and do drugs.

I hear hushed whispering and sigh, knowing more than likely my mom's buying drugs. My gaze travels around the area, across the road, along the front of the house. I notice a strange, jagged, circular pattern painted on the metal along with a sign that reads: Enter at your own risk. Those who dare step in never get out.

Part of me thinks the warning is a joke, but a small part of me starts to get a little anxious about who lives in this house.

"Okay, are you guys ready for this?" my mother asks, drawing my attention back to her.

The door to the house is wide open, but the person who answered has stepped back so I can only make out their silhouette and what looks like a head of red hair. It seems so dark and smoky inside, as if there are no open windows or ventilation.

"Go on." She has something in her hand and a nervous look on her face as she flicks her wrist and motions at the door. "Get in there."

Sadie moves forward first, and I hear a cackle from

inside. The sound triggers something deep inside me, a warning.

Something's wrong.

Don't go in. Don't go in.

I run for her with my hand extended, reaching to grab her and pull her back, but the house starts to fade away—everything does—and bleeds red.

Bleeds red.

Don't go in there.

Blood.

Don't go.

Blood everywhere.

Close your mind. Trust me, you don't want to see what's about to happen . . .

My eyes shoot open as I gasp for air, but my lungs are constricting, and I can't get any oxygen.

"Help," I gasp, rolling to my side, clutching at my chest.

Dr. Gardingdale is above me, his eyes wide as he pats my back and tells me to, "Breathe. Just breathe. Air in. Air out. In. Out."

He repeats the mantra until I calm down, and then he moves back and gives me room.

I sit in the chair with my feet planted on the floor and my head in my hands. "I was remembering the day my mother dropped us off at the house," I finally say. "But the memory would only go up until the point where Sadie ran inside, and I went in after her. Then it shut down . . . All I could see was red."

I hate that, no matter what, my mind refuses to let me see what happened in that house. All I know is a female there had bright red hair and disgustingly long nails. They also didn't—don't—like it when people leave their group, even those who didn't enter of their own freewill.

He studies me closely as the music changes from the sound of ocean waves to the lull of a waterfall. "I think that's going to be all for today." He seems distracted as he stands up from his chair and walks over to his desk. "I'm starting to get concerned, though, that we might be putting too much pressure on your mind." He collects a prescription pad and a pen from his drawer. "I'm going to write you a prescription just in case you have another panic attack like that."

"I won't take the pills." My legs are wobbly, and my stomach is woozy as I push up from the chair and work to get my footing.

He leans over the desk, pressing the pen to the paper. "I'm not saying you have to take them, but you'll have them on hand just in case."

"She was buying drugs the day she dropped us off. She was high and needed her next fix, so she sold her kids out to a fucking bunch of evil people." I stuff my hands into the pockets of my jeans. "So, trust me when I say I won't take the pills."

He sighs but drops the pen and turns to face me. "Well, just know that the option is there and that there's no shame if you decide to take them."

"Okay." I nod then start for the door.

He scoops up his office keys from the desk. "Let me walk you to your car."

Ever since the incident in the parking lot where a chunk of my hair was stolen, he has been walking me to my car. He always locks his office up first, even though he goes back inside afterward.

After he locks up, we exit the building and cross the parking lot toward my car parked out near the back row, even though the entire area is vacant.

"It was more crowded when I came here," I explain,

glancing up at the sky now painted with stars.

"You're usually my last client of the day," he replies, reading a message on his phone.

When we near the car, I fish the keys from my pocket and push the key fob. The headlights flash across the dark parking lot as the doors unlock.

"I'll see you next Tuesday," I say, pulling the driver's side door open.

He nods absentmindedly as he turns back toward the office building. "Take care, Ayden. And, if you need anything at all, call me."

"I will." I lower my head to climb in but pause when I spot a blank piece of paper on the dashboard. I pick it up and flip it over. Invisible fingers wrap around my neck, and suddenly, I can't breathe again.

Those that step in, never get out. We're going to torture you until you break. Just like we did to your sister.

I drop the note to the ground and scramble back, scanning the parking lot. Even though the note wasn't signed, I know who left it. The Soulless Mileas, a group of people who held my siblings and me captive in that house I saw in the memory just minutes ago.

"Wait, something's wrong," I call out to Dr. Gardingdale. "There's a note."

He reels around, nearly dropping his phone. "Where?"

I point to the ground at the piece of paper, my eyes trained on the trees, the buildings, the bushes, every place someone could be hiding. "They must have put it in there while I was inside," I say as he crouches down to examine it without picking it up. "I don't know how, though. The car was locked."

He straightens his legs and stands up then slowly circles the back end of the car. He walks around the front and down the side, inspecting every inch while dialing a number on his phone. He halts near the passenger side and moves closer, lifting his head to look on the roof. "Your sun roof's open." He glances at me from over the car. "Did you leave it open?"

"Maybe . . . I was honestly pretty distracted when I drove here." Distracted by the heavy make out session I had with Lyric right before I drove here. My thoughts were lost in her and the way her lips felt against mine. How soft her skin was against my hands. The soft whimpers she kept making. "I'm sorry."

"You don't need to be sorry. None of what's happening is your fault." He puts the phone up to his ear and starts chatting with the police to report the incident.

It's the second one he's had to report in two months, and I'm starting to wonder exactly how many more incidents are in my future. If the note holds any truth to it, then probably a lot.

I'm never, never going to be free
Until I die,
Or they capture me.
I'm not sure what ending's worse.

CHAPTER 2

FOUR HOURS LATER, I'M IN the police station with Lila and Ethan, waiting for Detective Rannali—the person working my brother's murder case and my sister's kidnapping—to come speak with us about what happened tonight.

"I wish this could have just waited until morning." Lila restlessly jiggles her foot up and down as she scans the busy room full of officers. She has flour on her jeans and shirt because she was cooking for a wedding she's catering when she received the call to come here. "It's too late for him to be out on a school night."

"Honey, I think, considering what happened, it's good that they want to tackle this tonight." Ethan places his hand on her knee to settle her. "Be thankful they're not shoving it aside."

"I am." She ceases bouncing her leg. "I'm just really tired of all of this and those damn people. Why can't they just leave us alone?" Regret fills her eyes as she looks over at me. "Sorry, I know I'm making this worse."

"You don't need to apologize." I slump back in the seat. "Besides, I'm the one making this worse. I brought this on everyone."

"Don't you dare say that," she starts to protest, but stops talking when Detective Rannali strolls up.

His white, button-down shirt is wrinkled, his tie is crooked, and his hair is disheveled. "Sorry to make you wait. It's been a long day." He nods his head at his office door. "Come inside. There's some stuff I'd like to talk to you about."

The three of us simultaneously rise to our feet, file into his office, and take a seat in front of his desk. Once everyone gets settled, he opens a folder that contains the note I found tonight.

"So, ever since this all started, we've been wondering why the Soulless Mileas are so fixated on you—leaving notes, stealing your knife, taking your hair—yet they never actually make any threatening moves. We've had some theories, but we weren't positive." He glances from the note to me. "This note is starting to confirm our suspicions."

"And what are you suspicious of?" Lila asks, grasping onto Ethan's hand for support.

She has been doing that a lot lately, revealing just how much stress this ordeal has been putting on her. It makes me feel so damn guilty all the time because it's my fault. I brought these people into their lives. I brought this stress into their lives.

The detective closes the folder and overlaps his hands on top of it. "When I was first put on your sister's case," he speaks directly to me, "I remembered interviewing this woman in the neighborhood who believed the people who took Sadie stalked her first. She reported seeing people breaking into the house. I didn't look into it too much, because the source had ended up being highly unreliable. But, over the last few weeks, I've been noticing a pattern."

"They're doing the same thing to me." My fingers curl around the armrests of the chair, and my fingernails scrape at the wood. "And, eventually, they're going to try and take me."

Lila gasps, covering her mouth with her hand. "That's not what's going on," she says in denial.

"I never said that," the detective says with caution. "I just said that there are some similarities between your case and your sister's. And the note, well, it's just more proof that you need to start being extremely careful."

"How can I be more careful?" I ask, dumbfounded. "I already spend no time alone. There's an alarm in the house. My therapist walks me to my car."

"We'll do more to keep him safe." Lila places a hand on mine. "It's going to be okay."

"No, it's not." I stand up, ignoring their protests to come back as I exit the office.

I want to walk out the front door of the station and just start running until my legs give out. Run away until I feel safe. But nowhere is safe, and running away is only going to put me in harm's way. So, instead, I wait for Lila and Ethan by the glass entrance doors. They don't show up for another thirty minutes, and by then, Lila looks like she's been crying.

"Is everything all right?" I ask her as she strides up to me.

"Everything's great." She folds her arms around me and yanks me close, despite my rigidity. "Everything will be okay."

Lies. Lies.
Everyone lies.
Lies to save me.
Lies to break me.
Lies to make me ache.
How many more lies are in my future?

"What do we do now?" I ask Ethan from over Lila's

shoulder as she continues to hug me so tightly I can barely breathe.

"The only thing we can do," he replies, wrapping an arm around his wife. "Go home and make a plan that will keep you safe."

I nod in agreement for his benefit. But no matter how many plans they make, I'll never truly be safe.

Those that step in, never get out.

Never, ever, ever.

CHAPTER 3

THE MOST DEPRESSING SONG OF all time is playing in surround sound. Definitely not my choice of music, especially when so much dreariness haunts Ayden's life already. Every day, he's plagued by the fact that the same people who kidnapped him and his siblings over four years ago are holding his sister. The same people have also been tormenting him for the last several months by breaking into his house, stealing his hair, and as of three days ago, leaving him creepy notes in his car.

With my sketchpad propped open on my lap, I stare across the room at him, assessing the pain he tries to keep hidden while drawing the shadows of his smoldering dark eyes framed by the longest, darkest eyelashes I've ever seen.

Today, he's dressed in all black and sporting the leather bracelets that match mine—Christmas presents we gave to each other a few months ago. Each stroke of my pencil captures the pain concealed below the surface of his strength.

As I'm shading his eyes, the iPod shifts to the next song, which turns out to be as equally energy draining as the first.

"Who picked out this playlist?" I climb off the sofa and pad over to the stereo that's below the flat screen mounted on the wall.

Ayden peers up from the notebook he's been scribbling in for over the last hour, sweeping wisps of his inky black hair out of his eyes. "I thought you did."

"Yeah, right. These songs are too depressing for me to be listening to at the moment." I frown at the stereo. "My mom must have turned it on before she took out the sugar junkie clan for dessert."

The Gregory's kids are staying over for the night while Ethan and Lila are away at their son, Everson's, football game. At fourteen-years-old, Everson is living his dream already, playing quarterback for the middle school league. While the Gregorys wanted to take the whole clan with them, they thought it'd be best if they stayed behind, considering it's a school night. Lila acted like a nervous wreck when they dropped everyone off and gave my mother an hour-long lecture about keeping Ayden in the house at all times with the alarm on and an adult always around.

After dinner, my mom suggested everyone go get ice cream, but Ayden and I stayed behind with my dad who retired to his office about thirty minutes ago to put together a band line-up for his club.

I tap the skip button, moving to the next song, "My Heroine" by Silverstein. "Much better."

"Much better?" Ayden cocks his brow. "It's as slow as the last one."

I hold up a finger. "Give it a minute." I sway my hips to the slow rhythm of the song while sweeping my hands through my hair. When the tempo quickly picks up, I grin cockily at Ayden. "See. Much better."

He chuckles, a rare but breathtaking sound. Then he sets his pen and paper aside on the coffee table and stretches his arms above his head. "Do I lose points against me for not knowing that?"

"Hmmm . . ." I thrum my finger on my bottom lip as I amble across the living room toward him. "I might consider letting you keep all your points for a small fee, of course."

"And what's the fee?" he asks, mildly amused.

I straddle his lap and announce my fee with my actions. He briefly tenses from the contact then relaxes when I tangle my fingers through his hair.

"There. Much better," I whisper. "I don't like you being so far away."

He offers me a small smile. "I wanted to sit by you, but I worried your dad would maybe get mad or something."

"That we were sitting on the couch together?"

"I don't know . . . yeah. I mean, I'm worried maybe they'll figure out we have something going on."

"Have something going on?" I playfully tease. "I'm not sure what you mean. What's going on?"

He stares at me, unimpressed. "I mean our relationship that they don't know about yet."

"Oh, right. I completely forgot about that." I smile innocently at him, and he pinches my side, causing me to yelp. "No fair." I pinch him back, right on his chest.

Tension ripples through his body as he stiffens from my unexpected touch.

"Sorry." I quickly apologize. "I don't know what I was thinking."

"I-it's okay," he stammers through a loud exhale. Then he takes my hand and lines my palm right over his thundering heart. "You just surprised me. That's all . . . You can . . . I'm fine with you touching me on the outside of my shirt. You know that, right?" His off-pitch tone reveals exactly how difficult it is for him to say that.

Touching Ayden is a gift.
One I'm grateful he gives me.
I just wish I could have it all the time.
Every day and night.
On and on and on.
Forever.

I lean forward and place a kiss on his lips. His breathing accelerates as he grasps onto my hips, and I smile to myself, secretly loving that I can make him react like that.

"Maybe we shouldn't do this here," he mutters as I kiss him again. "Your dad's in the next room, and your mom could walk in at any moment."

"Don't worry about them." I rock my hips against his, eliciting a groan from him. "Only stop if you want to stop."

Please, please, don't stop.

Ever, ever, ever.

His protests shift into throaty moans as he deepens the kiss, entangling our tongues, tasting me deeply while his hands travel up and down my sides. His fingers trace each bump of my ribs before drifting down to the hem of my black and purple dress. His fingers tremble as he fiddles with the bottom, something he usually does.

Having more than likely suffered from sexual abuse while being kidnapped, intimacy is complicated with Ayden. Touching me is less of a problem than getting touched himself, but he's always a bit unsettled.

"Do we need to slow down?" I ask, then steal another taste of his lips.

"I don't know." He puts a sliver of space between our mouths, breathing hotly against my lips. "It's getting easier. Sort of. I mean, I don't panic as much, and I feel like I want . . ." He trails off, his eyes glazed over and pupils dilated, as if he's high from the kiss.

High on our kiss.

Dazed by our connection
And the overpowering heat
Of our bodies,
Our souls.
Intoxicated by love.
God, how I wish,
Wish that were the truth.

After searching my eyes, his lips return to mine, and his hand slides underneath my dress, silently answering my question. I fall into his touch, desperately tumbling into a place I once dreamed about but now know exists.

Love.

I'm pretty sure I'm in love with Ayden, but fear has stopped me from telling him, terrified that my declaration will freak him out.

He cups my ass, pushing me closer until our bodies conform. I slide my arms around him then trace my fingers up and down the nape of his neck, kissing him with everything I'm feeling, hoping it'll be enough to get it out of my system.

When his mouth leaves mine, I make a raspy protest, but words get lost as he places tender kisses down my jawline to my neck. He sucks and nips on the flesh, causing my body to swelter with overbearing heat.

"Ah . . . This feels so good," I moan with my head tipped back, clutching onto his shoulders and wishing the moment would never end.

But as soon as the wish surfaces, the front door opens, the alarm goes off, and the moment goes poof. We scramble apart, breathless, our clothes and hair in disarray. I stumble across the room back to the sofa, smoothing my dress back into place. Dropping down on the cushion, I quickly scoop up my sketchpad and pencil right as the alarm gets silenced.

My mother, Fiona, and Everson enter the living room from the foyer while my father comes hurrying in from the hallway.

"What's going on?" he asks as he rushes in. "Why's the alarm going . . . ?" He trails off when he sees my mom. "That was a quick trip."

"Yeah, we just went through the drive-thru." My mother gives a suspicious glance between Ayden and me. "What have you two been up to?"

Shrugging, I press the tip of my pencil against the paper. "Nothing. Just chillin.'"

"Sure you were." She exchanges a look with my father, and for a flash of an instant, I wonder if they know exactly what Ayden and I were up to. "Did you check on them at all while I was gone?"

My dad shrugs at her. "Not really, but the alarm was set so I'd know if they tried to leave."

"I'm not worried about them leaving."

"Then what are you worried about?"

Hello, Captain Oblivious. Even I get what she's worried about.

She presses him with a look, but he still appears lost, either clueless about what my mom's implying or unwilling to accept it.

"I have a few things I've got to take care of," he says to her, backing out of the room. "Meet you upstairs in, like, twenty minutes?"

My mom heaves an exhausted sigh. "All right."

He waggles his eyebrows at her, and then the two of them exchange a look meant only for them to see, even though there's a room full of eyes.

"Wow, way to be obvious, you two," I say to break the awkward silence in the room.

My mother shoots me a dirty look, and I flash her a

smirk.

"She's just like you," she tells my dad. "You know that, right?"

"I do." He grins, pleased. "And I'll take that as the highest compliment." He winks at me before turning and disappearing down the hallway.

My mom brushes her auburn hair off her shoulder then turns to me. "I'm going to go upstairs to take a shower. Try to behave. And have everyone in bed within the next hour."

I give her a salute. "Yes, boss."

She rolls her eyes but smiles before walking off toward the stairway. Moments later, I hear the alarm beep, meaning she set it.

Once all the parentals are out of the room, Fiona, the youngest Gregorys, plops down on the sofa beside Ayden. Kale hurries up to me, hands me a bowl of caramel swirled ice cream, then sits down on the armrest.

"I brought you ice cream." She gives Ayden one of the cups. "I got cookie dough because I know it's your favorite."

Ayden stares at the bowl with his brows knit. "How'd you know it's my favorite?"

Fiona rolls her eyes. "You think you're so mysterious, Ayden, but let me tell you, you kind of aren't." She shovels a spoonful of ice cream into her mouth then flashes him a grin. "You said something about it being your favorite during your birthday."

"Did I?" Ayden wonders, diving into his ice cream. "I don't remember telling anyone that."

"You told Lyric, just like you tell her every other secret of yours." She kicks her feet up onto the coffee table with a sassy smirk on her face.

Ayden and I share an amused look because Fiona is

a typical thirteen-year-old—full of rebellion, a sassy attitude, and keeps everyone on their toes.

"Just like you share everything else with her, including your body," she adds with a giggle.

Ayden and my eyes snap wide open, and she erupts in a fit of giggles.

Kale chokes on his ice cream. "Jesus, Fi, where's your filter?"

"I don't share my body with her." Ayden's voice cracks.

Technically, he isn't lying. I haven't touched Ayden anywhere other than on the outside of his clothes. I, however, have been very giving with my body.

"Fiona, why would you say that?" I ask coolly, stirring my ice cream.

She dabs the tears of laughter from her eyes. "Because it's true. Everyone knows it."

I lick a heap of ice cream off the spoon. "Who's everyone?"

She shrugs indifferently. "Me, Kale, Everson, half the kids at school."

"What about my parents?" I ask her. "And yours? Do they know?"

She shakes her head. "I don't think they know yet. They're pretty oblivious when it comes to these sorts of things."

I kick back on the sofa with my feet propped under me and stuff a bite full of ice cream into my mouth. When our relationship started heating up, Ayden and I agreed it'd be for the best if we kept it a secret for a while. With our families being so tight, we know that the moment they find out, they'll start giving us rules and having expectations. At eighteen-years-old, we want to have a normal relationship without parents getting involved and making everything all awkward.

"I wouldn't get too relaxed if I were you," she remarks. "Sooner or later, they're going to find out, and it'd be better if you guys told them; otherwise, you're going to hurt their feelings. You know how sensitive they can be."

I catch Ayden's gaze. "She's probably right."

He squirms uncomfortably. "Yeah, maybe." He shoves a bite of ice cream into his mouth and stares at the fireplace, lost in thought.

I open my mouth to ask him if everything's okay, but Kale speaks first. "Ayden, could you help me with something?" he asks, quickly hopping to his feet.

Ayden tears his gaze off the fireplace and blinks up at him. "What's up?"

Kale scratches his nose, appearing as uneasy as Ayden. "Can we talk about it upstairs in the guest room?" His gaze skims over Fiona and me. "In private."

"Sure." Ayden flicks a glance in my direction before he rises to his feet, looking as squirrely as the first day we met. "I'll see you in the morning."

I frown after he hurries out of the room like it's on fire. "I wonder what that's about."

"Kale has a crush on this girl at school," Fiona explains, misinterpreting what I meant. "But, since he's a weirdo, he needs Ayden's help trying to get this girl's attention. I don't know why he asked Ayden, though. He's just as much of a weirdo as Kale." She gives an elongated pause. "We all kind of are." Her eyes sparkle with mischief as they land on me. "That includes you, too, you know. You're seriously as insane as the rest of us."

"I never claimed to be sane." I jab the spoon at the ice cream, still stuck on why Ayden seemed all squiggly. "Besides, normal is so overrated. Trust me. I have a few friends who are normal, and I'd rather poke my eye out than live their lives of going off to college as soon as I graduate, getting a normal job, and eventually starting a family."

With senior year nearing the end, it's all everyone talks about anymore. Going off to college to pursue a degree that will give them an average job with stable pay.

"You don't plan on going to college?"

"No. At least, not until I see what I can do with my music career."

"Isn't that sort of risky?"

"Yeah." I balance the bowl on the armrest. "But I'd risk my sanity if I didn't at least try."

"Does your mom and dad know about this?" She sets the cup of ice cream on her knee and starts side-braiding her long, brown hair.

"I've mentioned it a couple of times," I tell her. "They're a little bit more hesitant than I am that it'll all work out."

"Figures. Parents so don't understand dreams." She secures the braid with an elastic.

"What's with the third degree, anyway? You're thirteen. Aren't you supposed to be worrying about crushes and makeup and stuff like that?"

"I do worry about that stuff, but as an aspiring artist, I also worry about my art and whether or not becoming an artist is in my future."

"I'm sure it is." I stand up with my sketchbook in my hand. "Your sketches are amazing."

"So are yours and your mother's." She collects the cup off her lap and hops to her feet, tugging at the hem of her yellow dress. "Can I see what you're drawing?"

I hesitate. The detailed drawing of Ayden feels very private and intimate, but then I realize it doesn't really matter since she already knows about our relationship.

"What the hell." I hold out my sketchpad for her to see.

She examines it closely, and a smile spans across her face. "It looks so much like him it's crazy."

I grin at her approval, tuck the sketchpad under my arm, and motion at her as I head for the stairs. "Come on. Let's go get ready for bed, and then I'll let you look at more of them."

She skips after me. "Thanks, Lyric. You're the best neighbor-who's-like-a-sister ever."

"Yeah, yeah," I start up the stairway, "you say that now, but I'm sure you'll change your mind like you do every other day."

She giggles. "Yeah, you're probably right."

After we're in our pajamas, we get situated in my room. Since we only have one guestroom in my house, Ayden and Kale are staying in it, so Fiona is camping out on my floor in a sleeping bag. The lights are off, but she uses her phone as a flashlight while she flips through my sketchpad.

"There's so many pictures of Ayden." She turns another page. "Lyric?"

"Yeah?" I answer sleepily.

"Do you love him?"

"Love who?" I yawn, already half asleep.

"Ayden."

I freeze mid-yawn and open my mouth to say no, but the lie won't leave my lips.

"It's okay," she reassures me, "I won't tell anyone."

I smile to myself as I roll over and close my eyes. I fall asleep to the sound of turning pages and my mind filled with a thousand lyrics.

So soft are his lips,
Like rose petals and velvet.

The taste of him is indescribable.
The feel of his body almost unbearable.
When he kisses me, I swear I'm dying.
Out of air, body aching, knees shaking.
More, more, more,
Always craving more.
Love, it's like an addiction,
Consuming the mind.
Love, love, love.
I'm so in love with him.

CHAPTER 4

I'M WOKEN UP IN THE dead of sleep by violent shaking. Still half stuck in dreamland, at first I think it's an earthquake, but as my eyes adjust to the night, I realize it's Fiona.

"Lyric, wake up." She gives my shoulder another shake.

"What's wrong?" I sit up, rub my eyes, and then glance at the clock. "Dude, it's only four o'clock in the morning. What the hell, Fiona?"

"It's Ayden," she says, her eyes wild with panic. "He's in trouble."

Just like that, I'm wide awake, like my body has been hotwired.

"What's wrong?" I fling the blankets off my body and spring from the bed.

"I had a dream about him," she whispers, hugging her arms around herself.

I instantly relax. "I'm sorry you had a nightmare, but seriously, you can't wake me up this early." I'm not a morning person at all.

"It wasn't a nightmare," she huffs in frustration, stomping her foot on the floor. "It really happened."

I sink down on the edge of my bed, yawning. "What happened?"

"Ayden . . . I was dreaming about him sleepwalking outside, and then the dream came true." Pale moonlight trickles through the window and highlights the fear in her expression.

"I know nightmares can be scary," I say in the most sympathetic voice I can muster at this early of an hour, "but you have to remember that they're just that—nightmares."

"It wasn't a nightmare." She marches up to the window and points at something outside. "If you don't believe me, then take a look for yourself."

My heart immediately starts pumping blood through my body at an alarming rate. I rise to my feet, pad over to the window, and peer down at the ground. At first, all I see is nightfall covering the neighborhood. But as I strain my vision, I spot a figure next door, standing out on the Gregory's front yard.

No, not Ayden. He's not supposed to leave the house and definitely not in the middle of the night.

"Ayden . . ." I whirl to Fiona. "Go wake up my mom." I run out of my room, down the stairs, and cringe when I realize the front door is wide open, and the alarm has been turned off.

Ayden knows the code, so I'm guessing he did it somehow while he's sleepwalking.

What the hell?

Even though it's April, the cement is cold against my bare feet as I race down the driveway and around the fence dividing our yards. The road is dimly lit by lampposts that offer just enough light so I'm not running around blind.

As I approach him, my pulse soars. Wide-eyed and out of it, his lips are moving as he mutters under his breath. I've found Ayden sleepwalking before, and like the first time, he's talking about stuff I don't understand.

"We're not going to let you out that easy," he mutters, staring dazedly at a car on the corner of the road. "No one leaves us. Ever."

I struggle over what to do. I know better than to wake him up; otherwise, he might flip out. But I need to get him back into the house somehow.

I reach out to touch his arm, hoping to subtly guide him back without waking him, when he turns his head and looks at me.

"We're going to come for you," he mutters. "And you're going to wish you never escaped . . ." He blinks his eyes, and then his lips part. "What the hell?" In a panic, he glances around at the houses. "Where the hell am I . . . ? How did I . . . ?" His enlarged eyes lock on me. "I don't . . ."

Shit. He's waking up and panicking.

"It's okay." I cautiously inch toward him with my arms open, preparing to hug him, but he skitters away from me with his hands out in front of him.

"How the fuck did I get out here?" he demands in a harsh voice, his eyes watering up as he gasps for air. "I don't understand."

I keep my hands in front of me while stepping toward him. "You were sleepwalking, I think. But it's okay. Everything's okay."

He clenches his hands into fists and sucks in a breath to fight back the tears, but a few escape and cascade down his cheeks. "I'm so sick of this. I feel like I'm losing my goddamn mind."

"I know, but it's going to be okay." I have no idea what else to say. No clue what to do. I feel so helpless at the moment.

"I'm so sorry." His head slumps forward as he starts

to cry.

"You have nothing to be sorry about." I loop my arm around his back and steer him toward my house. "Let's get you inside."

Nodding, his arms wraps around my waist. We hike around the fence, up the driveway, and to the front porch. I only let him go to shut the front door, but freeze when I notice the car on the corner that Ayden was staring at now has the headlights on.

I watch as it flips a U-turn and peels off down the street. With everything that has been happening, I wonder if it isn't a coincidence that the car drives off the moment we head back inside. Could it be someone stalking Ayden again?

"Lyric, what's going on?" My mother's voice floats over my shoulder.

I lock the door then turn around. She has on a robe, her hair is a tangled mess, and her tired eyes are bouncing back and forth between Fiona, Ayden, and me.

I hurry and explain what happened, making sure to include the car. She tells me not to worry, that it was probably one of the neighbors heading off to work, but her eyes show her concern.

"Let's all get back to bed, and we can talk it about in the morning, okay? When Lila and Ethan get home," my mom says, ushering us toward the stairs. "I can't believe you managed to turn the alarm off in your sleep," she mutters quietly.

"I'm sorry," Ayden apologizes as we ascend the stairs. "I don't know how I did it, either."

"Don't be sorry," my mother says from behind us. "This isn't your fault, sweetie."

Ayden bites down on his lip, not saying anything else.

"Are you okay?" I whisper to him.

"I don't know," he mumbles under his breath, loud enough that only I can hear.

I graze my fingers along his arm. "I'm here if you want to talk about it in the morning."

He nods, and then we part ways at the top of the stairway. Fiona follows me into my room and slides back into the sleeping bag while I climb into bed.

By the time I pull the covers over me, the sun is kissing the edges of San Diego and glowing across the sky, casting rays of light into my room. Restless, I stay awake to write, silently expressing what I can't say aloud, allowing myself to get lost in my words.

"Lyric, I'm scared," Fiona says so abruptly I jump and chuck the pen I'm holding like I'm some sort of spastic ninja.

"Jesus, I thought you were sleeping." I set down my journal, lean over to the side, and peer down at her. "You don't need to be scared. Ayden's fine."

"That's not what I'm scared about." She tugs the sleeping bag up higher as she gazes up at the ceiling. "I'm scared I'll have more nightmares if I shut my eyes."

"You said you dreamed that Ayden was sleepwalking?"

"Sort of," she replies vaguely. "Then, when I woke up, I saw him out on the front lawn."

This isn't the first time she has said something strange to me. There was an incident when Ayden was sleepwalking and screaming, and Fiona said she felt his scream, whatever that means.

"Does this kind of stuff happen to you a lot? I mean, do you dream about things that happen?"

"I don't dream it . . . I feel it happen." With her eyes opened so wide, she looks utterly horrified. She abruptly bolts upright and snatches hold of my hand in desperation. "You can't tell anyone that. Promise me, Lyric." When I don't agree right away, she tightens her hold on my hand. "This is important. I need it to stay a secret, just like you need the fact that you're dating Ayden to stay a secret."

I have no idea what's going on. If she's blackmailing me. If she's crazy. If I'm crazy because I kind of believe her.

"All right, I promise," I say with reluctance. "Just as long as you keep quiet about me and Ayden."

"I will." She releases her grasp on my hand and lies back down on the floor. "Thanks, Lyric." She rolls over on her side, and a minute later, she's fast asleep, breathing softly.

Wigged out by the last few hours of events, I grab another pen from my nightstand drawer and return to my journal to write. My thoughts drift from what Fiona told me to what happened with Ayden. The pen floats fluidly across the paper, pouring out my soul and the deepest fears I don't dare utter aloud.

How do I save him
When the world has so much control?
Spinning through life, a turbulent force,
Sucking him down into a dark hole.
Sunlight spills upon me,
Drowns me in warmth.
I outrun it for as long as I can.
He's falling into the dark, begging to be saved,
Pleading for me to save him.
I reach for him,
But the sunlight devours me
And burns my hands,
Singeing me to dust.

CHAPTER 5

Ayden

LAST NIGHT WAS GOING OKAY until Lyric mentioned that we'd eventually have to tell our parents we're dating. I never really thought about it too much, but once she pointed it out, I realized she was right. One day, they'll find out about us, and I'll have to face my unworthiness. Deep down, I've always known her parents weren't going to be thrilled about the messed up guy next door dating their cheery, upbeat daughter. I was ruined the moment I was chained up in that house. Those days spent locked under that roof changed me, fucked me up, poisoned my skin with marks that will never go away.

To top off the declining night, I ended up sleepwalking to the front lawn, which was not only terrifying as hell, but also extremely dangerous, all things considering.

I have no memory of what happened until the point when Lyric woke me up, yet the moment Lila and Ethan return home the next afternoon, they expect me to recount the details to them.

After Kale, Everson, and Fiona are set up at the table, doing their homework, the three of us sit down in the living room with cups of coffee and cookies because Lila believes sugar eases tense situations.

"I really can't tell you too much about what happened." I pick at a loose thread in the knee of my jeans. "All I can remember is waking up and seeing Lyric."

Lyric, poor Lyric.
Worried out of her mind
As she stared into my eyes
And tried to read what was hidden in my mind.
What would she see if she broke through the lock?
What I witnessed all those days I was trapped in the dark?
I wish she never had to see that side of me.
Wish. Wish. Wish.
Wish I could be the guy she deserves,
The one who touches her with everything,
Gives her everything,
Could give her undying love.

"What about the car?" Lila brings the brim of a coffee mug to her mouth and sips. She's been pretending to be calm, but under the surface, I can tell she's frightened about the ordeal.

"I didn't really notice it." I stuff the rest of the cookie into my mouth then wipe my hands off. "Lyric did."

"Lyric said you were staring at it." Ethan threads his fingers through Lila's to comfort her. "And then it drove away the moment you got into the house."

"If that's what she said, then I'm sure it happened that way." I lift my shoulder and shrug, unsure of what they want me to say. "I swear, if I knew more, I'd tell you, but I'm just as confused as you." And terrified out of my mind.

I'll never admit that aloud, though, because then they'll only worry about me more.

I've lived with the Gregorys for over two years now, and they're some of the nicest people I've ever met. Always wanting to keep me safe. Always trying to protect me.

"We know you'd tell us if you could remember," Lila says, setting the cup of coffee down on the table. "I just think what we really want to make sure of is that you're okay. I know it's got to be hard, being stalked by these people and always worrying if . . ." She smashes her lips together as she emotionally tears up.

The clock ticks in the background. Out the window, the sun is shining across the clear blue sky, cars zip up and down the street. A neighbor is shouting at a dog, and a lady with bright red hair is strolling down the sidewalk. Her hair reminds me of blood and almost throws me back into a memory of when I ran into that house. I almost let the images through, because I want to help my sister, want to remember who the people were that took us. But my body constricts, forcing the images to fade away.

"I'm not sure what you want me to say other than I'm fine." I blink my attention away from the window, pick up my cup of coffee, and gulp down the hot drink.

"Okay." Lila casts a glance at Ethan. "Still, it has to be really, really stressful, especially when we don't know if they're going to show up again."

She seems fairly adamant about pointing out the danger of the situation, and I'm not sure why. She knows I understand, so there has to be some other reason.

"Ethan and I worry about you," she continues. "After the note and the car being out there last night, we think it might be a good idea if you aren't alone very much."

"Haven't I been doing that already?" I ask. "Especially after getting that note the other day and then talking to the detective."

"Yes, but . . ." She glances at Ethan again. "We just want to make sure you understand the importance of you following the rules and being safe."

"Yeah, I understand the rules. Have for a while." I

glance back and forth between them. "Is there something you aren't telling me?"

It wouldn't be the first time they've kept stuff from me in order to try to protect me from the harsh reality.

"We're not keeping anything from you." Ethan leans forward in the seat and rests his elbows on his knees. "We just want to make sure you're being safe, and you're taking care of yourself mentally. We think you've been a little too quiet these last couple of months."

"I've always been quiet." *Where are they going with this?*

"We know that, but it seems like, ever since you found out about your sister, you've been even quieter."

"We just want you to know how sorry we are that this is happening," Lila adds, her eyes welled up with tears. "I know it's got to be hard, especially after what happened to your brother."

I flex my fingers as my hands begin to tremble.

My brother, gone forever.

Gone, gone, gone.

Just like my sister might be.

After we all miraculously made it out of the house alive, only one of us might survive.

Or maybe none, depending on the outcome.

It isn't like I haven't ever thought about it—that the Soulless Mileas could get ahold of me again—I've worried about it every hour of every day for the last four years. The note increased the fear, though, and made the idea very real.

"We just want you to know that we're here for you if you ever need anything." Lila stands up, crosses the room, and takes a seat beside me. "We love you, Ayden. If you need anything at all, you can let us know, and we'll do whatever's in our power to make it happen."

It's a nice offer, but what I want isn't in their power—a normal life with my sister and without the painful reminder of the past branded on my flesh.

Then a couple of ideas strike me from out of nowhere, ideas I've contemplated before but have been too afraid to ask.

"There actually might a couple of things you can do for me." I sit up straighter in the chair. "Could you ask the detective if I can read the letter my sister wrote? I want to know what's on there."

Lila's expression fills with remorse. "I'm not sure they'll agree to that, seeing as how it's evidence." She places a hand on my back, a motherly gesture, but still, the contact causes me to tense.

"Could you at least ask?" I ask, one step away from begging her. "It can't hurt to ask, right? And maybe it could help me figure out what I'm getting into since she wrote the note right after she was kidnapped."

"If that's what you need, then I guess I can ask." A deep frown etches her face, and worry lines crease the corners of her eyes.

Knowing Lila, she's probably worried how I'll react to reading the letter, hence the hesitancy. It isn't for her to decide, though. I *need* to know what's in the note my sister was forced to write and mail to the police while she's being held captive somewhere by people who are skeletons of human beings and once tried to drain our souls dry.

"Thanks." I scratch at my side, preparing to ask my next question. "I also want to get the tattoo on my side covered up . . . the one they put on me."

It's a big step just asking for it, but I've wanted the tattoo removed forever. The only thing stopping me has been my fear of being touched during the inking and of tumbling into a memory. I want to believe I have the hidden strength to do it, though.

Lila glances at Ethan. "What do you think?"

"I actually like the idea of getting rid of it." He digs his phone from his pocket. "I have a buddy who owns a tattoo parlor down by where I work. He does good work. I could take you in to see what it would take to get it covered up."

"Thanks. That'd be great."

I know it won't solve my problems, but the idea of having the tattoo gone gives me the strangest sense of peace.

A taste of freedom
From the bleeding ink
Staining my skin
Like the blood on their hands.
Gone, gone, gone,
The ink is fading away.
Maybe after it's erased,
I can finally feel like I was actually saved.

After Lila and Ethan agree to my requests, I collect the car keys to head to my therapy appointment.

"You're just going straight there, right?" Lila checks while walking me to the door.

I shake my head as I grab my jacket from the coatrack. "Yeah, I don't have band practice tonight." Throwing a wave over my shoulder, I open the door and step outside beneath the clouds.

"You'll call me when you get there, right?" Lila asks, following me outside. "And text the therapist to come walk you in if no one's around?"

"Yeah, I know the drill." I stop at the end of the walkway, studying her. She has her arms folded tightly around her, and her gaze is continuously inspecting the houses across the street. *Odd.* "Is everything okay?"

"Of course." She smiles stiffly. "I was just making sure that car wasn't out here. Lyric said it was a black, newer model, right?"

"I think so." I eye her warily, not believing her story. "But you do realize that description fits every other car in this neighborhood."

She sighs. "I know. I really wish she could have gotten a better look at it."

Raindrops start to fall from the sky, and I pull my hood over my head. "It could have been someone going to work."

"Yeah, it could have," she replies, seeming doubtful. Her eyes rise to the stormy sky, and she shields her hair from the rain with her arm. "Anyway, you get going. I'm going to be here all day, so if you need anything at all, then call."

Nodding, I jog up the driveway toward the black, newer BMW, which kind of proves my point about the car. With everything that's happened, though, I can't blame them for being concerned. I just wish I wasn't such a burden, always causing stress and worry.

Lila remains on the front porch, watching me back onto the road and steer toward the main street.

I make the drive toward the therapist's office across town with the radio up, listening to one of the playlists Lyric made for me. Being in the car alone always makes me edgy, and I'm always checking in my rearview mirror for some sign someone is tailing me.

Today, I swear a massive maroon SUV with tinted windows matches my every turn and lane change. But right as I start to panic, the vehicle veers down a side road.

Breathing easily, I flip on the blinker at the next road and take a right, driving into a rundown neighborhood located a few miles away from my therapist's office.

A light drizzle of rain sprinkles from the clouds as I park the car in front of the house that was the last address listed for Sadie.

The house is boarded up and painted with jagged circular symbols that match the tattoo on my ribs. The home resembles most of the surrounding structures on the street, so the entire area is extremely creepy. In a strange way, the place reminds me of the home I grew up in and how damn lucky I am to be living where I am now.

I know it isn't the best thing to be here, but I can't help myself. Something about the place terrifies me yet draws me to it.

I've been making the detour for the last month. Every time I stop by, I contemplate going inside and looking around in the hope that I get a better understanding of what Sadie went through while she was living here. But I've never gotten the balls to even get out of the car.

I remain in the car, staring at the peeling paint, wondering if it was put there after Sadie was kidnapped or if they did it beforehand. The detective said our cases are similar, and that they stalked her first before taking her, but I still don't know exactly how it happened.

I don't know
Anything
About her
Other than my heart aches for her.

A year younger than me, Sadie should be a junior in high school, having fun, going to parties like I used to before I got put on lockdown. I haven't seen her since we were removed from that house four years ago, and I don't know what her life has been like since then. Looking at the homes around me, I'm guessing it hasn't been great.

I gawk at the house for ten minutes straight before I put the car in drive and start to pull away.

"I promise I won't let anything happen to you," I whisper to Sadie from across the room.

"How? You're tied up, too," she cries through the darkness, her voice weak.

Chains, chains, chains bite at my flesh.
Peel back the skin, reveal what's inside.
Look at me raw, see the truth in my eyes.

"I don't know how, but I will, Sadie. I swear."

Broken promises,
Cracked and ruptured.
Left behind,
Like dust on the floor.
I'm sorry I lied.

I slam on the brakes and strangle the steering wheel as the memory crawls under my skin. Fueled with the need to see what's hidden in the house, to understand just how badly I let my sister down, I shove the car back into park, fling the door open, and climb out.

Raindrops splatter across my face and drip from my hair as I hike up the lopsided driveway. When I reach the side door of the house, I glance around to make sure no one is watching me before opening it.

The smell of mold and rot engulfs my nostrils as I step over the threshold and inside what looks like a kitchen. The floorboards groan under my boots as I inch my way into the darkness.

Sticking my hand into my pocket, I remove my phone and turn on the flashlight app to get a better look around.

The cupboards are hanging crooked on the walls, the countertops are torn up, and shards of glass cover the floor.

I carefully maneuver my way through the kitchen and into the living room, the atmosphere growing darker as the outside world slips away from me. To my right is a stairway, but most of the steps are missing. I veer in the opposite direction toward a closed door tucked behind a raised wall. Painted across the wall are words that are way too familiar: *Running away is like running in circles. You can't escape once we've found your soul, and soon, you'll end up back in the same place.*

A cold shiver courses through me. I heard those words whispered during the weeks I was trapped.

Panicking, I turn away, but stop mid-turn.

No. I need to go through with this.

Wheeling back around, I inch toward the door, noticing an *S* carved in the wood right above the doorknob.

No, not Sadie.

My phone buzzes a few times, but I ignore it, needing to go through with this. I wrap my fingers around the metal knob and, with a deep breath, push open the door.

The stench of the room smothers the air from my lungs, heavy and weighted like death. I cough, covering my mouth with my arm as I glance around the small room with caved in walls and a rotting floor. In the middle of the mess is the metal frame of a bed. I can almost picture my sister sitting on it day in and day out, waiting to be saved, but no one ever shows up, and soon she's taken away to a far worse life than even this.

Tears sting my eyes. I know it isn't a memory, but thinking about what she must have gone through—is still going through—aches deep inside me like searing hot metal against my bones.

As I veer toward a panic attack, I spin on my heels and rush out of the house. By the time I burst back into the rain, I'm quivering from head to toe as fear pulsates through me. I run down the driveway toward my car, needing to get the hell out of here. Rain pours from the sky and soaks through my clothes as my boots splash through the puddles.

"Excuse me. Do you live here?" A woman wearing a

bright red raincoat with the hood pulled over her head is suddenly at the end of the driveway.

I slam to a stop and hurry and wipe my eyes with my sleeve, trying to catch my breath. "No . . . I was just . . . I knocked on the door, but no one answered," I lie, unsure of what else to say.

She glances at the home then at me. "You know it's vacant, right?"

"I figured that out, yes." As casually as I can, I move to the right to swing around her, knowing if I stand near that house for too long, I'll lose my shit.

"Didn't the boarded up windows and spray paint kind of give that away?" she asks, sidestepping and blocking my path.

Red flags pop up everywhere.

My eyelashes flutter against the rainstorm as I skim her over. She's medium height, a little on the thin side, and is wearing black rain boots. Her hood is pulled so low I can hardly see her face, but her voice sounds gruff, like a heavy smoker.

Do I know that voice? Or am I just being paranoid?

Her hair isn't red like blood, red like the woman who always wanted to touch me. That's the only sense of comfort I have at the moment, but hair dye can easily fix that.

I duck my head to get a better look at her, but she steps back, stuffing her hands into her pockets.

"You better be careful. This place isn't safe." She spins on her heels and runs down the sidewalk away from me.

"Hey!" I call out, hurrying after her.

I don't know why, but I have this crazy feeling that she might know something.

She picks up her speed as she nears the end of the block. I bring my pace from a jog to a sprint as she makes a left and disappears behind a fence. By the time I reach the corner, she's gone.

"Shit!" I curse, kicking a street sign.

"Ayden."

I freeze then turn around, shielding my eyes as I squint through the rain at Lila who's standing a few feet away from me, wearing her coat and carrying an umbrella.

"I . . . Why are you . . . ?" I look around the street and spot a maroon SUV parked at the entrance of the neighborhood, the same car I thought was following me. "What's going on?"

"Shouldn't I be asking you the same question?" She shakes her head with dismay. "Get in the car. We need to talk."

I look back in the direction the woman vanished. "There was someone here, talking to me. It seemed like she was warning me about something."

Lila leans forward and peers down the street while positioning the umbrella over both of our heads.

"They're not there anymore," I explain. "But it was a woman, and—I don't know—I have a bad feeling about her."

She frowns as she looks back at me. "This entire place is one bad feeling. Now get in the car so you can explain to me what the hell you were thinking coming here."

The walk back to the car is painfully slow and quiet. By the time we climb inside, the SUV is pulling away, and the rain has slowed down.

"Who is that?" I ask, pointing at the vehicle.

"That was an undercover detective," she says, slamming the car door.

"What?" Suddenly, their little not-being-alone speech makes much more sense. "Why is he following me?"

"Well, for starters, we want to make sure you're safe. And secondly, because Dr. Gardingdale informed us that you've been late to the last eight sessions."

"You could have just asked me what I was doing."

She elevates her brows at me accusingly. "Every time we ask you about anything, you tell us you're fine. Plus, you tracked down this place"—she nods her head at the house—"all by yourself. You searched for your sister's address for months, and Lyric was the only one you ever told. So, how could I possibly know you'd tell us the truth if I asked?"

Okay, she has a point.

"We needed to find out where you were going since you won't ever tell us anything." She tosses the umbrella into the backseat, and then her eyes narrow at me. "I hate being this kind of mom—the one who gets angry at her children—but seriously, what the hell were you thinking, coming here by yourself?"

"The police investigated this place after Sadie was taken," I remind her as I rev up the engine and flip on the wipers. "They didn't find anything suspicious other than the paint on the outside and inside."

"Other than the paint." She gapes at me. "Ayden, that paint all over the house matches that mark on your side, the one put on you against your will. That's not a little thing."

"I know." I lose my voice as guilt creeps up inside me for upsetting her. "But I just wanted to see for myself."

Her expression slightly softens. "I understand that you want to know what's going on—we all do—but you can't go around looking for stuff on your own. Not after what's been going on and that note . . ." She trails off, shaking her head.

I flop my head back against the headrest. "I get that I fucked up, but I feel like I'm losing my damn mind. Every day, I wake up worried something's going to happen to me. Or worse, the police will knock on our door again, only this time, they'll be there to tell me my sister's been found dead."

She's quiet for a while, probably trying to figure out what the hell to say to my out of the blue confession.

"I get that it's hard." She gently places a hand on my arm, and for once, I don't flinch. "But wandering off by yourself isn't going to help. You need to let the police do their job and focus on yourself and getting better. Talking like this—telling me how you feel—that's a start. I've never heard you be so open."

"I think I'm just getting tired of keeping everything locked in all the time." I shut my eyes. "It's hard just to focus on myself when it feels like anyone could be them. Like that woman I just saw."

"What did she say to you exactly?" she asks, cranking up the heat. I recap the last five minutes to her, and she frowns when I'm finished.

"Honestly, I'm not that worried. This area is very sketchy, and it could have easily been a nervous drug dealer or something. But I'll go let the detective know about her, and maybe they can track her down."

I draw the seatbelt strap over my shoulder. "How long have I been followed?"

"Only since the note."

"How long am I going to be followed?"

"Until we know you're safe." She nods as she sticks her hand into her coat pocket and retrieves her phone. "Besides, they're hoping the next time they try to do something, they'll catch them in the act."

"So, they're watching me all the time."

"For the most part." She gives me a sidelong glance. "So no more running off to dangerous places." She reaches for the door handle. "Now, go straight to your appointment and then home. Nowhere else. Don't go looking for that woman. Let the police handle it."

"All right," I reply, because I don't really have any other choice.

"Thank you for making this easy." She hops out into the now sprinkling rain.

"Wait. How did you get here?" I ask, leaning over the console.

"The detective called me the moment he figured out where you were going." She lowers her head to look at me. "When I got the call, I hopped in my car and drove as crazy as Ella to get here."

"Where's your car?"

She points diagonally across the street, and I easily spot the back end of her silver Mercedes.

"Oh." Through the rain and the distraction of the woman, I must have somehow missed the obvious.

"I'll see you in about an hour and a half." She closes the door, and just like that, our conversation ends.

As I make the short drive to therapy with the SUV tailing me, I feel like I've been put on probation. Having come from a home where, most of the time, my siblings and I ran wild, I feel strangely okay that. For the first time in a long time, I feel kind of safe.

Ten minutes later, I enter the office where my therapy sessions take place. The rain has let up by the time I walk in, and sunlight sneaks through the clouds and glimmers through the windows.

"Hey, Ayden, how have you been?" Dr. Gardingdale greets without looking up from the filing cabinet he's sifting through.

"Good." I drop down in the chair across from his desk.

He glances up at me. "You don't sound good." He glides the filing cabinet drawer shut, pulls out a chair, and then sits down. "Is something wrong?"

Out of habit, I shake my head, but words slip out of my mouth on their own. "Did you tell Lila I was showing up late to sessions?"

"I did," he answers shamelessly. "I was concerned that you might be doing something that could harm your wellbeing."

"Why would you figure that?"

"Because of something you said at your last appointment."

"What did I say exactly?"

"That you were thinking about going and looking for your sister yourself."

"I said that?" Why can't I remember that?

"You were under when you said it," he explains, checking the time on the wall clock. "It was during an amnesia therapy session."

I attempt to remember, but come up blank. "Why didn't you tell me?"

"Because you were upset when you woke up." He tugs on his red and blue striped tie, loosening it. "It was the session where you—"

"Cried," I finish for him.

I cringe at the faint memory of me waking up to the branding iron. The pain was unbearable. I could still feel it when I woke up.

"I didn't want to upset you, but I thought I needed to tell your mother about what happened and about being late to sessions." He pauses, giving me an opening to explain where I've been.

"I think maybe I should reconsider that slip I signed, giving you permission to discuss certain things with the Gregorys."

"Is that what you really want?"

I hesitate then shake my head. "No, not really. They

don't deserve to worry like that."

"I think that's a wise choice." His phone buzzes, and he silences it without looking at it. "So, is there anything else bothering you? Maybe at home? Or at school?" His light questions are his way of easing into the darker stuff, which always comes later in the hour.

"No . . . not exactly . . ." I trail off, uncertain how much talking I want to do today. It's been such a stressful day already. "Nothing's really wrong at home or school."

It's not as easy as it sounds
To confess my darkest worries,
My fears of who I am,
My fear of never being good enough.

He slips on his glasses. "Remember, I can't help you unless I know what the problem is." When I still don't answer, he adds, "Do you want to talk about your sister? I don't usually like to dive into the complicated stuff, but if you need us to, we can. I know what's going on with her has to be stressful. Plus, you've been putting a lot of pressure on yourself with this amnesia therapy because of what's happened to her."

I wipe my sweaty palms on my jeans. "That's not what I was going to say . . . but I do worry about her. All the time, actually. I even went to that address she used to live at . . . That's why I've been late."

Shock flickers across his face, but he keeps himself professionally composed, his voice remaining even. "Can I ask why you've been going there?"

I shrug. "I was curious where she lived and what her life was like up until she was taken. Plus, in this weird way, it made me feel close to her." I only realize the truth when the words leave my lips.

Deep down, I knew going in that house wouldn't help find Sadie. It was the last place she lived, the last place she might have had a life.

"That's understandable," he says. "It has to be hard on you having not seen her for years, only to find out she's been kidnapped."

"I feel like I hardly got to know her. I was fourteen when we were taken, and she was only thirteen. My older brother was almost sixteen, but still, it seems like such a short amount of time . . . time I'll never get back. And, with my brother, I'll never have a chance to get any more time at all." I force down the lump in my throat.

"I've been dreaming about her a lot . . . Sadie. She's in a house on this hill, and she's tied up and hurt. I can hear her, but . . . I can't help her. All I want to do is help her, and I feel like, if I can just see what's around the house, then I'll be able to find her. But I never have the dream long enough for me to figure out the exact location."

"Are you sure it's a dream? Perhaps it's a memory."

"I honestly have no fucking idea anymore. Sometimes, it's hard to tell what's really happened and what's a nightmare. Sometimes, I feel like my mind gets all jumbled because it's overthinking too much, if that makes any sense."

Lightning booms from outside, causing me to jump. Out the window, the clouds have rolled in again, blocking the sunlight from the earth.

His forehead creases. "I know you're not going to be happy about this, but I've been considering maybe having you take a break from the amnesia therapy."

"What?" I jolt upright in my seat. "No, I can't do that. Please, don't make me do that."

He offers me a sympathetic look. "Ayden, I'm sorry to say this, because I know you want to help find your sister, but I think we might be putting too much pressure on you, and the brain doesn't do well with stress."

He scoots his chair forward and crosses his arms on

his desk. "It was stress and the pain from the situation that made you forget to begin with. Perhaps a little break might be beneficial and might actually help you have an easier time remembering, if that makes sense."

"I don't want to stop the therapy yet, not when my memories are starting to surface on their own." I shift my weight in the chair. "I've actually been thinking a lot about that experimental therapy you told me about, the one Lila doesn't want me to do. I'm eighteen now, though, so doesn't that mean I technically don't need her permission?"

"Legally, you don't need the permission from a guardian, but I wouldn't advise it. Like I said, your brain needs rest." He removes his glasses and cleans the lenses with a rag he fishes from a drawer beside him. "I'm not saying we're going to stop forever. We can go back to the therapy in time."

"My sister doesn't have time," I croak, my emotions thick in my throat.

"Finding your sister isn't solely your job. The police are doing everything in their power to find her."

"The longer she's gone, the less likely she's . . ." My chest aches just thinking about it, deep wounds hidden beneath the scars.

There were so many scars on all of us when we were pulled out of that house. So many scars showing just how truly evil they were.

"I think we need to start working on some relaxation exercises," he says as he watches me fight to get oxygen into my lungs.

He puts his glasses back on, collects a pen and notebook from the drawer, and then stares at me for the longest time before asking, "Can I ask what you were going to say to start with? I asked you what's wrong when you walked in, but we never made it to what you were going to say."

I gradually inhale then exhale before I can speak. "I was going to say what's been bothering me is . . . Lyric."

"The girl you've been seeing?"

"Yeah. We've actually been dating in secret."

"Why do you feel the need to keep it a secret?" he asks, jotting something down in the notebook.

"We've been saying it's because our parents are really close, and if we told them, they'd start setting all these rules, but . . ." I sketch the scars on the back of my hand, faint white lines put there by fingernails.

"But what?" he treads cautiously. "Remember, in order for me to help you work through the problem, you have to discuss it with me."

A deafening breath escapes my lips. "I'm starting to realize my reason is a bit different than hers."

"How so?"

"I don't know . . . I think I'm just worried about what's going to happen when her parents find out. Lyric . . . She's so happy and full of life. She can make anyone laugh, and everyone loves her. Me,"—I internally cringe—"well, I'm not like that at all."

He writes down a few more notes. "So, you think you don't fit well with her?"

"No, I think she's—that I'm—" I rub my hand down my face, releasing a trapped a breath. "Look, I know I'm not good enough for her."

His hand stops moving across the paper as he peers up. "And what does Lyric say about how you feel?"

"I haven't told her, but if I did, she'd tell me I'm wrong, because that's the kind of person she is."

Silence stretches between us as he slides the notebook aside and overlaps his hands on his desk. "Can I ask why you feel unworthy?"

"Because she's too good for me," I reply with a shrug.

"I thought that was pretty clear."

"I think it's only clear to yourself," he explains, meticulously assessing my expression. "I think that, perhaps, because of the verbal abuse with your birth mother and with the trauma you endured in your past, your self-perception is a little distorted."

"I think my past is part of the reason I'm not good enough for her," I disagree with him. "I think I have this dark, fucked-up past that's made me a fucked-up person who doesn't deserve to be with someone who's so happy and good. God, I can barely let her touch me without freaking out. " The truth slips out of me like venom. My breath turns ragged, and my heartbeat skyrockets. "And, if we do make it too far with the physical stuff, I have to battle down this ugly, wrong feeling inside me. I don't want to be this way, though. I wish I could change it . . . just get past it."

"Our past doesn't shape who we are, and as for the not being able to withstand physical contact, that's perfectly understandable considering what happened to you. I know we haven't outright talked about the abuse you went through, but I think maybe, when you're ready, we should start discussing it."

"But how can I discuss something I'm not positive ever happened? I just assume it did because of how I feel inside and through bits and pieces of the memories I can remember."

"We don't have to discuss the details. We can just discuss your feelings." He grabs his pen and paper again and scribbles down some notes. "I think that's something we'll work on in your next session. In the meantime, I'm going to teach you some relaxation exercises to help calm yourself down when you're having a panic attack."

"I wish it were that easy, because I want her to be able

to touch me, but I just don't see it working." I nervously crack my knuckles. "I always panic whenever things get too far."

"It'll take some time, but I have all the confidence that you'll eventually get to a place in your life where you'll be able to handle physical contact. Do you want to know why?" he asks, and I nod. "Because you want to get better. I can tell. And wanting to overcome something is the first step to getting there."

I hope he's right. God, do I hope. But until I see proof, I won't be able to believe it.

"What about my memories? I don't want to stop doing the therapy." Don't want to give up on Sadie.

"We're not stopping," he promises. "We're just taking a short break and giving your mind some time to settle."

I curl my fingers in and stab my nails into my palm as guilt crashes through me.

Sadie, I'm so sorry.
Sorry, sorry, sorry.
Sorry I can't find you,
Sorry I've forgotten,
Sorry you have to suffer.
If I could, I'd take your place.
God, how I wish it were me instead of her.
What I wouldn't give to make that happen.

CHAPTER 6

"I LOVE THE SMELL OF spring," I declare as I inhale the delicious scent of the air. "It always makes me smile."

"Everything makes you smile." Ayden hands me a rag with a hint of a grin on his face.

It's been a week since he sleepwalked, and for the most part, he seems to be okay. I'd put money on it, though, that he still feels guilty about the ordeal. Guilty because he worried everyone. Guilty because he freaked me out. My dear, shy boy, always worrying about everyone except himself. I wish I could talk to him about it without upsetting him, but after seeing him cry, I worry mentioning anything will trigger a nerve.

His parents—who I call Uncle Ethan and Aunt Lila, even though we're not related—must have had the same thought process as me, because they seem pretty hush, hush about what happened.

"That's not true." I collect the rag from him and duck my head under the hood of my 1970 Dodge Challenger. My dad and I have been working on fixing it up since December, and I'm hoping to have it drivable soon. "Bugs don't make me smile. Or frowny faces."

He snorts a laugh. "Frowny faces? Only you would say frowns don't make you smile."

"That's because I'm that awesome." I pull the dipstick out and wipe it off with the rag before dipping it back inside the oil.

"That, you are," he remarks, moving up behind me.

"And don't ever forget that, my friend." I remove the dipstick, glance at the oil level, then put the stick back in. Wiping my hand off with a rag, I step back from the car. "It looks like it might—" My back bumps into Ayden.

He hardly ever instigates contact first, expect on rare, amazing, wonder-filled occasions, so I allow myself to enjoy the earth-shattering moment and breathe in the feel of his body heat.

I smile stupidly when he doesn't move away. "Whatcha doing?"

"Nothing." His voice is uneven, revealing his nerves. "I was just . . ." He releases a breath then places his hands on my hips. Surprisingly, his fingers are steady. "I just wanted to touch you." He rests his forehead against the back of my head and inhales deeply. "And to make sure you're okay."

"Okay about what?" My eyelids drift shut as I lean into his touch.

His simple touches are better than light.
They awaken my body and bring it to life.
More. More. More, my body is craving.
The addiction is potent, consuming, aching.
Leaves my body wanting, pleading, shaking.
Sometimes I feel like I'm withering, fading.
Fading. Fading. Fading.
Into him.

"About . . . about what happened the other day . . . when I sleepwalked." His fingers grasp onto me, and his chest crashes against my back as his shallow breaths turn ragged. "I know I probably freaked you out. I've been meaning to ask you about it, but I didn't want to upset you, so I decided to wait until stuff cooled off."

"I'm not upset about what happened." And not surprised one little bit that my theory about him was right. I turn around and loop my arms around him. "I'm just worried about you and how you're handling it."

"I'm fine," he swears, searching my eyes for my true feelings. He forgets, though, that I'm like an open book. "It's not anything I haven't dealt with before. But you... What did I say to you exactly while I was asleep?"

"Nothing I could really understand."

"Are you sure? Because, if I said anything weird... Then I want to know."

"The whole situation is a little strange," I admit. "You were completely out of it, yet you were standing there, talking and... crying."

"I cried?" His mouth curves to a frown. "I'm so sorry. I can't believe I did that in front of you."

"Stop worrying." I lure him closer to me with a jerk, the movement rougher than I intended. "You have nothing to be sorry about. You sleepwalk. So what? We all have our weird, little quirks."

He cracks a small, adorable smile. "And what are your weird, little quirks?"

"Um, hello, isn't that kind of obvious? I'm *always* as freaking cheery and sparkly as the sun is on crack, trying to spin everything and everyone into sugar and rainbows with my smile. Albeit, it's an adorable smile." I flash him my pearly whites. "I bet it's kind of blinding and gets a little tiring to deal with all the time, though."

"It'll never get tiring." His mood shifts as his gaze drops to my lips. "And your smile's beautiful."

I have to take a moment to catch my breath; otherwise, my voice will wobble like mad-crazy. "You can kiss me if you want."

"Can I?" He tries to tease, but his voice comes out raspy.

Leaning in, he places his lips against mine, giving me a featherlike kiss.

"That's it?" I jut out my lip when he pulls away.

Sucking in a few calculated breaths, his hands glide around my back, and he fumbles with the hem of my tank top. "It's getting late, and your parents will be coming home soon. I don't want them to find us making out in the garage." When I crinkle my nose, he adds, "Lila and Ethan aren't going to be home for a while, though, so . . ."

"So, what?" I play dumb and totally get rewarded when he blushes.

"I thought we could, you know . . ." He lifts one hand to nervously massage the back of his neck. "Go up to my room for a while, and"—his blush deepens—"continue kissing."

I choke on a giggle. "I knew what you meant from the beginning, but it was fun watching you get all weirded out."

He jokingly scowls at me. "That was kind of mean."

"Yeah, I know. It's a good thing you love me." I instantly want to kick myself for dropping the L-bomb. I know the word makes him squeamish.

He stares at me, his expression unreadable, as silences encompasses us.

"So, yeah, let's go inside," I say awkwardly after a soundless moment goes by.

Not saying anything, he laces our fingers together and steers me out of the garage, down my driveway, and toward his house. He pauses when we're about to walk inside and suddenly looks down at the end of the driveway.

I track his gaze to Miss Finkleson, our neighbor across the street, watering her garden in her bathrobe. "What are you looking at?"

"Making sure my . . . babysitter isn't around." He tensely massages his neck.

"Babysitter? Dude, what are you talking about?" I squint at his expression. "Did you get high with Sage today?"

"No." He sighs, his hand falling to his side. "Because of everything going on, an undercover detective has been following me to make sure I'm safe. I didn't know it, though, and got caught going somewhere. Lila made it seem like, because I fucked up, I was going to be watched all the time, but I haven't noticed the car around for the last couple of hours."

"What were you doing?" I wonder. "When you got caught?"

He pulls an oh-I'm-so-busted expression. "Hanging out in front of that house Sadie last lived at. Figures the day I decide to go inside is the day they followed me. Lila was really fucking pissed off at me."

He went into that house?

A detective is following him?

To keep him safe?

I bite down on my lip hard as reality crushes down on me and causes my eyes to water up.

"Lyric, what's wrong?" He lowers his face closer to mine, searching my eyes. "Are you . . . ? Are you *crying?*"

"No," I lie, sucking back the waterworks. "I'm almost crying."

"Almost crying?" He frowns. "What'd I say that upset you?"

"It's not what you said. It's what you didn't say, which

I know is a really cliché girlfriend thing to whine about." I blink up at the sunlight filtering through the sky, only because I can't look him in the eye at the moment. "I hate that you keep stuff from me. You going to that house is like the Internet hacker all over again."

"No, it's not." He cups my face between his hands, forcing me to look at him. "I didn't tell you about this, because I was still trying to figure out for myself why the hell I felt the need to go there all the time." He smooths his hands down my cheeks, down my neck and shoulders, leaving a trail of heat all the way to my waist. "I realized I was searching for something I'd never really find, so I won't be going back."

"Good. You should have never gone there by yourself, ever. Not with all this stuff going on. It's too dangerous."

"I couldn't go back even if I wanted to. Not when that detective is keeping an eye on me." He contemplates something. "It was weird, though. While I was there, a woman came up to me and told me it wasn't safe for me to be there. But it was raining, and she had the hood of her coat pulled up so I couldn't see her face."

"That's strange," I agree, trying not to go all crazy-girlfriend on him. But he has me incredibly worried that he's going to do something stupid. "Did you tell Lila about her?"

"Yeah, she called Detective Rannali, and he said he'd look into it, but I guess the area where the house is has a high crime rate, especially with drugs, and he seems pretty convinced the woman was just warning me to get the hell out of the area."

I step closer, eliminating the space between us. "Ayden, promise me, the next time you're going to try something questionable, you'll tell me first. I know you have this whole belief that you need to do everything alone so you won't burden everyone with your problems, but I want to be burdened. No, I *need* to be burdened."

He presses his lips together and nods once. "All right. I promise."

"Thank you." I free a breath of relief. "I always need to know you're okay." I step back and twine my fingers with his. "Now, let's go inside and make out."

His lips threaten to pull upward as he turns and leads me the rest of the way to the back door. I can feel the beat of his heart pulsating from his fingertips as we enter his house.

It's quiet inside, soundless inside.

"So, no one's home at all?" I ask as we kick off our shoes in the foyer.

He shakes his head, giving me a nervous, sidelong glance. "Nope, everyone's gone for at least another hour."

Biting back a smile, I let him steer me into the kitchen. The air smells like cinnamon and chocolate, and I spot a plate of cookies on the counter.

"Yes! Cookies!" I exclaim a little too excitedly. Aunt Lila owns her own catering business and is an amazing cook. "I love it when she bakes."

He laughs at me as I swipe a cookie from off the plate. Then we start up the stairway.

As we reach the top of the stairs, he smiles at me from over his shoulder as I stuff my face with gooey chocolate. "Good?"

"Delish." I lick my fingers clean, making exaggerated smacking sounds.

He watches me in complete fascination, his eyes burning with something I don't quite recognize.

I lick my last finger clean. "Are you okay?"

He blinks and then clears his throat. "Yeah, I'm good."

I eye him suspiciously. "Wait. Are we having another

office moment?" I restrain a laugh when he uncomfortably shifts his weight, a flush creeping up his cheeks.

Back in the day, before we were dating, he got a hard-on while I was straddling his lap. Being slightly intoxicated, I pointed it out and embarrassed the crap out of him.

"Honestly," he starts, carefully calculating his next words, "we've had a lot of office moments over the last few months."

Acting like a ridiculously silly girl, I grin. "Really?"

"I don't know why you look so shocked," he quickly says, looking off over my shoulder. "Just looking at you is—does—turns me on. But kissing and touching you . . ." He blinks back at me. "But, yeah, anyway . . ." He waits, looking hopeful that I'll let him off the hook.

Even though I love teasing him, I decide to go easy on him. "So, anything else interesting happening in your life that I should know about?"

He contemplates it, climbing to the top of the stairs. "Well, I'm getting my tattoo covered in a few days."

"Really?" I ask excitedly.

He nods, excited himself. "I'm a little nervous about . . . well"—he gestures at his side where the tattoo is hidden beneath his shirt—"the whole process."

I offer him an encouraging smile. "You'll do fine. I know it. And, if you want, I can go with you and hold your hand."

"Actually, I was kind of hoping you'd sketch the cover up tattoo for me." He skims his finger along the inside of my wrist, causing me to shiver. "It'd be nice if you'd go with me, too, though."

"Of course." I puff out a stressed breath. "Man, I'm feeling a little bit nervous."

"About what?"

"About creating something that will permanently be

on your body. Just think, every time you look at it, you'll think of me."

His brow arches questioningly. "And that's a bad thing?"

I shrug. "That all depends on stuff."

"Stuff like what?"

"I don't know, like if we break up one day or something."

He studies me with his dark eyes, and my skin starts to heat; not with a blush, but with lust. My heart pumps fast, dances in my chest, creates a rhythm of its own, a beat that would make a fantastic song.

"I think I'm okay with something you draw being on my body forever." Without warning, his lips come down on mine hard, giving me barely any time to process more than a single thought about what he's said.

I have zero time to suck in a breath as his tongue slips into my mouth. He kisses me fiercely, passion burning, scorching through my body, silk spilling through my veins. It's the kind of kiss with zero planning, the kind of kiss that means so much. The kind of kiss I'll hold onto forever. The kind of kiss everyone should experience at least once in their lifetime.

My hands find his shoulders, my fingertips delving into the fabric of his shirt as I try to keep my legs from giving out. As if he senses my inability to stay on my feet, his hands travel down my body, trembling the entire way, and he grips onto my thighs. With a deep inhale, he holds onto me tightly and picks me up.

When his body begins to quiver, I start to lower my feet to the ground, but he constricts his grasp on me, holding me in place. He counts to five under his breath then presses me closer until so much heat is coursing through me I can barely breathe. So, so much heat. I feel like I'm drowning in heat, yet I want to sink farther, let the warmth take me down and hold me there forever.

"Where are we going?" I whisper against his lips as he starts to move somewhere.

Pressing me even closer to him, he slides a hand underneath my butt. "To my room." His voice is uneven, off-pitch, gravelly.

I link my feet behind his back as he stumbles blindly down the hallway and kicks open his bedroom door. I get lost in the kiss, the feel of his hands, the beat of his heart slamming through his chest and against mine. I get so lost I barely notice anything around me until we're falling onto the mattress.

His solid body lands on top of me, but his arms brace the weight of his fall. He pulls back to look down at me, breathing heavily, and panic flashes in his eyes.

"Are you okay?" I ask, cupping his cheek. "We can slow down if we need to. We always can."

"I'm fine." He gasps for air, battling to calm down. Once he's settled, he stares at me with strands of his hair in his eyes. "I know we can always stop, but I . . . I think I want to keep going."

I sweep his hair out of his eyes and let my hand linger on his scruffy cheek. I'm not sure what he means. Keep going? How far? More kissing? More touching? More . . . ?

My thoughts dissipate as his lips return to mine, and he gives me a deliberate, sensual, soul-stealing kiss. His hand wanders up the bottom of my skirt, slowly, slowly, slowly. Every brush of his fingers, every caress of his tongue is deliberate, which makes every second that much more erotic. His fingers stop moving the moment they reach the hem of my panties. He never takes it farther than this, and I haven't asked him to, even though I want to. Badly.

I gasp and wiggle below him, desperate for him to

touch me more. For me to be able to touch him. Touch, touch, touch him all over. I want to touch him like he touches me.

Knowing he'll more than likely stop me, I dare to slide my fingers down his back and fiddle with the hem of his shirt, stealing a touch. When he doesn't budge, I test him further, delving my fingers under the fabric and caressing his bare flesh. I hold my breath, waiting for him to panic, which makes the kiss instantly turn awkward because I eventually have to suck in a huge breath.

"One . . . two . . . three," he whispers under his breath then kisses me deeper, kisses me through the awkwardness and back into the intensity of the moment.

I'm not sure what's up with the counting, and I don't really care. He's letting me touch him more than I ever have. I grasp onto the moment, inching my hands up his back and tracing a soft path up his spine. He either shakes or shivers from my touch—maybe a little bit of both.

"I can stop," I tell him when his breathing shifts to erratic.

He takes a few measured breaths. "No . . . You're okay. I can do this."

I sketch a line up and down his back. "So, are you . . . ? I mean, you can touch me." I actually blush. Yeah, I, Lyric Scott, blush. It's something I thought would never happen, and it feels so freaking weird.

Thankfully, Ayden's face is too close to mine to notice.

He nods, either to himself or to me, before he slips a finger into my panties. Nerves bubble in my stomach, about to burst. I try to prepare myself, but the instant he slides a finger inside me, I'm lost.

Gone. Gone. Gone.
Lost inside you.
Lost inside me.

Lost inside us.
I feel so alive.
Breathing, heart beating,
Needing, needing, needing.
I can hardly breathe,
Can hardly think
Past the pleading, pleading, pleading.

By the time I return to reality, I'm out of breath, and my pulse is soaring. Ayden is staring down at me with so much desire blazing in his eyes I barely recognize him.

"Was that okay? I mean, you don't regret it, right?" He smooths strands of my blonde hair out of my eyes.

"No regrets at all," I assure him breathlessly, fighting back a grin, but eventually, a smile plasters across my face.

His fingers splay across my cheek and he traces a line below my eye. "You're so beautiful. I just . . ." He sighs and rolls off me.

"What are you doing?" I pout, rotating on my side.

He stares up at the ceiling with his arm draped across his forehead. "I just worry about you all the time. I mean, you're so happy and outgoing, and I worry I'm going to ruin it."

"You don't ruin anything, and you need to stop saying that."

"Not even when you can't touch me?"

I roll over to him and swing my leg across him, pushing myself up and straddling him. "I can't touch you, huh?"

His hands mold to my waist as he grasps on to me. "You know what I mean. We can't even take our relationship further." His cheeks redden as he looks away.

"We can't?" I challenge, reaching for the bottom of my shirt. I lift it up and tug it over my head, shaking out my hair. "I think we take it further every day."

His breathing speeds up as his grey eyes drink me in.

"I've been working on some stuff to help calm me down when I'm panicking," he whispers. "I want to get better for you."

"Is that what the counting is about?"

He nods. "My therapist taught me some breathing exercises and stuff."

"While I love that you're trying, I still need you to know that it doesn't matter to me. I want to be with you, no matter what."

He leans up and kisses me, his hand sliding around my back. I shiver from the graze of his fingers against my flesh as he fumbles with the clasp of my bra. Once he gets it unfastened, the straps fall from my shoulders, and the cool air nips at my skin. Even though I'm pretending to be as cool as a freaking cucumber, my heart slams against my chest.

"Tell me if I need to slow down," he whispers against my lips.

Instead of telling him to go further, I grab his hands and place them on me. He groans from the touch, seeming in pain. But he has to be enjoying this since I can feel his happiness pressing between my thighs.

"Your skin's so soft," he murmurs, caressing the sensitive spot of flesh to the side of my breast.

I softly sketch his jawline with my fingertip. "So's yours. And, one day when you're ready, I'll be able to touch you like you touch me."

His hands continue to explore my body, his fingers scorching hot against my flesh. "What if I'm never ready?"

"You will be, Ayden. You've come a long way already."

He sucks in a breath through his nose then pushes up and slams his lips to mine while his hand glides to my breast, his thumb grazing my nipple.

"You taste like cookies," he breathes softly through kisses.

"You taste like . . ." I trail off at the sound of a startled gasp from behind us.

"Oh, shit." I scramble off Ayden, grab my shirt, and press it to my chest.

"I'm sorry," Lila says from the doorway with her hand over her eyes. "I should have knocked first."

"No, you shouldn't have," Ayden sputters, bolting upright in the bed. "I mean, you shouldn't have had to, because we shouldn't have been in here, doing this . . . doing stuff." He rakes his fingers through his hair. "I'm so sorry."

Lila remains quiet with her hands over her eyes. "Okay, here's what we're going to do. I'm going to give you guys exactly one minute to get dressed and meet me downstairs. Then we're going to have a talk. And, Lyric, I'm calling your parents and having them come over, as well."

I pull a face. Great. This is going to be so awkward. "Okay."

"Good." She hurries away, leaving the door wide open.

I quickly put my bra on then yank my shirt over my head. "Well, looks like the cat's out of the bag now," I say as I hop off the bed.

"This is so bad." Ayden stands up, wrapping his arms around his head, freaking out.

"Yeah, but we were going to tell them eventually." I adjust my shirt into place.

He paces the floor in front of his bed. "But not like this . . . not after she saw me. And I need to prepare myself for how disappointed your parents are going to be."

"Disappointed?" Confused, I step in front of him, forcing him to stop moving. "Why would they be disappointed? A little angry, sure, but they'll get over it."

He gulps. "Not over what happened. With me. I doubt

they're going to be happy that you're with me."

I gape at him. "Are you kidding me right now?"

"I know who I am." He refuses to look at me, staring at a poster on the wall. "I have so many problems . . . My life is so fucked up. You're so perfect, and they're not going to want me ruining that for you."

"First of all, I'm not perfect, and my parents definitely don't think I am. There've been many lectures and punishments proving how imperfect I am, just like everyone else in the world. And, second of all, I honestly think they've been expecting this to happen between us."

He shakes his head, his jaw set tight. "I highly doubt that."

I roll my eyes. "You're being ridiculous right now, and I'm going to prove it."

I grab his hand and march for the door, ready to face the music. Ready to prove him wrong.

He is good for me.

Everyone knows it.

Everyone knows just as much as I do that we're meant to be together.

CHAPTER 7

I'M A NERVOUS WRECK GOING downstairs. Even though I knew our relationship would eventually be discovered, I expected it to happen later on and definitely not under such embarrassing circumstances. Now, they're really going to start keeping an eye on me.

"Dude, breathe," Lyric mutters under her breath as we reach the bottom of the stairway. "Everything's going to be fine."

I wish that were true. Tonight was so amazing—touching her like that, watching her fall apart beneath me. She tastes and feels so good that, if I had my way, I'd spend every hour of my life feeling her skin and kissing her.

Life would be so much easier if that were possible, but that's hardly plausible. The reality of the situation is ugly and brutal and is about to become a whole lot more so.

My heart is hammering in my chest as we walk into the living room. Our hands are linked together, but the moment I catch sight of Ethan and Lila, I wrench mine away.

Lyric sighs at my movement then plops down on the sofa, appearing completely comfortable.

"So, what's the punishment?" she asks, crossing her legs and relaxing back in the sofa.

"That's for your parents to decide," Lila replies with aggravation written all over her face. "But I'm just going to say that you are way too comfortable about the situation, young lady."

"I'm not too comfortable. Not really," Lyric protests. "I just know that this shouldn't be as big of a deal as you guys are going to make it. I mean, from the stories I've heard you guys and my parents tell each other when you guys drink too much wine, you all had sex by the time you were our age."

Lila's lips part in shock. "You're having sex?"

"No, we're not," I interrupt, my voice higher than normal. "We were just . . ." I trail off, my cheeks warming with my mortification.

Ethan offers me a sympathetic look, seeming about as uneasy as I am.

"Whether we are or aren't having sex is beside the point." Lyric shoots me a dirty look from over her shoulder. "The point is that we're legally adults, and if we were having sex, it wouldn't be the end of the world."

I press her with a stressing look. *You're making this worse,* I mouth.

She carries my gaze with determination, but then sighs. "Fine, I'll let us get our lecture. I was just trying to prove a point."

Lila and Ethan sit with their mouths hanging open, at a loss for words. The room goes so silent everyone can probably hear the thunderous beat of my heart.

After a minute passes, I sink down on the opposite side of the sofa from Lyric. When the front door swings open, though, I spring up from the sofa and decide to sit on the chair across the room, way, way far away from Lyric.

"So, what'd they do now?" Mr. Scott asks, rubbing his hands together as he enters the room.

Beside him, Mrs. Scott doesn't look as relaxed. I almost wonder if she already knows what's going on.

"I . . ." Lila starts, but stops herself. "Well, I guess there's no easy way to put it other than I caught them, um, messing around in the bedroom."

Mr. Scott's expression instantly plummets. "You caught them doing *what?*"

I slouch lower in the chair with my head ducked and fix my attention on the floor.

"It wasn't that big of a deal," Lyric intervenes. "It's not like we were having sex or anything."

"Not that big of a deal." Mr. Scott seems irritated, which kind of surprises me.

Out of the two of them, he has always been more laid back than Lyric's mother.

"Oh, don't seem so shocked," Mrs. Scott says, sounding calmer than all of them. "She's eighteen, and her best friend's a guy she spends every waking hour with. Sounds a little bit familiar, doesn't it?"

"You were nineteen," Mr. Scott argues. "And that was different. We were both more mature than her."

"Hey," Lyric argues, offended, "I'm mature."

"Yeah, okay. We were so mature," Mrs. Scott talks over Lyric, her voice dripping with sarcasm. "We never did anything reckless at all."

"Well, okay, I get your point, but still . . . You and I aren't like our parents," Mr. Scott replies defensively. "We have rules. We need to put those rules into play and ground her or something."

I still haven't looked up, my eyes trained on the floor as I wait for one of them to say something negative about Lyric being with me. But they continue on about their pasts as if they've forgotten about the problem and the other people in the room, listening to their every word.

Finally, they must remember that other people are around, because Mrs. Scott hisses, "Maybe we should talk to Lyric about this at home."

"Sounds good to me," Mr. Scott agrees, clearly annoyed.

I don't look up even though I feel Lyric's eyes on me.

"They're gone. You can look up now," Ethan says after the front door clicks shut.

I elevate my gaze to find that Ethan and Lila are watching me with concern. Their change in demeanor throws me for an unexpected turn.

I wait for them to say something, punish me, tell me how badly I messed up. Instead, they remain silent for a mind racing amount of time before they exchange a look, and then Ethan gets to his feet.

"You want to go out to the garage and help me change the oil in the truck?" Ethan asks me, although it's not really a question.

Nodding, I stand up and follow him through the house and out the back door. It's past seven o'clock at night, and usually, the family is sitting around the table, eating dinner. I'm guessing tonight we might be breaking the routine, though.

Ethan doesn't say much as we start working on the oil. I hand him tools whenever he asks for them and help him when he needs it. So much time ticks by that I don't think he's going to bring up what happened. When he finishes, he cleans the oil off his hands, and then an uneasy look crosses his face.

My lecture and punishment are coming, and I tell myself I can handle it, that I've been through way worse.

"So, you and Lyric, huh?" He tosses the rag aside on the shelf and shuts the hood of the truck. "Can't say I'm that surprised."

"I'm sorry I messed up," I tell him because I don't know what else to say. The fact that he doesn't think it's surprising is baffling to me.

He reclines against the front of the truck with his arms folded. "You didn't really mess up. I was young once, too. I get it."

I rest against the shelf behind me. "I'm not sure Mr. Scott would agree with you. He seemed pissed. I'm afraid he's not going to let me spend any more time with her."

He waves me off. "He'll get over it. He just needs some time to cool off."

"If it helps, I promise nothing like that will happen again."

"Don't make promises you can't keep." He heads for the door. "Just make sure that you're careful with stuff, okay?"

Is this some sort of subtle safe sex talk? Why isn't everyone freaking out more?

"Okay," I reply uneasily as we leave the garage.

When we reach the porch, he stops to pat me on the shoulder. "You're a good kid, even if you don't always think so."

I feel lost. It somehow feels like he knows my fear of unworthiness. "Thanks." I start to wonder if maybe Dr. Gardingdale was right. Maybe my unworthiness is in my head, my own inner demon that no one else can see. I only wish I could find a way to get completely past it.

Wish on a thousand stars that, one day, somehow, my life will be normal.

CHAPTER 8

DINNER IS PRETTY NORMAL. THE only exception is Fiona teasing me about Lyric, but I can handle that. Thankfully, Kale has moved on from his crush on Lyric, so I don't have to worry about him getting upset.

"I can't believe you guys fooled around with the door open," Fiona teases with a smirk as she butters a roll.

"Fiona Gregory," Lila warns as she passes the bowl of corn to Everson, "leave your brother alone."

Fiona dramatically rolls her eyes but does as she's told, keeping her lips zipped.

"Now, let's talk about something else," Lila says cheerfully. "Does anyone have anything exciting happening in their life?"

"I finally asked Mandy out," Kale says, cutting into his steak. "We're going to a movie on Friday, if that's okay?"

"Who's Mandy?" Ethan asks, pouring himself some wine. "I thought you had a thing for Lyric." He pulls a whoops face. "Sorry, I probably shouldn't go there, right?"

"I stopped liking Lyric when I found out Ayden was dating her." Kale reaches across the table for the butter.

Lila stares at Kale in shock. "Wait? How long have you known about them?"

Kale gives a noncommittal shrug. "I don't know. For, like, a couple of months."

Lila's eyes narrow on me. "You two have been together for *months?*"

"Um . . ." I rub the back of my neck. "Kind of."

"I figured as much when I saw you guys backstage at the concert," Ethan absent-mindedly remarks as he drenches his steak in barbeque sauce.

"And what happened backstage?" Lila seems to grow angrier by the second.

Ethan sets down the bottle of sauce then picks up his fork and knife. "I thought I caught them when they were about to kiss."

"Why didn't you say anything until now?" she asks, sounding hurt.

"Yeah, I'm sorry about that, but I knew, if it was true, everyone would act all crazy, which you guys did." He starts slicing his steak. "I figured I'd let them tell you when they were ready and give them some time without constantly being pressured."

Lila's shoulders slump in defeat. "All right, you have a point." She frowns as if greatly disappointed by that fact. "You're off the hook."

"Thanks," Ethan says, shooting me a discreet smile.

I chuckle under my breath and reach for the bowl of potatoes.

"So, I want to go to football camp this summer," Everson announces, breaking the silence.

I'm extremely grateful as the conversation shifts from me to him. I remain fairly quiet for the rest of dinner, lost in my thoughts about what happened in my bedroom with Lyric. How she traced her fingers up and down my back. How I was terrified out of my mind, afraid of the memories clipping at the surface. Afraid because . . . It felt too

fucking nice. I found myself wanting to explore more, and that scared me out of my goddamn mind.
I've never felt like that before.
You make me feel things I didn't know were real.
How can that be possible?
I thought I was never going to be whole again,
That I'd remain a broken shell,
Cracked in places that could never be fixed.
Now, everything I believed is withering,
Fading into something I can't explain.
Please, please, don't let me down.
Give me hope
And let me fade away.

"Ayden, are you all right?" Lila interrupts my thoughts.

I rip myself from my daze, realizing I'm the only one left at the table.

"Yeah. Sorry. I guess I just zoned off." The legs of the chair scrape against the tile floor as I scoot back from the table.

"Okay." She picks up an empty bowl and carries it to the sink. "Would you mind helping me do the dishes? There's something I'd like to talk to you about."

I start stacking the dirty plates on the table. "What's up?"

"Well, I talked to Detective Rannali about letting you read the letter your sister wrote, like you asked." She opens the dishwasher and places a few plates inside. "Unfortunately, they can't let you read the letter yet, because it's important evidence as of now."

Even though I was expecting that answer, it's still frustrating.

"Okay, thanks for trying." My shoulders sink as reality crushes me down into the ground.

Down. Down. Down.

Into the dirt,
Burying me alive, right along with the hurt.
Suffocating, smothering, where is the air?
Hidden with the pain in a sea of despair.
Down. Down. Down,
Into the dirt.
Pull me from the despair, help me survive.
Please, someone help me.
Don't let me die.
Lift me from the darkness and into the light—
Out of the dirt, out of the pain, away from the hurt.

    She abruptly folds her arms around me. "I know life's been hard on you, and while I really don't ever want to walk in on you like that again, I'm glad you're with Lyric. You deserve the best, Ayden, and I know Lyric makes you happy, which is why I'm not going to punish you over what I walked in on tonight." She clears her throat. "Just promise me you two will be careful."

    This is quickly turning into the most mortifying conversation I've ever had.

    "Okay, but . . . never mind."

    She moves back to look at me. "No, go ahead and say it. I need to know that you feel comfortable enough with me."

    "It really isn't that big of a deal." I wave it off. "Forget I said anything."

    "Is it about Lyric or . . . sex?"

    "What? No. It's definitely not that." I make myself look her in the eye. "It's about Sadie and the case. I just want to know more about what's going on."

    She stiffens. "Look, Ayden, I know you're worried about her, but the police are doing everything they can to find her. They even tracked down that woman you ran into in that godawful neighborhood and brought her in for questioning."

"What'd they find out?"

"Nothing much." She grabs another plate out of the sink and sticks it in the dishwasher. "The woman said she saw you go into the house, and she thought she'd warn you to stay away from it, considering what happened there. They already knew what went on there, though, so her statement didn't help with the case."

I gather a few dirty cups out of the sink and hand them to her. "But I want to know exactly what happened in that house. No one's flat out told me the details."

She remains quiet while she stacks the cups on the dishwasher rack. "The police believe Sadie was taken from that house by the group of people who took you guys when you were younger, and the foster parents she was living with at the time of the kidnapping were drug addicts and didn't notice she was missing for over a week, so it instantly put a hitch in the case."

A week? She was gone and entire week, and no one knew?

My heart is splitting in two
And bleeding out
Because she never knew
Just how good life could be.

I grip on to the edge of the counter to keep from falling down. "Didn't they notice all the paint and stuff on the walls?"

"They might have, but . . ." She sighs heavily. "When people are on drugs, they can get too caught up in their addiction."

"My mother was an addict," I utter quietly with my head lowered. "She was like that sometimes, so I get it. But still, it pisses me off."

"I know it does, sweetie." When I glance up, her heart

looks like it's breaking for me. "What can I do to make you feel better?"

"The only way I think I'll ever feel better again is when they find her." Forcing myself to suck it up, I stand up straight. "There's some stuff on the Internet about the locations of some of the places the Soulless Mileas hang out at, and I think you should mention them to the detective the next time you talk to him."

Her brows knit. "I didn't know you were looking up that sort of stuff on the Internet."

"No one really tells me anything, so I thought I'd find out some stuff for myself." I hand her a dish soap tablet from the box beside the sink, and she drops it inside the dishwasher.

"We tell you what we feel is a healthy amount." She closes the dishwasher door and pushes start. "Does your therapist know you've been doing this?"

"No. The only person I've told is Lyric and now you. I didn't think it was that important."

"I think you should tell him so you two can talk about the stuff you've read. It can't be easy . . . reading about that . . ." The way she says it makes me wonder if she has been reading stuff, too. She grabs a dishtowel and begins wiping down the counters. "Maybe I'll mention it to him myself since I have to go in for a visit, anyway."

A pucker forms between my brows. "Why are you going in for a visit?"

She winds around the kitchen island, cleaning up spilled sauce on the tile. "To discuss your amnesia therapy." She stops scrubbing and looks up at me. "Your father and I just feel like maybe you should stop doing it since there hasn't been a lot of progress, and it seems to be increasing your stress."

"It's not increasing my stress." The last thing I ever want to do is stop with the therapy, and if Lila gets involved, there's a slim chance I'll ever be allowed to do it again. "And I can't do that to my sister—stop trying like that."

"You've been sleepwalking more ever since you started the treatment. You sleep less. And now I find out you're looking up stuff on the Internet. It's not healthy."

"Nothing about any of this will ever be healthy, but I might be able to be less stressed if the police find her." I contemplate my next words carefully. "Which is why I think you should reconsider letting me try that experimental therapy."

She swiftly shakes her head. "We've already talked about it and decided it was too risky."

I grit my teeth, biting back my anger. I don't agree with her, but at the same time, I feel guilty for even thinking about going against them. The Gregorys were kind enough to take me in when they knew I had so many problems, and I owe them for that. The last thing I need to do is yell at her.

"I'm going to go up to my room and work on my homework." I swing around her and stride for the stairway.

"Ayden, please don't be angry with me," she calls out. "We're doing this because . . . because we love you."

I smash my lips together so forcefully my jaw aches. Despite the fact that I once had a mother and father, I've never actually had anyone say they love me like that. I don't even know how to respond, so I don't say anything, hurrying up the stairs and locking myself in my room.

Lock yourself up.
When are you ever going to learn?
The only way to be free
Is to give in.
The only way to be free
Is to surrender.

CHAPTER 9

ABOUT AN HOUR INTO WRITING my English essay, I decide I need a break and get on my computer. I open up the webpage I've looked at every night for the last couple of weeks that contains an article about the Soulless Mileas and their rituals and beliefs. On the top of the page are photos of houses, backyards, the shore—the pictures I mentioned to Lila.

I shut my eyes and try to summon locked up memories.
The house on the hill
Bleeds through the ground,
Saturates the dirt,
And drips from the trees.
The red river flows down the grass
And to the ocean.
Waves crash against the sand,
Erasing the blood
And carrying it away.
But a faint trail still remains.
The house on the hill
Waits to be found,
Waits to tell its secrets
Of shackles and nails,

Stories of torture and pain.
Drip.
Drip.
Drip.
"What is that, Ayden?" my sister whispers through the darkness.

The only thing I can see is the bright pink ribbon in her hair.

I open my mouth to tell her, but my voice gets lost in the sound of the dripping.

"Ayden, can you hear me?" she whispers. "I think... I think it's blood. Oh, Ayden, I think it's my blood."

My eyes snap open as my body trembles from the memory—my sister's plea for help. I glance at the computer screen and examine the photos closely.

"Where are you, Sadie?" I whisper, my eyes locking on a photo of a house settled on a shallow hill.

I try to picture the people inside it, but my memory shuts down. The strange thing that doesn't make sense to me is that the house we were trapped in was the one in my neighborhood and not on a hill. That's where I remember being dropped off by my mother, and that's where we were picked up, yet sometimes, I see us in other places and wonder if we were moved around somehow.

Overwhelmed with emotion, I leave the computer desk and seek comfort in my guitar. After I get situated on my bed, I pluck the strings with my fingertips and sing aloud, something I only do behind closed doors.

"Burning, burning, burning,
My body is in flames.
The fire igniting,
Burning me with rage.
I want the fire out,
Beg the clouds to drench me in rain.

Yet, when I look up,
The sky is fucking tame, no rain in sight.
So the fire keeps on burning,
Blazing, blazing, blazing,
Until it kills me eternally."

I frown at my words. With everything going on, I need to pick myself up, not drag myself further down into depression.

What I need is Lyric.

Glancing out my widow, I look over at her house. Her bedroom light is off, which means she's probably downstairs with her parents. I'm curious what her punishment is, but too nervous to text her and ask. Worried she'll tell me her parents won't let her see me again.

Sighing, I reach for my journal and turn to a page I've been scribbling in for the last week or so. I place my guitar on my lap again, line my fingers with the strings, and open my mouth.

"Lyric, Lyric, Lyric,
Her name pours through my veins.
Her laughter, her smile,
It's enough to drive me insane.
The way she looks at me,
It doesn't make sense
Why she would want me.
I don't understand.
She's so beautiful, so wild, so full of light.
Every time we touch,
Everything feels right.
Every time we kiss,
My head spins out of control.
I try to hold on, but I eventually fall.
Falling, falling, falling,
I'm falling into her.

Falling so blindingly, so helpless, so willingly.
Please, God, please, let me keep falling."

I stop strumming the strings as my phone buzzes on the nightstand. I set the guitar aside and check the incoming message.

The second I see her name, I smile.

Lyric: So, I just had a super awkward safe sex talk that lasted over an hour. What about you? Did you get punished?

I rest against the headboard and type a response.

Me: Ethan kind of the did the same thing with me, only his lasted about fifteen seconds. That's the only punishment you got? Your dad seemed pissed off.

Lyric: He was freaking out, but honestly, it was kind of funny. I think he's having issues with me growing up or something. My mom was pretty chillax, though. Which I was kind of surprised about. I mean, she's usually the one doing all the scolding and punishing, but she seemed more worried that we're being careful.

Me: You told them that wasn't an issue, right?"

Lyric: Whoops. I knew I was forgetting something.

Me: Please tell me you're kidding! Your dad's never going to let me see you again if he thinks that.

Lyric: You should know that I'm kidding. I like my jokes, but I'm not a liar. And FYI, my dad wasn't upset because he thought I was sleeping with you. He was upset about the concept of his daughter having sex. They both seemed super relieved that it was you I was caught with and put a lot of the blame on me.

I think they think I'm a bad influence on you, which might be kind of true. They like you, dude, even if you did get caught feeling their daughter up.

Me: Still, we should probably be a little bit more careful from now on.

Lyric: I'm good with being careful, just as long as there's going to be a from now on. You seemed freaked out, Shy Boy, and that stuff you said about my parents being disappointed that I was with you . . . It makes me sad that you see yourself like that, that you can't see how good you are.

Me: I'm sorry I freaked out. What can I do to make it up to you?

Lyric: Hmm . . . Let me think. How about admitting that you're good enough for me?

Me: I'm being serious. I want to make it up to you.

Lyric: And I'm being serious. I want you to say it.

When I don't respond right away, another text buzzes through.

Lyric: I'm being serious. Say it or else.

I can't help myself.

Me: Or else what?

Lyric: Ah, I think I'm being challenged.

A pause then another message comes through.

Lyric: If you don't tell me that you're good enough for me, I won't kiss you for a week.

I chuckle.

Me: Fine. I'm good enough for you. There, are you happy?

Lyric: I'm really happy, actually. Not only did I get you to say it, but now I know how much you love my kisses.

Me: You should have known that already.

Lyric: Maybe I did, but it's nice to know for sure. I have to go. My mom is making me watch a show with them. God knows what it's about. Probably a tutorial on how to accurately put a condom on or something.

I shake my head, grinning. Leave it to Lyric to get me to smile even when I've had the most depressing night.

When we say goodbye, I put my phone away and spend the next hour working on my homework. By the time I fall asleep, I think I'm feeling better until I sink into a nightmare of the woman with hair that matches her blood red fingernails.

Drip.
Drip.
Drip.

"Close your eyes and prepare yourself, Ayden." Fingernails slide across my hands, up my arms, and down my chest, making my gut twist with disgust. "I'm going to break you apart and make you bleed."

CHAPTER 10

IT'S FRIDAY NIGHT, WHICH MEANS concert time for my band, Alyric Bliss. Well, concert might be a stretch. Basically, we have a gig at Infinite Bliss, my father's club, opening for another band. We play five songs total, and my dad is making us sing our own stuff in order to prep us for when we record.

"You look nervous." Sage, the drummer of our band, remarks. With his blue hair, multiple piercings and tattoos, and edgy clothing, Sage looks the part. "I thought you'd be over your stage fright by now."

"I *am* over it." When I peer out at the packed room, my body contradicts my words as a thousand butterflies on crack start to flutter inside my stomach.

"You pointing it out isn't helping, so stop being a dick," Nolan, our bassist, tells Sage while twisting the knobs of the bass he's holding. Nolan is a little less grunge and more boy band-ish: spikey blond hair and blue eyes with these crazy full lips that don't seem like they should belong to a guy. But he plays a sick guitar solo, so he's cool in my book.

Sage tosses a drumstick in the air then catches it like a baseball. "I'm not being a dick. I'm just stating the obvious—that she looks nervous for it being our seventh performance." I scowl at Sage, and he raises his inked hands in front of him. "Sorry, I'll stop saying it."

"Thank you." I peer back at the floor, and my stomach drops again.

Even though I won't admit it aloud, Sage is right. It seems like I should be over my stage fright by now, yet before every performance, I feel as jittery as I do when I drink too much coffee.

"And where the hell is Ayden?" Sage says from behind me. "He should have been here by now."

"He'll be here," I assure him. Still feeling a little concerned myself, I decide to text him.

Me: We're on in like 40. You're on your way, right?

When he doesn't reply right away, I start to get all twitchy. With the Soulless Mileas out there constantly tormenting him, it's hard to remain calm whenever he goes MIA.

After five minutes drag by, I squeeze through the mob of intoxicated people to get to the bathroom and check my appearance. I'm not really a makeup girl, but I reapply the kohl liner around my bright green eyes and dab on some lip gloss. Then I comb my fingers through my long, blonde hair, smooth my hands over my black shirt and plaid skirt, and tighten the laces on my red boots. The last thing I ever want to happen is tripping over my shoelaces.

After I'm done, I push out the door and head back to the stage. As I'm passing the bar, I notice a woman staring at me. She's very model-esque: long legs, flowing blonde hair, and bright blue eyes.

"Hey," she says, giving me a tentative wave.

"Um . . . hey." I have no clue who she is, but she acts like she knows me.

"You don't know who am I, do you?" she asks with a mixture of amusement and nervousness.

I shake my head. "Sorry."

"No worries." She rises from the barstool, scooping up a half-filled wine glass from the counter. "I'm Ava. I used to know your mother and father back when they lived in Wyoming. I was out here visiting and heard your father had a club, so I thought I'd stop by."

The name doesn't ring a bell, but my parents rarely talk about the people they knew back in Wyoming.

"That's cool. You should track my dad down and say hi." I scan the bar then the hallway that leads to my dad's office. "He's around here somewhere, more than likely in his office, but he wanders out here during performances."

"Lyric!" Sage hollers from the backstage area with his hands cupped around his mouth. "Time to get your ass up here!"

I roll my eyes at him. "Sorry. I guess I have to go. But, seriously, go say hi to my father. I'm sure he'll want to chat with you about the good ol' days or whatever."

She offers me a small smile when I wave, and then I hurry through the crowd. My heavy boots clunk against the steps as I dash up the stairway to the backstage.

"Dude, Sage, my bro, my friend, what are you thinking, screaming across the stage like that?" I ask as I duck behind the curtain. "My dad's not going to be happy with you acting like a spastic mad man."

Sage gives me an innocent look. "I tried to text, but you didn't answer."

I check my phone and realize the battery is now dead. "Has Ayden texted you yet?"

Sage shakes his head. "And I've texted him like fifty times."

As I grow even more worried, I open my mouth to tell

Sage to hand me his phone so I can call Lila and Ethan, but then the door to our right swings open.

Ayden rushes inside with his guitar case in hand. "Sorry, I'm late. My car was being a pain in the ass and wouldn't start." His hair is dripping wet, water beads his skin, and his soaked grey shirt clings to his body.

I gawk at him like a pervert.

If you want to see perfection,
Just look right in front of you.
So gorgeous and flawless
With dark, haunted eyes,
Lips that taste so intoxicating,
A body that . . .
Good God, that body.
I want touch it, run my hands all over him.

"Lyric, did you hear what I said?" Ayden interrupts my lustful thoughts.

I rip my eyes off his body. "Nope, not a damn word."

He inquisitively glances down at his shirt then back at me. "You okay?"

"Yep, I'm great. I was just"—I shrug—"checking your sexy body out."

Astonishingly, he doesn't blush as our gazes meld. It's been a week since we got caught in his bedroom, and we've been trying to behave ourselves, but behaving has increased the sexual tension to about an . . . oh, eleven hundred.

Sage clears his throat and shatters the moment into oblivion.

Even though he seems fine with Ayden and me being together, sometimes, when we show a little PDA, he gets annoyed.

"Why didn't you answer your texts?" Sage asks Ayden as he stuffs his drumsticks into the back pocket of his jeans.

Ayden blinks his attention away from me. "You texted me?" When Sage nods, he pats his pockets. "Shit, I must have left my phone at the therapist's office."

"You scared us," I tell Ayden. "Or at least me. I think Sage was more worried we wouldn't have a guitarist."

"Hey, I was kind of worried," Sage gripes. "I'm not that big of a douche."

"Fine, we were all worried." I lower my voice and lean in toward Ayden. "I thought something bad happened."

"It wasn't anything like that. Just car trouble, like I said. Everything's fine, though. The detective following me around helped me jumpstart it." He shakes his head, showering me with water.

"Gee, thanks for the shower," I tease, raising my hand to wipe the water off my face. "Is he still keeping an eye on you?"

"Yeah. Lila says it'll only be for a bit longer since nothing has happened in the last few weeks." He steps forward and gently brushes his fingers across my cheeks and lips. "I need you not to worry about me so much. I don't want you to panic every time I'm late." He places a featherlight kiss on my mouth. "I hate thinking that I stressed you out."

He tastes minty and smells like rain. I breathe in the scent and taste, softly sighing against his mouth like a lovesick girl.

"I can't stop worrying about you." My eyelashes flutter as he tangles his fingers through my hair. "It's part of the job title as your best friend."

A soft groan slips from Ayden's lips as his hands travel down my back.

Sage clears his throat again. "Get a room, would you? Jesus, it's like one step away from watching porn."

Ayden shakes his head at Sage. "So, what did I miss?"

he asks me as he sets his guitar case on the floor.

"Well, we go on in, like, thirty," I tell him then shoot Sage a conniving smile. "And Sage has been pissing his pants that you weren't going to show up."

Sage glares at me. "Yeah, right. You're the one freaking out, and not just about Ayden."

"What else are you freaking out about?" Ayden asks me with concern.

I give a shrug. "I already told you that I still get nervous every time we're about to perform."

"What can I do to help?"

"You could talk to me about something else. Take my mind off stuff."

Nodding, he takes my hand and leads me back to the corner of the room. When he sits down on the floor, he pulls me down with him so we're sitting across from each other.

"So, I've been talking to my therapist about that experimental therapy I told you about a while ago," he starts, resting against the wall.

"The one Lila doesn't want you to do?" I crisscross my legs and rest back on my hands.

He nods, fiddling with the leather bracelet I gave him. "But I'm not really sure she has any say in it anymore."

My head cocks to the side. "What do you mean?"

"I mean that I'm eighteen and technically don't need a guardian's permission to go through with the therapy." He leans forward and tugs on my arm, so I sit up straight. Then he laces his fingers through mine. "I don't want it to come to that," he says, staring down at our hands, "but, at the same time, I can't stop thinking about Sadie and how, if I could just see the people's faces, then maybe the police could track her down and make some arrests."

I take a minute or two to prepare myself for what I'm

going to say next. "I get what you're saying—I really do—but what are the risks, exactly? I mean, how dangerous are we talking?"

"There's a short list of them," he answers with hesitancy. "Like memory loss and stress on the heart, but if the therapy's done right, then nothing should go wrong."

I make a mental note to search online for the side effects. If they're bad, then I'm going to talk him out of it. The last thing I ever want is for him to get hurt or, worse, lose him. My heart aches just thinking about it.

"Look, I get that, no matter what, it's kind of risky. And it's not going to be easy . . . seeing the stuff I've forgotten. I know my mind blocked it out for a reason." With his free hand, he scratches his head. "But I don't think I could live with myself if I didn't at least try. And I really need you to support me and be there for me."

Dammit. He said he needs me. There goes my plan of talking him out of it.

"All right, I can do that, I guess. But I'm not going to lie; I'm scared of what's going to happen. I don't . . ." I swallow hard. "I don't want to lose you." *Because I love you.*

I'm in love with you.
Love you so much
I feel like I'm going to combust,
Shatter into pieces that scatter
Through the wind and rain,
Blow away and get lost.
Lost, lost, lost
In my love for you.

Now he's the one to gulp. "You won't. I promise."

"Hey, you two love birds, we're up!" Nolan shouts mockingly from behind us.

I crinkle my nose. "Sometimes, I wish you and I could

just be a duo."

He smiles thoughtfully. "That'd be nice, but considering I can't sing, it'd be more of a solo and a half band."

"It still sounds better right now." I push to my feet and tug my skirt into place. "Those two are getting on my nerves."

He strokes my cheekbone with his finger. "Want me to throw a basketball at them to see if I can get them to shut up? I mean, I do still owe you for that."

Smiling, I ponder the idea. "While I know you're kidding, I'm seriously considering it."

"Well, let me know when you decide," he jokes, crouching down to unlatch his guitar case. "I'm going to go hurry and dry off the best I can before we go on."

"Why? You rock the wet shirt look pretty well."

He keeps his head tucked down. "Maybe, but I'd feel super awkward."

"Well, you look sexy when you're awkward, too." I plant a kiss on the top of his head then squeeze through the curtains and skip off to set up with Sage and Nolan.

A few racing heartbeats later, Ayden joins us and hooks up his guitar to the amp while I adjust the microphone stand. The lights beam brightly and blind me to the point where I can hardly see anyone in the room. Still, I know they're all out there, and those crazy ass butterflies in my stomach start taunting me again.

Thankfully, about a minute later, Sage slams the sticks against the drums, and Ayden strums the strings of his guitar. The sounds of the instruments block out my focus on the audience as my lips part.

"Rush. Rush. Rush.

My heart is rushing like the rain,

Erasing every ounce of pain from my body

And spilling it below me.

My sins bleed into the water,
Soaking through the ground.
Rush. Rush. Rush.
I close my eyes and feel myself disappear.
A skeleton of myself, a ghost of my soul,
I'll never give in to anyone.
I'll never go through this again.
Rush. Rush. Rush."

The lyrics are more morbid than what I normally sing, but I wrote them on a whim while I was bored one day and watched way too many depressing movies. When I sang it to my dad, he thought it rocked awesomeness, so I shared it with the band.

It's the first time I've sung it on stage before. The upbeat tempo has the crowd going wild, dancing and head banging, feeding me with the fuel I need to really get into the performance.

By the time I sang our full set, I'm dripping with sweat and grinning as I bounce backstage. Sage and Nolan high-five me on their way out, but Ayden seems a bit distracted. He passes by me without so much as a glance in my direction.

"What's up?" I chase after him, back past the curtain and to the flat area near the exit doors.

He carefully sets his guitar in the case. "It's nothing." His brows dip. "I just . . . I just had the strangest feeling someone was watching me, but I can't figure out why."

"Did you maybe see someone in the crowd that you know?"

"No, it's not that . . ." He trails off then shakes his head. "Never mind. I'm just being paranoid." When he faces me, he forces a smile. "Let's go celebrate your amazing performance."

"You sure?"

"Yeah, I'm sure. I want to celebrate my awesome performance, too." His lips quirk with genuine amusement.

I thrum my fingers together evil-villain style. "Hmmm, whatever shall we do?"

"Party." Sage appears out of nowhere like a freaking ninja with a bottle of champagne in his hand.

"Dude, did you jack that from the bar?" I reach for the bottle.

He dodges out of my reach. "Actually, I stole it from my mom's fridge. She has at least ten bottles of it, so she won't notice." He looks down at the bottle. "Although, I wish it were a bottle of Bacardi." He shrugs then grips the bottle in front of him and, with his thumb, pops the cork.

The bottle hisses and foam shoots all over the floor. I jump out of the path of the spraying foam while Sage takes a swig then offers me the bottle.

I take the drink from him. "I'm down, but you've totally got to take the fall for the mess on the floor if my dad finds out. I'm already on thin ice with him." I angle my head back and chug some champagne.

"Why? What'd you do?" Nolan asks, intrigued, as he joins our circle. He snatches the bottle from me after I lower it from my mouth and downs at least a quarter of the bottle.

I shrug, giving a discreet glance at Ayden. "Just some stuff."

"Stuff as in . . ." Sage's shifty gaze moves back and forth between Ayden and me questioningly. "Okay, never mind. Forget I asked." He pats his pockets. "I think I'm going to go outside and smoke." Which is code for him going outside, smoking, then hooking up with the first decent looking girl he can find.

He strides toward the exit door and pushes outside. Nolan throws back another swallow of champagne then shoves the bottle at me and hurries after Sage.

I take another sip then turn to Ayden. "You want some?" I ask, even though he more than likely will decline.

Neither of us are big drinkers, and Ayden doesn't like doing it because he feels like he's acting like his old self, the person he was before Aunt Lila and Uncle Ethan adopted him. So, I'm a bit startled when he grabs the bottle from me and takes a few swallows.

"You're suddenly in a weird mood," I remark as he hands the bottle back to me.

"I'm feeling pretty okay right now, maybe even good." He laces his fingers through mine then stares at our interlocked hands with the faintest smile on his lips. From the sight of it, my insides get all gooey, like melted chocolate. "I was thinking we could hang out tonight and talk."

Interesting, since he has never been a big talker.

"Okay, you want to go home, then, and hang out in one of our rooms? Or did you have something else in mind?"

"Remember the spot near the bridge that we used to hang out at back before we could drive?" he asks, and I excitedly bob my head up and down. "I was thinking we could go there."

Goddamn those butterflies. They come to life the moment he says it. What the hell are they expecting to happen exactly?

"Yeah, we can do that." I raise the bottle to my mouth and throw back a couple more sips. "I'll go tell my dad we're leaving and meet you at the car?"

Nodding, he collects his guitar case, and we part ways. I head down the metal stairs to the main floor, past the busy bar, and down the hallway right as the next band starts playing. Music flows through the building like warm honey and vibrates the floors.

"They have a good beat," I comment aloud. "But we

are definitely better." I abandon the bottle of champagne before I reach the last door. "Hey, old man," I tease as I enter my dad's cluttered office. The walls are decorated with old music memorabilia, and the desk is covered with papers and wrappers. "I'm taking off. Just wanted to make sure you didn't need anything."

My dad glances up from some papers on his desk. He's sporting his bedhead/fauxhawk, and he has a half empty beer next to him. "I actually needed to talk to you . . . Is the rest of your band still here?"

I shake my head and sink down in a chair across from his desk. "Nah, Nolan and Sage are doing God knows what, and Ayden's waiting for me out in the car."

My dad scrunches his nose. "You guys are going straight home, right?"

"We might make a stop or two on the way."

He frowns in disapproval. "I'd rather you go straight home."

"I won't be out late." I flash him a devious grin. "And don't worry, I put that condom Mom gave me in my pocket."

His skin pales. "Lyric, that isn't funny."

"It kind of is, though."

He rakes his fingers through his hair. "You're too much like me. It's driving me crazy."

"You used to think that trait was endearing." When he continues to veer toward a meltdown, I decide to let him off the hook. "Look, I wasn't lying the other night when I said I wasn't having sex yet, so would you please chill out? You're a cool dad and everything, but this whole awkward, freak-out thing you've been doing for the last week is making you lose mad cool points."

He rubs his hand down his face, leaving red marks on his skin. "I just don't want you to mess up your life by making a mistake."

"I won't. I promise." I draw an X across my heart. "Now, can you tell me what you wanted to talk to my band about, because it's been driving me crazy since you said it?"

"I said it a whole minute ago." He pauses, and I can tell he wants to bug me more about being careful but decides to drop it. "I think I might have an opportunity coming up for you guys."

I lean forward in the chair, eager to hear more. "What kind of an opportunity?"

His fingers wrap around his beer. "A tour kind of opportunity."

"Are you shitting me?" I bounce up and down with excitement.

"No, I'm not shitting you." He opens his drawer, pulls out a paper, and slides it across the desk to me. "It's this summer. It's not a huge tour or anything, and the bands are pretty unknown, but I think, for your first gig, this could be a really good thing."

"A really good thing." I snatch up the paper, jump from the chair, and run around the desk, throwing my arms around him. "This is the most awesomest thing ever."

He hugs me back. "Don't get too excited yet. You still have to see if everyone in your band can go, and we have to check with your mother and make sure it's okay. I know she's been talking to you about college."

"Yeah, and I told her I didn't want to go straight out of high school."

"I know, but we still have to discuss this with her. She needs to be on the same page. And there'd be a ton of rules you'd have to follow. I don't care if you're eighteen and an adult; I'm not helping you get on the tour unless you agree to my rules."

"Fine by me," I say without zero hesitation because I want this more than anything.

"All right, we'll discuss them after we talk to your mom and your band. Ayden might be a little tricky, considering everything that's going on, but maybe if I talk to Ethan, it might help get everyone to agree to let him go."

"Thank you. Thank you. Thank you." I pull away, beaming from ear to ear. "I'm going to go tell Ayden now and track down Sage and Nolan tomorrow, but I bet they'll be in." I head for the door with a huge smile on my face, but then suddenly remember something. "Hey, Dad. There was a lady at the bar earlier. She said her name was Ava, and she knew you from Wyoming. Did she stop in and say hi?"

"No . . ." His forehead creases. "I'm sorry, but how did you end up talking to this person?"

"She stopped me when I was walking by. I think she recognized me or something." Now that I say it aloud, though, it seems odd. How did she recognize me when I've never met her?

"How did she, though?" He scratches his head. "I don't talk to anyone who still lives there except your grandma and grandpa."

"Maybe they're the ones who showed her a picture of me or something."

"Did she give a last name?"

"No, she didn't give me a last name. She was around Mom's age."

"Are you sure it wasn't your mother?" he jokes, still edgy.

"Ha, ha, you're a freaking riot, old man." I wrap my fingers around the doorknob. "No, it wasn't Mom. She had blonde hair and these really blue eyes."

He rubs his scruffy jawline, seeming baffled. "Do me

a favor and go straight home with Ayden until I can find out who she is."

"Should I be worried?" I ask, opening the door.

He pushes back from the desk and rises to his feet, stretching out his legs. "I'm not sure, but the best thing to do is be safe."

The excitement over the tour gradually fades as my dad follows me out of his office. We check around the floor area and the bar for the woman, but she's nowhere to been seen. So, he walks me to Ayden's car and sends us on our way after we promise to drive straight home and nowhere else.

"I'm sorry we don't get to go to the bridge," I tell Ayden as he steers the car down the busy road toward our neighborhood.

Lampposts reflect in the cab and shimmer across his face as we pass by stores, houses, and people strolling up and down the sidewalks, the city alive and awake.

"It's okay." He shrugs it off as he shifts gears. The rainstorm has cleared, but the roads are wet, and puddles splash against the tires. "I get why your dad's worried. I just wish I could have seen this woman myself."

"Why?"

"Because . . . Maybe I would have recognized her. Maybe that's why I felt uncomfortable on stage. I could sense I was being watched."

"You think she might know the people who . . . ?" I nervously bite on my fingernails.

"I don't know. At this point, I'm starting to question every person I pass by on the street." He taps on the brakes to stop at a light.

"We should find something relaxing for you to do tonight." I reach for his hand.

"Like what?" Interest lights up in his eyes.

"I don't know . . . We could drink some more champagne if we can steal a bottle from the fridge. And then we could hang out in the hot tub. The damn thing never gets used, and it's supposed to be relaxing, right?"

His eyes enlarge, and I remember why we never use the hot tub. Ayden can barely stand being shirtless in front of anyone, which leaves water activities out of the picture.

"Never mind. Let me think of something cooler."

"No . . ." His fingers twitch against mine. "I mean, we can try it. I'm supposed to be trying new things, anyway."

"Says who?"

"Says my therapist."

"All right, if you're okay with it, then let's do it." I raise my knuckles for a fist bump.

Ayden laughs, but taps his knuckles against mine.

"What else did you want to tell me?" he asks as he drives forward through an intersection. "When you came out to the car with your dad, you said there was some awesome news you needed to tell me."

"Oh, it's more than awesome news, but I'm going to make you wait until we get home. Build the anticipation." I prop my feet up on the dashboard and tip my head to the side to stare out the window at the stars peeking through the clouds.

I don't know how many times I've gazed up at them, making wish after wish that I'd one day get to live out my dream of being a singer. I never really thought they'd grant me my wish.

Stars, stars, shining above,
I've whispered to you
So many times,
Told you my secrets
And sold you my soul
In exchange for guidance.

Stars, stars, shining above,
I'll tell you another
Wish from the heart
Then close my eyes
And blow out the light
And wait for you in the dark.

CHAPTER 11

ABOUT A HALF AN HOUR later, I'm sitting on the edge of the empty hot tub out in my backyard, wearing my favorite black bikini. Apparently, because no one ever uses the hot tub, my parents drained it. Since I have no clue how to fill it, I sit with my feet inside, trying to figure out what to do. My mom is working late at the gallery, so I was able to steal two beers from the fridge—my parents aren't really champagne kind of people.

Ayden went inside his house about ten minutes ago to get changed into some shorts. Honestly, I'm not one hundred percent sure he's going to come out, not when he thinks we're going to get into the water and he's going to have to strip off his shirt in order to do that.

The hot tub has a stereo built into it, so I mess around until I find the perfect song, "The Ocean" by Manchester Orchestra. Then I pop the top off the beer, sit back, and wait, hoping I don't have to wait forever.

Two minutes later, my phone buzzes from beside me. Figuring it's Ayden, I pick it up, preparing to read a rejection on my hot tub offer. Instead, the message is from Maggie, a friend from school.

Maggie: I thought u said u were coming to my party.

Me: I said I would try, but some stuff came up.

Maggie: U mean sexy goth boy stuff?

Me: Yeah, sort of.

Maggie: U can bring him.

No, I really can't. With all the drama going on, there's no way Ayden's parents will let him go party it up without parental supervision.

Me: Sorry, we're already busy.

Maggie: Now, I like the sound of that. It's about time u two bumped uglies, just like I'm about to bump uglies with Sage.

Me: Okay, first off, bump uglies? Seriously? That's what you call it? Secondly, Ayden and I aren't having sex. We're just hanging out in my backyard. And thirdly, Sage???? WTF?

Maggie: What? He's hot.

Me: Yeah, but you two hate each other.

Maggie: There's a thin line between love and hate.

Me: Not really.

Maggie. Oh, whatever. Sage is hot, and if I want to fuck him, I can.

Me: Sorry. You're right. I didn't mean to sound so bitchy.

Maggie: Apology accepted. Now, let's get back to you and Ayden not having sex. Why the hell not?

Me: Because we're not ready.

Not entirely true. Sometimes, I feel like I am ready, but I know for a fact Ayden isn't.

Maggie: Yeah, right. So is it u or him? I'm guessing him since u asked me last week what it was like.

I scrunch my nose at her message and consider putting my phone away.

In a moment of sheer curiosity, I asked her about sex. Not because I'm clueless. I just wanted to know firsthand how bad it hurt in case, one day in the far, far, far away future, Ayden and I end up having sex.

Me: Hey, I have to go. My parents need me.

I put the phone down on the brim of the hot tub. It buzzes a few more times before Maggie gives up. I'm not upset with her or anything. It just doesn't feel right discussing my and Ayden's relationship with her when she doesn't have a clue what's going on with him, and it's really none of her business.

A half a beer later, Ayden finally wanders into my backyard. He's wearing a pair of black board shorts and a green T-shirt. His black hair is damp and hangs in his eyes.

"Did you shower?" I lean forward to get a better look at him.

He ruffles his damp hair into place. "Yeah, I wanted to wash the rain out of my hair." He hoists himself up beside me, plants his bare feet into the empty hot tub, and discreetly but thoroughly checks out my body. Then his gaze drops to our feet. "What the hell? Where's the water?"

"Yeah, so apparently, my parents drained it because no one ever uses it." I hand him a beer. "I did manage to steal a couple of these, though."

"So, what do we do now, then?" He pops the top off

the beer and slants his head back to take a swallow.

I stare at the sad, pathetic excuse for a hot tub. "Do you know how to fill it?"

He shakes his head. "I've never even been in a hot tub before."

"Not even back when . . ." I bite my lips to stop myself from mentioning his past.

"Back when I lived with my birth mother?" he asks, scratching the back of his neck. "It's okay, you can ask me stuff if you want to. I've been working on it in therapy . . . I mean, with that kind of stuff."

"Like hot tub stuff?"

"Yeah, like hot tub stuff." He scoots toward me until our knees are touching.

I stifle a smile because I can tell he did it on purpose, needing to touch me.

"And to answer your question," he says. "My birth mother wasn't really the take-her-kids-swimming type, and that includes hot tubs."

"So, what did you do for fun, then?" I swallow a little bit more beer then balance the bottle between my legs.

"Get into trouble." He gives a half-shrug. "You remember what I looked like when we met, right? That was basically who I was for the longest time."

"What do you mean by trouble, exactly? I know you drank, smoked, and got into fights, but any arrests I need to know about?" I dazzle him with a smile so he'll know I'm messing with him.

"No, no arrests." He relaxes back and stares up at the sky while sipping his beer. "My mother wasn't a good mother, and you already know that I didn't know my dad, so basically, my brother . . . my sister, and me just ran wild from the day we were born. We got into a ton of trouble all the time and did a lot of shitty stuff. Sometimes, I worry it's all going to catch up with me."

"My dad doesn't really know his dad, either. I guess he left his family when he was like six and started a new family. And, from what I understand, my mother's parents were neglectful, although my grandpa turned his life around."

When he looks at me in puzzlement, I get to the point. "What I'm trying to say is that, from some of the stories I've heard over the years, they got into a *ton* of trouble, but they turned out just fine. For parents, they're actually pretty cool." I clink bottles with him. "So, I'm betting you'll turn out just fine. In fact, you kind of already have."

"I still have a long ways to go before I'm fine, but I'll admit that I'm getting better."

My jaw drops in mock shock as I place my hand over my mouth. "Did you just say something nice about yourself, Shy Boy?"

His lips quirk. "Maybe."

I grin like I've just won the freaking lottery. "You should do it more often."

He remains quiet as he gazes at the night sky. Most of the clouds have thinned, and the stars and moon glimmer vibrantly above us.

"So, you want to hear my news?" I ask abruptly. "Because it's pretty big and epic."

His head cocks to the side as his attention falls to me. "Let's hear it."

Unable to conceal my enthusiasm any longer, an absurdly huge smile takes over my face. "It's about the band and a tour."

"*Really?* What one?"

"I think it's called the Rocking Summer Blast Tour or something like that. I have a paper in my room about it. My dad actually got us the gig, and it's not the biggest, most popular line-up, but it could help us get a foot in the door. Plus, imagine how cool it would be. You and me on the road, twenty-four seven, singing and writing lyrics while we see the country. We could have this super awesome duet at the end of our performance." When he doesn't say anything right away, I add, "Isn't it exciting?"

He doesn't seem that excited, more like disappointed. "I'm not sure if I can go . . . not when my sister's still out there."

I have no idea what to say to that. Honestly, I don't think there's anything I can say. He's clearly suffering over his sister, and I'm not about to try to convince him he's wrong for feeling that way.

"What can I do to help?"

He shrugs. "There's nothing anyone can do except wait for the police to find her." He grows quiet for a minute, studying the scars on the back of his hands. "Sometimes, I think about going to look for her myself"—he stares across the yard at his house—"tracking down every place connected to their name and seeing if she's being held at any of them."

My expression plummets. "I think you should just let the police do their job."

"I'm not saying I'm going to. I was just telling you I think about it sometimes."

"When you think about doing stuff, you usually do it." My sharp tone surprises me, almost as much as how afraid I am that he's going to actually go through with what he said.

He jerks back, thrown off by outburst. "No, I don't . . . I was just telling you because"—hurt masks his expression—"I thought that's what we did."

"Yeah, we do." I swing my legs out of the hot tub, hop down onto the grass, and cross my arms, staring him down.

"But you keep doing things like tracking that hacker down and going to that house, so when you say things like you're going to go track down these places, I get worried you're actually going to do it."

"I'm not going to go looking for them. I just need to do"—he balls his hands into fists, staring above us, as if cursing the stars—"something. I'm so sick of waiting around until they finally decide to take me. Like today at the concert. I was fine until I was around a bunch of people. Then all I kept thinking is how someone could be watching me in the audience, waiting to make their next move, just like they did to Sadie. Did you know they kidnapped her right out of her home?"

"They're not going to take you!" I shout, startling the both of us. I try to calm myself down, but it's like there are these waves inside me, roaring and swirling, and I feel like I'm drowning in the center of it. "Nothing's going to happen to you, and you're not going to go look for these places. Promise me you won't do it. Ever."

His eyes widen as he gapes at me in horror. That's when I realize tears are pouring from my eyes and down my cheeks. We hardly ever fight—I hardly ever fight with anyone—but the idea of him doing something stupid that could potentially lead to me losing him is making me feel like I'm losing my damn mind.

I can't ever lose him.
Ever. Ever. Ever.
Let the ocean take me away and drown me in rage.
I'll give myself away,
Just as long he stays safe.
And never, ever goes away.

"Lyric, I get that you're upset, but—"

"No, you don't get it," I cut him off, sounding calmer. "You don't care about yourself, so I don't think you realize how much it would kill me if something happened to you, because you don't think someone can care about you that much. But I care about you that much."

"It wouldn't kill—"

"I love you." Probably the worst moment ever to say it, but what's done is done and I'm not going to take it back. Honestly, I kind of feel better, like I got a few tiny rays of sunshine back.

I step toward him, feeling calm as a summer day. "If you care about me at all, you'll promise you won't go looking for these places, and you'll let the police do it." I lift my hand and hitch my pinkie toward him. "In fact, you'll pinkie swear on it."

He opens his mouth in a protest, but then his jaw snaps shut. He does the movement repeatedly, as if I shocked his voice right out of him. Then he searches my eyes for something with his face contorted in puzzlement.

"All right," he finally says as he loops his pinkie with mine. "I pinkie swear I won't go look for the places and will just talk to the police about it."

I suck back my tears. "Good."

A moment or two drifts by before we pull away. Another handful of seconds tick by before anyone says anything.

"Can I kiss you and make it better?" He chews on his bottom lip, mulling something over. "I don't like seeing you cry, especially when I'm the one who caused it."

I dry my tears from my cheeks then nod, and he seals his lips to mine, giving me the softest kiss.

The longer we kiss under the stars, the more I feel at peace. It doesn't matter if he didn't say I love you back. I wasn't expecting him to. I just needed to let him know how much I care about him, and I think I did exactly that.

Besides, deep down, in his own way, I think he might

love me. I can tell through his little touches, kisses, smiles, and how he agreed to do something tonight that he didn't really want to do, but felt he needed to because he didn't want to see me hurt.

Words are just words
That pass across lips.
Actions show more
Than words ever can understand.
Ayden's actions are beautiful,
And tell me all I need to know,
Feed my soul and give me hope.

"What can I do to make tonight up to you?" he asks when we finally come up for air.

"You don't need to make anything up to me." I hitch my arms around him. "We had our first fight. So what? It was bound to happen sometime."

"Okay, then what should we do to celebrate"—he glances at the hot tub—"because I think sitting in the hot tub is off the table."

I thrum my finger against my lip. "I have an idea."

He eyes me over with suspicion. "You have that look in your eye."

"What look?" I bat my eyelashes innocently.

He gives me a blank stare. "The look that means you're about to get us into trouble."

"I promise we won't get in trouble. You might not be too thrilled about it, though."

Before he can press for more details, I snatch ahold of his hand and drag him toward his house.

As we're rounding the fence, I notice a maroon SUV parked in front of his house.

"So, that's the infamous detective?" I smile at the car and give a little wave.

"You're such a weirdo," he jokes then steers me

toward the backdoor of his house.

The alarm goes off when we enter, and he hurries through the darkness to turn it off. I flip on the lights and bend down to untie my boots.

I feel him move up behind me before I actually see him.

"Hey." I stand upright, my back aligning with his chest.

As he circles his arms around my waist, the air feels electric, sharp zaps biting at my skin.

He rests his chin on my shoulder. "So, what did you want to do?"

"I was thinking we could work on that song we've been writing . . . and you could sing it for me."

"I knew you were up to something, but I already told you I can't sing."

"I'll be the one to decide that." I start to turn around to head for the kitchen, but he tightens his hold on me.

"Are you sure that's what you want to do?" There's a playfulness to his voice that's got me really curious where he's going with this.

"Yeah, you kind of owe me." It's a lie. He doesn't owe me anything, but I really want to hear him sing.

"Oh, yeah?" His lips dip toward my neck. "How do you figure?"

"Because you . . ." My eyes roll back, and my knees almost buckle as he sucks on the side of my neck.

The harder he sucks, the more difficult it becomes to keep my legs under me. Fortunately, he has his arms around me and keeps me from toppling to the ground.

"You sure you still want to hear me sing?" His warm breath falters against my neck. "Because I could . . . I could keep doing this."

After I regain my breath, I glare at him from over my

shoulder. "Don't try to play me like a sucker. I know you're trying to distract me, and it's not going to work." I slip out from under his arms and grab his hand. "Now, get your ass upstairs and sing for me so I can see if I'm ever going to be able to live out my dream of doing a duet with you." I haul him toward the kitchen, giving a playful glance over my shoulder. "And, when we're done, you can suck on my neck some more as punishment for trying to play me."

"I'm all for the sucking on the neck part, but don't say I didn't warn you about the singing thing."

"Let me be the judge of that."

Even though I have no clue what his singing voice sounds like, the dreamer side of me believes it's going to be low and smooth, like honey, and absolutely, one hundred percent dripping with sexiness. He may not agree with me, but he has zero confidence and doesn't believe anything about him is good.

When we enter his room, I release his hand and cross my arms, refusing to let him off the hook, even when he gives me his sad, puppy dog eyes.

"All right, Shy Boy, show me what you've got."

CHAPTER 12

I LOVE YOU. **SHE SAID** she *loves* me.

Love. Love. Love.

At first, I thought she was kidding.

I could see on her face that she wasn't, though. I thought about talking her out of it, telling her she really doesn't love me—couldn't—but the longer I stared at her, the more I could see how truthful she was being. There was no way I was going to be able to talk her out of it.

It was that look that made me pinkie swear that I wouldn't go looking for those places. I will keep my word, too, no matter how bad things get, because she's Lyric and I . . .

I, what exactly?

I think deep down I know just how much I care about her.

Enough that I would give up almost anything.

Lyric watches me as I situate on the bed with my guitar on my lap. Her eyes are lit up with anticipation that my voice is going to sound amazing, and I feel bad that, in a moment, I'm going to let her down.

"Are you sure you want me to do this?" I ask, lining my fingers along the strings. "Because, once I sing, there's no going back. That dream of yours will forever be crushed."

She bounces down on the foot of the bed. "Just do it, Shy Boy." She snaps her fingers impatiently. "Stop procrastinating."

She's still wearing her bikini, and the sight of her skin and curves is a nice distraction from the fact that I'm about to sing in front of someone for the very first time.

"All right, but don't say I didn't warn you." I lean back against the headboard and think of which song to play. My instinct tells me to go with a cover song, but then I figure, if I'm doing this, I might as well go all the way and sing one of my own songs.

As I open my mouth, I have no idea which song is going to come out.

"Stuck in the dust
Of a soul that was crushed,
I silently bleed in the stillness.
Aching inside, most days I feel like I'm losing my mind.
I'm dying inside.
And no one can help me."

I play a few more chords as I sing the chorus.

"Stuck in a sea of pain,
I thought nothing would ever change,
That my life would always be this way."

My fingers strum the strings.

"You blindsided me out of nowhere,
Right when I was about to surrender to the darkness,
Swallow it down with a handful of pills and sink to the bottom of the water.
Take away the pain so I can't feel it anymore.
So close to the edge,
You offered me your hand and dragged me to the

shore."

I stop playing, even though the song isn't finished, because Lyric is crying. Hot tears spill down her cheeks as she hugs her knees to her chest.

"Fuck, I'm sorry." I set my guitar aside and scoot down to the bottom of the bed beside her. "I don't know why I picked that song. I should have sung something different. Something happier."

"Is it true?" More tears stream from her eyes and down her cheeks. "Did you really think about taking your own life?"

I want to lie to her, but she deserves better.

"I used to, but I haven't thought about it since . . . well, since you and I became friends."

"Oh, Ayden, I never knew it was that bad for you." She slides her legs to the side of the bed and throws her arms around me.

"It's not that bad anymore." I breathe in the scent of her as I wrap my arms around her. "I promise."

I close my eyes and breathe in the truth. Yes, there's a ton of bad stuff going on in my life, but the darkness that used to grasp me by the ankles and wrists has lightened. The pain isn't so heavy, the scars easier to bear. But, if I'd never met Lyric and the Gregorys, I'm not sure I would have ever made it here to this moment.

"Your voice is beautiful, by the way," she whispers. "Even better than I thought it was going to be, so now you have no more excuses not to sing with me."

I want to argue with her, tell her she's wrong. My voice isn't beautiful. I can't sing with her. Instead, I decide to nod and enjoy the moment I almost didn't have.

CHAPTER 13

THE WEEK IS FAIRLY UNEVENTFUL, maybe even a little on the normal side. By Friday, I no longer have a detective tailing my every move. I make sure to do everything I'm supposed to and don't wander off. My life consists of school, band practice, therapy, family time, and Lyric.

Lyric, Lyric, Lyric. I spend all my free time with her, yet it still never feels like enough. I don't know what's happening to me exactly, but something is definitely changing.

"Knock. Knock. Knock." Lyric raps her hand on the doorframe as she strolls into my bedroom with her sketchbook tucked under her arm. She's wearing a short purple dress, her leather jacket, and black platforms. Her hair is wild around her face, and her lips are stained pink and look absurdly tempting. "Happy tattoo day, Shy Boy."

I prop my guitar against the wall, swing my legs over the edge, and stand to my feet. "Did you finish up the sketch?"

She bobs her head up and down enthusiastically. "I did. You want to see it?"

"Of course." I reach to take the sketchbook, but she dodges out of my reach.

A slow, conniving grin spreads across her face. "It'll cost you."

My arm falls to my side, and my lips twitch with amusement. "What's the price?"

She taps a finger against her lips. "Let me think about this. Something pretty awesome, of course, since this is a freaking amazing sketch. Not money. Not anything materialistic. How about a cookie . . . ? No, that doesn't seem very awesome. I could always make you do a striptease."

"Lyric"—laughter bursts from my lips—"just tell me what you want."

"Oh, fine. Take all the fun out of this." She fakes a pout, but her smile almost instantly lights up her face again. "It'll cost you a kiss."

"That's it?"

"What can I say? Your kisses are pretty valuable."

Insert awkwardness on my part. I've never been good with compliments.

"I don't think my kisses are that valuable, but if that's what you want, then I'll give it to you." I step forward, slide my hand around her back, and reel her in for a kiss.

The kiss is quick, but leaves me breathless. When I start to move away, Lyric's arm snakes around my back, and she pushes me right back against her.

"A little bit longer, please," she begs, arching her chest toward me.

I easily give her what she asks and slip my tongue inside her mouth, kissing her the way she deserves. The kiss goes on for seconds, minutes, hours . . . so long I lose track of time.

Out of breath, I finally have to pull away, giving her bottom lip a gentle nip. She shudders in my arms, and I nearly stop breathing.

God, how can I be alive when my heart is beating so

quickly?

"Okay, that definitely earned you the reward of seeing this." Her voice is gravelly. She clears her throat before opening the sketchbook and hands it to me. "So, what do you think?"

Lines trace the pages and form shapes and swirls, dark and bright shades and vivid colors, patterns that all surround a fiery gold and red bird with its wings spread wide.

God, this must have taken her forever.

"It's a phoenix," she explains, "which is supposed to mean rebirth and strength. I thought it was pretty fitting."

That's how she sees me? For some reason, the thought causes my heart to swell inside my chest.

I smooth my hand over the page. "It's amazing. More than amazing. I don't even know what to say."

"So, you like it?"

"It's perfect. I don't think you could have done anything more perfect." I shake my head in awe. "God, Lyric, this is amazing. I mean, I know you're talented, but . . . This must have taken you days to draw."

"Nah, it didn't take that long." She waves me off. "But I was freaking out that you would hate it."

"No, I love it." *I love you.* I shake the thought from my head and thank her by kissing her again.

"Oh, a bonus payment." Her lips move against mine as she cracks a joke.

"You can have as many bonus payments as you want. I owe you a ton, anyway, for putting up with my shit the other night. I should have never upset you like that. I didn't realize that you . . ." I kiss her again and again, tipping her head back and tangling our tongues, her lips hot and inviting.

Moaning, she grips at my arms and clutches onto me as I lower her to the bed.

"As much as I love where this is going," she murmurs as her back is just about to touch the mattress, "on my way up here, I was told to make sure to tell you that we have to leave in no less than five minutes; otherwise, we'll be late for your appointment."

I grunt in response, and she erupts with laughter.

"I've never heard you sound that frustrated before. That was pretty funny."

"You think that's funny?" My hand skates around to her ribcage, and I tickle her.

"Hey!" she gripes, writhing below me. "That's not fair."

"How do you figure?" I tickle her again, secretly loving how her hips thrust against mine every time she moves.

"Because I just gave you the most awesomest sketch of a tattoo ever. That definitely earns me a no-tickling-for-a-while pass."

"Oh, fine." I tickle her a few more times then push off her and offer my hand.

"Are you nervous?" she asks as I pull her to her feet.

"Yeah," I admit with a shaky breath.

"Don't worry, I've heard it can be more of a high than painful," she says as I slip on my boots.

"I'm not worried about the pain. Pain's fine." I rake my fingers through my hair as we head out of my room and toward the stairs. "I'm just worried about, you know"—I gesture at my side—"my shirt pulled up and someone being that close to me and touching me. What if I freak out or something?"

"That's why I'm going with you," she reminds me as we reach the bottom of the stairs. "I'll hold your hand and keep you so entertained with my charming personality that you'll barely pay attention to anything else. I've even been saving up some juicy gossip for this particular occasion."

"Since when do you gossip?"

"Since this morning when all hell broke loose at the Scott's home."

I bend over to lace my boot. "Is everything all right?"

"It will be as soon as the drama passes."

"You guys ready to go?" Ethan asks as he strolls into the kitchen, swinging the car keys around his finger.

"Surely-durely," Lyric singsongs. When I stand upright, she grabs my hand and jerks me toward the door. "Come on, let's go get the past taken off you."

TWENTY MINUTES LATER, ETHAN IS parking the car near the side of town that is enclosed by small shops and restaurants. Ethan owns the one on the corner, a few blocks down from the tattoo shop.

Inside, the windows and walls are decorated with different drawings and images, and in the center of the room is a display case. In the back corner is a curtain, and I can hear a needle buzzing from behind it.

Ethan starts chatting with his buddy, Cole, whose arms and neck are covered with ink.

"Is it doable?" Ethan asks as Cole studies Lyric's sketch.

"It'll definitely take a couple of sessions." He examines the drawing closely then looks at me. "Can I see the tattoo you have now? I just want to make sure this will cover it up."

I glance at Lyric, who gives me an encouraging smile, then step forward and lift up my shirt, revealing the inked patterns that form a jagged circle along my scarred skin.

Cole bends over and squints at the tat. "Whoa, that is probably one of the worst tattoo jobs I've ever seen." He stands upright and frowns at Ethan. "On the phone, you said it was homemade, but I didn't think it would be that bad."

"So, you can't fix it?" Ethan asks, casting a concerned glance in my direction.

My muscles ravel into knots. All this time, I was so focused on getting the actual tattoo that I didn't even consider it might not be able to be covered up. The idea of having it on my body forever sends my stomach dropping.

Cole rubs his jawline. "I didn't say that. I just said I didn't expect it to be that bad." He lowers his hand. "I can cover it up, but the raised scarring will still be there."

"That's fine," Ethan says, crossing his arms. "We didn't expect you to be able to cover up all the scars. We just don't want to be able to see any of the ink that's already there."

"Well, then that works." He looks at the drawing again as he backs up toward the curtain. "Let me go get this drawn up, and then we'll go from there."

"You going to be okay?" Ethan turns to me after Cole disappears through the curtain.

I sink into a chair near the front door. "Yeah, I'm just a little nervous."

"That's understandable. If you need anything, just say so, okay?"

I nod, and he stuffs his hands into his pockets then wanders off to look at the framed sketches on the wall.

I lower my head, rest my arms on my knees, and take a few measured breaths, trying to calm myself down.

Lyric plops down beside me and nudges my boot with her foot. "So, I learned interesting stuff today."

"About your family?" I raise my head up to look at her.

She shakes her head. "Nah, I'm saving that juicy story

for when you're actually getting the tattoo. But this story is mildly entertaining. It's about Sage and Maggie."

My brows dip. "I thought they hated each other."

"Well, apparently, there's a thin line between love and hate, or so I've been told. And they fooled around at a party a while ago." She tucks a lock of her hair behind her ear. "Sage told me about it today in class, which FYI, I think he's starting to see me as a dude. He kept giving me all the details about Maggie's hot body, which I so didn't want to hear."

I laugh because she's so far from wrong. "He doesn't see you as a dude. He's probably just trying to make you jealous."

She rolls her eyes. "No way. I can tell he's over me. He even asked for her number."

"Sage asked for someone's number? He's always telling me he doesn't do relationships." Unless he could have Lyric, which I still think is what his behavior is all about.

"Apparently, he changed his mind. It's kind of funny, though. The two of them hook up with more people than I can count. They almost seem perfect for each other in this weird, sick, whore-ish way."

"I don't know . . . It kind of sounds like a disaster to me. I mean, neither of them have ever been in a relationship for more than a minute." And I still don't believe this is about Maggie.

"True, but I have hope."

"That's because you're you."

She smiles at that. "I am pretty amazing."

"Yes, you are." I stretch my legs out. "So, have you told Sage and Nolan about the tour?"

She hesitates then shakes her head. "Not yet."

"Why not?"

She crosses her legs and reclines back in the chair.

"Because I'm waiting for you to agree to go."

"Lyric—" I start.

"My dad said we have until after we record our album. I'm giving you until then to decide. If you want to go, then I'll tell Sage and Nolan."

"I'm not going to—"

She covers my mouth with her hand. "I'm not asking you for an answer right now, so don't give me one." She lowers her hand and sits back in the chair. "Give it a few weeks, and then you can tell me your answer."

I puff out a breath. "Fine."

But, unless my sister's found, I won't go. I can't take off, hit the road, and live an amazing life while I know Sadie is trapped in darkness somewhere.

For the next twenty minutes or so, Lyric and I chat about lighter things, like the song she's decided we're going to sing together. Listening to the sound of her voice and watching her talk animatedly, I fall into another world filled with ease and calmness. But the moment Cole walks out from the curtain, the bubble around us pops.

"Come on back, and let's get this put on you," he says with a nod of his head.

My knees shake as I stand up and cross the room. When Lyric laces our fingers together, I feel the slightest bit better, until Cole tells me to take off my shirt so he can put the sketching on my skin and make sure we get it in the right place before we start.

I glance between Cole, Ethan, and Lyric, knowing I have to do this since the tattoo is on my side, but knowing doesn't make it any easier.

"I can step out if you want me to," Lyric whispers softly enough so only I hear her.

She's never seen me with my shirt off, but if I'm going to have her in here with me while I get the tattoo, then it's going to have to happen. I guess it's time to rip the band-aid off and get over one of my biggest fears. Having her here while I get the tattoo was my decision. Plus, she loves me, and I need to hold on to that.

"No, you're fine." I take my fiftieth nervous breath of the day, grab the collar of my shirt, and pull it over my head.

By the time I get it off, my pulse is racing so fast I swear I'm going to have a heart attack. It's the first time anyone has seen me shirtless since I was freed from that house except on a few rare occasions when Lyric walked into my room without knocking. I'm terrified, yet I've made this huge step forward.

Forward, forward, forward.
Please, just let me fly
Instead of falling off the cliff.

Lyric dips her head to catch my gaze. "You okay?"

"Yeah . . . I think so." I cringe at the wobbliness of my voice.

My heart races violently the entire time Cole aligns the drawing on my ribcage. I hope that, by the time I lie down in the chair, I'll relax, but that doesn't end up being the case.

Instead, I become nervous over the needle. I stare at the ceiling, deeply inhaling and exhaling while trying to picture myself in a calm place—near the ocean, in the mountains, all alone. It's a relaxation technique Dr. Gardingdale taught me, but it doesn't help. By the time the needle pokes my skin, I almost bolt from the chair.

Nails, biting nails,
Scrape layer after layer,
Peel away your soul.
You'll never be the same again.
We'll make sure of that.

You'll be tainted.
I don't want to be tainted. I want to be whole.
I'm stronger than that. I have to be stronger.
Or else what do I have to live for?

"Hey, look at me." Lyric's comforting voice draws me away from my thoughts.

I open my eyes and find her staring down at me.

"Do you want to hear my story now?" she asks in a calm, soothing voice.

As I stare into her bright green eyes, a calm rolls over me. "Yeah, tell me the story."

She smiles, drags a chair over, and sits down beside me, holding my hand. "So, guess who the blond woman at the bar turned out to be?"

I hear the buzzing of the needle, distantly feel it, but feel her more potently. "Who?"

"My dad's half-sister."

"*What?* Where the hell did she come from? I thought your dad was an only child or something."

"Remember how I told you that he hasn't had contact with his father or his new family in forever. Well, I guess his half-sister decided she wanted to see him. She recognized me because she saw pictures on the Internet and tracked my dad down that way. I guess she chickened out last weekend, though, after talking to me. Then she showed up at his studio last night."

"What happened?"

"At first, my dad was irritated and thought she was there because she needed something. But, when he realized she was genuinely there to see him, they chatted for a while. I guess she wants to be part of our lives."

She props her elbows on the edge of the chair and rests her chin on her hands. "She said she's wanted to meet him for a while, but she was afraid my dad would be upset with her because their dad's such a fucking bastard. Plus, we lived so far away that it made it hard to just stop by. Then her husband got transferred to San Diego, and she decided she no longer had an excuse. She has kids, too. I think a daughter and a son. I'm not sure about all the deets, but I guess we're supposed to hang out sometime or something."

"That's so weird . . . that he suddenly has a sister." So weird, but I'm jealous.

The jealously is short-lived, because my skin starts to burn from the needle, and my eyelids start to close as I plummet toward the darkness.

Lyric pulls me right back out, delicately placing her palm on my cheek. "Hey, look at me."

When I open my eyes, my gaze locks with hers. I wait for her to say something, but instead, she intensely carries my gaze. I feel myself falling again, only someplace different. Someplace new.

Feel, feel, feel your heart beating.
It feels so free
With her eyes on you.
Nothing else matters.
Time has vanished.
The past doesn't exist.
The pain and the wrong is gone.
Feel, feel, feel yourself sinking.
Not into the darkness
Where the chains pull you down.
But into the light
Where your heart is waiting to be found.
Found, found, found.

I'm not sure how long I lay in that chair, but it's enough time that my legs are wobbly when I stand. Once I get my footing, I stare at my reflection in the mirror. The outline of the tattoo inks my ribcage. Through the twists, lines, and dark curves of the feather and beak, the scars are still visible, yet I feel lighter inside, different, less bound. I took a massive step today.

Ethan thanks Cole for doing a kickass job then makes me another appointment to get the outlines shaded while I put my shirt back on. Then I leave the back room with Lyric, and we head for the car.

During the drive home, Lyric and I sit in the backseat with our hands clasped. The contact of her skin lulls me into a relaxing state as I lean my head against the window and watch the buildings and houses drift by.

My thoughts drift to Sadie. I wish she could have been here with me, getting her tattoo covered up. I vow to myself that, one day, when she's found, I'll take her to do just that. I'll help her feel free from the darkness like the Gregorys and Lyric have helped me.

Freedom, is that was this is? Have I finally found something I never thought existed? Is it possible that one day I'll be free?

All I can do is hope.

CHAPTER 14

SOMETHING CHANGED IN AYDEN THE day he got the outline of his tattoo. He became more at ease, as if the mark on his ribcage had been weighing him down. Don't get me wrong, he's still my shy boy who is holding onto a lot of pain and constantly worries about his sister. But he has been smiling more, which has to be a step forward, right?

A couple of weeks drift by before he goes in to get the shading done. I want to go with him, but the appointment falls on the day my family and I are meeting my father's sister and her husband.

They arrive at the house around five o'clock to have dinner, dressed to impress. Seeing my aunt again, I wonder how I ever could have missed the family resemblance. My father and her share the same blond hair and sky blue eyes and joking mannerism to the point that the relation is almost uncanny.

Around six, we gather around the dinner table to eat. Outside the window, the sun is setting, and next door, the Gregory's driveway is vacant, which means Ayden is still getting his tattoo. As soon as I see that car, though, I'm bailing out to go over there.

"So, where are your kids?" I ask Ava as I pick at my chicken.

"They're actually still back in New York with their grandparents," Ava explains, wrapping her fingers around the wineglass. "We wanted to get settled before we brought them out here."

I wonder if she means with the grandfather I've never met. I don't ask, though, since I can tell the subject is making my dad uncomfortable.

"We'll definitely have to bring them over when we get them out here," she continues after taking a sip of wine. "I think you and my oldest would really get along. He's really into music."

Funny, I wonder if my dad got his musical talent from his dad, then.

"Does he play anything?" I ask, scooping up a glob of mash potatoes.

"He plays the cello," her husband, Glen, answers, poking his fork into the salad. "And he used to play the flute when he was younger, but when he reached fourteen, he gave it up. Said he was too old for it."

"I play the violin," I tell them. "Maybe we could rock out sometime, orchestra style. Unless he plays symphonic rock."

"I think I've heard him mention something about that before." He exchanges a look with Ava who shrugs.

"Beats me." She sets the wineglass down. "He goes through a new phase every other week. The only thing he's stuck with is the cello."

"How old is he?" I reach for a roll.

"He's fifteen," Ava replies as my mom refills her glass with wine.

"So, Kale's age," I remark. "Sounds about right."

Kale goes through phases like no other. Like that girl

he had a crush on a month ago. He's moved on from her and is already focused on someone else.

"Who's Kale?" Ava wonders, picking up the glass again.

I open my mouth to reply, but I see headlights pull into the Gregory's driveway and turn to my mother. "Ayden's home. Can I go over and see how everything turned out?"

She glances at Ava and her husband then starts to protest, but Ava interrupts.

"Don't keep her here on our part." She winks at me, reminding me so much of my dad it's weird. "We have plenty of time to catch up."

"Fine. Go." My mom gets up to gather the dishes as I push back from the table. "You should tell Lila and Ethan to come over later and chat for a while." Chat is code for drink wine and reminisce about the good ol' days.

Nodding, I take my dishes to the sink and rinse them off then hurry for the back door.

"Don't stay too late," my mom calls out as I step outside. "And make sure to keep Ayden's door open."

"Okay!" I roll my eyes then shut the door and jump the fence.

I walk in without knocking, a bad habit of mine. Aunt Lila and Uncle Ethan are in the kitchen, chatting about something.

"Hey," Aunt Lila greets me when I close the back door. "How'd everything go with the family dinner?"

"It seems to be going okay, but that's usually the case when wine is involved." I slip my sandals off and walk into the kitchen. "They said you two should go over and chat for a while."

"I think we could do that for a bit, right?" Lila says to Ethan. "It is the weekend, and no one has practice or anything."

He shrugs as he moves for the cupboard. "It's fine by me. I'm not working this weekend."

"Is Ayden upstairs?" I ask, walking backwards for the stairway.

"He is." Lila eyes me warily from across the kitchen. "If you go up there, you better make sure you keep that door open."

"My mother said the exact same thing." I pause at the bottom step. "How'd his tattoo go?"

"He seems okay," Ethan answers, opening the fridge. "I think he handled it better when you were there, but he still did pretty okay today."

Ethan's version of okay can be a little iffy since he's fine with almost everything.

Without saying anything else, I turn around and trot up the stairs. When I reach Ayden's closed bedroom door, I knock as I walk in, something I've done since the day we met.

He's sitting on his bed, writing in his journal with his leg stretched out and his back propped against the headboard.

"Hey," he says, smiling at me.

"Whatcha doing?" I plop down on the bed beside him, roll on my side, and prop up on my elbow.

"Just writing about what happened today." He closes the journal, tosses it on the nightstand, and lies down facing me. "About how good it felt to get that damn mark all covered up."

"Hey, we're going over to your house for a little while." Lila pokes her head in, suspicion crossing her face as she eyes Ayden and me on the bed. "Would you two mind sitting on the floor?"

Ayden sighs but climbs off the bed, and I begrudgingly follow. He takes a seat in his computer chair, and I sit down on the trunk near the foot of his bed.

"Everson and Kale are sleeping over at a friend's house," she informs us. "And Fiona is downstairs in the den watching some weird documentary about psychics. Keep an eye on her, please, and keep this door open at all times."

She pushes the door open all the way before backing toward the hall. "I'm going to set the alarm, but if you need anything at all, we're right next door. We shouldn't be long." She steps back, pushing on the door again, even though it's already open to the wall.

"They'll be gone for more than a while," I say once I hear the front door shut. "Ava and her husband are there, and you know how chatty Aunt Lila is with new people. Plus, they have the wine out."

Ayden chuckles as he spins the chair from side to side. "That's okay. They should enjoy themselves. I think I put a lot of stress on them today."

"So, how did today go?" I ask, leaning back on my hands.

"Okay." He rakes his fingers through his hair. "I mean, it would have been better if you were there, but I made it through it and feel pretty good right now."

"Can I . . . ?" I bite down on my lip, wondering if I should ask.

"Can you what?" he wonders with his forehead creased.

I let my lip pop free. "Can I see the tattoo?"

He hesitates before his fingers drift toward the bottom of his dark grey T-shirt. "Yeah, sure."

"Are you sure?" I double check. "You don't have to show me if you don't want to."

"No . . . I want to." He grips the fabric. "Besides, you should get to see your artwork." Summoning a deep inhale, he lifts the shirt up and slips one arm out of the sleeve.

Bright red and gold ink splatters up his side along with intricate shades that contrast with the dark lines of the feathers and cover the mark.

"It's gorgeous." *You're gorgeous.* "Cole did an amazing job." I climb off the trunk and move in front of Ayden to get a better look. "Man, I so need to get a tattoo." Instinctively, I reach forward to touch him, but realize he's probably not going to like that, so I pull back.

Ayden catches my hand. "I want to try something," he whispers, his voice strained.

I nod, even though I don't have a damn clue what he's about to do. Don't care, though. Let him do whatever he wants with me.

He slowly guides my hand back to him and, with an uneven breath, places my palm on his chest. His heart is hammering and slams against my hand.

I don't say anything. I can barely breathe, knowing how significant this moment is to him—to us.

"Your skin's so soft," I utter, afraid to move my hand and ruin the moment.

His hands slide to my hips, and his fingers inch up my shirt. "So's yours." He traces his finger back and forth along the speck of flesh.

A shiver courses through me, and I suddenly can't breathe.

Air ripped from my lungs.
Heart bleeding.
I need to see all of him,
Every inch,
Feel the softness of him against me.
I want it so badly my soul aches.

I start to draw back because it seems like we could both use a break from the intensity, but my hands have other ideas, and my fingers drift up his chest. When he doesn't protest, I inch my hand higher, keeping our eyes locked, making sure he's all right. I don't want to push him. If he so much as even looks like he's freaking out, I'll stop in a heartbeat.

When his eyes snap wide, I jerk back. "Sorry."

"No, it's fine." He counts to three under his breath then, with a swift yank, removes his shirt. "I want to . . ." His breath falters as I take in the sight of him.

While he was getting his tattoo, I tried my best not to stare. Right now, all I do is stare. Stare, stare, stare forever. He's not ripped like a jock or sculpted like a model. He's lean and toned and has a few scars on his skin. He's the most perfect thing I've ever laid eyes on, and it almost makes me cry that he's mine.

"You're so beautiful." I gently place my hands on his chest and his skin feels warm against my palms.

He shivers from my touch. "I want to feel you, too"—he takes a few shallow breaths—"against me."

I want to ask him if he can handle that, but I don't think he'd ask if he didn't actually want to. And I want to, too. So, so much, I can hardly stand it.

I step back and shut the door. Then I head back across the room toward him, lifting my shirt over my head.

His grey eyes soak me in as I fumble with the clasp of my bra. Once unfastened, I lower the straps from my shoulders and toss it on the floor. Then I turn to his iPod on the dresser, scroll to my playlist, and select "Youth" by Daughter.

"This seems like the kind of moment that needs a song," I explain when he gives me a puzzled look.

As I climb up on his lap and put a leg on either side of him, he struggles to breathe evenly, and my heart slams against my chest. He's nervous. I'm nervous. This isn't a big deal just for him. I've never been this far with a guy before, and I'm glad Ayden is my first. Glad I get to experience a lot of my firsts with him.

He smooths his hands over my sides as I loop my arms around his neck and press my chest against his. The skin-to-skin contact is better than I could have ever imagined in my crazy, imaginative mind.

He's warm enough to thaw a thousand icebergs,
Liquefy the world into water,
Melt the coldest of hearts,
Chip away at frigid souls.

He gasps as I clutch onto him. Then he slips his arms around me, presses me closer, and buries his head in the crook of my neck, kissing my hammering pulse.

A few tears land on my shoulder as he starts to cry.

"I love you," I whisper just loud enough for him to hear.

He doesn't say it back, but he embraces me with everything he has in him, and I know it's his silent way of saying it back.

CHAPTER 15

SATURDAY NIGHT MIGHT HAVE BEEN one of the most amazing nights I've ever had. Spending the night with Lyric in my arms, simply holding each other with our bodies connected, surpassed every good experience. She said I love you again, and I almost said it back.

The words burned on the tip of my tongue,
Scorching metal,
Ready to brand our souls
Forever.

I didn't quite make it there, but I'm not too upset with myself. In fact, I'm probably the happiest I've been in a long time.

All that changes Monday morning when I open the car door to go to school. In the center of the driver's seat is a piece of paper wrapped by a faded pink ribbon.

Knife
Hair
Sadie
Sacrifice.

It's time we finally talked, Ayden. Meet us as the Golden Center Docks tonight at 10:00 if you ever want to see you sister again. And make sure to come alone.

"Sadie," I whisper, my hand trembling as I tumble into a memory.

"Ayden, help me!" she cries through the darkness.

I can't see her anywhere.

Where is she? Where is she? Where is she?

I search the darkness and see a woman with blood red hair.

Red hair, like blood.

Then I see Sadie chained to a wall, her pink ribbon stained with drops of blood.

"We're always watching you."

I blink from the memory, my body quivering as I jerk my hand back. I can't touch it, not when there might be fingerprints.

My gaze skims the neighborhood, searching for a face I can't remember. Since it's early May, the neighborhood is buzzing with the summer air, and people seem to be everywhere. Short, tall, thin, heavy, a guy with blonde hair, a woman with red hair, and it feels as if they're all watching me.

Blood, blood, blood everywhere.

Red nails.

Red hair.

Blood, blood, blood.

I run up the driveway to the house, throw open the back door, and stumble into the kitchen.

"Ayden." Lila's head snaps up from her breakfast, and her eyes widen as she shoves the chair back from the table. "Oh, my God, what happened?"

"A letter," I barely get the words out as I point at the back door. "There's a letter on the seat of the car."

Ethan is storming for the back door in less time than it takes me to suck in my next breath. "Stay here," he warns as he rushes outside, slamming the door behind him.

Lila hurries over around the table to me as I sink down in a chair.

"The note . . ." I lower my head into my hands, guilt crushing my chest. "It had my sister's hair ribbon on it . . . It had to be hers."

Lila kneels down in front of me and folds her arms around me. "Everything's going to be okay."

Five minutes ago, I would have agreed with her.

"No, it's not," I croak. "The note said that, if I want to see my sister again, I have to meet them at the Golden Center Docks tonight."

"Don't worry. That's not going to happen." Lila hugs me tightly until Ethan comes back in.

She stands up, and the two of them exchange a hushed conversation in the doorway. After they're done with their discussion, Ethan rushes upstairs while Lila ducks into the living room to make a phone call.

When she returns to the kitchen, she sits down in the chair beside me.

"Ethan's going to get everyone off to school before the police show up," she tells me. "Detective Rannali is going to come here and collect the note, search the area, and dust for prints. He wants you to be here to ask you some questions, though."

I nod, balling my hands into fists underneath the table, wishing I could go back to Saturday night and have Lyric hold me again.

"I wish the detective was still watching the house. It's like they were waiting for them to leave to make their next more." When I say it aloud, I realize how true that might be.

"You should text Lyric and tell her she'll need to find a ride," Lila says, watching me like a hawk, as if she expects me to crack apart like I used to. "Ayden, everything's going to be okay. We're going to take care of this."

I want to break apart, shatter into pieces, but I'm stronger than that. I can feel the strength where the fresh ink stains my flesh and in the lingering memories of Lyric's lips against mine and the feel of our flesh touching.

Strong.

Strong.

Strong.

I dig my phone out of my pocket and send Lyric a text.

> *Me: I can't take u to school this morning. Something came up. Sorry.*
>
> *Lyric: Everything okay?*
>
> *Me: I'll talk to u at school, okay?*
>
> *Lyric: Okay.*

I know she's probably worried now, but I don't want to give the details of what happened via text.

I put the phone away then spend an hour waiting for the police to show up and another hour after that for them to dust for prints. The entire time, I'm trying to figure out what to do about the note. As risky as it is, I think I need to do what they requested and meet them. Am I terrified out of my goddamn mind? Yes. Will I hate myself if I don't do it? Yes. The biggest problem is going to be convincing Lila to let me go.

After the police are finished dusting for prints and the letter is bagged, Detective Rannali sits down in the living room with Lila and me to ask me some questions—if I've seen anything suspicious, if I know why they sent me the letter.

When he's finished, I have a few questions for him about Sadie and the case. Call it a last resort to the inevitable—that I'm going to have to meet those people at the dock.

"What about those pictures on the website?" I ask. "Have you looked into those? It seems like someone could find them if they went looking for them."

"We've done some research into that, but all the places have yet to be tracked down." He clicks his pen and presses it to a notepad he fishes from his suit jacket pocket. "And, Ayden, let me stress that you searching for those places is not an option. We believe that was what your brother was doing right before he was murdered. We've had some witnesses give us statements that he was on some sort of mission to find his sister."

"How did he even know she was taken?" I wonder, taken aback.

He went looking for her? Risked everything to find her?

"I think the two of them somehow managed to remain in contact. We pulled your brother's phone records, and Sadie sent him a text a few days before she was taken."

Sadie and her bad feelings. She was always having them and was usually right. She had a bad feeling the day we were taken, warning us that something bad was about to happen.

Sadie.
Sadie.
Sadie.
I'm going to help.
Please, just hold on.

"We're still investigating into it more." He writes something down then glances at Lila. "I have to ask about the amnesia therapy. How has it been coming along? The last update we received was quite a while ago."

"That's because he stopped the therapy," Lila replies

curtly, folding her arms. "We didn't see the need for him to keep doing it when there wasn't any progress."

"As of now, that therapy might be the only thing that will help us identify the perpetrators." He seems irked. "I wish you would have informed us that he'd stopped it."

"What about what the note said?" I intervene. "Are we going to talk about that?"

His irritation lessens, as if he were waiting for me to bring it up. "I was planning on mentioning it, yes. I want to know how you feel about it."

"He's not going to meet those people anywhere," Lila snaps. "I'm not going to let him."

"I'm eighteen," I mutter, knowing I'm going to upset her and loathing myself for having to do it.

In the end, this is about saving Sadie.

Lila narrows her eyes at me. "I don't give a shit how old you are. You're my son, and you'll do what you're told."

"Living a life where I could be kidnapped is just as risky," I point out. "I need to do this. Maybe, if I do, it'll lead us to Sadie."

Lila tears up. "I can't let you risk your safety like that. If you go there . . . alone . . ." She shakes her head. "No, I won't let you do it. I can't lose you."

"He wouldn't be alone," the detective chimes in. "We would have officers around the area. The Golden Center Docks couldn't be a more perfect area for this. There are trees and plenty of other places to hide. Plus, it's secluded from the city."

Lila glares at him. "I'm not letting you use him as bait."

"I'm not being used as bait," I insist. "I need to go there for my own sake. Do you know how bad it would eat away at me . . . ? How bad it does eat away at me that I can't save her? She's there, and I'm here. She's suffering, and I'm not."

"Ayden, I . . ." She has no clue what to say to the truth of my words.

"Besides, if we do this, it could lead to some arrests and maybe put an end to this," I press. "I—we—could all finally have a fucking normal life."

It might be the biggest and longest speech I've ever made, and there's definitely a shock factor to it.

Lila sniffs back tears. "I just want you to live the life you deserve without all this pain."

"Then let me do this for myself. For my sister." I shut my eyes and take a deep breath. "For my brother."

When the room grows quiet, I open my eyes.

She's staring out the window, her eyelashes fluttering against the tears. Detective Rannali catches my gaze and gives me an encouraging look. I don't give a shit about him, though. I'm not doing it for him. I'm doing it for my sister and myself. And for my brother.

"I want assurance that no harm will come to him." She looks over at the detective. "I won't agree to this unless you can give me that."

He nods. "Of course." He tucks the pen and notepad into his pocket. "We're not going to put your son at risk. We'll do this safely, and if anything looks suspicious, then we'll pull him out."

Lila's gaze lands on me. "You have to promise me the same thing. If at any time something seems wrong, you'll leave."

I nod, some of the tension alleviating in my chest, but it's replaced by fear.

Am I really going to do this? See them again? The people who stole my life from me?

Her gaze elevates to the ceiling as she dabs her eyes.

"I hope I don't regret this," she mutters. "I don't know what I'd do if I lost you."

Even though I'm not the touchy feely type, it seems like the kind of moment where I should give her a hug, so I wrap an arm around her and give her a pat on the back.

"Thank you . . . and not just for this. For taking me in and making sure that I didn't . . . well, you know."

I'm not sure if she knows just how much I appreciate what they've done for me. Maybe, if my brother and sister could have found this, things would have turned out differently for them. Maybe, if tonight goes well, my sister can still have this in time.

"Oh, Ayden." She pulls me against her, crushing my chest.

Usually, I squirm, but I decide to let her have a moment. Truthfully, I kind of need one, too. Even though I'm strong, I'm still terrified out of my goddamn mind that something will go wrong. Unlike a couple of years ago, I have a lot to lose.

My family.

My music.

A career in music, even.

Most importantly, Lyric. I don't even know if I could function without her, not with how close we've gotten.

She holds me up when I'm falling,
Stills me when I'm tumbling,
Calms me when I'm cracking,
Gives me air when I'm suffocating.
Lyric, she somehow takes the pain away
When everything is crushing down on me.
How I ever lived without her, I have no idea.

The problem is, I'm worried how she's going to react when I tell her what I'm going to do. She flipped out when I told her about the photos. Maybe I should keep this to myself for now.

After the detective leaves to go get his team prepped for tonight, I stay home with Lila and help her clean the house. Scrubbing down the counters and the floors distracts us from the massive cloud hovering above us.

Finally, after the kitchen and living room are sparkling, we sit down at the table to eat some sandwiches.

"I don't want to tell Lyric what I'm doing tonight," I tell her, picking the crust off the bread. "She'll worry about me, and I don't . . ." I swallow hard. "I don't want her to have to go through that."

Lila nods, picking at her food. "I think we should probably keep it from Fiona, Kale, and Everson, too . . ." She shuts her mouth and stares down at the plate. "Ayden, are you sure you want to do this? The police, they'll keep looking for her. They're not going to give up."

"I know they're not going to, but how am I supposed to live with myself if I don't go?"

"This might not go as you plan. You know that, right?"

I nod, sucking in a deep breath. "I know that, but it's worth the risk."

She nods, still staring at her food.

A silence sets in like an ominous doom.

CHAPTER 16

I LEAVE THE HOUSE BEFORE Lyric gets home and drive around town with Lila while she runs some errands. I know, if I see Lyric, then there's a chance I'll break down and tell her everything, so it's a good thing we take off before that can happen. Still, when she sends me a text, I feel like the world's biggest asshole for lying to her.

> Lyric: *All right, dude, why weren't you at school? What's going on?*
>
> Me: *Nothing. I didn't feel well, so I stayed home.*
>
> Lyric: *Why aren't you home now?*
>
> Me: *Lila took me to the doctor.*
>
> Lyric: *Is everything all right? Now u have me worried.*
>
> Me: *Everything's fine. I just have a cold.*

There's a pause before the next message buzzes through.

> Lyric: *R u sure that's all that's going on? U seem like you're being a little vague and sketchy.*

Me: I swear everything's fine. If I'm feeling better by the time I get home, u can come over.

Lyric: Okay.

Her one word response means she's more than likely buying my bullshit. I just hope she isn't too angry when I do go home and have to explain everything to her.

After we finish running errands, Lila drives me to an old diner located near the Golden Center Bridge to meet with Detective Rannali so he can give me a rundown on how the night will go down. He already gave us strict orders to make sure we aren't followed by anyone when we go, and during the thirty-minute drive, Lila is a nervous wreck, constantly checking the rearview mirror, changing lanes, and taking the longest route possible.

By the time we pull up, it's late enough that the sun has set, and the city around us glows against the night. Only an hour left, and then I'll be standing on the dock, facing the people who haunt my nightmares.

Or will I?

Now that I think about it, I can't remember any of their faces nor have I seen any of the people who have been tormenting my life for the last few months. What will happen when I finally see them? Will I know them? Will I remember that I know them? According to some of the stuff the detective has told me, the Soulless Mileas are a decent sized group of people.

"How are you feeling?" Lila asks after she parks the car in front of the diner.

"Fine," I lie, unbuckling my seatbelt. When she presses me with a stern look, I sigh. "Fine. I'm terrified out of my goddamn mind."

"You can always not do it," she says with hope in her eyes. "No one will be upset if you back out."

"That's not true. I'll be upset with myself." I reach for the door handle to let her know I'm going to go through with this.

Sighing, she turns the keys and shuts off the engine. "Just so you know, I'm going to be there, too. I already told Detective Rannali that I'm not going to let you do this unless I can be close."

"All right." I push the door open and climb out of the car.

She gets out, too, and meets me at the front of the car. Then we walk into the diner. The hostess seats us in a booth, tucked away in the corner of the room where the lighting is low. The place has a total of five customers, which is probably why the detective picked this place to meet.

"Anyone hungry?" he asks after the waitress places menus in front of us and leaves.

I shake my head. "Not really."

Lila reaches over and flips open the menu. "You're going to eat. I don't want you doing this on an empty stomach. You need your strength."

Giving her what she wants, I order a plate of fries and a soda. She orders nothing for herself, and the detective asks for a glass of water.

"So, I first want to assure you that the location of the dock couldn't be any better," the detective starts after our drinks have been delivered. "There are trees and bushes surrounding it, and there's also an old, vacant building nearby. My team has already scoped out the place and set everything up. Nothing appeared suspicious, so I have no reason to believe this won't go smoothly."

"The note said to come alone, though," Lila reminds him. "Aren't you worried that's going to cause problems?"

"The only problem I foresee is that no one shows up."

He reaches for his water and takes a sip. "There was no threat to the note, though, which I found a little odd. I'm guessing they assume Ayden will just listen to them."

"But I don't even get why they want him to meet them," Lila says, folding her arms on the table. "What exactly is the point of making him come out here to meet them?"

The detective exchanges a look with me from across the table. I can tell he's thinking the same thing.

"I know this isn't what you want to hear"—he leans back in the booth—"but we believe it's their way of coaxing Ayden out to a desolate place so they can try to take him without making a scene." When Lila's eyes widen, he adds, "Don't worry. We're not going to allow that to happen. I have ten of my best men all surrounding the dock."

"You better not mess this up," Lila says, being all hardcore. "If anything happens at all, I'll track you down and cut off your balls."

The detective appears highly amused by the threat. "Duly noted." He turns to me. "I need to go over a few things with you. First and most importantly, under no circumstances are you to get into a vehicle with anyone."

"You think they're going to ask me to do that?" I ask, stirring my soda with my straw.

"It's a possibility, yes."

"Can't you just arrest them when they show up?" Lila absentmindedly steals a fry off my plate and pops it into her mouth.

He puts his hands out in front of him being very down-to-business. "We will arrest them, but we have to be careful and move slowly so we don't spook them. We want to make sure that this ends with us getting Sadie back. You have to understand, these people aren't your typical criminals. They have heavy beliefs that bind them to each other.

Cracking down on them and trying to get them to out the rest of the group isn't something that's going to easily happen. In fact, from all the information I've collected on them throughout the case, more than likely, they'd easily go to jail to keep their secrets."

Lila swallows hard. "All right, I'll trust your judgment, then."

"Thank you," he says. "Now, Ayden, I want you to listen carefully."

He gives me rule after rule: no acting spooked, keep calm, no trying to take matters into my own hands. He acts as though I'm going to flip out when the person shows up and try to kill them. While I briefly ponder the idea, I would never do something like that.

By the time he's given me the rundown, there's ten minutes left before go time. I've eaten probably a total of five fries and feel sick to my stomach.

"Are you ready for this?" he asks me after he pays the bill.

I shrug and then nod. "As ready as I'll ever be."

The detective and Lila leave the diner first, getting in his unmarked car and driving down to the location. I climb in Lila's car and remain in the parking lot for five more minutes before backing out. Then it takes me three minutes to get to Golden Center Docks and another two to get out of the car.

I reach the dock that stretches out over the water with no time to spare, which is exactly what I was hoping for. The last thing I want is to be standing out here in the open, terrified to fucking death.

The water laps under the wooden dock I'm standing on, and the trees enclosing the area sway with the wind. The sky is dark, the moon full, and the stars bright. In the distance, I spot the building the detective mentioned.

Every now and then, I hear a noise and wonder if it's the person meeting me here or if it's the police. I can't really tell. In fact, I can't really tell much of anything other than I'm edgy as shit.

Finally, at around a quarter after ten, I spot movement from the path that leads down to the dock. I turn and watch as the figure descends the shallow hill and heads straight for me. My muscles seize up, and I want to run, but force myself to stay put.

When the person reaches the edge of the dock, I realize I'm cornered. The only place for me to go is in the water. Whoever it is has all the control, which instantly makes me think it's someone from the Soulless Mileas.

They slowly make their way toward me, each step premeditated. As they get closer, the moonlight casts across them, and my jaw drops. They're wearing a red raincoat with the hood pulled over their head and black rain boots.

She stops halfway down the dock, leaving at least ten to fifteen feet between us.

"Hello, Ayden."

"You're the person who was at that house," I say with my eyes trained on her. "The one who warned me the place wasn't safe."

"It wasn't safe," she answers calmly in the same gruff voice she used that day. "It wasn't time for you to go yet."

A chill slithers up my spine.

"What do you want?" I ask, daring to take a step toward her. "Why did you ask me to come here?"

"I didn't ask you to come," she replies, taking a step back. "You were chosen to come."

"You were chosen, Ayden," she whispers in my ear. "You were chosen for this since the day you were born."

I blink from the memory and step toward her, my legs shaking. "It was you . . ."

"Close your eyes," she says. *"This is going to hurt."*

I stop in the middle of the dock. "You were there."

She shakes her head. "No, I wasn't. I'm here now, though."

She speaks like everyone else in my memories, her words wrapped in riddles.

"Tell me why I'm here," I demand, my voice echoing around us.

She glances at the water behind me, and then her gaze slides to the trees. "Ayden, you've been a bad boy." Her eyes land back on me. "You were supposed to come alone."

Shit.

She turns and races off down the path toward the direction she came. I run after her without thinking, refusing to let her get away. Tree branches whip at my face as I keep my eyes on her, tracking her as she swings left then right before veering into the trees.

I dive in after her, the leaves and branches thick around my face. I know somewhere in the midst of the trees there are officers, but I can't hear or see anything other than the woman laughing from somewhere.

"You want to know why we picked you?" she asks, her voice sounding as if it's coming at me in every direction. "You want to know why?"

"No." I whirl left then right, scanning the area for her. "I want to know what you've done with my sister."

"Your sister?" she asks with a cackle. "I don't think I know who you're talking about."

"You're lying," I growl, stumbling deeper into the trees. "Tell me where she is."

"Hmmm . . . Let me think. Locked in a house, swallowed by the darkness, where no one has ever killed, yet blood stains the floors and the walls."

"Fuck you!" I shout, lunging in the direction of where

it sounds like her voice is coming from. Instead, I end up bumping into a tree.

I hear the sound of officers yelling my name from somewhere close by and shout out, "I'm over here!"

"And here's another little secret I'll let you in on." Her voice floats from the trees ahead of me. "Your blood is tied to us, Ayden. And not because your mother gave us to you. Your blood has tied you to us from the moment you were conceived." Footsteps dance around me. "Ever wonder who your real father is?"

"No." I cover my ears with my hands as I sink to my knees.

"Ever wonder why we chose you?" she whispers in my ear. *"Ever wonder why your mother gave you up so easily?"*

"No. No. No." Rage crashes through me as I jump to my feet. "I'm not going to let you get away with this."

"We already have," she whispers from right behind me. Then something hits me hard on the back of the head.

Love, love, love.

I never got a chance to say I love her.

My eyes slip shut as I begin to fall.

Then everything goes black.

CHAPTER 17

SOMETHING'S WRONG. I COULD TELL from the moment Ayden sent me the text this morning. The worry only magnifies when I step foot into my house. For starters, both my parents are home, and Ethan is here along with the three youngest of the Gregorys. When I ask them what's up, they give me a vague, "We're just hanging out" answer.

Ayden also didn't show up for school. He said he was sick, but I'm not buying it. Something's definitely up.

"So, when are you guys going to fess up?" I announce while everyone's sitting around the table, eating pizza.

"Fess up to what?" my dad replies, acting all breezy.

"Whatever's going on with Ayden." I pick a pepperoni off a slice and drop it back into the box.

"Nothing's going on," Ethan says, staring distractedly at his pizza slice.

"You're lying. I can tell." My eyes travel across him, my dad, then land on my mom.

She shakes her head. "Lyric, nothing's wrong. Ayden's just sick and went to the doctor." She checks the time on the microwave. "Lila did say she had to run a few errands, and they were going to be a little late."

"Whatever. Don't tell me, then." I finish off my pizza then chill in the living room for a while with my sketchbook.

I work on a drawing of a tattoo I'm thinking about getting until around nine thirty or so when Fiona and Everson walk in. They have backpacks in their hands and frowns on their faces.

"Something's definitely up," Everson says as he drops his pack on the floor and sinks back in the chair. "It's too late for them to be gone."

I thrum my fingers on the top of my thighs. "Did Ayden seem sick this morning?"

Fiona shakes her head as she unzips her backpack. "No, he seemed fine." She pulls out a thick textbook. "My parents seemed freaked out, though. My dad was acting like a weirdo the entire drive to school, and he gave us this huge lecture about being careful and keeping an eye out for anything weird today."

"It probably has something to do with the fact that the police were at our house this morning." Kale appears in the doorway with a slice of pizza in his hand.

I turn the volume of the stereo down. "How do you know the police were at your house?"

He shrugs, sinking down into a chair. "I was hanging out at one of my friend's houses across the street, and his mom asked me about it."

I bite down on my lip and pull out my phone to send Ayden a text.

Me: When r u going to b home?

When he doesn't answer, an uneasy feeling gnaws in the pit of my stomach. I know he's told me time and time again not to worry about him, but I can't help it. I love him, and not knowing where he is drives me crazy.

I get lost in my thoughts as I flip through songs while everyone works on their homework. I've always had a rather overactive imagination, and it conjures up a thousand different horrible scenarios of what could be going on.

When my mother walks into the room and motions me to come over, I suddenly realize that maybe my imagination was right. Perhaps something terrible has happened.

She points at Fiona, Kale, and Everson, then puts her fingers to her lips, indicating for me to be quiet before leaving the room. I causally get up and wind around the sofa.

"Where are you going?" Fiona asks, glancing up from the textbook.

"To get a snack," I reply, hoping I sound calm.

"Grab me something, too, would ya?"

I nod. "Sure."

She smiles and returns to her homework while I hurry and sneak out of the room. When I get into the kitchen, my mother is sitting at the table with her phone clutched in her hand, and my dad and Uncle Ethan are hurrying for the back door.

"What's wrong?" I ask.

My dad motions for me to come with them. "We need to go to the hospital."

I feel as though someone has punched me in the stomach and knocked the wind out of me. "What happened?"

Worry is written all over his face as he grabs the car keys off the counter. "There's been an accident. I'll explain on the way. We need to go."

Bile burns at the back of my throat as I slip on my shoes and follow them out the door. We climb into my dad's 1969 Chevelle, and he breaks almost every traffic law as he flies down the street and onto the freeway.

"Would someone please tell me what's going on?" I

finally say after ten very long minutes go by.

My dad glances at Ethan who looks as though he's about to be sick.

"Go ahead and tell her." He grabs his phone out of his pocket and sends a text. "She's going to find out eventually."

Sighing, my dad focuses on the road and begins telling me a horrible story about a letter and a meeting and basically a plan that consisted of Ayden risking his life.

By the time he's finished, I almost ask him to pull over so I can throw up.

"But he's all right?" I ask Ethan, sliding forward in the seat to look at him.

"I'm not sure. Lila . . . her text said . . ." He shakes his head. "I never should have let him do it."

"Knowing Ayden, he would have done it without you," I tell him. "I think he believes it's his job to save his sister."

"I know." Ethan's phone vibrates in his hand, and he glances down at the screen. When he sighs in relief, I know it has to be good news. "I just got an update from Lila. Ayden's okay. He hurt his head and had to get stitches, but other than that, he's going to be fine."

I breathe freely for the first time as I lean back in the seat. I hadn't realized how worried I was until now. Worried more than I ever have been.

Love, it's like a drug
I can't live without.
I thought I was stronger.
But love, it owns me now.
Without him, I feel so lost.
Without him, I don't feel whole.
Love, love, love,
What have you done to me?

CHAPTER 18

DESPITE LILA'S MANY PROTESTS, AFTER I get the stitches put in my head, I talked to Detective Rannali who has been waiting in the emergency room with us. She watches him like a hawk from the corner of the room, ready to yell at him the moment he says something that pisses her off even more.

"Are you sure you didn't get a positive ID on the woman?" He pulls the curtain shut to give us some privacy.

I shake my head. "All I know is that she was wearing a red raincoat and black rain boots. She had a voice like a heavy smoker." I reach up to scratch my head then remember I can't because of the stitches. "I know she was the woman who was at the house, though. The one who warned me about being there."

"Can you recount what was said by her?" he asks, grabbing his pen and notebook from his pocket.

I replay everything I can remember her saying, and he writes it all down.

"I don't get how you guys didn't catch her, though," I say after I'm finished. "She was right there with me in the trees."

"We still have a team out searching the area," he says.

"But I have a theory that she might have had a boat nearby. We have some people out on the water, searching, and we did find a red raincoat tossed in the bushes near the shoreline."

"You said he was going to be safe," Lila interrupts, crossing her arms and staring him down. "And that nothing bad was going to happen, yet the woman got away, and my son's in the hospital."

"And I'm greatly sorry about that." He clicks his pen and tucks it away. "But I also told you that I couldn't predict everything that was going to happen, only what I hoped would happen."

She shakes her head, enraged. "You lied."

"Why do you think she said that thing about my real father?" I slide off the bed and plant my feet on the ground, steadying myself as the world starts to spin underneath me.

"Take it easy, Ayden." Lila holds onto my arm. "The doctor said you need to move slowly for a little while."

"I'm not sure," the detective answers, stuffing his notepad back into his pocket. "Do you know who your real father is?"

"I thought I did." I lean against the bed for support. "But my mom was the kind of woman who might have lied about stuff like that."

He mulls over something, and I know what he's thinking, because it's probably the same thing I am. That my real father might have something to do with this. He might be part of the Soulless Mileas.

"I'm going to do a little searching into you," he says, drawing the curtain back. "I'll keep you updated, but in the meantime, I'm going to send a detective to keep an eye on Ayden."

His words don't soften Lila at all. In fact, her face reddens with anger.

"If this escalates into something worse . . ." She jabs a finger at him.

"I know. I know. You'll cut off my balls." He swings around her and heads for the doors that lead to the waiting room.

After he's gone, Lila turns to me. "'How are you feeling?" She squints at my face to examine my eyes. "The doctor says we need to keep an eye out for a concussion."

"I know. I was right here, remember?" I ask, starting for the door.

"I know. That was a test to see how your memory is." She walks ahead of me and pushes the door open so I can go through.

"My memory's fine." But that's not the truth.

I may be able to remember tonight, but I still can't remember that time in the house. Part of me wonders now if the reason why I blocked it all out isn't just because of the trauma and horrible things that happened to me in that house. Maybe my mind is trying to protect me from the pain of who was behind it all.

Could it be my real father who chose to break me, his own flesh and blood?

As soon as I step foot into the waiting room, my worries momentarily vanish, and all my thoughts center on one thing or person, anyway.

"Ayden." Lyric's eyes light up when she sees me. She sprints across the room, pushing people out of her way to get to me. When she reaches me, she throws her arms around me and almost knocks me to the ground. "I was so worried . . . I don't even . . ." She stops talking and holds me tightly.

"Careful, Lyric," Lila says from beside us. "He might have a concussion."

Lyric starts to pull back, but I place my hand on the

small of her back and press her closer. "She's fine," I tell Lila.

I won't let her go.
Not until she knows.

Ethan gives me a pat on the back while Lyric remains latched on to me.

"I'm glad you're okay." Her eyes are red like she's been crying.

I've been crying, too, but not because I've been worried for my safety. I cried during the ride to the hospital because the woman got away. My hope to find Sadie got away.

Lyric and I remain joined at the hip as we pile into her dad's car. Lila rides with us, too, because she refuses to let me out of her sight.

"I'll come back for the car in the morning," she says as she climbs into the backseat with Lyric and me.

Ethan nods in agreement as Mr. Scott drives forward and out onto the road. Everyone stays pretty quiet during the drive, and the sound of the tires and the lull of the radio fills up the silence.

Lyric keeps her arms around me and her head resting above my heart. I count to ten under my breath, over and over again. Not because she's touching me. Not because I'm having a panic attack. But because the need to tell her how I feel is about to combust inside me.

I thought I was going to die tonight,
Be buried in the trees
Beneath the stars and the moon
For only the sky to see.
My body would sink into the dirt
And be stilled in the silence forever.
And in the midst of my mind,
I knew I'd never be able to tell her.

It's well past midnight by the time we make it home. Everson, Kale, and Fiona are asleep on the Scott's couch and floor, and Lyric's mom looks worried out of her mind.

"Let them sleep," Mrs. Scott says to Lila. "I'll call you when they wake up tomorrow."

Lila nods gratefully. She has bags under her eyes, her blonde hair has slipped from her braid, and she looks drained dry. Even Ethan doesn't look in that great of shape.

I want to make this easy on them so they can get some rest, but there's something I have to do first.

"Can I talk to Lyric for a moment?" I ask as Lila leans down to kiss Fiona on the head.

"Of course." She moves to Kale, pulling the blanket over him. "Just make it quick, please."

I nod then steer Lyric toward the stairway.

"Where are we going?" she asks as I take her hand and lead her up the stairs.

"I have to tell you something." I move slowly; otherwise, my head throbs. My heart, on the other hand, races violently inside my chest as I mentally go over what I'm going to say to her. Preparing doesn't do any good, though, because the moment we make it into her room, and she looks at me with her stunning green eyes, my mind blanks out on me.

"I-I love you?" I stutter, sounding more like I'm asking a question than declaring my feelings for her. As soon as the words leave my lips, I want to smack myself in the head. "God, that sounded awful."

"No, it didn't. It was perfect." Her hands glide up my chest, and she links her arms around my neck. "I love you, too."

I seal my lips to hers, kissing her deliberately, savoring the taste, feel, scent, the warmth of her as I back her to the bed and lay her down. I know we don't have a lot of time, but I need a moment to feel her beneath me, know she's here.

Know that I'm still here.

I thought I was never going to have this again. Now that I know what it feels like to think I've lost it—her—I don't know what I was so afraid of. Being with her is better than music, poetry, words spilled on pages.

This is . . .

Perfect.

"I need you to do me a favor," I say, pushing back to look down at her.

She nods, her lips swollen from the kiss, her chest heaving as she struggles to catch her breath. "Whatever you need, I'm here for you."

She says exactly what I knew she would say. I just hope she'll keep her word.

"I'm going to call Dr. Gardingdale and make an appointment to do the experimental therapy, and I need you to be there for me, because I know Lila's not going to. Not after tonight."

"Ay"—she hesitates—"are you sure that's a good idea after what just happened?"

"That's the thing." I push up, sit down on her bed, and pull my knee up to rest my arm on my leg. "Tonight could have been avoided if I had just done the damn therapy to begin with."

Lyric sits up beside me, combing her hair into place. "You know I'll be there for you if you need me." She lays her hand over mine and threads our fingers together. "I just need you to be sure you want to do this."

I turn and look her directly in the eyes so she'll know how truthful I'm being. "I want to do this."

She grasps onto my hand and shuts her eyes. "Then I'll be there for you."

"Thank you." I lean in and kiss her before moving off the bed and retrieving my phone from my pocket.

"You're calling him now?" she asks, standing to her feet.

I nod as I dial his office number. "I'll leave a message on his phone, but I need to do it now; otherwise, it'll drive me crazy."

I put the phone up to my ear, taking deep breaths and preparing myself for what I'm about to do. The cards have shifted now that I know my real father might be involved, and I'm even more terrified of what's locked away in the box in my mind.

I have to do it now more than ever.

I know what the risks are. Shock. More memory loss. Heart complications. There's a short list of other side effects, as well.

But it's time to take that risk. It's time for me to face my demons head on and find out what really happened to my siblings and me in that house. And who did it to us.

INSPIRING YOU

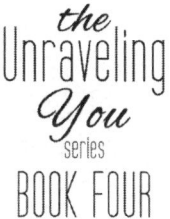
BOOK FOUR

New York Times and USA Today Bestselling Author
JESSICA SORENSEN

INSPIRING YOU
All rights reserved.
Copyright © 2015 by Jessica Sorensen

This is a work of fiction. Any resemblance of characters to actual persons, living or dead, is purely coincidental. The Author holds exclusive rights to this work. Unauthorized duplication is prohibited.

For information:
jessicasorensen.com

Cover Design:
Sarah Hansen, Okay Creations
www.okaycreations.com

Photography:
Perrywinkle Photography

Interior Design and Formatting:
Christine Borgford, Perfectly Publishable
www.perfectlypublishable.com

Something inside me
Guides me down a desolate road.
Leading to somewhere.
Leading into the unknown.
Nothing but darkness.
All, all alone.
Terrified to be found.
Fucking fearing the end.
Still, I make my way down that road.
Clutching onto the hope
Of reaching you one day.
It's all I have to hold onto
Until I get to you again.

"HEY, CAN WE TALK FOR a minute?" Lila, my adoptive mother, asks as she sticks her head into my room.

"Yeah, sure." I close the notebook that I scribble my thoughts and lyrics into. "Is something wrong?" I ask as I scoot to the edge of my bed and lower my feet to the floor.

She shakes her head as she walks into my room. "No, honey. Nothing's wrong. I just want to talk." She sits down beside me. "You've seemed kind of quiet at dinner lately, and with everything going on . . ." She sighs. "I just want to make sure you're doing okay with everything."

"I'm fine," I say, hoping I don't sound as guilty as I feel.

The truth is, a ton of shit is wrong, more than she realizes. Not only have the police found no new information on where my sister, Sadie, is, but I also have an officer following me around twenty-four seven. While I'm grateful they're protecting me, I'm not sure what the hell I'm going to do when Monday rolls around, and I have to go to my therapy appointment. Hopefully, I can think of a good excuse as to why I'm going to a doctor's office; otherwise, I won't be able to go through with my plan.

"I know but . . ." Lila mulls something over while staring out the window where the stars and moon have taken over the sky. "You just seem a little different lately." She looks at me, worry lines creasing her eyes. "Ethan and I are worried you might be holding stuff in, especially after you found out about your dad . . . And that letter you got the other day . . ." She shudders. "I know it has to be hard for you."

The letter that arrived in the mail the other day was addressed to me. Fiona was the one who collected it from the mailbox. Thankfully, Lila got a hold of it before anyone else did, noted the lack of a return address, and handed it over to the police. While I don't know what the contents of the letter are, I've noticed I'm being watched more closely, so I'm guessing it was another threat.

"Sweetie, I just want you to know we're not going to let anything happen to you." Lila pats my leg. "Your father . . . these people . . . they're not going to get ahold of you."

I do my best not to think about the father I never knew, and if he really is part of the evil group who once kidnapped my siblings and me and who still has my sister. Because, if I think about him too much, then I start thinking about *everything*. And the more I analyze everything, the more I get dragged back into the darkness I let own me for too long. And I don't want to be stuck in the darkness anymore. I realized that when a member of the Soulless Mileas lured me into the woods. I thought I was going to die out there in the dark, by myself, haunted by my fears I never overcame. When I didn't die, I promised myself *no more being afraid.*

No more fear.
Only fight.
Forever and ever.
No matter what
I'll fight until the end.

Lila sighs at my silence, her shoulders slumping forward with disappointment. "Are you sure there isn't anything you want to tell me?"

My stomach twists with guilt. *It's like she knows what I'm going to do.*

I shake my head. No, if she knew what I was up to, she'd put a stop to it. "I'm okay. I promise. I'm just a little caught up with graduating and stuff. There's a lot going on."

She smiles. "I still can't believe you'll be a high school graduate in just a few days. It seems like only yesterday we were bringing you home."

"Two years has gone by kind of fast, hasn't it?" I realize the truth of my words.

With all of this crazy shit going on with the Soulless Mileas, I haven't had time to step back and think about how quickly time flies. In just a few days, I'll be out of high school, and I have no clue what I want to do. Most of my time has been spent trying to find my brother and sister. My search for my brother ended painfully with the police finding his body near my old childhood home. They believe the Soulless Mileas played a role in his death, but since they can't track down any of the members, no one has paid for taking his life.

"It has gone by pretty fast. Too fast, at least for me." Her eyes tear up, and she unexpectedly throws her arms around me. "I'm so proud of you. You're such a strong, good person, Ayden. I'm so lucky I get to have you as my son."

I pat her back, not feeling as uncomfortable as I used to when she hugged me, but hugging is still out of my comfort zone. "Thank you . . . For saying that. It means a lot to me."

"I'm just saying the truth. You're an amazing person, Ayden Gregory."

I wonder how my graduation conversation would've went if my birth mother hadn't handed us over to those horrible people, if she were still alive, and my brother and sister and I were living with her. Would I even be graduating? Would I have ever truly felt what it was like to be loved and taken care of? I want to say yes. I want to believe my life with her wasn't all bad. And maybe it wasn't. There were some good moments that the four of us shared, but most of the good was lost in a sea of yelling, abuse, and neglect.

By the time Lila and I pull away from the hug, my eyes are burning with tears. I don't want to cry. I've been doing too much of that lately in the privacy of my room, whenever I think too much or when I have a nightmare about the past.

Lila dabs her eyes with her fingertips, wiping away smeared makeup. "Well, I just want you to know I'm here if you ever need to talk."

"I know," I say. "And I appreciate that, but I promise I'm just a little distracted by school and stuff."

"All right." She rises to her feet and reluctantly leaves the room.

The moment she shuts the door, I grab my pen and notebook and get out the clusterfuck of thoughts crammed inside my head. I hate lying to Lila—hate lying to anyone—but if I'm ever going to end this—fight until the end—then I need to go through with the experimental amnesia treatment. Hopefully doing so will bring back enough of my memories that, at the very least, I'll be able to positively identify some of the people who took me and my siblings over four years ago.

I just hope remembering doesn't break me again.

I won't let it pull me down.
I won't give in
To darkness.
Drown me all over again.
I'll fight and I'll fight and I'll fight
Against the rapids.
Against the terror.
I'll never surrender.

After I finish jotting down my thoughts, I put the notebook in my nightstand. Writing usually calms me, but I still feel restless as hell. I need answers. It's driving me fucking crazy not knowing what's going to happen next—what the Soulless Mileas next move will be.

I sit down at my desk and turn on the computer screen. With a few clicks of the mouse, I open a webpage filled with information about the group. I scroll through the updated pages and read a more current post. Lately, there's been a lot of rambling about sacrifices. It makes me really damn anxious and worried that Sadie is their sacrifice—worried I could be too if they get their hands on me.

"The sacrifice isn't just about giving up what we want," I read a section of the article aloud. "It's about giving up what we love. It's the ultimate sacrifice and the aftermath will cleanse our souls."

A chill slithers up my spine. Was it my father who wrote this? Is that what we are to him? His sacrifice to cleanse his soul?

I shake my head, anger blasting through me. Fuck him. He doesn't love us, no matter what his twisted mind thinks.

No matter how much I want to be strong, though, the pain of what my father has done nearly kills me every time I think about it. The air is strangled from my lungs, making it difficult to breathe. I need to remain calm, stop stressing, and give myself a few hours to forget about all the shit going on in my life.

Only one other thing can calm me down when I'm this worked up. Or one person, anyway. Lyric Scott, my best friend, my girlfriend, my everything really. I don't even care if I sound cheesy. Lyric is the best thing that's ever happened to me, besides being adopted by the Gregorys.

After I slip on my boots, I go downstairs to the kitchen.

Lila is standing in front of the stove baking something that smells heavily of cinnamon, and Ethan is sitting at the table sorting through some papers for work.

"Can I go over to Lyric's for a while?" I ask as I grab a can of soda from the fridge.

Lila looks up from the pan, hesitation written all over her face as she exchanges a look with Ethan. "It's kind of late, don't you think?"

Ethan glances at the clock. "It's only nine."

Lila glares at him. Clearly, that's not what she wanted him to say.

I pop the tab on the can. "It's just next door, and there's

an officer parked right outside . . . But if you don't want me to go, then I won't." The last thing I want is to stress her out.

Ethan shakes his head. "I don't think it's that big of a deal," he says to Lila. "And you can't keep him locked up forever. He's eighteen years old."

"Yeah, I know." She sighs, turning down the temperature of the burner. "I guess it's okay. Just make sure you make it home by midnight." She picks up a spoon and stirs whatever's in the pot. "Oh, and please keep Lyric's bedroom door open at all times."

"I will," I tell her, feeling slightly uncomfortable.

Ever since the Gregorys and the Scotts found out about mine and Lyric's relationship, they've been very adamant about an open-door policy. I'm okay with it, though, just as long as I get to see Lyric.

On my way out of the house, I pass by the living room. Fiona, Kale, and Everson are sitting on the couch, watching some sort of zombie movie on the flat screen.

"Where do you think you're going?" Fiona calls out when she spots me hurrying for the front door. At thirteen years old, she has a lot of spunk. In a way, she reminds me of Sadie, back before we were taken. Always playing around, always so excited about everything, and a bit over-dramatic at times. "Oh wait. I bet I know. You're going to see Lyric." She flutters her eyelashes, drapes her hand over her head, and flops back on the cushions. "Oh Lyric, I love you so much. I can't stand being away from you for more than ten seconds."

I shake my head, my lips quirking. "Lyric and I haven't seen each other all day."

"That might be a record," she says, sitting up on the couch. "Seriously, you guys have issues. When I start dating, I'm going to have a rule that we can only spend like two hours a week together."

Kale, who's almost sixteen, chokes on a laugh. "Yeah, I bet that'll never happen. With how dramatic you are, you'll end up being one of those girls who wants to spend every two seconds with her boyfriend."

"Hey, don't be rude just because you and Zoe broke up." She slumps back. "It's not my fault you got too clingy."

"I wasn't too clingy," Kale grumbles, pushing to his feet. "I just liked spending time with her." He squeezes by me and stomps up the stairs, slamming his bedroom door.

"Teenagers are so hormonal," Fiona says with an eye roll.

"You should cut him some slack," I say. "He's still really upset about the break up."

"He needs to get over it," Fiona replies. "He didn't even like Zoe that much."

"He might have." I lean against the doorway. "It seemed like he did to me."

"Yeah, well, he didn't," she says. "Trust me."

"Did you actually hear him say that?" I ask.

"Nope. I just know this stuff." She focuses on the television.

Fiona says these kinds of things frequently—that she just knows things she couldn't possibly just know. I once heard her tell her friend she believes she's a psychic, and while I'm not sure I believe in that kind of stuff, I can't help but wonder sometimes.

"Hey, you still coming to my game tomorrow?" Everson asks as I turn for the foyer.

He's fourteen years old and has been obsessed with football for as long as I can remember. His games are important to him and even though sports really aren't my thing, I want to go to his game, get out of the house, get some fresh air.

"I think I should be able to make it." I pat my pockets as I back toward the foyer again, making sure I have my phone on me, because I know Lila will text me a few times to make sure I'm okay.

"Cool." He stuffs a handful of popcorn into his mouth. "It might be the last one you ever get to see for a long time."

I pause. "How do you figure?"

He nonchalantly shrugs. "Because you're graduating and going on that band tour."

"I'm not going on the tour." Just thinking about my band, Alyric Bliss, going on the Rocking Summer Blast Tour makes my mood plummet. But I can't go with them. Not when the Soulless Mileas want me. Not when Sadie is out there waiting for me to save her.

"Yeah, right. You'll change your mind," Everson says. "I know you're going through some stuff and those crazy people are after you, but you like music almost as much as you like Lyric. And since she's going on this tour, you'll end up going."

I want to argue with him. Tell him he doesn't get it. That there's more to it than just some crazy people being after me. But a small part of me still hangs onto the hope that maybe over the next month my life will change, and somehow, I'll get to go on the tour. Lyric even insisted I go with the band to record next week. She said whether they replace me or not, I've earned the right to be on the album. My initial instinct was to argue, but I really want to be a part of this with them, so I agreed.

"I'll see you in a bit, okay?" I tell Everson then walk out the front door.

I make my way down the path to the driveway, the night summer air instantly making me sweat. As I'm rounding the fence to head next door, I spot a police car parked not too far down the road. The car is always there, watching my house, and when I go to school, therapy, or band practice, it tails me. I never get any time alone anymore, and I long for the days when I can walk down the sidewalk without being watched and without worrying that someone is going to grab me.

Live for the days when I can just *live*.

When I reach the side door of the Scotts' two-story home, I hear music blaring from upstairs, probably from Lyric's room. I rap on the door several times before I give up and just walk in. I don't cross paths with Mr. or Mrs. Scott as I make my way upstairs and to Lyric's room, something I'm thankful for, considering Mr. Scott seems uncomfortable every time I'm near his daughter. Lyric says it's because he's worried we're having sex. I want to tell everyone that they have nothing to worry about, that because of my fucked up past, I'm not sure when I'll be ready to have sex. I used to think I'd never get to a point in my life where I could even think about having sex. But when I met Lyric, some of that fear was overpowered by want.

Want, want, want
All the time.
I want her so badly
I'm losing my mind.
With all the desire
And heat
Pulsating through me.

I feel like I'm stuck
Out on a wire.
Wanting to stay on
Yet wanting to fall.
Fall, fall, fall

Right into her.
God, please let me fall.

I can't help but smile as I reach Lyric's bedroom. Her door is open, "Holocene" by Bon Iver is playing from the stereo, and she's sitting on her bed strumming her guitar and singing along with the song. Her long blonde hair flows over her bare shoulders, and she's wearing a pair of red shorts, a black tank top, and the leather bracelets we gave each other last Christmas. She's so beautiful that I have to catch my breath.

Instead of walking in, I linger in the doorway and watch her play, getting lost in her singing. Lyric has an incredibly beautiful voice that gives our band an edge. I could probably listen to her sing all day long, if she'd let me. While she's okay with her stage fright, she gets nervous when people watch her sing, including me. She conquers the fright, though, every time she steps up on stage, which makes her that much more amazing.

As the song ends, she scrunches up her nose, clearly frustrated. She must be trying to work out something with the tune because the song turns right back on. She lines her finger to the guitar strings and her lips part, but she freezes when she notices me.

A smile spreads across her face, and her green eyes light up. "Hey, I was just thinking about you."

I don't know how she can look so happy to see me. She tells me all the time it's because I make her happy. That has to be a lie. Lyric is just an upbeat person. She smiles about ninety percent of the time, laughs the other nine percent of the time, and that one percent is for the rare occurrences when she's sad.

"Weird. I was just thinking about you too before I came over," I say with a small smile.

"That's because we can clearly read each other's minds." She sets down the guitar and stands to her feet, stretching out her arms and legs.

"If that's the case, then what am I thinking right now?" I ask as my eyes wander up and down her body.

"Hmmm . . ." She taps her finger against her lips with a sparkle in her eyes. "That you so want to kiss me right now."

My lips quirk in amusement. "How'd you guess?"

"Because it's always what you're thinking about," she teases as she crosses the room toward me. "Morning, noon, and night, you can't get my kisses out of your head. Because they're that awesome."

"And apparently mind controlling," I joke, already feeling better.

"Well duh. Awesome kisses have to have the awesome power of mind control; otherwise, what'd make them awesome?" She grins, placing her hands on my shoulders.

"Maybe your kisses are just awesome because you're you," I suggest, tucking a strand of her hair behind her ear.

Her attitude shifts from playfully joking to intensely wanting. I know what she wants, so I dip my lips and give it to her. I kiss her softly at first, but the longer our tongues tangle the more I begin to tip sideways on that wire. I just want to let go. Tumble off and never get back on.

I back her up, kissing her passionately until our legs bump the side of the bed. We fall onto the mattress and she giggles against my lips. The sound makes me smile, but the light mood immediately heats up again as my hands travel up and down her sides, across her breasts and her waist. I kiss her with every ounce of emotion I have in me, but my body trembles as she parts her legs and grinds her hips against me. I fight the urge to stop, refuse to let the past control me.

I won't go there anymore.
Back into the dark
Where I'm lost and all alone.
I won't let them control me anymore.

"My parents aren't home," she whispers against my mouth as I slip my hand under her shirt.

I nod, even though she wasn't really asking me a question. Not straightforwardly anyway. I know her well enough to understand what she wants without her flat out asking for it.

I push back, grab the bottom of her shirt, and fumble to pull it over her head. Once it's off, I toss it onto the floor.

She stares up at me with her intensely green eyes as her fingers wander to the hem of my T-shirt. "Can I?" Her voice is soft as she carries my gaze.

I swallow hard then nod, wishing she didn't have to ask. Wishing I was strong enough to just get over my issues so I could be the kind of laidback, carefree guy she deserves. But it'll take time before I'll ever be able to jump off that wire without the inner fight rising inside me. I'm starting to believe that one day I'll get there, though, which is more than I could say a few months ago.

She sits up and I lean back so she can pull my shirt over my head. Then she tosses it onto the floor and splays her fingers across the tattoo on my side. She traces the lines of the feathers that form a phoenix, then her hands skate downward toward the top of my jeans. I shiver out of fear, out of want, my mind racing so quickly I barely register when she asks if this is okay. I dazedly nod and she skims her fingers back and forth across my lower abdomen, just below my waistband before she tugs on my belt loop, pulling me against her as she collapses onto the bed.

I stick my hands out to brace the fall, but she yanks on my jeans again until I lower my lips to hers. I kiss her slowly, taking my time, memorizing every inch of her mouth as my hands explore her body. The longer the kiss goes on, the more complicated it becomes to breathe, but in the best fucking way possible.

I don't care if I die.
If I ever breathe again.
Just let this kiss go on forever.
Let it carry me away
To someplace better.
Where it's just Lyric and I
No past, only the future.
Let me be with her.
Let me get through this.
Let me get to a forever.

I move back to remove her bra, then I crash my mouth to hers again as our chests collide. A shudder ripples through my body from the skin-to-skin contact. Fear resides inside me, underneath a sea of want, stirring.

Don't forget.
Don't forget.
Don't forget.
What was done to you.
Don't forget that we own you.
Don't forget.
Don't forget.
Don't forget.

I won't let it consume me. Won't let the past ruin this moment.

No more. I'm stronger than this—than they *are.*

Shoving the memory out of my mind, I focus on her lips, how incredibly soft they feel against my mouth, how her warmth engulfs me, and the pleading whimpers she makes as my hand wanders to the top of her shorts. My fingers linger there for a while as I fumble with the button.

Once I get it undone, Lyric shimmies out of her shorts and kicks them onto the floor.

I take in her long legs, smooth skin, and beautiful green eyes. "I don't . . ." My fingers shake as I sketch a line up the inside of her thigh. "Are you sure you want me to touch you like—"

She pushes up and slams her lips against mine, answering my question. As we lie back down on the bed, my finger slips inside her, and I instantly become lost in everything that's Lyric. The way she lets me touch her. The way I'm the only one who gets to see her like this. The way she trusts me. How fucking gorgeous she is. How amazing her smile is. How amazing she is.

"Ayden." She moans my name as her eyes shut and she clutches onto my shoulders.

Good God, I'm about to lose it. Seriously. Somehow between the fear and uncertainty, desire has completely taken over. I don't even care that she's touching my shoulders, my chest, my stomach. All I can think about is getting to see her like this.

Once she comes apart, I brush her hair out of her eyes, place a tender kiss her lips, then roll on my side, letting my mind slow down.

"Are you okay?" she asks, rolling over and facing me.

I bob my head up and down. "I'm fine." When she still looks concerned, I take her hand and place it on my chest. My heart thrashes as my adrenaline soars. "I promise I'm okay." I swallow hard. "I love you and I trust you." To prove it to her, I move her hand down my chest, across my stomach, all over my scarred skin. It's tortuously confusing because I fear being touched yet at the same time, I want her to touch me more.

Want. Fear. Want. Fear.
So closely tied together.

How can I untie them?
And make them come apart.

"I love you too," she says.

Sometimes it feels so unreal when I'm with her, like I'm dreaming. Maybe I am. Maybe I'm really still stuck in that house and this is all just a dream, my mind's way of coping with what happened to me. If that's the case, then let me die in the dream, never wake up.

"No matter what you think, no matter how much you say you're not good enough for me, no matter what, I love you, Ayden," she says, as if she senses where my thoughts are heading.

Even though my body is quivering from her hands' exploration, my lips manage to turn upward. "That kind of sounds like the start of a song."

She leans over me, her hair veiling around my face. "What can I say? I guess you just inspire me."

"You inspire me too."

"We so sound like a cheesy love song right now." She grins as she sings, "You inspire me. I inspire you. Let's get together and run through a magical field of rainbows and butterflies."

I snort a laugh. "Don't pretend like you don't actually want to run through a magical field of rainbows and butterflies. I know how much you love them both."

"Okay, you might be right. But let's never, ever include rainbows and butterflies in our songs."

"*Our* songs?" I ask with a cock of my brow. "As in plural? Because we've only written one so far."

"You and I have a lot of songwriting in our future." As if she senses me tensing, she adds, "Ayden, I know you say you're not going on this tour, but I'm still holding onto the hope that you will." My lips part in protest, but she talks over me. "And even if you don't make it, I'll still be back in a few months, and we're going to pick up right where we left off. Nothing's going to change between us."

Reality seeps in and my body trembles even more.

Misreading my fear, she starts to withdraw her fingers, but I place my hand over hers, securing her palm against my chest.

"It's not that," I say in an uneven voice. "It just scares me . . . Thinking about being away from you for three months."

"It scares me too," she admits, giving in easily as I wrap an arm around her and pull her closer so our bodies are aligned perfectly.

Surprisingly, I stop shaking and a warm calm settles inside me. I give myself a moment to breathe in the inner peace, to let it really sink through me, because I don't get to experience calm very often.

"I know you think I'm being naively silly," Lyric whispers. "But I'm still hoping we won't have to be apart. That you'll go in on Monday and do this experimental therapy treatment, and the police will be able to find your sister."

I know that it's not going to be easy. That it may take several tries for the treatment to work. That if it does work, it might be like opening Pandora's Box, and my mind will be so fucked up that I'll be back to where I started before I came to the Gregorys'. There's also the possibility something could go wrong. That I could end up in shock, with more memory loss, or even heart failure. The risks are why Lila won't let me go, and why Lyric looks like she's going to throw up every time the treatment is mentioned.

"Hey, it's going to be okay," I tell her when I note the paleness of her skin.

"You don't know that for sure." She buries her face into my chest. "I don't want anything to happen to you."

"Nothing's going to happen to me." I smooth my hand

over the back of her head, wanting to promise her I'll be okay no matter what happens.

But I can't bring myself to lie to her.

CHAPTER 2

I'M SO WORRIED ABOUT AYDEN, my stomach hurts. My heart . . . God, my heart is having the most trouble. I'm not sure how to convince it everything will be fine, that keeping this secret for Ayden is the right thing to do. I want to tell someone so they'll stop him from going through with the treatment, but it feels selfish to do so. Not being able to help his sister has been silently killing him. If this treatment works—if he can remember enough to save his sister—then maybe he'll be able to finally, *finally* live his life in peace.

"You smell like vanilla cupcakes." My voice is muffled as I press my nose against his bare chest.

Ever since he told me he loved me, he's been getting better with being touched. But he still trembles sometimes, and when things get really hot and heavy, we have to stop before he veers toward a panic attack. Right now, he's extremely calm, though, at least for him, so I'm going to savor this moment for as long as he'll allow it to continue.

He tangles his fingers through my hair. "That's because Fiona sprayed me with some girly perfume crap this morning. She used so much of it that it soaked through my shirt."

I laugh, nuzzling closer to him. "Really? Why'd she do that? Just to torture you?"

"She said I needed to sweeten up. That I was acting too grumpy and sour."

"Why were you acting grumpy?" I cross my fingers that he'll open up and tell me.

"I don't know . . . I think I'm just stressed and have been taking it out on everyone."

I inch to the side so I can set my palm on his chest and feel the rhythm of his heart. "Stressed out about the therapy?"

His heart slams against my palm. "I'm stressed out about a lot of things."

I angle my head back and look up at him. "But right now, you're worried about the therapy."

"Are you trying to play therapist?" he teases even though his pulse is still racing.

"Maybe." I push up, straddling him, and my pulse accelerates as his gaze drinks in my chest. "I just know how you are . . . that you shut down sometimes and don't talk about your feelings. What you're doing Monday is super huge, and I just want you to know that you can talk to me, and hopefully, I can help make you feel a little less nervous." I sweep my hair to the side and flash him a grin. "Making people feel better is one of my many talents."

"And just how are you planning on making me feel better?" he asks, grazing his fingers across my breasts.

Like every other time he touches me, butterflies lose their mind inside my stomach. "Well, I wasn't planning on doing *that*, but if that's what you want then . . ." I trail off as I lower my lips to his. "I'll give it to you."

A husky moan escapes his mouth as I suck on his bottom lip. He cups the back of my head and draws me closer, sliding his tongue into my mouth. My body doesn't feel like it's under my control anymore as I rock my hips against his. He groans, but stiffens. I know he wants to do this just as much as I do—I can feel his hardness through his jeans. But wanting and having are two different things with Ayden, and I wait for him to stop us, like he usually does.

But after counting under his breath, he kisses me more fiercely as he grinds his hips against mine. He repeats the movement over and over again, moaning and gripping onto my waist. My hips move rhythmically with his as I lose myself in him. My hands drift down his chest and to the top of his jeans. I want to touch him like he touches me.

Touch him, touch him, all over.

Never let him go.

I wait for him to stop me and when he doesn't, I undo the button of his jeans. His stomach muscles tense, but he continues kissing me. With a nervous breath, I dip my hands inside his boxers.

He groans something incoherent about trusting me as his body trembles. I worry I've pushed him too far, but then he seals his lips to mine and kisses me so forcefully I swear I'm going to have a bruise. I fall blindly into the moment, part of me wishing I never had to return. That I could just stay this way, him and I in this perfect place where he lets me touch him.

If only I could hold on forever.

Hold onto him forever.

He's come too far

Just to fall all over again.

I can't lose him.

The fear is always there in the back of my mind that therapy is going to change him, remind him why he has such a difficult time letting people touch him.

What if I lose him?

"You're not going to lose me," he breathes raggedly as he blinks up at me, his eyes glossy, like he's high from our kisses.

"Did I say that aloud?" I sound breathless. "Sorry, I thought I was talking to myself in my head."

He chuckles. "You know that makes you sound kind of crazy."

"Good for me you already love me," I tease. "Crazy or not, you're stuck with me now."

"That's perfectly okay with me," he says. "Just as long as . . . as long as you're okay with being stuck with me."

I don't answer with words. I answer with a kiss.

We make out for at least another hour before we put our clothes back on and lie down on my bed side by side.

"You should just spend the night," I say as I trace the folds of his fingers.

"I wish I could, but I don't think your dad would appreciate coming home to that."

"My dad's way more chill than he was when he first learned about us."

"Yeah, maybe . . . But since I want him to stay chill, I think I should probably not be in your bed when he gets home."

I jut out my lip, knowing he's a sucker for the move. "That sounds like no fun at all."

He laughs, shaking his head as he rolls on his side. "As much as I love giving you your way, I can't this time."

"Oh fine." I sulk. "Can we at least do something fun tomorrow, though?" *Before Monday when everything could change.*

"I actually promised Everson I'd go to his football game with him." He strokes my cheekbone and my eyelashes flutter uncontrollably. "You should come with me."

"To a *football* game? Blah." I make a face. "But if

that's what you're doing, then count me in." I dazzle him with a grin. "Man, it's a good thing I love you."

A small, rare smile graces his lips then he kisses me again.

"You taste minty," he whispers against my mouth. "And kind of sugary."

"That's because I just ate mint chocolate chip ice cream before you came over."

He takes another taste, before propping up onto his elbow. "Tell me something happy. I need happy right now."

"Happy, huh?" I drum my finger against my lips. "Well, today at school, I won an award for that project I entered in that art contest."

"Really?" The pain in his eyes briefly diminishes. "That's amazing, Lyric, seriously."

"Yeah, it's pretty cool. The sucky part is the award came with a scholarship, which I have no use for at the moment. My mom wasn't very happy about it, which I guess I get. I mean, she's an artist, and it's pretty baffling to her that she has a daughter who's turning down an art scholarship. I had to explain to her that while I love to draw, I'd much rather be singing and spreading my awesomeness through music, even if sometimes the thought of singing onstage makes me want to puke."

"Don't be so hard on yourself. You've been doing amazing with your stage fright."

"Yeah, I guess so." She mulls over something, seeming reluctant. "Can I ask you something?"

"You can ask me anything."

"What do you want to do?"

His fingers trail down my neck to my chest. "What do you mean?"

I roll on my side and hitch my leg over his hip. "I mean, when we graduate. Do you think you'll go to college ever?"

"Maybe . . . I actually haven't really thought about it too much."

"Well, now that you are thinking about it, can you see yourself tied down with classes?" I ask, eager to hear his answer.

"Not really." He contemplates his answer. "I honestly just want to play my guitar. It makes me feel calm inside and happy."

I smile at that. "I don't think you've ever said that before."

"Said what?"

"That something makes you happy."

"You make me happy too," he says softly.

"It's nice to hear you say that, Shy Boy. " I wink at him. "My life is now complete, which makes me very, very happy."

A ghost smile rises on his lips. "Good, I'm glad you're happy."

"Of course I'm happy. I get to be here with you."

I expect him to argue that there's no way I could be happy with him, but surprisingly he doesn't.

Progress.

We spend the rest of the night talking and stealing kisses until midnight rolls around and he leaves to go home. I watch him through my window as he rounds the fence and heads up his driveway, only turning away when he's made it safely into the house.

Like everyone else, I constantly worry that at any moment those creepy people who are after Ayden are going to slink from the shadows and steal him away. Every night when I close my eyes, I dream of the days when I won't have to worry about losing him. That he'll be safe. That he'll be free of them.

Because I know those days will come,
I won't let myself believe anything else

SUNDAY FLIES BY QUICKER THAN
and before I know it, Monday arrives. Ayden's
ment is after school, and I'm severely distracte
classes, stressing over what's going to happen.

"Why are you acting all twitchy?" Sage, the dr
in my band, asks during math class.

"I'm not acting twitchy." I lie, unsure what to tel
since he doesn't know much about Ayden's situation.

He rakes his fingers through his blue hair, eyeball
the pen I'm tapping madly against the desk. "You aren
huh?"

I cease the tapping and slump back in my seat.
"There's just some stuff going on, and I'm having a hard
time handling it."

He shoves up the sleeves of his grey shirt, revealing
the multiple tattoos on his arms. "That doesn't sound like
you. You always seem like you can handle anything."

"I try to, but I can't always be perfect." I flash him
my pearly whites. "Everyone's got to have their flaws, and
while mine are super small, I do have them."

"I wasn't saying you have to be perfect . . . I was
just . . ." He studies me, fiddling with a piercing in his
brow. "Is this about Ayden?"

Sage used to have a crush on me so whenever he mentions Ayden, things get a little weird and uncomfortable. But right now, I'm more concerned he might know what's been going on with Ayden. I have no idea how he'd know, but Ayden is a private person and would freak out if Sage or Nolan, the bassist of our band, found out.

"No." I glance at the clock. "Everything's fine with Ayden."

"Are you sure?" he questions, staring me down. "I know you've been struggling with him leaving the band... You've been distant at tryouts. It's got to be hard, trying to replace him."

"It's not about that." I chew on the end of my pen. "Well, it does kinda suck balls that we have to replace him, especially when everyone that's tried out sucks balls too."

"I think that might be the meanest thing I've ever heard you say." He seems amused by the fact.

"Why? I don't tell *them* they suck balls." I sigh when he keeps grinning at me. "Okay, I know I'm being a total Debbie downer right now, but seriously, how are we supposed to rock this tour if our guitarist can't carry a tune? We need to find someone spectacular. Or at least someone who can hit all the notes."

"Would you relax? We'll find someone," he reassures me, sitting back in the chair.

I don't want to find someone. I want Ayden.

The idea of being on the road, touring, is freaking amazing, and I know I'll go even if Ayden can't. But being away from him for that long is going to be torturous. Plus, the people who've tried out are in no way as musically talented as Ayden.

"But you might have to stop comparing everyone to Ayden," Sage says. "We might just have to settle for someone who's not as good as him."

"I know," I say, even though it kills me. It's time for me to start sucking it up and being the ever-so-amazing optimist I know I can be. "That one dude with the green hair might have potential."

He grins. "There's the Lyric I know."

"She's just a little tired." I pretend to take a bow. "But

she decided she needed to quit hiding being her exhaustion and make a grand appearance.

We bust up laughing, but then the teacher forces us to quiet down.

A half an hour later, the final bell rings, dismissing school for another day. I hurry out of the classroom and zigzag through the packed hallway, making a beeline for Ayden's locker. I try not to freak out when he's not there. While he promised me I could go with him to the therapy appointment, I worry he'll pull a classic Ayden move and try to go without me, thinking he's protecting me somehow.

I bounce up and down on my toes, scanning the people lollygag through the halls, and then watch amusedly as Sage makes a U-turn when he spots my friend Maggie heading in his direction. The funny thing is, she does the same thing when she notices him. The two of them have acted so awkward since they almost hooked up. From what Maggie told me, they were both so wasted it ended up being a disaster, and they've barely been able to look each other in the eye ever since.

"What are you smiling about?" Ayden asks, appearing by my side out of nowhere, like a freaking ninja.

He's wearing a pair of black jeans and a grey shirt, and strands of his dark hair hang in his eyes that carry so much sadness. Although not as much as they used to.

"It's nothing," I say, shamelessly checking him out. "I was just laughing at Maggie and Sage and how they run away from each other every time they're about to cross paths."

He spins the combination and opens his locker. "I told you it'd never work out between them."

"Yeah, I know, but I kind of hoped it would." I slip my arm through the strap of my backpack and shrug when he shoots me a *really* look. "What can I say, I'm a dreamer." I sing the last part. "Who wants everyone to find love."

He laughs, but his expression conveys his nerves.

"How are you doing?" I recline against the locker beside his as I wait for him to put his books away. "I mean, are you nervous?" I shake my head. "Sorry, that's a really lame question, isn't it? Of course you're nervous."

"No question you ask is lame." He bumps the locker shut and slings his backpack over his shoulder. "I'm a little nervous, but at the same time, I'm kind of not . . . It's strange . . . I've been carrying so much pain and fear around with me ever since I came out of that house, but just the idea that maybe I'll finally put some of this behind me makes the pain and fear feel less heavy . . . If that makes any sense."

"It makes perfect sense." I lace our fingers as we make our way down the hallway toward the exit doors. "You're going to let me hold your hand while you do the treatment, right?"

"If Dr. Gardingdale will let you." He dazes off, and God knows where his thoughts are headed. Probably somewhere dark and filled with self-torture.

I need to distract him.

"My parents are going on a trip to Paris with my aunt and uncle," I say as we step outside into the sunlight. "They're going while I'm on tour, though, so I don't get to go."

"Sucks for them," he says, looking at me. "They're going to miss out on all the fun that would have come with bringing you."

I press my hand to my heart, giving him my best playful grin. "Hey, that's what I said too. But they just don't get it." I lower my hand to my side. "It's good, though, that my dad's spending time with his half-sister. And I have cousins now, so that's cool. There was just too much pressure being the only child in the entire extended family."

"Pressure?" he asks as we reach his car.

"Yeah, you know, to carry on the family name as awesomely as my rock star dad did. My grandma's said it to me a couple of times." I don't really feel *that* pressured. My parents and grandparents have always been cool about not pressuring me to be anything other than myself. I'm just trying to talk about anything other than the treatment and the tour.

"I'm sure you'll do fine." He opens the passenger door for me. "You're already going on a tour and you're only eighteen. That's a pretty amazing accomplishment." He smiles, but it's forced.

I know he wants to go on the tour. Wants to live a normal life. Well, as normal of a life as any other band member.

Hurts, hurts, hurts,
All the time.
Watching him silently hurt.
The pain, the despair
He carries inside
It's got to be making him lose his mind.
Driving him to the edge
Of a place I can't let him go.

"Yeah, I know." My mood goes kerplunk as I climb into the car.

Only a few more hours and then it's time. Only a few more hours and I might lose him.

Ayden suddenly freezes as he ducks to get in, and his gaze sweeps the grassy area across from the parking lot.

"Is everything okay?" I track his gaze to a woman wearing a red raincoat, standing in the midst of a sea of people dressed in summer attire. "Do you know her?"

He stares at her a beat longer, only looking away when

the woman turns and gets swallowed up by the crowd. "Stay here." He closes the door and jogs back to the cop vehicle parked a few spaces behind us.

He says something to the officer before walking back to the car and climbing in.

"What was that about?" I ask as he shuts the door.

"I'm not sure, but the woman who chased me into the woods . . . She was wearing a red raincoat." He starts up the engine and locks the doors. "I don't think it was her, but I still thought I'd tell the officer."

My muscles ravel into knots as I skim the people around the quad and the parking lot. "What if it is her?"

"It's going to be okay." He places a shaky hand on my knee. "But we need to wait here until the officer comes back."

I gulp. "How long do you think it'll take him to check everything out?"

He shrugs, looking out the window. "That all depends on if he can find the woman or not." His jaw tightens as he shakes his head in dismay. "Lyric, I'm so sorry for putting you through this."

"Don't start," I warn. "You're not putting me through anything. It's not your fault those people are insane and won't leave you alone."

"It's kind of my fault, though, if it's my father who's in charge of their group," he utters quietly.

I reach over and set a hand on his scruffy cheek. "None of this is your fault. Trust me. Kids aren't responsible for the bad stuff our parents do. If that were the case, then I'd be responsible for every time my mom gets a speeding ticket when she decides she's going to race some dude in a sports car. Or when my dad secretly smokes in his office."

"Smoking and speeding tickets aren't really the same as kidnapping and murder."

"Ay." My heart is breaking for him. "You're the sweetest guy I've ever met in my entire life. You'd do anything for the people you love, so trust me when I say you're in no way responsible for anything that your father does. You need to stop being so hard on yourself."

He blows out a breath. "Maybe you're right."

"Of course I'm right." And a little shocked that I convinced him. "I'm always right, even when I'm wrong."

A half smile surfaces. "There you go again. Making up your own rules."

I open my mouth to keep going, but the officer knocks on the window, scaring the bejesus out of me. Ayden jumps too and quickly rolls down the window.

"It's all clear," the officer, who's probably in his mid-twenties, says as he leans down and looks inside the car.

"You found the woman in the red rain coat, then?" Ayden asks, still tense.

"I tracked her into the school," he says, nodding. "She's actually the art teacher, Miss Merrybellton, or something like that."

"And she was wearing a raincoat?" Ayden gapes at the officer in disbelief.

"I'm actually not surprised," I tell Ayden. "Miss Merrybellton can be a little," I circle my finger around my temple, "off her rocker sometimes. She's always trying all these new styles. Today must be inappropriate weather attire day."

"Well thanks for checking on it," Ayden says to the officer, his eyes still wide with fear and worry.

"That's what I'm here for. And it's good you told me. We need to check out all suspicious activity," the officer replies then steps back. "Now you should probably head home."

Ayden rolls up the window, pushes the shifter into reverse, and backs out of the parking space.

He's silent for most of the drive, which instantly puts me into worry mode. But every time I strike up a conversation, he gives me one or two word responses that lead to nowhere, and I worry he might be regressing.

My thoughts drift to my life before Ayden. I've always been a happy, positive person who's had a good life. My mom and dad have been the rock stars of parents, always showing me unconditional love. I've always been able to chase my dreams. I've always had a roof over my head. But even with everything, I still felt something was missing. That something was Ayden.

I didn't know it back then. Didn't realize it when we first met. It took me time to get there—took us both time. And now that I have it, there's no way I'm going to lose it.

When we get home, Ayden parks the car in front of the garage then twists in his seat to face me. "We have to leave in a half an hour." He chews on his bottom lip as he glances at the door of his house. "I'm not sure what to tell Lila since I normally don't go to appointments on Monday's."

"Just tell her you're stressed and need to talk to someone," I suggest, unbuckling my seatbelt.

"But how do I explain why you're coming with me? And why we're going to a doctor's office instead of the normal therapy office building."

My jaw just about smacks the floor. "We're going to a *doctor's* office?"

He slips the keys out of the ignition and opens the door. "It's just a precautionary measure in case something unexpected happens."

"I read a little about this treatment, and from what the articles said, you'll be put under sedation. Is that true?"

"I'll be under but I'll still be able to talk, at least from what I understand. But I think I'll be really out of it." When he sees the panic in my eyes, he cups my face between his hands. "Everything's going to be okay. Nothing's going to happen to me."

I swallow the lump wedged in my throat. The last thing he needs to be doing is worrying about me. I need to chill on the freaking out. "I'm okay. It's just a little scary thinking about what they're going to do to you."

He presses his lips together. "Are you sure you're okay? Because if it's too much for you, you don't have to go—"

I put a finger to his lips, shushing him. "I'm going with you. There's no way you're talking me out of it." I lower my hand to my lap. "And just tell Lila I need to spend as much time with you as I can before I leave for the tour."

"But what about the doctor's office thing?" He points over his shoulder at the cop car that's been tailing us since we left school. "Because they're going to follow us and report where we went the moment we park the damn car in front of the office."

I peek back at the cop car. "Are you sure you just can't tell Aunt Lila what we're doing?" Aunt Lila isn't really my aunt, just like Uncle Ethan really isn't my uncle. My family was just so close with the Gregorys from the moment I was born that I started calling them that.

"If I tell her then she'll never let me go through with it," he says with heavy remorse. "And I have to do this."

I try to bring out my sunshine and positivity as I rack my brain for a solution to our problem. "Just tell her you're taking me to a doctor's appointment. That I have to get a shot and need you to hold my hand."

"And what happens when she talks to your mom and finds out that was a lie?" he asks warily.

I shrug. "We'll face the music when it happens, but

right now, let's just get through this one appointment."

"Are you sure you want to do this?" he double checks. "Because everyone's going to be pissed when they find out we lied."

"Of course I'm sure." I wink at him. "I got your back, dude. Always and forever."

That gets him to smile. I just cross my fingers that his smile will still exist after the therapy session.

AN HOUR LATER, WE'RE SITTING in a waiting room at a busy doctor's office waiting for Dr. Gardingdale to arrive so we can get this show on the road. Ayden is about a million times more nervous than when he got his tattoo, which is saying a lot. But he's not the only one that's so jittery they can't sit still. It didn't help that when we left, Fiona blindsided me as I was getting into the car.

"I know what you're doing," she said with her hands on her hips.

I caught Ayden's gaze from over the roof of the car. "Look, Fiona," I turned to her and lowered my voice, "you can't tell anyone, okay? This is really important."

"I know it is. And I know I can't say anything to anyone, not when this could set Ayden free," she said simply. "I just wanted to give *you* a head's up that Ayden's going to need you to be calm for him. That it's important you don't freak out, even when things look bad."

For the second time today my jaw nearly hit the ground.

Her words have been stuck inside my head ever since, playing like a scratched record.

"What exactly did Fiona say to you in the driveway?" Ayden asks, leaning closer to me and keeping his voice low.

"It wasn't important." I pick up a pamphlet that's on the table to the side of me to busy myself with something since I can't seem to sit still.

"But she said she wasn't going to tell Lila and Ethan, right?'" A flush creeps up on his cheeks as his gaze drops to the pamphlet in my hand. Then he starts bouncing his knee up and down as he averts his gaze to the floor.

"No, she said she knew she couldn't tell anyone, whatever that means." I look down at the pamphlet to see what's causing him to blush. I try not to laugh, because out of all things, I grabbed one about safe sex. Seeing an opportunity to alleviate some of the tension, I decide to tease him a little. "It might have some good tips in there." I nudge his shoulder with mine. "Maybe we should read it."

He massages the back of his neck, muttering something under his breath before elevating his gaze to me. "You think we should?" The blush is still there, but his voice is surprisingly steady.

His unexpected question catches me off guard and I feel my own cheeks warm, which rarely happens. Usually I have mad skills in the chillax department, but just thinking about having sex with Ayden makes my heart go all glowy crazy in my chest like a cracked-out unicorn.

"I don't know." I fiddle with the edge of the pamphlet. "Maybe. The other night things did get a little . . ." I rack my brain for the right word that will sum up what happened Saturday night, but then decide to be funny, because we need funny right now. "Bow chicka bow wow."

He snorts a laugh. "I guess that's one way to put it."

"You're okay with what happened, right? I mean, I know that was a huge step for you." I fold and unfold the pamphlet, feeling super fidgety. "I just don't ever want to push you into doing stuff."

"Lyric, I swear to God I'm fine." His expression grows intense, his gaze boring into me. "You've never, ever have pushed me into doing anything that I didn't want to do." He blows out a frustrated exhale. "You've always been so patient with me, even when you shouldn't have to be."

I slip my fingers through his. "Ayden, I love you. Being with you is amazing. It's not about *having* to do stuff. It's about *wanting* to."

He nods his head up and down, his gaze dropping to the pamphlet in my free hand. "Still, it's getting easier . . . I mean, with the intimate stuff."

I lock eyes with him. "How much easier?" My voice is steady, but my heart's an erratic mess.

He opens his mouth to answer, and dear God, I'm eager to hear what's about to leave those lips of his, but an older dude wearing a bright-ass orange tie and tan slacks enters the waiting room, and Ayden instantly jumps to his feet.

"You haven't been waiting too long, have you?" Dr. Gardingdale asks Ayden, tucking his briefcase underneath his arm.

Ayden shakes his head. "Not too long."

"Good. Good." Dr. Gardingdale seems nervous, his gaze flicking back and forth between Ayden and me. "It's nice to see you again, Lyric."

Ayden reaches back, grabs my hand, and pulls me to his feet. "I hope you don't mind that I brought her."

"It's fine," he says, waving at us to follow him as he heads toward the door near the front desk. "Ayden talks very highly of you, Lyric. And it might be good that you're here. You seem to have a calming effect on him."

My gaze slides to Ayden. "Do you talk about me with him?" I'm not offended. Just curious what he could possibly have to say about me while he's in therapy.

He lifts his shoulders and shrugs. "You're a huge part of my life. Of course I talk about you." He holds the door open for me, looking a little sheepish. "Besides, like he said, you have this crazy calming effect on me, so whenever I get too stressed, I just start talking about you."

That makes me smile. I stand on my tiptoes, give him a quick kiss, then tuck the pamphlet into the back pocket of my shorts. He totally notices and his cheeks flush a deep red.

"You're so adorable when you're embarrassed," I say, taking his hand as we follow Dr. Gardingdale down the hallway lined with rooms.

"I'm glad you think so," he replies, his cheeks still pink. "Because I find it really fucking annoying."

I kiss his cheek just because I can.

When we reach a room at the end of the hallway, Dr. Gardingdale motions us inside, then closes the door. It looks like a normal check-up room; plain white walls that surround a bed, a blood pressure machine, and a couple of chairs.

"We're going to hook you up to the monitors so we can keep track of your heart rate while you're out," Dr. Gardingdale explains as Ayden sits down on the bed. "Dr. Milleperton is also going to be putting in an IV as well so we can inject the sedative."

"An IV?" I ask in shock. "Is that really necessary?"

"This is an extreme treatment that requires some mild medication," Dr. Gardingdale says as he sets his briefcase on the counter near the sink. Then he turns to Ayden. "Now, are you positive you want to do this?" he asks. "Because there's still time to change your mind."

Ayden lies down, resting his arms on his stomach. "I'm not going to change my mind."

My heart speeds up, thrashing in my chest.

Tell me what I'm supposed to do
To make this ache go away.
A gnawing warning in my heart,
Begging me to listen.
Soft whispers through my mind.
Tell me a story of where this is heading.
Tell me a story of my life without him.
Dark colors, no light, pure emptiness,
That's what the whispers promise me.
I've never been so confused,
So lost before.

When the doctor comes in and hooks the IV and heart monitor to Ayden, I consider texting Aunt Lila. Consider running out of the room and bailing on the situation because I'm freaking out. But this isn't about me. This isn't about how I feel. This is about Ayden.

So, I take his hand, trying to be there for him the only way I can. "I love you," I whisper. "So much."

"I love you . . . too . . ." He trails off as he slips into unconsciousness.

CHAPTER 3

"TRY TO KEEP YOUR MIND clear," Dr. Gardingdale says as my hazy mind bounces back and forth between consciousness and unconsciousness.

"I'll . . . try . . ." My lips feel so numb, like they're detached from my face. In fact, my entire body feels like it doesn't exist.

"Good. Now try to picture the house you were kept in, if you can." Dr. Gardingdale's voice sounds like it comes from somewhere nearby, but I can't tell where he is—where anyone is. "But I don't want you to push yourself too hard, Ayden. If at any moment you feel like this is too much, just let me know."

"Okay . . ."

Where's Lyric? I want to say. *I want to see her. Want to make sure she's okay. She looked so worried the last time I saw her.*

But I can't see a damn thing. Can't feel anything. I just exist in an ocean of darkness threatening to pull me under the violent waves. I try to fight, try to keep above water, but eventually I succumb and have no choice but to go . . .

Down . . .

Down . . .

Down . . .

Images flash through my mind, memories long forgotten of my brother, my sister, and myself. We're playing at the park, stealing candy from the gas station, painting the rocks in our yard to look like a rainbow, racing through the grassy field to the side of our home.

Then the memories shift away from my home life. I see myself in school, hanging out with my friends, and the time I walked home with Lacey Marlleron, a girl I had a crush on when I was thirteen. I relive getting into trouble when I was caught shoplifting. I see myself fighting with my mom over wanting to see my father. Fighting with my brother when I stole his skateboard and broke it. Fighting with Sadie over the bowl of cereal.

I see it all . . .

A life lost . . .

I see the fall . . .

That leads me straight to where the darkness all began . . .

And I plummet straight into it . . .

"You want to see?" Someone whispers in my ear. "Maybe if you're lucky, I'll take the blindfold off and let you look at your new home."

I start to tell them no, that I don't want to see anything ever again, but I have duct tape over my mouth. I want to scream. Beg them to tell me where my sister and brother are. I try to move, wanting to run the fuck away from this place, but metal cuffs bind my hands, and I'm weak from dehydration and starvation.

"Don't fight the pain, Ayden." Fingernails pierce into my hands, and I feel a warm trail of blood trickle down my skin. "The pain is the easy part."

I scream through the tape and kick my feet. Stop. Touching. Me.

I'm so sick of being touched. I never want to be touched again.

But she puts her hands on me again, letting them wander, before she removes the blindfold from my eyes and rips the tape off my mouth. "Open your eyes and meet your home."

I shake my head. No. I won't do it. Won't do what she tells me.

She stabs her nails into my hands again, this time deeper. Searing pain shoots up my arms and rips through my body, and I bite down on my tongue until I taste blood.

"Open your eyes," she warns, digging her nails even deeper.

I feel pathetically weak as I give into her request and open my eyes.

It's the first time I've seen the light of day in who knows how long. But with the dark curtains hanging over all the windows, hardly any light flows through the room covered in strange circular symbols. The carpet has stains on it, red stains that look like blood, and so much dust and dampness is in the air that it's hard to breathe.

"Hello, Ayden." A man is sitting in a chair in the middle of the room, and he smiles at me. "It's been a long time."

What? Who the hell is this guy?

"You're probably wondering who I am," he says, rolling up the sleeves of his stained shirt. "I was hoping you'd remember, but from the look on your face, I'm guessing that's not the case."

I eye him over, noting that he has the same eyes and hair color as me. A chill goes down my spine and my feeble body trembles.

"It's not really your fault. It's your mother's. She knew the deal when she had you—that she was supposed to raise

you with the knowledge of who I am, then hand you over when it was time—but clearly, things didn't happen that way," he continues, snapping his fingers as he glances to my right. *"Don't worry, though. I'm about to take care of it."*

I turn my head to see what he's looking at and my gut churns.

"Please don't do this, Jerry," begs my mother as a woman with bright red hair and fingernails violently shoves her into the room. My mom trips over her gashed up bare feet and falls forward. With her hands bound, her face slams against the dirty carpet. Instead of getting up, she sobs, her body wrenching. "Please, don't do this. I'll do anything if you just let me go."

"No more bargains." The man rises to his feet and stalks toward her. "Your bargains aren't worth anything."

She lifts her head, tears streaming down her cheeks. "I gave you our children, didn't I? Just like I promised I would."

I forget how to breathe. How to think. Our *children? That means . . .*

"Dad?" *I gape at the man, horrified and disgusted.*

He glances at me, and even though his eyes are like mine, they look unfamiliar, cold. Without saying anything, he grabs my mother by the arm, drags her to the chair, and pushes her down, then kneels in front of her.

"I know I gave you the children to take care of, but you haven't been raising them how we discussed. They know nothing about us or our beliefs." *He exchanges a look with the red-haired woman, and she grins before rushing down the hallway. He focuses back on my mother, gripping onto her legs.* "When I gave you the money to take care of them, I specifically remember stressing how important it was that you taught them about our way of life and about the sacrifice they'd be taking part in. But after talking to them, I see you haven't even told them who I am."

"I can give you the money back." A hysterical sob wrenches from my mother. "Just let me give you back the money."

"Give me the money back?" He cackles, a sound that sends an icy chill through my body. "We both know you spent that money on drugs a long, long time ago."

"I can borrow some from someone if you'll just let me go." When he remains silent, she cries, "Please, Jerry!"

"I have a better idea," he says as the woman with red hair returns to the room.

"No... No... No..." Tears pour out of my mother's eyes as the woman hands my dad a syringe.

"What's the matter?" He snatches hold of my mother's arm and twists her wrist. "I thought this is what you wanted? That you'll do anything to get your hands this."

"Leave her alone!" I shout, trying to wiggle my hands free from the cuffs. The metal bites against my wrists as I struggle and the scratches on my hand burn. But I keep fighting, refusing to sit here and watch him hurt her.

The woman in the corner snickers then sits down beside me. "Don't worry. It'll be over soon."

I'm not sure if she's talking about it being over for my mom or for me. It doesn't matter. I can't let either happen. I have to be strong.

"Just let her go and I'll do whatever you want. Learn about you and your ways," I plead with my dad as tears stream down my face.

"Oh, I know you will. But I can't have your mother messing that up for me. There was a lot of planning that went into bringing you, Sadie, and Felix into this world. You were supposed to be ready for the sacrifice. It wasn't supposed to be such a fight. You were supposed to be ready to cleanse your soul." He looks at my mom then plunges the needle into her forearm.

I tell myself he just injected her with drugs. That she'll wake up like she always does whenever she shoots up. But as her body slumps to the floor, her skin turns sickly white. Her eyes open and veins map her rapidly paling skin.

A blood-curdling scream rips from my chest. "No!"

"Wake up, Ayden," someone says. "You need to wake up."

I desperately try to open my eyes, try to blink the image of my dead mother away, but all I see is her lying on that bloodstained carpet where she took her last breath.

"Open your eyes, Ayden . . . Please . . ."

I'm trying. I'm really am.

Please, please let me get out of here.

Please don't let me die in this place.

CHAPTER 4

I ZONE OFF AS I hold Ayden's hand, recollecting every moment we spent together. It's funny, but when I really analyze our past, I can see that I fell in love with him way before I realized it.

That revelation puts a smile on my face. Then Ayden's body gives a hard jerk, and I'm yanked back to reality.

"Wake up, Ayden," Dr. Gardingdale says, rushing up to the side of the bed. "You need to wake up."

Ayden's body spasms and his eyelids start fluttering as if he's trying to wake up, but can't get his eyes open. Then the heart monitor starts beeping and panic skyrockets through my body as my worst fears are right in front of me.

"Open your eyes, Ayden . . . Please . . ." I beg, gripping onto his hand.

Please don't let me lose him.
Don't take him away from me.
Just let me close my eyes
And pretend this is all a dream.

Dr. Gardingdale tells me to move out of the way, and I sink down in the chair. I've read information about this treatment, and my mind races with all the horrible things that could potentially happen. He could go into shock.

Suffer from heart failure. Or worse, completely lose his memory,

What if he forgets everything?

Everything is moving in fast motion as the doctor starts talking medical talk while he injects something into Ayden's IV. I try to stay calm like Fiona said, but then the word "coma" comes out of the doctor's mouth and something inside me shatters. Tears stream out of my eyes as I slip out of the room to call Aunt Lila, knowing it's the right thing to do.

"Wait, Lyric, slow down," she says as I sputter out what happened. "I can't understand what you're saying."

I take a few measured breaths, trying to pull myself together. "A-Ayden did the treatment—the one you d-didn't want him to do. We're at a doctor's office down on First and Peach Way Lane. You need to get down here."

"He did *what*?" she exclaims. "Lyric, please, tell me he's okay."

"Just get down here, okay?" I tell her as the door behind me opens. Dr. Gardingdale steps out and motions for me to come back in. My chest tightens and air is ripped from my lungs. "Is he okay?" I ask him.

He nods. "You can come back in if you want to."

"Lyric, put Dr. Gardingdale on the phone," she demands before I hang up.

"Okay." My fingers tremble as I hand the phone to Dr. Gardingdale. "Ayden's mom wants to talk to you."

Sighing, he takes the phone and starts reassuring Aunt Lila that Ayden's all right.

I squeeze by him, rush into the room, and relief washes over me. "You're awake." Tears pour out of my eyes at the sight of him sitting on the bed as the doctor checks his heart rate.

Ayden's bloodshot eyes widen at the sight of my tears.

"Lyric, I swear I'm fine." He opens his arms, indicating for me to come to him. "Please, stop crying. I hate seeing you cry."

Against the doctor's protests, I climb into the bed beside Ayden and rest my head on his chest, listening to his heartbeat. "I'm not going anywhere unless I have to," I tell the doctor. "So you might as well continue checking him."

The doctor sighs. "Fine. Just take it easy on him until I can check all of his vitals."

I nod and press my body closer to Ayden, breathing in his scent and warmth. "I thought you weren't going to wake up."

He rubs his hand up and down my back, tracing the length of my spine. "For a moment, I thought the same thing too." His voice cracks and he clears his throat. "But I'm okay now. Everything's okay."

I push to my elbows and peer up at him, trying to read his vibe. "Did it . . . Did it work?"

His gaze welds with mine as he nods. "I saw the house . . . I saw them."

I suck in a sharp breath. "You saw the people who took you?"

He nods again. "I saw the woman who . . ." He blinks down at the scars on his hands then looks back at me. "And I saw my father . . . Saw him . . ." He swallows hard. "Kill my mom."

I stop breathing, and for the first time in my life, I'm speechless. My poor, sweet Shy Boy. Why does he have to keep going through so much pain? He's already been through so much already.

He brushes my hair out of my eyes. "I'm okay. I don't want you to worry about me . . . Everything's going to be okay now." He traces his fingers across my jawline. "I just really want to go talk to the detective."

"Your mother can drive you down there just as soon as I make sure you're one hundred percent okay," Dr. Gardingdale says as he enters the room, shutting the door behind him.

"You called my mom?" Ayden's brows knit as he stares at Dr. Gardingdale. "Why?"

"Actually, that was me." I pull a guilty face as Dr. Gardingdale hands me back my phone. "Sorry, I panicked."

"It's fine . . . I needed to call her anyway, considering what happened." Ayden sighs exhaustedly, his head slumping back against the bed. "I just don't like that she's probably worried as hell right now. I hate worrying her."

"I know you do, but trust me, we love that we get to worry about you." I sit up and press my lips to his.

I'll kiss him over and over again
Every second I get a chance
After what happened
How can I not?
How can I ever not be with him?

"Are you okay?" Ayden checks as he studies my face closely. "You look pale."

"I am now," I say, sitting down beside him. "You might have a real problem though."

His head angles to the side as his face contorts in confusion. "And what's that?"

"That you're never going to get rid of me." I thread our fingers together. "I'll never want to leave your side again after what just happened."

He chuckles, the tension momentarily vanishing from his eyes. "I'm perfectly okay with that problem. In fact, I think I should never, ever get rid of it."

"Good, because it's not going anywhere." I rest my head against his shoulder and close my eyes, breathing in the moment.

It's such a small thing, being here with him, but it feels so immensely important, because he's still him.

I just hope to God he stays that way.

CHAPTER 5

EVEN THOUGH IT MIGHT SOUND insane, I thought I was going to be stuck in that memory forever. Then I heard Lyric's voice, pulling me back to her. When I opened my eyes, there she was, leaning over me with worry in her eyes.

Thankfully, the longer I grasp onto her the more she settles down. If I could, I'd stay this way forever. But I know I need to get to the police station so I can tell Detective Rannali about my father and give him descriptions and a name.

My father. I involuntarily shudder at the thought of what he did to my mother. All this time I thought she died of a drug overdose, that she did it to herself. But my father killed her, just like he probably killed my brother. What really gets to me, though, is that the entire fucking thing was planned. That my mother had us so she could give us to these horrible people. That my father actually believed I was supposed to be ready to take on his whacked out beliefs.

I suddenly feel less guilty about what happened and really, really fucking angry. It's hard to sort through all my emotions when I'm so fucking torn.

Hate or not.
Guilt or fault.
Live or rot.
I don't know what to do.
What kind of person I am.
Who to blame.
Myself?
My mother?
My father?

Suddenly, the door bursts open and Lila barges inside with Ethan right behind her. Her anxiety is written all over her face, her eyes are wide, and her hair's a mess like she ran in a windstorm to get here.

"Ayden Gregory," she starts as she storms toward my bedside. A scowl etches her face as her lips part, but then she whispers, "I'm so glad you're okay."

Lyric scoots out of the way as Lila throws her arms around me and hugs me so tightly I can barely breathe.

"Don't you ever scare me like that again," she says with a few tears dripping down her cheeks.

Ethan gives me a pat on the shoulder and a sympathetic look as Lila continues to strangle me with her death hug. I notice Ethan's eyes are a little red, like he was crying before he got here. It makes me feel like the world's biggest asshole, because Ethan hardly ever gets too emotional, so he had to be extremely worried.

"I'm sorry," I apologize to both of them. "I just needed to do this, and I knew you'd never let me."

"You're damn right we wouldn't have." Lila steps back and motions at the monitors around the room. "Because I knew something like this would happen."

"But I'm fine." I sit up and wince as my muscles groan in pain.

"I don't care if you're fine." She wipes the tears from

her eyes with the back of her hand then waves a finger at me. "You won't do this treatment again."

"I don't have to do it again." I swing my legs over the edge of the bed. "I know who's been after me and who has my sister. I know what they look like and know one of their names."

Lila's eyes pop wide as her hand falls to the side. "The treatment worked?"

"Well, I don't remember everything." And I don't want to. After what I saw, all that pain and ugliness, I think it might be better if what happened to me is left locked in that box in my head. As long as my mind will let things be that way. "But I remembered enough." I stand up and the blood rushes from my head. "I need to go talk to Detective Rannali."

Ethan steadies me by the shoulder as I teeter sideways. "Careful. The doctor said that your body went through a lot of stress today."

"Maybe we should wait until tomorrow to go to the police station," Lila says, eyeing me over as if I'm going to break at any moment. "After you've rested."

"I'll never be able to rest until I talk to him." I force myself to straighten my stance. "Please take me there. I need to go. Now."

She and Ethan trade a questioning look, and then Ethan shrugs. "He's probably right. He'll be able to relax more after he talks to the police. He's been waiting a long time for this."

Lila shakes her head, still furious and upset, "Fine. But we're going to make this as quick as possible. I want to get Ayden home."

Home. The word carries so much more meaning now. I'm so damn grateful to have a safe place to call home.

AFTER LILA IS REASSURED AGAIN and again that my health is okay, Lila and Ethan drive me to the police station. I want Lyric to go with me, but after the whole lying ordeal, her parents told her she needed to go home. I worry she's in trouble, but she assured me that she could handle what her parents consider punishments.

At the police station, we're forced to sit in the waiting area while we wait for Detective Rannali to return from a case he's out working on. I can hardly sit still, just thinking about how this might be reaching an end. That maybe they can finally find Sadie. Make some arrests. Give my brother some justice.

"I wish he'd hurry up." Lila bounces her foot up and down as she scans the busy room. "I want to get Ayden home."

"I know, but you need to relax." Ethan places his hand on her knee to settle her down. "Try to stay calm for him, okay?"

"I'm fine," I say, picking at a hole in my jeans.

"Don't say that," she says, startling me. "I know you can't be fine, not after what you must have . . ." She sucks in a breath as her eyes water up again. "After what you saw."

"It wasn't that bad," I lie with my head tipped down. I shut my eyes and take a deep breath as the images try to resurface. "I didn't see that much."

She wraps an arm around me. "That might be true, but I know seeing any of it has to be difficult."

She keeps trying to console me until Detective Rannali finally shows up. His blue shirt has a coffee stain on it, his silver tie is loose, and his hair is disheveled. "I came here as soon as I could." He seems eager as he nods his head at his office door. "Come inside please. I'd really like to hear what happened with the session today."

The three of us rise to our feet, file into his office, and take a seat in front of his desk. Once everyone is settled, he opens a folder that contains the information and details of the stuff that's been going on over the last couple of years.

"I didn't know you were going through with the session," he starts as he searches his desk drawer for a pen. "But I'm glad you did. And I'm glad it worked."

"Don't treat this situation like it's a good thing," Lila snaps, being protective of me like she usually is whenever we're talking to the detective. "He could've been seriously hurt."

The detective clicks the pen and presses the tip to a yellow notepad. "I understand that. I'm just glad this all worked out."

"I didn't remember everything," I chime in as Lila grows more irritated by the second. "But I did remember some of the faces and a name."

He jots down a few notes, nodding. "How about you recount the details to me, and then we'll start going through some photos of possible suspects. If we can't get anywhere with that, we'll start working on a composite sketch."

I shudder at the idea of seeing my dad or the woman with red hair again, even if it's just in photos. But I nod, knowing I have to do this. Knowing this could be the lead they need.

I hurry and give him an account of what I saw while I was under. When I get to the part about my father killing my mother, the room grows so quiet you can hear everyone's heavy breathing.

"Ayden, I don't even know what to say." The detective shows the slightest bit of compassion. "This must be so hard for you."

"Say you're going to find him." I curl my fingers inward, balling my hands into fists, battling back the tears burning in my eyes. "Say you'll find him before he tries to cleanse his soul with Sadie's life, or whatever the hell he has planned for her. Then when you find him, you'll make him pay for everything he's done."

"I'll do everything in my power to make that happen," he assures me.

"Did you know about this cleansing soul thing?" I ask, gripping the armrests. "Did you know he—that the Soulless Mileas wanted to sacrifice someone they loved because they believe it'll cleanse their souls?"

His prolonged silence answers my question.

"You knew, didn't you?" I shake my head, struggling to keep my cool. But I hate how much I've been lied to throughout this investigation, how much they've left me in the dark.

"Over the last couple of months, I've learned enough about these people that I've had a hunch for a while what they're intentions have been," the detective says, setting his pen down on his desk.

"Do you think that could be why my brother was murdered?" My voice comes out off pitch, wavering, jam packed with the sadness and anger I'm carrying inside me. "Do you think he was one of my dad's sacrifices?"

"At first I wasn't sure, but over the last couple of weeks we've stumbled onto some evidence that opens that possibility," he explains. "But Ayden, that's about all the details I can give you right now about your brother's case."

"And what about Sadie?" My tone is clipped. But I don't give a shit. I'm so sick of him not telling me what's going on. "Is she going to be next?"

He doesn't answer, instead pushing to his feet. "I'm

going to need some more information from you, but I'd like to get you started on looking through some photos."

Lila turns to me, her skin pale. She seemed like she was going to faint when I told everyone my mother had us for these people and their sacrifice. I'll admit, telling that part hurt worse than nail scratches, broken bones, and wounded souls.

"Ayden, I can't believe . . . I don't know what to . . ." She struggles for words. "Sweetie, I'm so sorry."

"You don't need to say sorry. This isn't your fault." My voice is strained. "What's done is done and I just want to forget about it and move on. But after I help find my sister."

She nods, covering her hand over mine. "You can move on from this. In fact, I promise you that you will."

"I hope so." God, I hope so. Hope my sister's alive. Hope that through all the darkness, there will be a light at the end of the tunnel.

I'M FUCKING RESTLESS AS I get situated in front of the computer to scroll through photos. Blood roars in my eardrums as I wrap my fingers around the mouse. Lila is just as anxious, pacing the floor behind me while Ethan tries to get her to relax.

"Honey, you need to calm down," he says, wrapping an arm around her and steering her toward a chair.

"I'm trying." She bites her nails, looking at me. "Do you need anything? Water? A snack."

I'm not hungry but clearly she wants to help me. "Water sounds good."

Nodding, she springs to her feet and hurries off toward the vending machines just outside the room.

Ethan slumps back in the chair, letting his head rest against the wall. "I love that woman to death, but she doesn't handle stress very well," he mutters.

"I'm sorry," I say, knowing it's my fault. "For putting you guys through this."

"Stop apologizing, Ayden." He raises his head to look at me. "We're glad we get to be here for you. We just want you to be safe."

Nodding, I focus back to the computer. One photo after another, I sort through so many they all start to blur together. I'm there for so long that I worry maybe I won't find them.

But then my heart slams to a stop.

"That's him." I point at the photo on the screen of a man with the same eyes and hair color as mine.

"Are you sure?" the detective asks, leaning over my shoulder to look at the screen.

He looks younger in the picture, but I can still tell it's him. "Yes, I'm positive." My heart goes from a complete standstill to beating uncontrollably. "That's the man who killed my mother. That's my father."

See his face.
It's branded in my mind
Like the tattoo on my side
Put there to remember.
You never wanted me to forget.
Guess what. I didn't.

CHAPTER 6

IT'S BEEN A COUPLE OF days since Ayden did the treatment. For the most part, everything's been quiet in our lives. There hasn't been much drama, and we weren't even grounded for sneaking off to the therapy session. But Ayden is getting restless, waiting for something to happen with the case, although he won't say much about it.

I spend a lot of time trying to cheer him up, and from the outside it seems like it's working. But in the back of my mind, I worry he might not be dealing with stuff. It has to be hard for him. After finding out all those things about his parents. After seeing what they did. Finding out that his father paid his mother to have him.

My heart breaks for him and the pain he has to be going through.

"Did you hear anything I just said?" my friend, Maggie, asks me.

We're sitting in front of the school beneath the tree, lounging in the sun. We're supposed to be in class, but since it's the final day of school, and then I'll officially be a high school graduate, my English teacher let us have a free period.

"Not really," I answer truthfully, stretching my legs

across the grass. "Sorry, I'm just a little distracted."

"You're always a little distracted." She rolls up her shirt to the bottom of her bra so the sun hits her stomach. "And I think I know why."

"Really?" I ask with skepticism. *There's no way she could possibly know.*

"Yep. It has something to do with a certain sexy Goth boy you can't keep your hands off of." She rests back on her hands, smiling smugly.

I relax against the tree behind me. "Okay, enlighten me then. Because I have no clue what you're talking about."

"Oh, you so do." She pulls her glasses down, looking at me from over the top of them. "I can see it in your eyes every time the two of you are within a mile of each other."

"See what?" I say innocently, only so she'll have to say it aloud.

"You know what I'm talking about." She sits up and tucks her legs under her. "But if you want me to say it then I will. I'm talking about S.E.X. *Sex.*" She raises her voice loud enough that the people around us can hear her. "You want to have *sex* with Ayden. You want him to put his—"

"All right. All right." I cut her off, laughing. "I get it."

"But do you really get it?" she asks, retrieving a tube of lip-gloss from her purse.

"Maggie, I love you to death, but I'm totally not following you."

She applies a coat of gloss then smacks her lips together. "I'm asking you if you get how much the two of you need to get your freak on."

"Okay, we've talked about that reference," I say. "No calling it getting our freak on. It makes it sound so gross."

"Sometimes, it is gross." Her nose scrunches. "Like with Sage."

"Don't go there." I point a finger at her. "If you tell me

things, I might not be able to look him in the eye anymore. I need to be able to do that for the sake of the band."

"Fine." Her eyes sparkle mischievously as she sits back in the grass. "I won't tell you all the horrible details just as long as you admit you want to have sex with Ayden." When my lips remain sealed, she adds, "If you want, you can call it making love, but I kind of wish you wouldn't." She pulls a face like the idea is appalling.

"Fine, I'll admit it, just as long as you'll drop the subject of my sex life."

She grins, bouncing up and down. "So you're saying it's true? You're thinking about having sex with Ayden?"

I nod, trying not to smile idiotically. But the idea of being with Ayden like that makes me grin. "I think about it a lot."

"Think about what a lot?" Ayden asks from right behind me.

Maggie smirks at me then bats her eyelashes as she looks up at Ayden. "About you and her getting your freak on."

I glance over my shoulder at Ayden and offer him an apologetic look. "Just ignore her. She ate too much lip gloss today."

"Hey, I don't eat it," she protests. "I use it to draw attention to these bad boys." She smacks her lips.

Ayden's never been a fan of Maggie, and he simply stares at her before focusing on me. "Why aren't you in class?"

I shrug, picking at the grass. "We got a free period so we thought we'd come chill in the sun. What about you?" I look at the parking lot behind us where I think he just came from. "Did you just get back from somewhere?"

"Yeah, I did." His gaze flickers in Maggie's direction.

I get to my feet, reading his mind, because we're in

sync like that. "Hey Mags, I'm going to go talk with Ayden for a bit. Catch you later, okay?"

"Oh whatever." She stands up, brushing the grass of her legs. "I know you two are going to go make out in the car." She winks at me before strutting across the grass, giving her ass an extra shake as she walks by a group of football players.

"We need to talk, huh?" Ayden asks, his brow cocking.

"I could tell that you wanted to." I gently tap the side of his head. "Remember, I can read everything going on in there."

A soft laugh escapes his lips, but he quickly turns serious. "I do want to talk, actually." He gives a quick scan of the campus yard. "But maybe somewhere where there aren't so many people around."

The air is stifling today and I'm roasting like a beast, even in my purple tank, denim shorts, and gladiator sandals. "I am in desperate need of some air conditioning." I loop my arm through his. "How about we go sit in your car?"

He nods and we start across the grass, the sunlight flickering between the tree branches canopying above our heads. Neither of us speaks as we cross the parking lot and get into his car. I can tell something's stressing him out, and that he's stuck in his own little Ayden world of despair. I don't push him to confide in me, though, figuring he's been pushed too much already. If he wants to talk, then we'll talk. If he wants to sit in the car with me and simply hold my hand, then that's what I'll do.

He turns on the engine to crank up the air, then sits back and cracks his knuckles while gazing out the window.

"I'm sorry Maggie's a perv," I say as I prop my feet against the dash.

He glances at me from the corner of his eye. "I'm used

to Maggie and her mouth. In fact, my day would seem oddly incomplete without hearing at least one dirty remark from her."

"Well, that's a huge change for you. Usually, you get irritated when she opens her mouth."

"I said I was used to her, not that I wanted to be used to her." He's smiling and it's so beautiful and rare that I have to grin along with him.

"I think I might be with you on that," I say. "Can you believe she tried to tell me everything that happened between Sage and her? And I'm talking *everything*. Could you imagine? I'd be scarred for life."

"Sage would be so pissed if she did." He rests his head back and stares at me for a heartbeat or two, his eyes smoldering so intensely I have to catch my breath.

I never thought it could be like this.
That love could be so raw and potent.
So intoxicated.
So mind erasing.
My breathing is fading.
My heart isn't cooperating.
Anymore.

"I found out something . . . about the case," Ayden says with a heavy sigh. "Lila actually pulled me out of class to tell me. Then she made me go talk to Dr. Gardingdale to make sure I was handling everything okay."

I practically get whiplash going from joking about Sage and Maggie's dirty rendezvous to talking about the case.

"What happened?" I sit up straight, my feet falling to the floor. "Did they find them? Did they find your sister?"

He reaches forward and gently places his hand on my arm. "Lyric, calm down. Nothing has happened yet. They just got a lead."

"But that's good news, right?" *Please, please, let it be good news.*

"I'm not sure." He seems so calm, which is strange. "Maybe. The detective said he'd give me an update when he had one. It might take a few days, though."

"Are you sure everything's okay?" I ask him for the eleventh-hundred time since the amnesia session. "You've seemed sort of, I don't know, sedated lately."

"That's not a bad thing," he assures me with a forced smile. "It's good to be calm, right?"

I nod, but I'm not buying it. I have a hunch Ayden's cool-as-cookie-dough-ice-cream behavior is like a calm before the storm. I want to press him to talk, but worry I'll only stress him out more.

What do I do?
To get through to you?
To get inside your head?
See your thoughts.
Feel what lies under your skin.
In your veins.
In your heart.

The bell rings and I sigh as we get out of the car to go to class.

"If you get a free period, meet me out front, okay?" Ayden asks as we part ways in the hall.

"Surely durely." I throw him a wave over my shoulder, then make a quick pit stop at my locker to douse myself in perfume because I'm one sweat away from having a serious case of BO. As I click open my locker, a piece of paper floats out and lands on the floor by my feet. Not thinking too much of it, I bend down to pick it up and realize it's a letter.

We found the way to Ayden's heart. Make sure to pass along the message.

My attention whips up, and I cast a panicked glance up and down the hallway, skimming the faces of everyone. I swear I see a blur of red race out the front door, but I'm not about to chase the person down.

I grab my phone out of my pocket and run straight for Ayden.

CHAPTER 7

"LYRIC, WHAT'S WRONG?" I GAPE at her as she races up to me in the hallway, her eyes wild with panic.

Panting, she hands me a piece of paper while dialing someone's number on her phone. "This was in my locker." She hunches over, bracing her hands on her knees as she catches her breath.

My hands shake as I read the note. *We found the way to Ayden's heart. Make sure to pass along the message.* More fear than I've ever felt pulsates through me. They left this in Lyric's locker. My Lyric. God fucking dammit!

"Fuck." I kick the locker, then grab Lyric's hand and guide her with me as I stride down the hallway and burst out the exit doors.

"Where are we going?" she asks as she jogs to keep up with me.

My gaze is everywhere, taking in every person, every door, every vehicle. "I'm getting the police." Getting her to safety.

When I reach the police car, I startle the officer when I rap my knuckles on the window.

He rolls the window down, his brows knitting. "Ayden, is everything all right?"

Shaking my head, I hand him the note. "This was in Lyric's locker."

He reads the letter and mutters, "This sounds like a threat." He curses then hops out of the car. "You two go wait in the main office while I check the area." He calls for backup as we jog across the yard, parting ways at the entrance door.

"Do you think they're still around?' Lyric asks as we hurry down the now empty hallway and toward the main office.

"I don't know." I keep ahold of her arm, never wanting to let her go. "I honestly don't think so."

Her eyes are wide as she works to keep up with me. "Why?"

"Because I think this is another way of them messing with my head," I say as I yank open the door to the main office. "This has to be part of their plan. Every one of their moves always seems so calculated. So deliberate."

The question that's really bothering me, though, is how did they know about Lyric? The answer is fucking terrifying. That they've been watching me close enough to know how much she means to me.

I don't know what their intentions are with putting the note in her locker, but I have a feeling the move was deliberate. Maybe they're going to try to use her to get to me. Or maybe they think they can scare me into handing over myself by threatening her. If that's the case, then they're right. I'd walk straight into their hands if it means she'll be safe.

CHAPTER 8

AFTER I FIND THE LETTER, I call my mom while Ayden and I wait in the main office. The police make a huge scene as they search the school. Thank God it's our last day; otherwise, we would've had to spend the rest of our school days with everyone gossiping about what happened. While I can handle staring, Ayden, my Shy Boy, has trouble with extra attention.

Aunt Lila is the one who ends up picking us up, because she's closest to the school. But my mom, my dad, and Uncle Ethan are headed home.

By the time Lila arrives, the police have searched every nook and cranny of the school and surrounding area and found no sign of who left the note.

She doesn't say a word as she barges into the office and strides straight for Ayden. "This has got to stop." She throws her arms around him, hugging him tightly. "They can't keep doing this to you."

"They didn't do it to me." Guilt laces Ayden's voice. "They went after Lyric."

Aunt Lila looks over Ayden's shoulder at me, then she snags hold of my arm and tugs me in for a hug too.

"I'm so glad school's over," Lila whispers as she

continues to trap us in her death-grip-three-way hug. "Now we can keep an eye on you all the time."

"That's not completely true," Ayden says. "You have lives. You can't watch me all the time."

Aunt Lila is quiet, and I can almost see her wheels turning, trying to find a way to make it possible for her to be a near Ayden at all times. She must not arrive at a conclusion, because she says, "Let's get you two home, okay?"

We nod and follow her out to her car, leaving Ayden's vehicle there for Uncle Ethan and my dad to pick up.

Ayden barely utters a word the entire drive home, and I can see where this is heading. That he's blaming himself for the letter ending up in my locker.

"I know what you're thinking and it's not your fault," I hiss under my breath as Aunt Lila pulls the car into the driveway of the Gregorys' home. "So stop going there right now."

He turns his head away from the window, making eye contact with me for the first time in hours. "Lyric, they threatened *you*. I can't just forgive myself for that."

I scoot closer to him. "There's nothing to forgive. Nothing happened. I got a letter. So what. They didn't actually do anything to me. They just wanted me to pass along the message."

"You heard what the officer said," he whispers, self-torture rising in his eyes. "That letter was a threat."

I point at a cop car parked at the end of the driveway. "It's a good thing we have those then. Besides, they're always sending you threats and notes. This was probably just another way to try to get to you."

He crosses his arms. "I never should've dragged you into this mess."

"You didn't *drag* me into this mess. I willingly ran

head on into it, and I'd do it again in a heartbeat just as long as I got to be with you." I cup his chin in my hand, forcing him to look at me. "Now, you're going to chill out, and we're going to go inside and work on our songs so we can kickass at the recording tomorrow."

"But I—"

"No buts," I scold, but also smile to shine positivity to all the darkness trying to rain down on us. "We're going to go practice, then we're going to make out after we're all finished."

From the front seat, Aunt Lila clears her throat. "I'm going to go inside and give you two a moment. Please, don't stay out here too long." She opens the door to climb out. "And Lyric, I want you to wait with us until your parents come home. They don't want you leaving for any reason."

I salute her and she shakes her head like *oh Lyric, you're such silly girl*. Then she ducks out and closes the door.

I fix my attention back on Ayden. "Now promise me that you'll stop blaming yourself for what happened."

"It doesn't matter if I can forgive myself," he says, looking at me with those sad puppy dog eyes of his. "Other people are going to blame me."

"You mean my parents?" I ask and he nods. I link my arms around the back of his neck and slant toward him until our chests are flush. "I'll tell you what. If they blame you then you can sink into your self-pity. But if they don't, you have to stop blaming yourself. And I mean it. No self-blame. No sinking into your pain. No torture and despair."

He considers what I said, his lips twitching as he restrains a smile. "You know, you're starting to sound like a walking lyrical book."

"It's probably because I've been writing, like, all the

time. I want to come up with some fresh stuff that maybe *we* can use on the tour." I wait for him to argue about the *we*, and when he doesn't, I go back to our deal. "Now promise me you'll do it. Promise me you'll forgive yourself if my parents don't blame you." I lean back and stick out my pinkie.

He sighs, but hitches his pinkie with mine and seals the deal. "Fine, I promise."

"Good." I give my best prize winning grin because I know I've won the deal already, since my parents aren't the kind of people to ever blame Ayden for what happened. They like him more than Ayden thinks. They've always wanted me to be friends with him, even before we all met him.

I remember the day I was headed to meet Ayden for the first time. While I was walking over to the Gregorys' with my parents, I tried to get out of going, mainly because I was bored and wanted to do something fun. My dad said something to me that still gets to me when I really think about it.

"You're really lucky to have *every* single one of us," he said. "And you should really get to know the new kid. He's your age, and I'm sure he could use a friend with . . . Some of the stuff he's been through. You could be that friend for him. Do something good."

It's amazing how much I followed his advice. But being friends with Ayden was never about doing something good. It always came so naturally, as if we were supposed to be friends long before we ever met. And if anything, he's the one who did something good for me, by letting me into his world. It's always made me feel so special that he's trusted me so much.

After we get out of the car, Ayden and I go into his house and up to his room to work on our song that we're supposed to be singing together on our album, but we spend a lot of time kissing too. About a half an hour later, the crazed parent mob shows up and we're summoned to the kitchen. They tell Fiona, Everson, and Kale to go into the living room and work on their homework. After the room is cleared of the youngin's, Ayden sits down at the table with Uncle Ethan while my worried mom sideswipes me with a hug.

"Oh my God, I'm so glad you're okay." She circles her arms around me, squeezing so tightly I feel like my lungs are being crushed.

I give her a moment before I step back. "I'm fine, Mom. Would you relax? Nothing happened."

"I will not relax, Lyric Scott. We were so worried." She has yellow, green, and red paint spots on her shorts and tee and even in her auburn hair, which means she probably rushed away from one of her art pieces.

I feel bad that she had to bail in the middle of a piece. As an artist myself, I know when inspiration strikes, you just roll with it until it stops; otherwise you could totally lose the vibe.

"But I'm fine." I span my hands to the side and curtsey, trying to lighten the stressful tone taking over the Gregorys' kitchen. "See, one hundred percent okay."

My mom shakes her head exhaustedly. "You know, I'd ask you how on earth you could possibly joke at a time like this, but I already know my answer." She shoots my dad a look.

He's sporting his infamous bedhead/fauxhawk hair, a style that's unintentional and only appears when he's really stressed and has been raking his fingers through his hair.

He pulls a *whoops* face then shrugs. "Sorry, but you knew what you were getting into long before you married me." He turns to me, his amusement vanishing as his arms fold around me. "I was so fucking worried about you," he whispers in my ear so only I can hear.

"I know," I whisper back. "But it's okay. It was just a note."

"Still, we're going to keep an extra eye on you," he promises. "No going out alone or anything."

I nod my head up and down. "That's fine by me, but Dad? This isn't Ayden's fault." I keep my voice low so no one else will hear me.

"Of course it's not," my dad says, sounding shocked. "Why would you say that?"

"Because he thinks it is."

We hug for a second longer then step back, forcing ourselves to relax for the sake of the others.

My dad walks over to Ayden, who's sitting in a chair at the table, staring at the floor, looking so sullen I want to cry for him. "You're okay, right?" he asks Ayden.

Ayden glances up, looking startled by my dad's question. "Um, yeah, of course." He looks at Aunt Lila, Uncle Ethan, and my mom who are all staring at him with concern.

He may blame himself for all of this, but there's nothing but love for him right now. I just hope he can see it.

"Good. Good." My dad yanks his fingers through his hair, making the strands go even more askew. "If you guys want, we can move the recording to a later date."

"No way," I protest at the same time Aunt Lila says, "I think that's a good idea."

I scrunch my nose at her. "That is so not a good idea and it'll totally set us back for the tour."

She shoots me a warning look from across the kitchen. "Lyric, I don't think the tour is the most important thing right now."

"It might not be, but right now everyone is so stressed

out it's starting to give me a headache," I say, stealing a sugar cookie from the plate on the counter. "No one laughs anymore. Tells stories. Smiles. It's all stress over this. Stress over that. And I really think everyone just needs to take a chill pill and focus on some fun stuff in life, even if it's just for a few hours. Then you can all go back to acting twitchy and crazy." The four of them give each other curious glances, so I keep on rolling. "What I think we need is for all of us get in the car and go do something fun."

"And what do you propose this fun thing should be?" my dad asks, mildly amused.

"I don't know." I give a shrug. "I didn't get that far when I was mentally preparing my speech."

My dad looks at my mom who glances at Aunt Lila. Obviously, she's the ringleader in their quartet.

"It might be good for everyone to get some fresh air," she finally says after seconds tick by. "Just as long as we go someplace safe."

"And relaxing," I add, stuffing the rest of the cookie into my mouth.

"Hmmm . . ." My dad rubs his jawline. "I might know just the place."

MY DAD IS A KICKASS rock star/music producer, so when he said he knew a place that was both safe and relaxing, I was thinking maybe like a chill club that allows kids or perhaps a restaurant where the adults can drink a lot of wine. But nope. He takes us to Rock in Time Playhouse and Grub, which is pretty much a bedazzled pizzeria full of games, bouncy houses, and slides.

The second we step in, Fiona, Everson, and Kale race for the arcade section. Aunt Lila and Uncle Ethan chase after them while Ayden mutters something about needing to go to the bathroom.

"I'll be back in a sec," my mom says then wanders off to the bar to order a drink, leaving my dad and me to get a table and order food.

"You know we're all over twelve," I say to my dad as I point to the No Kids Over 12 sign beside the ball pit. "That so sucks. I want to jump in there like I used to do when I was a kid." Back when everything was so simple, so easy, so effortless.

He waves me off, heading for a corner booth. "That rule doesn't apply to us."

"How do you figure?" I ask as I weave passed the empty tables, following him.

"Because I know the guy who owns this place."

"Man, how many people do you know? Because it seems like a lot."

"It comes with the territory of running my own business." He slides into the booth and plucks a menu from a rack in the center of the table.

I plop down in the booth and cross my arms on the table. "I'm sure it might have something to do with the fact that you're a retired rock star."

"Perhaps." He fixes his attention on the menu.

"How do you do it?" I ask. "I mean, handle people giving you all these special favors and acting weird around you."

He shrugs, glancing up at me. "I'm not going to lie. Sometimes it's not easy and it gets tiring—it's part of the reason why I retired—but it was fun for a while."

"Do you think I'll be able to handle it? I mean, the environment." While I'm a pretty confident person, I value his opinion.

He rests his arms on the table as his mouth curves to

a frown. "As much as I want to say no and keep you home with me forever, I honestly think you'll do just fine. You're an amazing girl and very level headed." He grins at me. "Plus, you've got my charming personality."

"That I do. You're going to let me go, though, right? I mean, you're not going to try to keep me home, like Lila's doing with Ayden."

He shakes his head. "Of course not. Besides, I think it'll be good for you to get away from here for a while and have some fun. Your senior year has been really stressful."

"I know." I spin a saltshaker in my hand. "I just wish Ayden was going with me."

"I know you do, but you have to understand how hard it's got to be for him to even think about going when his sister still hasn't been found. Plus, I don't think anyone will be able to convince Lila to let him go."

"Yeah, I know." I sit back in the seat, trying not to let my disappointment get to me. While I'm bummed, I know Lila and Ethan have every right to worry about Ayden. And everyone's probably right. It's probably too dangerous for him to go. But the dreamer side of me can't help but think how much Ayden might regret missing out on this. He's missed out on so many life experiences already

Missed.

Missed.

Missed.

I'm going to miss Ayden.

I'm going to miss everyone.

"Dad, I'm really going to miss these talks of ours while I'm gone," I feel the overpowering need to tell him.

"I am too, Lyric." He chokes up. "But you know I'll always be here for you. Whenever you need to talk, just call me. In fact, I insist you call me at least once a day."

I stick out my pinkie. "Deal."

He hitches pinkies with me, offering me a small smile. "You know I'm the one who taught you how to promise this way, right?"

"I remember. I was four and you were promising me that you'd be home for my birthday even though you were on tour."

"You really remember that?" His eyes gleam with hope.

"Of course I remember. Just like I remember you never broke one single promise. You're an awesome dad. Always have been." I shoot him a cocky smirk. "That's why I turned out so awesome."

"You did turn out pretty freakin' awesome, if I do say so myself." He returns his attention to the menu, trying to discreetly wipe the tears from his eyes.

I really am going to miss him—miss everyone.

I glance at Kale and Everson freaking out over of a buttload of tickets pouring out of a machine, at Fiona and Ethan playing the arcades, and at my mom and Aunt Lila at the bar, sipping on wine, and laughing about something.

I smile to myself at how happy they all look.

Mission of Fun accomplished.

As I look back to my dad, I note all the tables around us are empty and a thought occurs to me. "Did you ask the owner if we could have this place to ourselves for the day?"

"I might have." He smiles as he reads over the menu.

"Nice job, daddy-o. I'm sure everyone will appreciate the down time."

But there's one thing missing from this picture of fun. Something I think I need to go check on.

"I'll be right back." I jump to my feet and wink at him. "Order me a beer while I'm gone."

My dad just shakes his head and mutters, "So much

like me."

I wind past the tables and burst into the men's room.

Ayden is leaning against the tile wall with his head tipped back, his gaze locked on the ceiling. He jumps at my sudden appearance, his eyes popping wide. "Holy shit, you scared me."

"No more sulking," I warn, aiming a finger at him. "You promised me if no one blamed you that you'd let it go."

"I wasn't sulking," he tries to assure me. "I was just thinking."

"About what?"

"About . . ." He drags his fingers through his hair and puffs out a breath. "About us."

My expression fizzles to a frown. "It's never a good sign when someone is over analyzing their relationship."

"No, it's a good thing this time. I swear." He strides toward me, stopping only inches away, panic gleaming in his eyes. "I don't want to be a selfish person, but I can't stop myself from wanting to be with you. When I saw that letter . . . I realized how easily I could lose you and how much it'd kill me if it happened."

I thread my fingers through his. "Then don't lose me. Be with me."

"It's not that simple." He lets out a frustrated breath. "Every time something happens, I can't help but worry that something bad's going to happen to you and it'll be my fault."

"Nothing's going to happen to me," I press.

"You don't know that for sure," he mutters.

"Okay, you know what, I don't." I tug on his arm, pulling him closer to me. "But something bad could happen at any moment, even while we're standing here. Like the roof could cave in and crush me. That wouldn't be your fault, and you can't control it from not happening."

"Why would the roof cave in?" he questions with a trace of a ghost smile.

I give a half shrug. "I don't know, maybe that foul stench is rotting it away."

He chuckles but then his mood nosedives. "I get your point, but I don't think you're getting mine."

"Okay . . ." I study him closely. "Could you explain it to me then, because apparently, my mind-reading skills are a little wonky right now."

"You were right about what you said . . . That no one smiles anymore. Not even you."

"I smile." I grin just to prove my point.

"But not as much as you used to."

"Ayden, that's not your fault—"

He places his finger to my lips, shushing me. "I'm not saying it's my fault. I'm just saying that you deserve to smile more, which I know you will when you're on the tour. In fact, I bet you'll smile so much you'll even get Sage to join in." He lowers his hand, tracing his fingers down my chin, to my neck, and the collar of my shirt. Goose bumps sprout across my skin, even though it's a hundred degrees in here. "But I want to be there to see you smile. I want to be the one smiling with you."

"I'm not quite sure what you're saying." Or maybe I do, and I just don't want to get my hopes up.

"Me neither." He sighs, frustrated. "I just wish I could experience all of it with you."

A glimmer of hope shines inside me. "Then experience it with me."

"But how am I supposed to do that with all the stuff going on?" Sadness consumes his face. "And what about Sadie? How can I just bail on her?"

"You wouldn't be just bailing. You've helped a lot.

And you can still help." I step toward him until the tips of our shoes brush. "You want to know how you do it? You just do it—you just go. You say to hell with the faulty roof, flip it the bird, and live your goddamn life."

"I wish it were that simple," he says quietly. "But no one would ever let me just take off. And what if the Soulless Mileas chase me down? What if I put everyone in danger?"

"Those are all possibilities, but so is the police finding the people who are doing this to you. They could find Sadie. This could all be over soon. You never know. That's the thing, Ayden, you never know about anything. Just like you never know if you'll ever have a chance to do something like this tour again. It might be a once in a lifetime opportunity. And if you want to go, then we'll find a way. Don't let anyone take away your life from you." I hold my breath, waiting for him to agree that he'll do it. Go with me on this crazy three-month journey lying ahead of me.

He doesn't flat out say it, but he does faintly smile and the tension in his body unwinds.

"We'll talk to our parents and figure something out if you decide you want to do this," I say, trying not to get too hopeful. Not until he says it aloud. "But right now, there's something way more important we need to do."

His forehead furrows as he stares at me. "And what's that?"

A wicked grin rises on my face as I haul him toward the door. "We need to go jump in the ball pit. Like, right now."

He laughs as I drag him out of the bathroom and through the restaurant. I don't slow down as we race for the ball bit. I just hold on until the edge and then jump.

CHAPTER 9

Ryden

WE LAND IN THE BALL pit, holding hands, and sink into a sea of plastic balls. When our feet hit the floor, Lyric laughs and pushes up to the top, like she's swimming in water.

"I always loved playing in these when I was a kid," she says as she twirls around in a circle, creating a funnel.

"I've never actually been in one," I admit as I pick up a ball and chuck into the air like a baseball.

"Well, now you can't say that anymore." She moves over by me. "Tell me one of your secret wishes."

I cock a brow at her. "One of my secret wishes?"

She nods, her green eyes sparkling. "I used to play this game with my dad when I was a kid. He would tell me his secret wish, then I'd tell him mine." She grins deviously. "He once told me that he secretly wished he could be a superhero for a day and wear a cape. I think he just said that, though, because he was trying to keep his wish PG."

I snort a laugh. "Why would I tell you my secret wish when you just outed your dad's?"

"Because you love me." Her bottom lip juts out and she bats her eyelashes at me as she clasps her hands in front of her. "Pretty please, Shy Boy."

I shake my head, but she's too damn adorable, and I can't help but smile. "You know that I know you do that on purpose, right?"

"Do what?" she asks innocently.

I touch the finger to her bottom lip. "Pout to get your way."

"Then why do you give me my way still?"

"Because I love giving you your way," I admit with a shrug. "I guess that's my secret wish. That I could always give you your way all the time. That I could give you what I know you want."

"You mean with the tour?" She catches my hidden meaning.

I nod. "I'm going to try to go for you, but I can't promise anything."

"Don't try for me." She loops her arms around me, angles her head back, and looks up at me. "Try for yourself."

Her long, blonde hair veils down her back, her green eyes glisten in the light, and her chest is pressed against mine. She looks so fucking beautiful right now, I could write a song about it.

Eyes so green
That carry love for me.
How is that even possible?
How can something so beautiful
Be in love with some like me?
And her lips, so perfect
I can't taste enough of them.
And when she touches me,
It's too fucking complicated to breathe.

"I'll try for both of us," I tell her. "Just as long as you do something for me."

"And what's that?"

"Kiss me—"

She crashes her lips to mine before I can even get the words out. Our tongues tangle as we sink into the pit. My hand skates down her side to her thigh and I lift her leg up and hitch it over my hip. She moans against my mouth as she grinds against me. I knot my fingers through her hair, feeling so comfortable being with her it's mind blowing. Just like the other night when she put her hands on me. It was the first time I ever allowed someone to touch me like that, and it was terrifying and incredible at the same time.

"Mom, Lyric and Ayden are making out in the ball pit!" Fiona announces as she steps up to the edge of the pit and points at us.

I softly toss a plastic ball at her, and she laughs, skittering out of the way.

"One day, when you're making out with your boyfriend," I tell her, "I'm going to get you back for that."

Fiona sticks out her tongue then skips off toward the game machines.

I spot Ethan and Mr. Scott heading our way. I don't think they're coming to yell at us for making out, but I'm not about to keep kissing Lyric when her dad could see us.

I sigh. "I guess that puts an end to our ball pit fun."

"You know they know we kiss, right?" Her brows arch. "In fact, I'm pretty sure they think we're having sex already, since my mom found that safe sex pamphlet in my nightstand drawer."

My lips part in shock. "She—You didn't—You told her we weren't having sex, didn't you?"

"I told her we weren't *yet*," she says. "But I've always been pretty close with my family, and I felt like I needed to tell her," she shrugs, "That we're getting really close to that point. At least I think we are."

I cast an unnerved glance at her dad as he busts up

laughing at something Ethan says. "Does your dad know too?"

"My mom and dad tell each other everything, so maybe." She tosses a ball aside then lines her chest with mine. "Would you relax? They know we're in love, and that we aren't just two teenagers getting their freak on."

"You told them we're in love?" I whisper, a mixture of fear and nerves.

"Not yet. But I'm sure they can tell. I should probably tell them, though." Her head angles to the side as she muses over something. "It's actually my secret wish. That I could shout it out right now and everyone could celebrate the love with us." She jumps up and presses a kiss to my lips.

She hasn't smiled like this in a while, and it makes me so fucking relieved to see her happy like this.

My lips turn upward. "Well, how can I argue with that?"

"Really?" she asks, her eyes light up.

I nod, a knot twisting in my gut. "Yeah, go ahead."

"Hey everyone!" She shouts with laughter ringing in her voice. "I love this beautiful boy right here. And guess what? He loves me too!"

I can't bring myself to look in the direction of Ethan and Mr. Scott. "I feel sick," I mutter.

"My declaration of our love is no reason to get sick," she says, playfully pinching my arm. "Now cheer up. This is a good thing."

"Do they look mad?" I whisper with my head ducked.

She stands on her tiptoes and peers over my shoulder. "No, but they're headed over here." Lyric's eyes sparkle mischievously as she returns her gaze to me. "We could always sink to the bottom and hide from them."

I nod. "Yes, please."

She takes my hand. "Ready. One . . . Two . . . Three . . ."

We jump up then dive down, pressing our lips together.

CHAPTER 10

THE ENTIRE NEXT DAY I'M so nervous and twitchy, people probably think I'm a spazz. But I can't help it. Today is an exciting day for everyone in my band. I just wish we didn't have that giant cloud constantly hovering over our heads, reminding us that a rainstorm could come at any moment.

Around two o'clock I head off to record my first album, and spend the next few hours with Ayden and my band at Infinitely Studio, my dad's recording studio, starting our career. We don't record every song that'll be on our album in one night, but we are planning to return within the next week to finish. Before we clock out for the day, I make sure Ayden and I do a duet, because, in my opinion, it's the best part.

"Are you sure you want to do this?" Ayden asks me as we prepare to go in and sing the song we wrote. "Because you can always back out."

"No way am I about to back out on one of my dreams." I plant my butt on the stool and put my headphones on, motioning Ayden to do the same.

He nervously sits down, slides on a set of headphones, and situates his guitar on his lap. I collect my guitar and get comfortable, disregarding Sage and Nolan gawking at us through the window.

"Ready?" My dad's voice floats through the speakers.

Ayden's been extremely jumpy around my dad, ever since I belted out that we were in love, and he flinches at the sound of my dad's voice. I don't know why he's acting all squirrely. No one has brought up our love declaration, except for my mom and she seemed pretty happy about it.

"I'm so glad you can just say it like that," she said to me as she worked on a painting in her studio at our house. "I had such a hard time expressing my emotions when I was younger."

"Really?" I was shocked because, for as long as I could remember, her and my dad have been happy and in love and not afraid to show the world.

She set the paintbrush down, nodding. "I had a lot of problems when I was younger. Thankfully, your dad stuck with me while I worked through them."

I couldn't help but think of Ayden and myself. He struggles sometimes with his emotions, but I'll never, ever give up on him. I want him. Forever.

I blink back to reality and lock eyes with Ayden. "Are you ready?"

He nods, his gaze fused to mine. "Whenever you are."

"We're ready whenever you are, daddy-o," I say through the microphone.

My dad gives me the go ahead, and I strum the first chord. Ayden follows my lead, and we play a few more chords, completely in sync, before I open my mouth and pour out my soul to the microphone.

"I never knew it could be like this, never thought such desire was possible, kissing the air from his lungs." My heart hammers in my chest. "And the heavens rain stars down on us, pieces of shimmering gold around us, pouring warmth all over us. Kiss me until I can no longer breathe. Raveling me up with you until I can hardly think. God, please fucking kiss me before I crumble to pieces."

We strum a few more chords, keeping the beat soft until it's Ayden's turn to come in. He summons a breath then opens his mouth and kisses the world with the beautiful sound of his voice.

"You make me weak. You make me strong. You make me ache. You make me feel so wrong. You make me burn for just a taste." His gaze burns into me, scorches my soul. "You make me, make me, so fucking insane. I can't stand it anymore. I want you all the time. It's always on my fucking mind. Please, just let me have you. God, please just say yes."

I nod. I don't even know why, other than I want him to have me.

He keeps his eyes on me until the song is finished.

I'm so riled up, I'm actually sweating.

My dad walks in, but I barely register what he's saying. I'm too caught up in Ayden, the sound of his voice, singing with him, singing one of *our* songs.

"You guys did a great job." My dad congratulates us with a huge-ass smile on his face. "Seriously, I'm not really a fan of duets, but that was pretty amazing."

"Thanks, Dad," I say, my gaze never wavering from Ayden.

My dad says a handful of other things about coming back in next week, but I hardly hear a word.

"Lyric, did you hear me?" my dad asks, looking at me with concern.

I blink my attention from Ayden and attempt to focus on my dad. "Nope. What's up?"

He sighs, sinking into a stool. "I asked if you want me to drive you home."

"We can just drive ourselves," I say as I slide off the stool to put my guitar in the case. "I know you have stuff to do."

"I'd rather you not drive home alone," he replies, crossing his arms. "It's late."

"I thought you had a meeting," I remind him. "That's what your secretary said when we came in here. And we won't be all alone. The officer will be following us."

"Yeah, I know." He frowns, actually pouting. "I forgot about the meeting. I wanted to take you out for ice cream or something."

"You can do it tomorrow," I suggest as I lock up my guitar case. "I can even clear my super busy schedule, just for you."

That cheers him up. "All right. I'll think of something fun to do." He turns to Ayden. "You can come too, if you want."

I smile as I tie my plaid over shirt around my waist.

You just got mad cool points, Dad.

Ayden glances at me, and I mouth, *come with us.*

"Sure. That sounds good, Mr. Scott." He picks up his guitar case.

"Call me Micha, okay," my dad insists. "Mr. Scott makes me feel so old."

"You kind of are old," I say. When he shoots me a nasty look, I add, "But the coolest old man ever."

He laughs, opening up the door. "Come on. This old man needs to get to work."

After we say goodbye to my dad, Ayden and I walk outside with Sage and Nolan to the parking lot. It's later in the evening and the sky is splashed with pink, orange, and gold.

"We so rocked today." Sage fist-bumps Ayden. "If we can sound like that on the tour, there's no doubt we'll get more tour offers."

Nolan tosses his drumsticks into the backseat of Sage's truck. "We did sound fucking awesome today, but what're we going to do when we have a sucky guitarist instead of Ayden?"

"Don't start," Sage warns, leaning against the back of his truck. "I already hear enough of that shit from Lyric."

"That's because it's the truth," I say, pulling my hair up as the heat instantly gets to me.

"Would you guys please stop arguing?" Ayden asks, shocking the three of us.

"Sorry, man," Sage says, holding up his hands. "I was just pointing out that they can complain about it all they want, but it doesn't fix the problem that we're going to be short a guitarist on the first fucking tour we got hired for."

"I'm sure they don't all suck," Ayden says, glancing at the screen of his phone.

Nolan shakes his head. "Yeah right. They're freaking terrible. Seriously. I've started wearing earplugs so I don't go deaf from the God awful noise they think is music."

"You wear earplugs?" I narrow my eyes at him and put my hands on my hips. "So not fair."

Sage sighs, retrieving a pack of cigarettes from his pocket. "You know, you could still change your mind, Ayden." He pops a cigarette between his lips, cups his hand around his mouth, and lights up.

Nolan perks up, rubbing his hands together. "Yeah, you could always do that. Make our lives easier."

Ayden fiddles with the leather bands on his wrists while staring at the ground. Sensing his uneasiness, I grab his hand. "We need to get home," I tell Sage and Nolan. "See you guys tomorrow."

Their moods deflate as they turn and get into Sage's truck. Ayden and I hop into his car without saying anything and he pulls out onto the busy road. I ignore the headlights of the cop car following us, and instead focus on stroking Ayden's palm during the entire drive to our neighborhood.

'That feels good," he murmurs as he steers the car into our subdivision.

"Yeah?" I brush my fingers across his skin again, tickling him softly.

He nods, his eyelashes fluttering. "It's relaxing."

"Maybe when we get home, I can give you a massage," I tease with a wink.

"Maybe," he says, surprising the crap out of me. He turns his head and our gazes weld. "What?" he asks. "Why are you looking at me like that?"

I keep looking at him the same way. "Looking at you like what?"

"Like you were when you . . ." His Adam's apple bobs up and down as he swallows hard. "Like you were when we were singing."

I rest my head against the seat, keeping my eyes on him. "Maybe because I feel the same way as I did when we were singing."

He grows silent as he turns the car into the driveway of his house. The lights are off, but my house is lit up and music is blaring.

"My mom's having a party," I tell him, unfastening my seatbelt.

"I know," he says, turning off the engine and headlights. "Lila told me about it earlier when she texted me and told me I could either go over to your house and wait for them to get home from Everson's practice. Or I could go inside my house, lock the doors, and set the alarm. But if I did that, I'm supposed to text her and let her know so she could give the police a heads up to keep an extra eye on me."

"How long is everyone going to be gone at practice?"

"At least until ten or so." He shrugs, looking over his shoulder at the police car parked in front of his house. "I guess there's a team barbeque after the practice."

For some insane reason, I think about that silly pamphlet tucked away in my dresser drawer. I don't know why it crosses my mind. Okay, maybe I do. "You want me to go to your house and wait with you? I'm sure my mom won't mind."

He stares at me, deciding his answer, before he unsteadily nods. My heart sprints so insanely I swear he can hear it.

We climb out of the car, meet around front, and link hands as we hike up the driveway. Once we get inside, Ayden texts Lila that he's home then we go up to his room and shut the door.

I turn around and face him, trying to figure out the right thing to say other then, *hey we should get our freak on.* I shake my head at myself. Seriously, I've been listening to Maggie way too much. For all I know, Ayden's thoughts aren't even headed in the same direction as mine.

He sets his guitar case down on the floor then glances around his room. "You want to watch a movie?" he asks me, his cheeks looking flushed.

Okay, so we're definitely not on the same page.

"Sure." I kick off my boots and flop down on his bed, trying to appear more composed than I am. "What are you thinking? Horror? Romance? A comedy? Or Rom Com?" I smirk wickedly, because Ayden hates Rom Coms.

He studies me, touching his fingers to his lips. "I don't know . . . Whatever you want to watch, I guess."

"How about no movies and just . . ." Something about the way he's looking at me, with hunger in his eyes, gives me the courage to get to my feet, walk up to him, and brush my lips against his. I half expect him to pull away—it's always a fifty-fifty chance with him. Instead, he deepens the kiss, groaning as he backs me toward the bed.

"We don't have to do anything if you don't want to," he whispers between our fervent kisses. "I don't want you to feel pressured."

My stomach does a flip as I smile against his lips. "You know I never do anything I don't want to do."

"I know . . . I just want this to . . ." His voice sounds strained. "For you to . . . For this to be perfect for you."

"Trust me. It already is." I collide my lips with his, and the kiss goes from slow and savoring, to reckless and nervous.

We fall clumsily onto the mattress and I giggle as our teeth clank together. He laughs, but the mood instantly turns serious again as he slips his tongue into my mouth.

I whimper as he bites my bottom lip, my back arching as I clutch onto his shirt, pulling him closer. His hands travel all over the outside of my shirt before I move back and pull it off. His fingers slide down my stomach and to the top of my jeans, and he fumbles with the button then the zipper.

By the time he strips me bare, I'm so nervous I'm shaking.

"A-are you sure you're okay?" he asks, his voice wobbly, unsteady, completely Ayden.

I nod, staring up at him. "I don't have anything though . . . Do you?"

He hesitates then gets up and walks to his dresser. When he returns, his shaky hand is carrying a condom.

"When did you get that?" I ask, trying to conceal my laughter over how guilty he looks that he has a condom.

He sighs, dropping the condom onto the bed as his eyes drink in every inch of me. "Lila made Ethan give some to me after they caught us fooling around that one time."

I prop up on my elbows, biting back a smile. "Well, as embarrassing as that must've been for you, I'm glad they did."

"You are?" His question isn't as simple as it sounds.

I nod then sit up and snag the hem of his shirt. He sucks in a sharp breath then raises his hands and lets me tug his shirt over his head. Once I get it off, I chuck it on the floor while he removes his jeans, leaving him only in his boxers. I take in the sight of him as I trace my fingers across his lean, but scarred stomach. I wish I could erase the pain of each one. Wish he never had to go through what he did.

Wish. Wish. Wish.
Wish upon a star.
Wish and wish and wish.
You can spend all your time wishing.
But then you'd be missing out on this moment.

He hooks a finger underneath my chin, bringing my attention to his eyes. He pauses, giving me time to back out. I'm not going to. Now that we're finally here in this moment, I never want to leave it.

"I-I love you." He leans forward and seals his lips to mine.

I love you too.
More than anything, Ayden Gregory.
You are it for me.

CHAPTER 11

I'M TERRIFIED OUT OF MY fucking mind as I put a condom on, lie Lyric down on the bed, and situate myself between her legs. My thoughts are racing a thousand miles a second as I suck in a breath and start to slip inside her. My entire body quivers and it makes me feel pathetically weak. Thankfully, Lyric senses my nearing panic attack.

She cups my cheek. "Look at me," she whispers, steadily carrying my gaze. "We don't have to do this... Not if you're not ready."

"No, I want to. I-I want to be with you," I say, looking into her eyes. "I love you."

"I love you too," she whispers with small, nervous smile.

I take a breath, then another, before moving slowly inside her, not wanting to hurt her, and not wanting to lose it. Because the panic is there under the surface, threatening to take hold of me.

I won't
Let it control me anymore.
This is my life.
This is where I want to be.
Only here.

With her.
As I rock inside her, she holds onto my shoulders, staring up at me with complete trust. It's the most incredible thing I've ever experienced. And, while I'm still scared to death, I feel different. Changed. I never want to allow my fear to make me miss out on any other amazing moments like this. I've spent so much of my life missing out on the good stuff, because I allowed the bad stuff to consume me.
No more.
Time to remove the cuffs from my wrists.
Time to free myself.

AN HOUR LATER, WE'RE LYING in my bed with our legs and arms tangled together. "This is for Keeps" by Spill Canvas is playing from the stereo, which I turned on because Lyric insisted this moment needed a song.

"I like this song," Lyric mutters as she rests her head against the crook of my shoulder.

I play with her hair as I gaze up at the ceiling, replaying what just happened between us. I'm still shocked that I wasn't dragged into an unwanted memory. It almost happened, but all I had to do was look at Lyric and the memory and fear faded.

"Are you sure you're okay?" Lyric props up on her arm and catches my gaze. "You've been really quiet."

"I'm fine." I sweep hair out of her eyes. "More than fine, actually."

She seems slightly insecure over something, which isn't like her. "You don't regret it, right?" she asks.

I swiftly shake my head. "Not at all. What happened . . ." The memory fills my mind of rocking inside her while kissing her deeply. "It was perfect."

"Good." She relaxes. "I need to write a song about this."

"About the first time we had sex?" I squeak, sounding pathetic.

"Don't freak out." She bites back a smile. "I won't use your name."

"It's not my name I'm worried about. I just want to be the only one who gets to see you like that."

"No one will see anything just from a song," she says, highly amused.

"That all depends on how descriptive you are."

"I won't be descriptive. I'll just write about how I feel."

"Which . . . Which is good, right?" I need to know—need to make sure she's okay with that just happened between us.

"Of course. What happened between us . . . It was really, *really* good." Even though she confidently maintains my gaze, a blush creeps across her cheeks. "We do get to do it again, right?"

My own cheeks heat as I nod.

We stare at each other for a heartbeat or two then I lift my head while pulling her against me, so our lips meet halfway. She groans from the connection as I grip her hip and roll her over, covering my body over hers. Right as things start to heat up again, though, my phone rings. I try to ignore it and continue exploring Lyric's mouth and body, but the damn thing won't shut up.

I grunt in frustration as I push back from Lyric.

She giggles as I climb off the bed to dig my phone out of the pocket of my jeans that are balled up on the floor.

"I love when you get frustrated like that," she says. "It's so adorable."

I smile at her as I swipe my finger across the screen.

But when I see I've missed over ten calls from Lila, I frown.

"Shit, it's Lila . . . She's called a lot." I dial her number as I put my boxers on. "She's probably freaking out that I didn't answer."

"Ayden!" Lila cries before I can even get out a hello. "Why haven't you been answering your phone?"

"Sorry, Lyric and I were practicing some of our songs, and I didn't hear it ring," I lie as I pick up my jeans and slip them on.

"I'm just glad you're okay. I was worried sick. I even called the police and told them to check on you, so don't be surprised when the doorbell rings."

Right on cue, the doorbell echoes through the house.

"Who is that?" Lyric wonders as she gets out of bed and starts getting dressed.

I hold up my finger, indicating I'll be right back then I step out into the hallway heading for the stairway. "They just rang the doorbell," I tell Lila. "I'm headed down to tell them I'm okay. I'm really sorry I didn't answer."

"It's okay. It's okay." Her tone carries an edge.

I pause. "Is everything okay?"

She hesitates before she utters, "Ayden, the police found your sister."

A wave of fear and relief rushes through me. "They found her? Where was she? Is she okay?" I struggle to get air into my lungs.

They found her.
But where?
Is she hurt?
Is she . . .

"She's alive," Lila says. "I don't know the exact condition she's in, but you can meet me down at the hospital and we'll find out what's going on."

"Did they arrest anyone?" I can barely hear over my deafening heartbeat. "Did they catch my father?"

"They said they made some arrests, but I don't know all the details. When the detective called, he didn't say much, but I'll get more information from him when we get to the hospital."

"I'll head there right now." I hang up and my legs buckle out from under me.

"Ayden." Lyric appears beside me. Her eyes sweep across me, as if she's checking for visible wounds. "What happened?"

"They found Sadie," I manage to get out.

She kneels down on the floor in front of me, moving slowly, as if she's approaching a skittish cat. "Is she . . . Alive?"

I nod and that's when I lose it.

Sadie is alive.
Sadie is alive.
She made it.
She survived.

I start to cry and Lyric wraps her arms around me and rubs my back.

I cry even harder. For Sadie. For Felix. And for myself. Because for the first time in my life I don't feel so weighed down.

I don't want to think it, because it feels wrong to after spending so much time being chased by the Soulless Mileas, but maybe, just maybe this will finally all be over soon.

CHAPTER 12

"LYRIC, WHY DON'T YOU HELP your dad in the kitchen while I finish saying goodbye to everyone," my mom says to me as I pace the foyer in my house, biting my fingernails.

I distractedly look up at her. "Huh?"

She heaves a sigh as she approaches me. "Honey, I know you're worried about Ayden, but wearing a hole through the floor isn't going to help."

"He said he'd text me and give me an update when he made it to the hospital." I check my phone again and frown when I see I have zero new messages. I wish I could've gone with him, but my mom and Lila didn't think that was a good idea since Ayden's going to be talking with the police. "He left over an hour ago." I tuck my phone away. "He has to be there by now."

"Honey, I'm sure he'll call you as soon as he can." She puts her hands on my shoulders and steers me toward the kitchen. "Now go get your mind off of stuff and help your dad clean up."

I begrudgingly go into the kitchen where my dad, Fiona, Everson, and Kale are cleaning up dirty dishes, food trays, and wine glasses left over from my mom's guests.

Uncle Ethan dropped the three of them off about twenty minutes ago and then headed straight for the hospital. He didn't say much, but I could see the concern on his face when he mentioned needing to get an update on Sadie's condition. I worry how hurt she is. How much they broke her. She's been with them so long . . . God, it's hard to think about the stuff she must have been through.

I begin wandering around the house, picking up stray cups and plates while my mom urges guests toward the front door, trying to get them to leave as quickly as possible without seeming like a total douchebag about it.

"How are you holding up after what happened?" my dad asks as I return to the kitchen with a stack of plates.

"Fine." I set the plates down in the sink. "I'm just worried about Ayden and how he's handling this."

"I'm sure he's fine." He gives my shoulder a squeeze. "He's a strong person."

"Yeah, I guess that's true." I think about all the obstacles Ayden has overcome in his life, including the one I just helped him with only hours ago when we were in his room.

"Why do you look flushed?" My dad questions, studying me closely.

I lean back, hoping to God he can't see the answer on my face. He can barely handle the idea of me having a boyfriend. I can only imagine what he'd do if he found out I just had sex.

"I'm just a little hot. I think I'm going to go turn the air conditioning up." I round the kitchen island, heading for the thermostat in the hallway. When I reach it, I don't turn the air up, since I'm not really that hot.

I slump against the wall and take a minute to collect myself. I'm just about to go back into the kitchen when my phone vibrates. I dig it out of the pocket, so eager to read the message that I drop the phone on the floor.

"Shit." I pick it up and swipe my finger across the screen.

Ayden: Hey, sorry I didn't text u sooner. Things have been crazy.

Me: But she's ok, right? I mean, your sister?

Ayden: I haven't seen her yet . . . I guess she had a broken arm that needed an operation. But the doctors said she should be fine. At least physically.

I squeeze my eyes shut as tears sting my eyes. Poor Sadie. I can't believe people can be so cruel, so brutal, so ugly. The only thing that gets the tears to stop is that I remind myself there's also wonderful, amazing, beautiful stuff in the world. That not everything is bad.

Me: Where did they find her?

Ayden: That's the strange part. She actually showed up at the police station.

Me: What???

Ayden: Yeah, she walked in and said who she was and that they let her go. Then she passed out. I guess the police had just raided the house she was being kept at and someone took off with her before she was found, but then they just dropped her off at the police station . . . It's so weird.

Me: That is really weird. Maybe the person who left her at the police station just panicked or something.

Ayden: Maybe. I don't have all the details yet, but I should be talking to the detective soon. Hopefully, he won't try to pull that secretive shit and keep me in the dark about stuff.

Me: Let me know how it goes. And come see me as soon as you get home. I know it's only been a few hours since you left, but I miss you. I'm seriously going to turn into one of those needy girlfriends.

Ayden: I miss you too. I wish you were here with me. I'd probably be a lot more relaxed.

Me: I can try to relax you when you when you get back.

Ayden: That sounds nice.

Me: Good. It's a date then.

For a split second, everything feels like it's going to be all right. Then another message pings through.

Ayden: I have some bad news, though. The police made a lot of arrests, but as of now, they haven't found my dad.

My fingers constrict around the phone. "Dammit."

Me: What are they going to do?

Ayden: Keep looking for him. And I have to be watched by an officer at all times until they find him.

My head slumps forward. I was so hopeful this was coming to an end, that Ayden was finally safe. But he'll never be until his dad's behind bars.

Me: I'm sorry, Ay. I really am.

Ayden: I hate this.

Me: So do I. But they have to be closer to finding him, right? If they've found all those other people.

Ayden: I hope so . . . I just really want this to all be over.

Me: Me too.

Ayden: I have to go. The detective just showed up. Call u when I'm headed home. I love u.

Me: I love u too.

With a heavy heart, I tuck the phone away and walk into the kitchen. Most of the plates and cups have been picked up and the air smells of lemon cleaner. Kale, Everson, and my dad have wandered off somewhere, but Fiona is at the table, munching on a cupcake.

"He's still sad," she remarks as I join her at the table.

I grab a cupcake off a platter and lick off a bite of frosting. "Who's still sad?"

She plucks a candy off the top of the cupcake and pops it into her mouth. "Ayden."

I peel the wrapper down and take a bite of the cake. "I don't think he's sad. Just stressed out."

"No, he's sad." She sets the cupcake on the table. "He's sad over his sister. And over you."

I freeze, mid bite. "Over me?"

She nods. "He's sad because he thinks he's going to lose you because he can't do stuff with you."

"Did you hear him say that?" I ask, trying not to get wigged out by her matter-of-fact attitude.

She simply shakes her head. "Nope, I felt it."

"You say that a lot. But I'm still not sure what you mean."

"It's hard to explain. And you probably wouldn't believe me if I tried." She sits back in her chair and picks up the cupcake again. "My mom knew about me, though. It's why she gave me up. Because I was a weirdo."

Her words make me pause. I know Fiona's story. Know her mother was a drug addict and Fiona was taken away from her, so I have no idea why she just said what she did.

"Do you want to watch a movie or something?" I ask, hoping to get her mind off stuff.

"Nah, movies are lame." Her mood abruptly lifts. "You want to help me with this art project I'm working on? Maybe we could even get your mom to help with it."

"Sure." I scoot back from the table and stand up. "Just let me go change into my pajamas and then I'll meet you in the living room, okay?'

"Thanks, Lyric. You're the best." She heads for the living room, but stops in the doorway. "You're kind of like the sister I never had. And just think, when you and Ayden get married, you'll be my sister-in-law."

She skips out of the room, leaving me shaking my head.

Marriage. I'm so not ready for that yet. Maybe a ways down the road, in like five or six years. Still, just thinking about the future, the possibilities, gets me excited. I just need Ayden here with me.

When I reach my bedroom. I'm extremely distracted as I slip off my sandals and turn on the light, and it takes me a second to notice something's different about my room. At first, I can't place a finger on what it is, only that I have an uneasy feeling. I glance at the floor, at the window, then the walls. That's when I spot the circular symbol painted just above my bed. The same symbol that the Soulless Mileas tattooed on Ayden's side.

I spin for the door to run downstairs, but crash into a hard, solid object. I trip backwards and open my mouth to scream, but the man I ran into quickly bends down and slaps a hand over my mouth.

"It's so nice to finally meet you, Lyric." A grin spreads

across his face.

Terror whips through me as I note the knife in his other hand, and I mentally calculate what I should do. There's no way I'm just going to give in to whatever he's planning on doing to me; no way I'm going down without a fight. So, I lift my leg to kick him right in the stomach, putting every ounce of strength I have in it.

He curses, falling down on me, and crushing me with his weight. But he recovers quickly and wrestles me to the floor. His hand slips from my mouth as he works to pin me down. I start to scream again, but he moves the knife to my throat.

"Don't give me a reason to kill you," he warns, his eyes darkening. "It would really make me angry, especially since I'm not the one who's supposed to kill you."

I swallow hard and the movement causes the blade to graze my skin.

He assesses me, then stands up, yanking me to my feet with him. Gripping me by the arm, he drags me to the dresser and cranks up the stereo so loudly I can't hear myself think—so loud no one can hear me scream.

"M-my parents are going to hear the music and come up here," I stammer as he grabs me by the hair.

He shakes his head. "You do this enough that they won't even give it a second thought."

Vomit burns at my throat. He's right. I've blasted my music for as long as I can remember, and my parents are so used to it by now that it hardly bothers them. What I don't get, though, is how he knows this.

"We need to get Ayden here," he says loudly over the music. "He's the one who's supposed to be doing this. He's the one who needs his soul cleansed."

I'm not quite sure what he's talking about, but I'm guessing it has to do with the Soulless Mileas and their ritual. My adrenaline skyrockets as panic sets in. *I need to get out of here. Now! Figure out a way, Lyric!*

"I have an idea," the man says thoughtfully as he backs me into the wall and lines the knife with my throat again. "Do you have your phone on you?"

Every instinct I have tells me to lie, so I shake my head.

His eyes darken and he roughly sticks his hand into my pocket and grabs my phone. A smile curls at his lips as he scrolls through my contacts and presses a few buttons.

While he's not paying attention, I seize the opportunity, bring my leg up, and knee him in the balls. He hunches over, gasping for air.

I bolt for the door, opening my mouth, "Help—"

I'm slammed from behind and shoved to the floor. I land hard on my face, but promptly flip over onto my back. The man jumps on me, his knee connecting with my stomach.

I gasp as the wind is knocked out of me.

"I guess it's going to be me, then." He pins my arms to the floor then raises his knife above his head.

I kick him again, refusing to give in, as I open my mouth to scream, praying someone will hear me.

CHAPTER 13

I'M STANDING IN THE BUSY waiting room of the hospital, waiting for my sister to get out of surgery while listening to Detective Rannali give me an update on what they're doing to find my father, when I get a text.

> Lyric: I have her. It's time to cleanse your soul, Ayden. And u better be a good son and come alone.

It feels like a knife has been gashed into my heart, and I'm bleeding out from the inside. I can't breathe. Can't get oxygen into my lungs as I painfully realize what the note left in Lyric's locker meant.

"Ayden, what's wrong?" Lila jumps up from the chair she's sitting in and rushes to me.

"My dad . . . He has Lyric," I croak as I hand her my phone.

She reads the message and her skin drains of color. "Oh God. This can't be happening. No . . . no . . . no . . ."

Detective Rannali grabs the phone from Lila. "What's going . . ." He trails off as he reads the message. "Shit."

I spin around, pushing people out of my way as I run for the exit doors.

"Ayden! Wait!" Lila chases after me with Ethan tailing

at her heels. "You can't go anywhere by yourself!"

I whirl around. "They have Lyric, Lila. I have to find her." I start to turn around, heading for the parking lot.

Her fingers fold around my arm and she forces me to stop. "We don't even know where she is."

"Then we have to find out—we have to find her." Reality crashes over me and I almost collapse to the ground.

God, please don't let him hurt her.
I don't know what I'd do if I lost her.
I'd crumple into dirt.
Disappear into an eternity of darkness.
Fade away into nothing.
I don't care if it makes me seem weak.
Just thinking about living without her.
It's killing me.

"We'll find her." Lila guides me back toward the doors. "But we need to be safe about it."

Ethan walks on the other side, staying close, like he's afraid I'm going to try to run off again. I want to. Want to get the hell out of here and find Lyric. No, not want. *Need.*

By the time we return to the waiting room, Detective Rannali has phoned in the report and is ready to take off somewhere.

"I need to call Micha and Ella," Lila mutters, staring into empty space, her eyes wide with fear. "Oh my God, what am I supposed to say to them?"

"I can do it," Ethan offers, retrieving his phone from his pocket.

"The Scotts are already informed of what's going on," Detective Rannali tells us as he picks up his suit jacket from a chair and slips it on.

"How were they already informed?" I match his stride as he takes off for the exit. "Did you just call them? What did they say?"

"They called the station about five minutes ago and reported a break in at their house," he says as the doors glide open. "I'm headed to their house now."

"Do you . . . Do know if Lyric's okay?" I ask as we step outside and head for his car.

"I'm not sure. I think they're still trying to detain the person who broke in."

"It's my dad." I smash my lips together as guilt crushes my chest. "The text said son."

He slams to a halt in the middle of the parking lot. "Ayden, you should probably stay here and wait for Sadie to get out of surgery."

I shake my head. "There is no fucking way I'm going to stay here until I know Lyric's okay." I want to be here for my sister, but I'll be useless until I'm one hundred percent certain Lyric's okay. "Lila and Ethan can stay here just in case she gets out before I get back. I *need* to go with you." More than I've ever needed anything in my entire life.

Detective Rannali glances back at the hospital, then sighs. "Fine, you can ride with me."

THE DRIVE TO LYRIC'S HOUSE is long and painful. I'm so wound up that I half expect my heart to give out on the way there.

When we pull up into the neighborhood, flashing red and blue lights are lighting up the entire block.

Detective Rannali parks the car as close to the house as he can get, then he turns off the engine and reaches for the door. "Stay here until—"

I barrel out of the car before he can finish.

"Ayden, wait!" Detective Rannali shouts after me as I run for Lyric's house.

I weave past cop cars and neighbors who've gathered around to watch the scene. Officers have formed a small line and are trying to keep everyone back, so I veer left and duck through an unguarded area near the fence line.

I'm not sure where to go, so I head for the back door. Right as I reach the steps, two officers exit the house, hauling out a middle-aged man in handcuffs.

He has the same eyes and hair color as me, his face recognizable from the memory. "Let me go. I didn't do anything wrong," he spats to the officers. "You're the ones who are wrong, for stopping me." He's walking awkwardly, like it's painful to move his legs, and his face and eyes are swollen, like someone beat the crap out of him.

I grind to a halt as fear and rage storm through me. "Where is she?" I growl.

"Kid, you can't be here," one of officers warns me, gently pushing me to stay back.

I follow them as they drag my father down the driveway and to a police vehicle. "You better not have done anything to her!" I shout.

"I was never planning on doing anything to her. It was supposed to be you. Your soul needs the cleansing. Not mine. I've cleansed my soul many, many times." His smile expands as he ducks his head and the officer forces him into the backseat. "I thought you could use Sadie. That her death could cleanse her soul, but then I heard you and Lyric say you loved each other for the first time, and I knew Sadie couldn't be your sacrifice. It had to be Lyric."

I fucking hate hearing him say her name, but taking in his words is even worse. The only way he could've heard Lyric and I say I love you for the first time is if he was either in the bedroom with us, or he bugged the room. Either option is equally as sickening, and it takes every ounce of strength I possess not to push the officers out of the way and strangle him.

"You're so fucked up," I snap, moving back as an officer steps in front of me and blocks my way.

"You need to keep back," the officer warns, steering me away from the car.

"You're part of me," my dad calls out. "And don't you ever—"

The officer slams the car door, locking my dad in the backseat. I stare at him for a second or two longer before I turn my back on him and start searching for Lyric.

I'm an erratic mess of nerves and anxiety by the time I find her parents standing near the back of an ambulance, staring inside, looking sick to death. Terror crashes through me as I run toward them and look inside the ambulance.

Lyric is inside, sitting on a stretcher, being examined by an EMT. When she sees me, her eyes light up, and she leaps to her feet, ignoring the EMT's protests.

"I've never been so glad to see you in my life," she says as she jumps into my arms and wraps her legs around me.

"Tell me you're okay," I beg as I clutch onto her for dear life.

She leans back to look me in the eye. "I'm fine. Just a few scratches, but it's mostly just carpet burn."

I carefully set her down, but only so I can examine every inch of her. She might have said she was okay, but I need to be absolutely certain. I don't see any wounds other than a few scrapes on her legs. Her eyes are a bit swollen, but I think that might be from crying.

"Ayden, relax." Her fingers caress my cheek, bringing my attention to her eyes. "I'm fine. I swear."

"What happened?" I swallow hard, my voice thick with emotion.

My body starts to shake

Breathing in her words.
The truth is potent.
The truth is raw.
The truth is real.
That I could have lost her.

She sighs exhaustedly. "He snuck into my room, used my phone to text you, then I kicked the crap out of him until he let me go. I think he had bigger plans, but after about ten kicks to the balls, he could barely breathe. Then my dad came in and beat the shit out of him . . ." Her muscles stiffen and her voice drops to a whisper. "For a second, I was worried he wasn't going to stop . . . That my dad was going to kill him."

A sick, twisted part of me wishes that had happened. But the last thing I want is for Lyric's dad to have blood on his hands.

"You're so fucking strong," I whisper, on the verge of sobbing. "And I'm so sorry you had to go through that— through any of this."

"Don't be sorry," she says firmly. "Just be glad, okay. That's all you need to be right now."

"About what?"

"That it's over."

It takes a moment for the full impact of her words to sink in. Then I pull her against me, promising myself I'll never let her go again.

CHAPTER 14

AFTER MY FATHER IS ARRESTED, the police spend the next day ransacking the Scott's and my house for any hidden cameras and recording devices. They find a few in Lyric's room and in my room. The idea that he was watching us makes me sick to my stomach, but like with everything else, it's something I just have to work on getting past.

As the rest of the week goes by, things slowly start to return to normal. Lyric and I spend most of our time attached at the hip, working on songs and simply relaxing, something we haven't been able to do in a while.

"You're staring again," she says to me while we're lounging around in her bed.

Her shirt is rolled up and her long legs are tangled with mine as we work on a new song. A little Nirvana is playing from the stereo, which brings back memories of the first day I met her. We also have all the windows open, mostly because we feel safe enough to have them open, and a warm summer breeze is blowing into the room.

"I'm sorry," I say, sounding very unapologetic. "I guess it's the song. It reminds me of the first day I met you and how I couldn't stop staring."

Her lips twitch with amusement. "Aw, the staring days. How can I forget those?"

"I was such a weirdo. Who knows why you became friends with me."

"Um, hello, because I'm a weirdo too. And as a fellow weirdo, your weirdoness barely fazed me."

I chuckle. "Well, I'm glad."

We grow quiet as we listen to the song, and my thoughts drift to everything that's happened over the last couple of years.

So much bad has existed in my life, yet there's been so much good stuff. Sometimes I got so lost in the bad that I couldn't see all the good, but I don't want that to be the case anymore. I want to experience my life. Breathe in every good moment.

"Tell me what you're thinking," Lyric whispers as she scoots closer to me.

"I'm thinking about how much you mean to me and how great you've made my life." I set down the pen I'm holding so I can drape my arm over her side. "And how I never want to lose you. How I want to spend the rest of my life experiencing good stuff with you to make up for all the bad things we've been through."

She chews on the end of her pen, a pucker forming between her brows. "That sounds nice. Really, really nice. And I hope it happens. I hope we get to spend a lot of time with each other doing all sorts of crazy things."

"It'll definitely happen." I smooth my thumb between her brows. "What's with the worried look?"

Hesitancy masks her expression. "I was thinking about your sister, actually... You're going to see her today, right?"

I nod, glancing at the clock. "I'll probably have to leave pretty soon."

I've visited Sadie a couple of times over the last few

days, but every time I go there, she's asleep. The doctors say she doesn't sleep very well, so no one's supposed to disturb her when she's out.

Lyric sits up, pulling me with her, then crisscrosses her legs. "Do you know what you're going to say to her if you get to talk to her today?"

I shake my head, closing my notebook. "I've gone over it in my head for years, what it was going to be like when I saw her again. I just never pictured it being in this kind of situation."

"I'm sure you'll do great." She gives my hand a reassuring squeeze. "And I think Sadie will probably just be happy to see you."

"But what if she's not?" I whisper. "What if she blames me for not finding her?"

"That's not going to happen, because it's not true. What happened wasn't your fault. It was *those people*." Her expression hardens.

"It might not be my fault, but I promised her I'd find her, and the fact that I didn't feels like I failed her somehow."

"You didn't fail anyone." She yawns. "And I have a feeling Sadie is going to agree with me."

"That's because you're an optimist." I laugh at her as she yawns again. "What's up, sleepy head?" I suddenly grow worried. "Wait, have you been having trouble sleeping?"

She stretches her arms above her head, her back arching. "No. I've been staying up late working on some new songs. I know it's morbidly twisted, but after everything that happened, my creativity sparked a freaking ton. I have so many ideas sloshing around in my brain that I don't even know what to do with it." She lowers her hand to her lap. "You want to read the song I wrote about that one night?"

"About the night my dad broke in?" I ask warily.

She shakes her head. "No, about the first time we had sex."

My body ignites with desire and need as I remember that night and the other nights we've spent together since.

"Hey, don't give me that look; otherwise I might start kissing you and we know where that leads." She points her finger at the open door. "And as much as I want things to lead in that direction, both of our parents are downstairs." She grins. "However, if you want, I can totally get some alone time later."

Just thinking about being alone with her causes my pulse to throb. "I definitely want that."

"Good." She leans in and brushes her lips against mine. "Now, do you want to read my song?"

I steal another kiss. "Of course."

Grinning from ear to ear, she flips open her notebook and sets it on my lap, pointing at which page to read.

Our bodies wind
Creating the perfect song
As your lips fuse to mine.
I could do this all night long.
Lie here
Tangled up with you.

So closely
No one will know
Where you start
And where I end.

My heart is pounding
With every stolen kiss
My mind is racing

Longing for a wish
That we could stay like this.
Always.

So closely
No one will know
Where you start
And where I end.

This moment with you,
God it's branded in my mind.
I want to keep it forever
Trap it inside
So it'll always be mine.
Forever.

So closely
No one will know
Where you start
And where I end.

"I want to sing it one day during a concert," she announces after I'm done reading it. "I won't do it, though, unless you promise to sing it with me."

I think she might be secretly asking a question without actually having to say it aloud. But I can't promise her I'll go on the tour yet. Not until I find out what's going to happen with Sadie. As of now, I have no clue what kind of condition she's in, and she doesn't even have a place to live. And I need to be here for her while all that is out.

"Maybe one day we can sing it," I say, shutting the notebook.

"Okay. Just as long as it definitely happens." She tries not to frown. "Tonight we're playing at my dad's club with a guy that Sage wants to be our new guitarist. You should come so you can see how bad we suck. Maybe you can give him a few pointers."

I can't contain my laughter.

"Hey, I'm not trying to be funny." She playfully pinches my side.

"I know you're not." My laughter dies down. "It's just the first time I've seen you be so pessimistic about something."

"Music is my life, and so is the band," she tells me. "And this guy makes us look like amateurs. We're going to be booed off the stage."

"I'm sure that won't happen."

"At least promise you'll be there tonight in case it does, so I can have a shoulder to cry on."

"Okay, I'll be there." I don't believe for a second that they'll be booed off stage, but if she needs me to be there then I will.

"Now kiss me, before you have to leave," Lyric demands, leaning in.

We steal a few more kisses before Lila shouts up the stairs that it's time to go.

"See you tonight," I tell Lyric as I collect my stuff and climb off the bed.

She nods, her lips swollen from my kisses. "Text me if you need anything. Even if it's just to talk."

I promise her I will, then I meet Lila and Ethan downstairs and we head out to the car.

On the way to the hospital, Lila asks me at least ten times how I'm doing. Like always, I tell her that I'm okay, but this time, I actually am. Yeah, I still have nightmares sometimes and there are moments when I cry, mostly when I think about my brother's death and Sadie in the hospital. Even my mother's death gets to me. But for the first time in my life, I actually feel free from the past now that it's behind bars. There are tons of charges against the people who tortured my siblings and me; charges ranging from murder to kidnapping. Detective Rannali assures me they have a solid case, which should keep my father and his followers there for a very long time.

"Ayden, we wanted to talk to you about something before we go in," Lila says to me after she parks the car in the hospital parking lot.

It's midday and the sun shines through the windows, heating up the car the moment she turns off the engine.

"What's up?" I ask, confused by how nervous she seems.

She trades a look with Ethan, and he twists around in the passenger seat to look at me,

"It's about your sister," he says to me. "And her coming to stay with us after she's released from the hospital."

"Detective Rannali was the one who suggested it," Lila explains, unbuckling her seatbelt. "But Ethan and I had already talked about it . . . I know she's seventeen and is almost a legal adult, but with everything she's been through . . ." She smashes her lips together, fighting back the tears. "We just thought it'd be nice if she had a place to call home."

Even though I try to fight them back, a few tears manage to escape my eyes. I want to say so much to them. Thank them for everything, for giving me a home, for not giving up on me when things got hard. For giving me a family. But I'm so choked up, I can only manage a nod as I scoot forward and wrap an arm around her.

She gasps in shock, because I normally don't hug.

"Thank you." I suck back the tears. "And I mean that. Thank you for everything."

"You don't need to thank us for anything," she says.

"You're our son, and we'll always be here for you."

We hug for a second longer before I move away. I clear my throat a few times and reach for the door to get out of the car.

As we walk into the hospital and toward Sadie's room, I go over in my head what I'll say to her if she's awake. It'll be the first time I've talked to her in almost five years and for some of those years, she was locked up in a house with people who tortured her. I worry there won't be any of that spunky, lively, carefree sister that I grew up with, and I won't have a damn clue what to say to her.

"Oh my goodness, she's awake," Lila says after she peers into Sadie's room. She steps back and turns to me. "We'll let you go in first and talk to her, okay? So we don't overwhelm her."

Nodding, I take a breath and step inside.

Sadie is sitting in the bed when I enter, staring out the window with a strange look on her face, like she's deeply contemplating something. She must hear me walk in, because she turns her head and looks over her shoulder at me.

We both freeze and just stare at each other.

She looks different, yet the same; her brown hair is still long and her face is covered with freckles. But there's a cast on her arm and a scar on her cheek, remnants that she's not the same Sadie I knew five years ago. That she's been beaten and tortured and God knows what else.

After a second or two goes by, I open my mouth to ask her if she knows who I am, but then she's already running to me.

"Oh my God, I thought I was never going to see you again," she cries as she wraps her good arm around me.

I start crying again, and it's ridiculously embarrassing. I seriously need to get a grip on myself. But the fact that she's here and alive, it's so fucking overwhelming I can't stop the tears from flowing.

She trembles as she hugs me, and I can sense that fear inside her, the fear of being touched. But she must be stronger than I was, because she keeps holding onto me.

"I'm so sorry," I say through my tears.

She shuffles back, giving me a quizzical look. "Sorry for what?"

"For not finding you." I wipe tears from my cheeks with the sleeve of my shirt. "I tried. I tried so fucking much, but no matter what I did, it all led to a dead end."

Her eyes pool with tears. "You didn't find me because they didn't want you to find me. There was nothing you could've done. As long as our . . ." Anger and fear flash in her eyes and her hands tremble as she balls them into fists. "As long as *he* wanted me there, I was always going to be there."

"How long . . ." I breathe in and out, trying to keep myself from crying again. "How long were you there?"

She turns her back to me, wrapping her arms around herself. "Ayden, I don't want to talk about this." She climbs back onto the bed with her feet dangling over the edge. "I've spent too much of my life surrounded by this shit, and now that I've finally gotten out, everyone just wants me to sit around and talk about what happened. I don't want to. All I want to do is forget about everything."

"I get what you're saying." I pull a chair up and sit down. "I forgot about what happened to us for a while and thought it was easier that way."

"You forgot?" she asks, her eyes widening. "Really?"

I nod. "Up until a few weeks ago, I couldn't remember any of the time we were in that house together."

"You're lucky then," she mutters, her shoulders slumping.

"I'm not so sure about that," I mumble. When she gives

me a confounded look, I add, "I couldn't remember because I was repressing everything, but it wasn't healthy."

"So you're saying you're happier now that you can remember?" she asks, confused.

"I still can't remember everything now, but what I did remember helped them track the people down." I slant forward in the chair and rest my arms on my knees. "I've learned over the past couple of years that running away from your feelings only allows them to grow and feed off you, and eventually they'll nearly kill you if you don't learn to deal with them."

"You sound just like I remember," she says softly, almost smiling. "You always had a poetic way of saying things."

"I did?"

She nods. "You did. It was always fun listening to you talk when you got really passionate about something."

"I'm glad there were fun times . . . Sometimes when I look back at the past, all I can see is darkness."

"There were a few good times I can remember . . ." She trails off as she scoots back in the bed and rests against a pillow.

"Are you tired?" I ask, getting ready to stand up and leave. "Maybe I should let you sleep."

She shakes her head and motions for me to sit down. "I don't want to be alone. But I don't want to talk about the past right now. I know you say it's not healthy, but I just can't yet, okay?"

If that's what she wants, then that's what I'll give her. "What do you want to talk about then?"

"You." A trace of a smile rises on her face, but pain and fear haunts her eyes. "I want to hear all about your happy new life."

"How do you know it's been happy?" I wonder

curiously.

"Because I can see it in your eyes," she says with a shrug.

"It hasn't always been that way, though."

"Then start from where it does get happy."

I rack my mind for the moment in my life where things turned around for me, where happiness felt within reach. "Well, I was adopted by this really amazing family," I say with a smile as I remember the day the Gregorys brought me home.

"Oh yeah?" She rotates on her side, cradling her casted arm. "Are they the ones who keep peeking through the doorway?"

I glance over my shoulder right as Lila walks by, trying to look casual as can be. I chuckle under my breath, turning back to Sadie. "That's Lila . . . My mom, I guess." It's strange to say that to Sadie, to call someone else other than our real mother my mom.

"She seems worried about you," she says. "She's walked past the room about a thousand times."

"That's just how she is." I pause, debating whether to tell her what Lila and Ethan told me in the car. "They want you to come live with us."

Her brows shoot up. "*What*? They can't . . . There's no way they'd want . . ." Her eyes water up again.

My heart aches at her self-doubt, the feeling of unworthiness of having something good.

"I think you should live with them," I tell her. "They're really nice people who'll help you get through this."

"Did they . . . Did they help you?"

"They did," I say. "And so did Lyric."

Her forehead creases. "Who's Lyric?"

How do I even begin to explain who Lyric is? The girl I'm in love with? No, she's more than that. Way, way more.

Not knowing how else to explain it to her, I start from the beginning, telling her about my journey with the Gregorys and how I fell in love with my best friend.

"So . . . you're in love?" Sadie asks after I'm finished.

I nod, fiddling with the leather band Lyric gave me. "I am."

She blinks, trying to hold the tears back, but they pour out of her eyes. "I'm so happy for you. I really, really am. I was so worried that maybe we both ended up broken and ruined but . . . Seeing you like this . . ."

I scoot forward in the chair and place an unsteady hand over hers. "I'm sorry. I didn't mean to make you cry."

"No, it's fine. I'm glad you did . . . And I'm glad you fell in love." She sniffles. "It gives me hope that maybe I'm not completely broken . . . That if you can make it, maybe . . . Maybe I can too."

It takes all I have in me not to break down and sob. "Sadie, you're going to make it. I swear to God you will. And I'll be there for you."

She cries for another minute or two before she pulls it together. "I don't want to cry anymore. Please, Ayden, tell me something that won't make me cry . . . Tell me more about your family . . . And Lyric . . . And this band and the tour . . . It all sounds so great." She sniffles as she dries her tears with the back of her hand. "I can't believe you ended up being musically talented. I remember when you tried learning how to play the flute. You sucked."

"Hey, I was eight," I protest. "And the only lessons I had were from Mr. Grangering. You remember him?"

"That grumpy old man that had a lot of cats," she says, nodding. "I didn't know he gave you lessons."

"The lessons really weren't that great since he got the harmonica confused with the flute. You should've seen him try to play it."

She laughs softly, but then her expression instantly plummets as terror flashes through her eyes. "I've always wanted to learn how to play the guitar . . . I thought about it a lot while I was . . . But I didn't think I'd ever be able to . . . Get the chance to."

"I can teach you," I offer.

"That would be amazing." She tries to smile but instantly frowns.

"Lyric can teach you how to play too," I offer, trying to keep the conversation going so she'll stay distracted from her thoughts. "She's actually just as good as me. Maybe even better."

"I want to hear her sing," she says. "When you were talking about it, all this excitement was in your eyes and I want to feel that excitement too."

"I'm sure there'll be plenty of chances for you to hear her."

"Maybe when you're on this tour thingy, I can go watch one of your concerts." Self-doubt seizes her expression as she grips onto the blanket for dear life. "W-well, just as long as I can stand backstage. I-I don't think I can stand being out in a crowd."

I completely understand where she's coming from. I remember the first concert I went to and how terrifying it was being in the crowd. Thankfully, Lyric was there with me and calmed me down.

"I'm not sure I'm going on the tour . . . I'm still deciding," I offer her a reassuring smile. "But you can definitely watch me play sometime."

"It's not because of me, is it?" she asks worriedly.

Not wanting to make her feel guilty over anything, I choose my next words carefully. "No, there's just some other stuff I need to do right now."

She shakes her head. "Ayden, please don't stop living

your life because of me. I'm so jealous of what you have, and I'd die if I knew I ruined stuff for you."

"You're not ruining—"

She cuts me off, clutching onto my hand in desperation. "Promise me you won't. Promise me you won't change your life because I'm here now. I don't want you to do that."

"But I want to be there for you," I say, choking up. "I don't want you to go through this alone."

"I'm not telling you not to be there for me. I-I'm just telling you to live your life. We were given a second chance, so promise me you'll do everything you want to do. That you'll be happy."

"I'll promise to if you promise to."

"I'll try," she whispers. "I'm not going to let them break me."

She's stronger than I expected, but I can still see pain hidden under the strength, the internal battle trying to consume her. And I need to be there for her, to make sure it never completely takes hold.

I SPEND THE NEXT HOUR telling Sadie about my life, because she doesn't want to discuss anything else. Then Lila and Ethan come in and introduce themselves. Sadie seems skittish around them and acts even more erratic when a nurse comes in to do a check up on her and to tell us visiting hours are over.

"Remember what you promised," Sadie says to me as I'm walking out of the room.

I turn around and nod. "Just as long as you remember too."

She smashes her quivering lips together and nods

before inching away from the nurse.

I hate leaving her alone, but she has to stay at the hospital for a few more days until she's made a full recovery.

Lila, Ethan, and I leave the hospital in silence. By the time we get to the car, it's late and the stars and moon are shining in the sky. Even though I might not make it in time, I ask Lila to drive me to Infinite Bliss so I can try to catch my band perform with their new guitarist.

As we make the drive across town, Sadie's words replay in my mind, the promise to be happy and live life. I know what that means, what makes me happy, but I want to be here for Sadie too and help her through what I know is going to be a hard time. Maybe, though, there's a way to do both.

"I have a favor to ask you guys," I say to Lila and Ethan before we climb out of the car to go inside the club.

"You can ask us anything," Lila reminds me as she shuts off the headlights. "Well, within reason of our capabilities."

I nervously explain my idea to them and then hold my breath as I wait for their answer. Is this a good idea? Is this really what I should do? I don't know if it is or not, but I guess I'm doing it.

Ethan glances at Lila with his brow raised. "What do you think?"

She shrugs then smiles. "I think he deserves it."

"All right, Ayden, you have yourself a deal," Ethan tells me with a grin. "Man, I'm so jealous. I've always wanted to go on a tour."

"Why didn't you?" I ask as I reach for the door handle.

"Because he hates crowds," Lila answers for him.

Ethan gives a shrug. "It's true. I never could get past all those damn people crammed into a room, sweating all over each other."

His statement does not surprise me, and honestly, I

kind of understand where he's coming from.

"Thank you for letting me do this," I say, opening the door.

"You deserve it," Lila replies as she collects her purse from the console. "Like I said, we'll always be here to help you. Don't ever forget that."

I have a smile on my face as I get out of the car, practically running as I head to tell Lyric the news.

CHAPTER 15

I TRY NOT TO POUT that Ayden missed the set, but I'm a tad bit sulky. I know he had a good reason for not showing up, though. That more than likely his sister was awake and the two of them are talking. I hope everything went okay. That Sadie's doing okay. That Ayden's doing okay with the guilt I know he feels over what happened to her.

I dig out my phone, deciding to text him.

> Me: Hey! Just wanted to c how everything was going. I'm guessing that your sister was awake this time?

He doesn't answer right away, so I put the phone into my pocket and head out of the backstage area and down to the floor. It's Friday night and the place is crammed with rowdy drunk people, dancing around, throwing back shots, and ordering drinks at the bar. We were the only live band playing tonight, so my dad has cranked up the music.

"Are you sure you just don't want to go home?" My dad shouts over the music as he struggles with whether or not to leave me out here alone. Ever since the thing with Ayden's dad happened, my mom and dad have been overly protective of me. I was actually worried they were going to try to stop me from going on tour. While they do seem a little more hesitant than they did before, they haven't tried to talk me out it. "Or I could stay out here with you and hang out?"

"I'm fine." I wave him off. "Go back to your office. I'm probably going to head home soon."

The bartender hands him a beer and my dad pops off the top. "Maybe you should come hang out with me."

"Dad, you have a meeting with the new band filling in for us," I remind him, dabbing my fingers under my eyes to fix my eyeliner that I know is smudged—it always is after I finish performing. "I probably shouldn't be in there while you guys discuss business."

"We could pretend you're my secretary," he suggests, checking the time on his watch.

"Dad, go, or you're going to be late." I shoo him toward the hallway. "I'll head home as soon as mom gets back from work." So I don't have to be in the house alone.

While Ayden's dad and many other members of the Soulless Mileas were arrested last week, I still feel unsettled, especially when I'm home alone. I went to a therapist the other day to talk, and I realized I might be more affected by what happened than I originally let on. The therapist told me we could have phone appointments while I'm on the road if I wanted to, and I agreed, just to make sure that the fear I feel will eventually fade and won't take control of my life.

After I finally convince my dad back to go to his office, I chill out on the balcony near the dance floor, trying to decide whether I want to dance yet or wait until I hear back from Ayden before I really let loose. Because I fully plan on dancing. Need to for the sake of my sanity.

"In just over a couple of weeks, we'll be on the road," Sage announces as he walks up to me. He's carrying a beer, and he has a dopey smile on his face, which probably means he's high. "Seriously, Lyric, why don't you look more excited?"

"I'm excited," I assure him, turning and resting my elbows on the railing. "I'm just thinking about some stuff. That's all."

Sage takes a swig of his beer then leans against the railing, staring at our new guitarist who's flirting with a woman twice his age. "Yeah, right. You're so full of shit. I know it's because Ayden's not here."

Not wanting to talk about Ayden not being part of the band anymore, I point at the beer in his hand. "Dude, you know you can't drink that in front of my dad. He's chill, but not that chill."

"I'll put it down if he comes over," he says, taking another sip. Then he turns to me, appearing hesitant. "You know everything's going to be okay, right? We didn't sound as bad as I thought we would."

"I know we didn't. In fact, with a little more practice, I think we're going to be able to rock it."

"Good, because I'm worried about you. You've been distant lately." He picks at the label on the beer bottle. "I'm worried you might change your mind at the last second and not go on this tour. And I know something's going on with Ayden. You guys are always acting strange, and I saw him talking to a police officer at school the other day."

"Sage, I'm not going to change my mind about the tour. I might be bummed Ayden isn't coming, but this has been my dream since I was like five years old and my dad taught me how to play the guitar." I shift my weight and tuck a few strands of my hair behind my ear, trying to figure out what to tell him about Ayden. "As for Ayden, you'll have to ask him what's going on. It's not my story to tell."

"Yeah, I guess I get that." He backs up toward the dance floor. "I'm going to go celebrate the beginning of what is going to be a fucking awesome journey. You should join me."

"I will in just a bit," I promise him. "I could use a fun distraction."

He grins then whirls around and dives into the mob.

I start to head for the bar to get a drink of water when my phone vibrates from my pocket. I fish it out and inch to the side of the room where it's a bit less grind-up-on-each-other so I can read the message.

> *Ayden: Yep. She was awake. Sorry I missed the band play. I just got so caught up in talking to Sadie. And I really didn't want to leave.*
>
> *Me: Don't apologize. U should be there with her.*
>
> *Ayden: Well, I'm not there right now. The nurse kicked us out because visiting hours were over and Sadie needed to rest.*
>
> *Me: R U home? I'll head there if you are.*

"Actually, I'm here." Ayden's voice sails over my shoulder.

A huge smile plasters across my face as I spin around and loop my arms around him. "Tell me how it went. I want to hear everything."

"I will, but let's go sit down," he says, brushing his lips across my cheek.

When I pull back, he places a hand on the small of my back and steers me toward the bar. We take a seat near the end where there are fewer people and the music isn't so loud. While Ayden asks the bartender for two cups of water, I seize the opportunity to study him, trying to determine if he looks upset or not. He actually looks pretty content, so I'm hoping the visit with his sister went well.

"I'm going to tell you what happened," he says, as if he reads my mind. "But there's something else I need to tell you first."

I pick up the glass of water the bartender sets down in front of me. "Should I be worried?"

He shakes his head, brushing a few strands of his dark hair out of his eyes. "This is actually a good thing."

"Okay." The silence is maddening as I wait for him to explain. "Ayden, please, pretty please with a cherry on top, tell me what's going on. The anticipation and build up is killing me."

He chuckles, so enjoying the slow torture he's putting me through. "Fine, but only because you pretty pleased." His fingers wrap around the glass of water, and he takes a sip before he says, "I'm going on the tour. Well, as long as you guys will take me back."

"Of course we'll take you back! I've never been so happy in my life!" I shout then roll my eyes at myself. "Well, okay, that might be a tad bit dramatic, but whatever. I'm super excited!"

He busts up laughing but then grows solemn. "I'm not going to be there the entire time. Well, I will for most of the performances, but I'm going to fly and drive back home whenever I can so I can spend time with Sadie."

"That's okay. You should spend time with her." Unable to contain my excitement, I jump onto his lap. "I'm just glad you're going."

"I am too." His hand slips around my back and urges me closer.

"You're doing this because you want to, though, right?" I ask. "Not just to make me happy. I know I've been a little whiney about you not going, but I never want you to do something you don't want to do."

"I want to go. I love playing my guitar. Plus, this is a

once in a lifetime opportunity I don't want to miss out on," he says. "But I'd be lying if I didn't say that part of the reason I want to go so badly is because of you. I can't be away from you for that long. And I want to be there for you, like all the times you've been there for me."

I lean back, looking him in the eyes. "I can totally accept that answer."

"Good," he says, then casts a glance over his shoulder toward the dance floor where Sage is jumping up around and failing his hands in the air. Then he looks over at Nolan just down the bar from us, chatting with a couple of girls. "I should probably go ask Sage and Nolan if they're cool with this. You guys did find a replacement, right?"

"But we never promised him he could go on the tour with us. Tonight was like a try out." I hop off his lap and tug him to his feet. "Trust me. They're going to be stoked you're coming." I pause before I drag him over to Sage. "Everything was okay with Sadie, though, right? I mean, as okay as anything can be in that kind of situation."

He wavers, biting on his bottom lip. "I think she's okay. Not great. I mean, I talked to her for hours, which has to mean something. But I could see the fear in her eyes, and she was really nervous around other people." He massages his chest with his hand like his heart literally aches for her. "She reminds me a lot of myself three or four years ago . . . And she refused to talk about anything other than me and my life . . . I worry she won't be able to recover from this if she doesn't deal with stuff."

"Ayden, I'm so sorry. I know it has to be hard for you to see her like that." And poor Sadie for having to go through what she has. It's such a horrible thing and I want to help her so much. Maybe I can. Maybe Ayden and I can help her get through this. "But look at you. You've changed so much since you first showed up at the Gregorys' house. If you can overcome it, I think she might be able to also."

"I just wish she didn't have such a difficult time ahead of her," he whispers, his beautiful eyes glossy with impending tears. "I think that's what makes this so hard. Me knowing how difficult it's going to be for her to heal. "

"I know . . . But we can be there for her. You and I . . . I want to help."

"I know you do, and I want you to help. She could use a friend like you even if she might not act like she does."

A smile tugs at my lips. "You mean like how you needed me?"

He nods, smoothing his thumb across my skin before he cups my cheek. "Lyric, there aren't even words to describe how lucky I am to have you in my life . . . If it wouldn't have been for you and your insane need to make me happy . . . I'm not sure I would even be here." He crushes me against his chest, hugging me tightly.

We stay that way for at least a full song, hugging each other, savoring the moment we could've very well never had. It's such a simple thing, a hug, just arms around each other, lungs breathing, hearts beating, two people standing in the middle of tons of other people all having their own experiences. But the moment feels so epically important to me, like this is the start to something bigger—a starting point to a long, twisty, but very exciting road.

I tip my head back to meet his eyes. "How about we go celebrate this ever so amazing time we have together by telling Sage and Nolan that you're back in the band? And then we can all celebrate."

"I'm just crossing my fingers they'll want to celebrate," he says as he follows me toward the dance floor.

I end up being right. Sage and Nolan are more than thrilled to have Ayden back in the band. Sage even does his celebration dance, which basically means he makes an ass of himself by attempting to break dance.

The night ends on a perfect note. And I have a feeling there's going to be a lifetime full of them.

CHAPTER 16

THE NEXT FEW WEEKS GO by fast. Most of my days are spent packing my stuff, practicing with my band, and helping Sadie adjust to living with the Gregorys and getting to know her as much as she'll let me. She seems to be doing okay in her new life, but she spends a lot of time in her room, listening to music. Lila has her in therapy three times a week, and I think Sadie might be taking something for anxiety, even though no one has flat out said it. I'd probably be less willing to go on the tour, but I remind myself that I'll be returning home next week to visit and the week after that.

Lila and Ethan have set up flights and car rides home for me, so I'll never be gone for more than a handful of days, and Lyric is even coming home with me some of those times. While Sadie insists it's unnecessary to come home to see her, I'd never be able to live with myself if I bailed out of her life for three months. And I want to get to know her when she's ready to let me in.

It's strange to think I'll be leaving soon. That I'll be out on the road, completely free to live my life without the threat of the Soulless Mileas trying to take me. Many of the members are in jail now and are being charged with many crimes. But the most relieving part is that my father is being charged with my brother Felix's murder and my mom's, something Detective Rannali informed me of during a phone call a few days ago. He also told me that my sister and I might have to testify during the case. I wasn't too happy about that, but I'll face it when the time comes. Right now, I just want to take things one step at a time and focus on the good stuff in my life.

The day finally arrives to say bye to everyone and leave for the tour. Saying goodbye to the Gregorys is hard, but saying goodbye to Sadie is the most difficult.

"Call me if you need anything at all," I say as I hug her goodbye in the driveway.

"I will." She puts an unsteady arm around me, doing her best to hug me back. We're both extremely nervous huggers so the moment is awkward, but I'm just glad we're here to experience it.

"And I mean it. Morning, noon, and night," I say. "I'll have my phone on me at all times. I want to be there for you. No matter what you need, just call me."

"Look at you, Shy Boy," Lyric says as she swings her leg over the fence and leaps into my yard. She has on a backpack and is carrying her guitar case, ready to hit the road. "You're starting to sound like me."

"That's actually a really good compliment." I hug Sadie for a second longer then step back. "Are you sure you're going to be okay?" I ask her.

Her eyes flick back at the Gregorys' home then she nods, hugging her arms around herself. "This place seems okay." Her gaze slides to Lyric and she timidly waves.

When the two of them met, they seemed to hit it off. I wish they had more time to get to know each other before we take off, wish Sadie and I had more time too. But I remind myself that I'll be back here next week, and the week after.

"Hey, Sadie." Lyric grins as she waves. "Did you get that old guitar I sent over?"

Sadie nods then flinches as a dog starts howling from one of the neighbors' yards. "I did. Thanks for giving it to me. You didn't have to."

"I know, but I wanted to." Lyric smiles reassuringly, making Sadie the slightest bit less uneasy.

I'm not surprised Sadie seems less nervous being around Lyric. Well, less nervous than she is around other people. It was Lyric's positivity that made me feel content even in the most unsettling times, and gave me hope that one day I could be happy too. I'm crossing my fingers it'll do the same for Sadie.

"Well, thank you . . . I-I'm really excited to learn how to play it," Sadie says to Lyric then she nervously backs away as a SUV pulls up in the driveway. "I think I'm just going to wait on the steps." She rushes back to the porch and sinks down on the stairs, eyeballing Sage and Nolan as they get out of the car.

Nolan walks around and opens the back of the SUV while Sage strolls up the driveway toward us.

"You guys ready to get this show on the road?" Sage asks, then his gaze darts to Sadie. "Who's that?"

"That's my sister," I say, picking up my bag from off the ground.

"They adopted someone else?" Sage asks with a crook of his brow.

"Kind of," I say, not ready to tell Sage the details of my life yet.

I sling my duffel bag over my shoulder and head down the driveway to load up my stuff. After we've gotten everything into the car, Lyric says goodbye to her parents while I give everyone in my family a hug.

Once I'm finished with the goodbyes, I slide into the backseat of the SUV with Lyric. She holds my hand as Nolan backs out onto the road.

"It's kind of funny," Lyric says, resting her head on my shoulder. "But you were doing this exact same thing a couple of years ago, only you were going to the house instead of away from it. It's crazy to think about."

She's right. The day I arrived at the Gregorys' I was sitting in the backseat of their SUV, feeling nervous and alone in the world. But that lonely, scared guy who feared life and hated himself isn't the person sitting in this seat right now. I'm so much different. I have dreams now. Want things. Have people who care about me. Who love me. Who are there for me.

I'm not alone anymore.
I'm not a ghost.
Who floats through life.
I'm a person
Who breathes the possibilities.
Who has hope.

"Not everything's the same." I sit back and hold Lyric's hand, knowing this is the start of an amazing journey.

EPILOGUE

Lyric

ONE MONTH LATER...

"ARE YOU READY FOR THIS!" I shout at the seemingly endless crowd.

They echo my enthusiasm, shouting and getting all riled up. There's even a mosh pit in front and some crowd-surfing going on.

Gripping the microphone stand, I turn around and look at Ayden. "I'm going to have my freaking awesome lead guitarist join me for this one." I grin at him as I motion him forward.

The crowd hollers again. After a month on tour, I'm learning that with the right amount of energy, I can get everyone pumped up over anything, even when it's almost a hundred degrees outside.

Ayden inches up to me, his gaze skimming my plaid skirt, black tank top, and knee high combat boots. Lust flashes in his eyes and he looks like he wants nothing more than to take me back to the motel room and have his way with me. I don't know how he can look at me like that when I have sweat dripping all over me, but I'm glad he can. Glad he's here with me.

"I can't believe I agreed to do this," he whispers when he reaches my side.

"Don't be nervous. You'll do great. And just think, after we're done, we get to hit the road and head home for a few days."

His mood instantly lightens. While we've had a lot of fun on the road, Ayden enjoys going back home and visiting his family. So do I, and I spend a lot of time talking and texting my parents. But I'm still happy to be here. To be living this experience.

Ayden suddenly frowns. "What if I mess up big time? There's so many people here."

"You won't mess up." I wink at him. "But if you do, just distract everyone by taking off your shirt and dazzling them with your sexiness."

He shakes his head, fighting back a smile. Then he wipes the sweat from his forehead and lines his fingers to the guitar strings.

I collect my own guitar, then stand beside him. "You ready?" I ask, bursting with excitement.

He nods, strumming a few chords. "But I'm only doing this because I love you."

I smile at him, then face the microphone and take a deep breath before I open my mouth and start to sing.

It's always amazing being on the stage, living my lifelong dream. It was definitely a crazy journey getting here, one full of bumps and unexpected turns. But I wouldn't trade any of it for anything because every single thing that happened got me right here to this moment. And it got me here with Ayden.

ABOUT THE AUTHOR

JESSICA SORENSEN IS A *NEW York Times* and *USA Today* bestselling author that lives in the snowy mountains of Wyoming. When she's not writing, she spends her time reading and hanging out with her family.

CONNECT WITH ME ONLINE

jessicasorensen.com
and on
Facebook and Twitter

OTHER BOOKS BY JESSICA SORENSEN

Isabella Anders Series:
The Year I Became Isabella Anders
The Year of Falling In Love (Coming Soon)

Unraveling You Series:
Unraveling You
Raveling You
Awakening You
Inspiring You

The Coincidence Series:
The Coincidence of Callie and Kayden
The Redemption of Callie and Kayden
The Destiny of Violet and Luke
The Probability of Violet and Luke
The Certainty of Violet and Luke
The Resolution of Callie and Kayden
Seth & Grayson

The Secret Series:
The Prelude of Ella and Micha
The Secret of Ella and Micha
The Forever of Ella and Micha
The Temptation of Lila and Ethan
The Ever After of Ella and Micha
Lila and Ethan: Forever and Always
Ella and Micha: Infinitely and Always

The Shattered Promises Series:
Shattered Promises
Fractured Souls
Unbroken
Broken Visions
Scattered Ashes

Breaking Nova Series:
Breaking Nova
Saving Quinton
Delilah: The Making of Red
Nova and Quinton: No Regrets
Tristan: Finding Hope
Wreck Me
Ruin Me

The Fallen Star Series (YA):
The Fallen Star
The Underworld
The Vision
The Promise

The Fallen Souls Series (spin off from The Fallen Star):
The Lost Soul
The Evanescence

The Darkness Falls Series:
Darkness Falls
Darkness Breaks
Darkness Fades

The Death Collectors Series (NA and YA):
Ember X and Ember
Cinder X and Cinder
Spark X and Cinder

The Sins Series:
Seduction & Temptation

Sins & Secrets
Lies & Betrayal (Coming Soon)

Unbeautiful Series:
Unbeautiful
Untamed

Standalones
The Forgotten Girl
The Illusion of Annabella

COMING SOON

Entranced
Steel & Bones
Forget Me Not (Sadie and Sage's story)
Iridescent (Fiona's story)

Made in the USA
Middletown, DE
10 December 2015